Dear Mollie & Tom:

My 81st year humble project

[signature]

PASSION

AND

PATHOS

PASSION

AND

PATHOS

JAHED RAHMAN

To order additional copies of this book, contact:
Xlibris
1-888-795-4274
www.Xlibris.com
Orders@Xlibris.com
797671

To Zeenat Shaheen Rahman, my loving wife

My Note

I started writing at a very late stage of my life. There were two imperatives for such an impulse and game change in life's penchant. The first one was the offshoot of location in a huge city, Chicago, housing almost one-third of Canada's total population. My wife and myself moved to Chicago, after living in Vancouver for seven years, with no apparent link with my professional background and earlier pattern of life. So I felt very lonely at the initial phase. Constrained by unfamiliar surrounding and evoking partial ability premised on school days endeavor to write plays, I ventured to writing as my way out.

The second one was propelled by an urge within me to leave behind a record of our family- from where we came, and who we are- for the benefit of our progenies, if one is interested to trace back. That initiation of 2013-14 slowly engulfed me in writing. And I contentedly continue to indulge in writing, and started enjoying it.

Life's progression mostly depends on subtleties and situations generally beyond control or choice of individuals. I am very much a product of that process. Things concerning life as riveted my present were beyond probabilities in the past, and have little bearings with my life then. I enjoy my present without traversing the past.

My present delight in life is premised on recently developed passion for writing. Writing also enables me to remain, without being an indulgent bystander, alert and active in pursuing other aspects of life, making total life and living a worthy one. I appreciate every bit of that though not a professional writer.

The book 'Passion and Pathos' is an outcome of that exertion. This is my fourth publication in a span of about five years.

The story primarily is premised on historic, contextual, and conceivable current realities of Afghanistan with the backdrop of al-Qaeda and Taliban phenomena. The principal character from Bangladesh went to Afghanistan, and became an al-Qaeda Mujahedeen after going through the process of orientation and induction in Pakistan.

He was astounded knowing that the country, with territories almost similar to present geographical coverage, has had been in existence for thousands of years.

More so, and contrary to current reality, Afghanistan had distinguished itself in the past, stretching thousands of years, as the flourishing base for various life philosophies such as Zoroastrianism, followed by Buddhism, and Hinduism, before the advent of Islam in the seventh century. That historical background made the character happy even though the same has been reversed in last hundreds of years by current priority for fighting, killing, destruction, and continuous conflict, demonstrating preference for guns, IEDs, and Molotov cocktails. Worst of all these is the apparent religious cover under which such atrocities are undertaken. That made the character angry and frustrated.

The topography, having conflicting features, mostly consists of barren plains, dust, snow, stone, boulders, and ranges of mountains. It remains both hostile and equally enchanting, influencing the way of life of its people. That made the character happy in a mixed way.

The story travels through the negative surrounds of tribalism and its impact on Afghanistan's pursuance of peace and progress, and in attaining its national identity and unity. Various tribes, being the decedents of many earlier dynasties and empires, have had their particular ways of life and living. Such life in homogenous territories, with languages playing the dominant role, caused and nourished the sustenance of belligerent priority to preserve those at any cost. Historically and ideally that sort of priorities and commitments provide necessary spaces for prolongation of emotion-laden conflicts, and tribalism thus continues to be both a pride and a problem for present Afghanistan.

Those resultant mixed settings caused unintended policy puzzles ideally providing spaces to super powers and its immediate neighbors to play with Afghanistan for achieving respective geopolitical priorities and sustaining those. That, along with tribalism, compound Afghanistan's prolonged political and military quagmire.

The story makes progression in this setting with heightened frustration and dismay of the main character concerning al-Qaeda and Taliban philosophies. He however experienced, during the journey process, inherent positive dynamics that were contributing to sustenance of al-Qaeda and Taliban movements notwithstanding negativities apparent.

The story highlights that opportunities in life is generally an uncertain occurrence. It brings to limelight how individual commitment and leadership can fundamentally influence the destiny of a group of people; and how energetic compassion can shape another life, burdened by the suspicion of being a terrorist, to one of academic excellence, thus making the world beautiful and worth living.

All these background, experiences and realizations formed the basis of the story. Its romantic elements, agonizing pressure, formidable challenges, positive responses of individuals, love and care of sympathizers and the like, form the core of the story having enigma of passion and pathos.

Many of the assertions stipulated and positions articulated in the story are those of the respective characters. They are neither absolute nor sacrosanct. But still there were enduring doubts about the appropriateness of making some of those observations on which opinions are likely to differ.

As I completed the first cut of the present book, I came across a speech delivered by Bhutanese Physician Prime Minister Lotay Tshering during his visit of Bangladesh in April 2019. The speech was given in Mymensingh Medical College of which he is an alumnus. In that speech, as I recall, he articulated, among others, "there is no 'right' or 'wrong' positions. It is primarily a question of 'opinion' (subject to understanding)." I am broadly inclined to agree with what the Hon'ble Prime Minister stipulated, and feel confident in retaining articulated positions on issues on which there may be differences of opinions. I am happy that I could take that staunch in telling the story with credence, some being pertinent.

In spite of comments otherwise, some of my friends encouraged me in continue writing. Naming them is not appropriate, but I know, and they know, who they are. I remain eternally thankful to them.

Jahed Rahman

MILIEU

Unlike some linguistic groups, Bangla-speaking (anglicized word being Bengali) people inhabiting Bangladesh and the West Bengal State of India are extremely proud and emotionally sensitive—other than respective religious roots of inhabitants—to their language and culture. Many cultural events and festivities are both related to and linked with months of the Bangla calendar. In that context, the first month of the Bangla calendar, known as *Baisakh*, carries a special significance and role. Baisakh coincides with mid-April to mid-May.

Following the elevated heat of Choitro, last month of the Bangla calendar, Baisakh symbolizes a month of infrequent but stormy localized recurrence of gusty winds along with hails and rains. Features and impact wise, it is analogous to tornado as is mentioned in weather science and literature. Consistent with name of the month and local practice, occurrences of such storms are known in Bangla as *kalbaisakhi* (similar to scary Baisakh). The localized happening of *kalbaisakhi* is routinely preceded by dark thick clouds typically in the northwest corner of the sky around the variable areas to be affected.

The second month, known as *Joishtho* and analogous to mid-May to mid-June, however, is a quiet one, typifying warm and humid weather conditions conducive to ripening of seasonal local fruits. There is normally no rain and storm around this period.

Albeit usual sedate weather features of the related period, the sky over Chittagong in Bangladesh, the place of Areem's intermediate college education, was besieged by low-lying sedentary patches of thick dark clouds, with the ground experiencing subsumed heat and uncomfortable

1

humidity. It was the early fourth week of June following the end of first academic year of Areem in college.

Such unusual weather occurrence in and around Chittagong was triggered by unexpected depression (low pressure) in the Bay of Bengal. The local weather bureau was broadcasting intermittent warnings about the onslaught of a severe cyclone accompanied by high tidal waves, urging people to take shelter in safe places. By evening time, the wind gained its velocity, reflective of the severity of a looming onslaught. The traffic on the road was minimal; and most commercial entities, including eating outlets, were closed.

The two-storied dilapidated hostel (something similar to a dorm) building of the college was very much in the thick of the storm; however, its limited respite was from surrounding old trees with slapdash branches hanging around. They were providing some local resistance to the wind with rain nevertheless pouring heavily. Smaller twigs and leaves were the immediate casualties, numerous being on the ground, mostly moving with each splash of the wind. It was all dark as the college was on its annual summer vacation, and all but one resident pupil left the accommodation. The snapping of electricity distribution lines earlier caused total blackout in the greater Chittagong area. This phenomenon of darkness coupled with heavy rain and wind made the surroundings a chilling one.

The lone occupant, having the southernmost room of the second story, was Areem Ahmed Shah Afridi, who just finished his first-year intermediate (akin to eleventh grade of the American education standard) course. Areem did not like the surroundings of his growing-up place in Dhaka but developed a liking for hilly Chittagong of Bangladesh. Banking on his performance in the board-conducted secondary school certificate examination, he convinced his father to agree to his college study in Chittagong. In the process, he received the most unexpected support from his new mother, who internally always wanted him to be away. Areem got admission into the Chittagong College easily and maintained academic excellence in initial college education. He earned a name in a rather short time. Related faculty members liked him enormously and spared no pain to guide him. When he told faculty members his desire to know more about possible USA education pursuits as well as the process, he was, as a special dispensation, allowed to stay for ten days in the hostel that was officially closed during the two-month-long summer vacation. It was clearly laid out that this special relaxation was premised on his spending time at the local outfit of the United States Information Service (USIS) and that he would be responsible for all his needs, including food.

Even though Areem was sure that he would not need all those ten days to have imprints about the process and possibilities of education in the United States, he was elated as that shortened his stay back at home. That feeling was driven into his mind even after receiving negative indications from his father earlier.

For students in general, and mostly those living in hostels or other private accommodations, vacations are always looked upon as welcome respites from limited and mundane quality of hostel food besides the opportunities to be with the known folks and in accustomed milieus. But that was not the case with Areem. He always preferred to keep that emotion private. Because of that, Areem had been rather tepid about returning home during vacations. While smaller vacations were malleable, this long summer vacation was a matter of trepidation and thwarting for Areem.

His father conveyed his displeasure about Areem's plan to stay back even when all facilities would be closed because of summer vacation. Taking hint from that indication, Areem acted quickly about convincing Father the need to stay the first ten days of holidays in Chittagong for matters related to USIS. He also advised Father that allowing him to stay in the hostel was exceptional and an outcome of help and support of faculty members. Areem, therefore, could not back off at this stage.

There was an unrelated issue of inquisitiveness beyond academic relevance on which he had little option but to be candid with those who inquired: that related to his name, especially the surname. Bangladeshi Muslim names, since Arabic based, generally end with Ahmed, Rahman, Chowdhury, Khan, Hossian, Ali, and the like. A surname such as Afridi is uncommon and sufficient to raise inquisitive queries. This was accentuated by slim and tall body frame and relative fair complexion of Areem, rather uncommon in the local setting. He had to explain these exceptions often to his close friends, teachers, and some other well-wishers but always exercised prudence in sharing details.

The backdrop of that narration was primarily premised on the skeleton diary that his grandmother left behind, and he accidentally got hold of that while looking for a land-related deed that his father desperately needed. It was after his secondary school certificate examination. As Father needed the deed and as Areem had spare time, he was asked to go through a hoard of papers and documents to find the deed. In that quest, Areem opened a wooden box kept in a remote corner and in a decrepit condition. He found the diary in that box being enfolded by the saree (five-and-a-half-yard fabric draped by Bangladeshi women to cover them) his grandmother wore during the first night of her wedding with Josh Mohammad, the grandfather. The note in the last page of diary details about the saree with desire that it should be given to her future granddaughter-in-law as a memento from her.

Neither anyone of the house was interested in reading an old document, nor did they care about an old saree. His father was preoccupied with business matters. To Father, the misplaced deed was more important than the diary of his late mother. Areem discreetly packed, took possession of them, and parked those in his room as his chattels.

During follow-on available time, he continued reading the diary, occasionally cuddling the saree too to have the feel of Grandma's touch. He was very impressed about the frankness with which she detailed her life with the grandfather. At the beginning of the diary, she wrote, "I shared frankly with my husband apprehension concerning coatings that could typify our conjugal relationship once we are gone. I also said that we should leave behind a record of our lives so that generations following us, if they so like, can have a reference document and be aware of real happenings that culminated in a relationship based on love and passion, rising above the immediacy of faith, language and race." During the depressing growing-up phase and as time permitted, Areem read and reread the diary to absorb its contents. Over time, both the diary and the saree became his most cherished treasures. He carried them wherever he went.

Possibly because of Hindu roots, where female learning was emphasized, his grandmother could very diligently record what she was told or experienced. Areem thus had a clear vision of the monumental and evolving pattern of lives and living of his grandparents.

His grandfather, Josh Mohammad Zakka Khan, hailed from the segments of Afridi tribe living in areas adjacent to Kohat civil district of North-West Frontier Province of Pakistan. Afridis are Pashtuns inhabiting a vast area comprising about three thousand kilometers of hilly terrain with a large concentration in Khyber Agency, Peshawar, and Kohat areas of the province. Pashtuns have a dominant presence in Afghanistan too, especially in its southern and eastern areas. The related and homogenous tribes are Khattaks, Orakzais, Wazirs, and Mehsuds. They are Sunni Muslims speaking generally Pashtun.

Josh Mohammad Zakka Khan was in Burma as an enlisted Indian army of the British Empire (one of the Indian infantry divisions), and his battalion was engaged in a bitter fight against the occupying Japanese forces in and around Arakan. That was the period of late 1943–1944, when the Second World War's Pacific scenario was at its zenith. As his battalion captured the small port of Maungdawon, the dogged and courageous commander decided for an early assault to capture two railway tunnels linking Maungdawon with the Kalapanzin Valley. That was a tactical move to unnerve the numerically superior enemy and create uncertainty in their planning and actions. In that battle, Josh Mohammad Zakka Khan fought furiously, valiantly provided needed cover to advancing forces while guarding a strategically important wooden bridge, and suffered multifarious injuries. In the absence of any meaningful field hospital, Josh Mohammad was brought and admitted into the Medical College Hospital of Calcutta for treatment.

Purnima, one of the few multilingual hospital ward nurses, was assigned to look after the immediate needs of Josh Mohammad's medical care plus monitor his health status until full treatment was planned and initiated. Because of his acute pain and interim high-dose medications, he was very weak and almost in a semiconscious status. He was totally oblivious of his condition and the place where he was. Two days after his admission, and as he opened his eyes in full sense, the first person Josh Mohammad exchanged looks was Purnima, who was standing by the side of his bed. She introduced herself as being the nurse in attendance and, in broken Hindi, said, "Thank Allah, you are in a stable condition notwithstanding the serious nature of your injuries, and the doctors will soon decide on the nature and type of your treatment. We will try our best." She continued saying with needed pause, "I come from a Hindu family of Bengal bordering Bihar Province. My father was a schoolteacher and a man of learning. He used to discuss with me regularly matters related to faith, living, social orders, and topics like that. He suddenly died when I was thirteen, and the family consequently was in total disarray, aggravated by penuries."

Purnima took a pause more to monitor Josh Mohammad's absorption ability of what she was saying and decided to go slow more with words but not ornaments of language. She continued, saying, "Being the neighbor of Bihar Province, I can speak and understand conventional Hindi. As a consequence of working in this hospital, I had both the need and opportunity to refresh that limited skill. Though at the heart of Bengal and most patients are Bangla speaking, we often have medical cases from different areas, and our main communication with them is either in broken English or in Hindi. If you so choose, you can communicate with me in Hindi but not in elongated sentences."

Josh Mohammad continued to look at Purnima unrelentingly as she was introducing herself. He, however, had no other thoughts or reactions. In responding to what Purnima said, he beamed politely and, as an escape, closed his eyes to avoid a possible discomforting situation consequent to his unabated looking at her.

He had a recurrent reflection. The ease and respect with which she said "Thank Allah," being a Hindu, amazed him. That was the most sincere statement projecting willingness to support someone in distress and expression of consolation avowals in initiating a possible dialogue of comfort with one totally unknown and in exacting health conditions.

The more that setting of Purnima's initial statement was evoked, the greater was his admiration.

No one in his extended family ever looked at him or cared about him with so much empathy and attention.

Josh Mohammad was from a relatively well-to-do family of his village settlement known as Dera Shabbir Khan. He transitorily educed his living in the midst of cousins and uncles in neglected milieu as he lost parents at infancy in an earthquake.

Parking all other thoughts aside, Josh Mohammad opted to enjoy the company and casual discourse with Purnima in broken Hindi using his exposure to Urdu language. Urdu, during that period, was the lingua franca of Indian army battalions. He formulated his discourse, focusing on the nature of his injuries, how he was brought to Calcutta, and the medical prognosis including chances of full recovery. Purnima detailed whatever she could but refrained from commenting as to the nature of injuries and the recovery prospects. She suggested that when the physician in- charge come for routine check-up the following morning, he could make the queries.

Josh Mohammad followed the advice and, in discussion with the visiting physician, inquired, through intermediation of Purnima, about his injuries and prospect of recoveries. The doctor was very truthful. Without hiding anything, he said, "You have multiple bone injuries in your lower body. We have given you a high dose of local anesthesia to minimize your immediate discomfort. An orthopedic surgeon is being assigned for your treatment. You would possibly need multiple surgeries over a period of time. The prospect, however, is good. If surgeries are successful, there is a positive chance of good recovery. In the meanwhile, be our guest for few months."

The visiting doctor took steps out with a reassuring posture but came back. He then said, "We are in touch with the military command of Calcutta. Your kith and kin have had been advised about your present location as well as your health status. So everything is under control."

Josh Mohammad laughed at himself. The doctor had no idea of his having no kin back home. His extended family was not at all concerned about him. His absence provided them the opportunity to grab his share of ancestral properties. That perhaps was one reason that his uncles encouraged him to join the Indian army of the British Crown, hoping that he would not return ever.

His initial days of pains and dizziness were passed without other stances. The arrival of two more severely injured infantrymen of the same battalion was not of much solace to him as they were from Central India, with language problem being the main impediment.

The only person he knew in Calcutta and the hospital was Purnima. He took occasional chances, in broken Hindi, to narrate his premilitary family life to and share his agonies with Purnima. As time passed, Purnima's ability to communicate with Josh Mohammad improved significantly, both by sign and words; but what impressed her most was his willingness to be familiar with Bangla language.

There were two successive major surgeries in the right leg of Josh Mohammad. Further surgeries, to be a total of six, were deferred to see the success of the first two as well as to give his fragile body a chance to gain some strength. He was doing fine under due diligence and care, among others, of Purnima.

By this time, both of them became very open and friendly. Josh Mohammad was candid in admiring without hesitation Purnima's long-flowing black hair, her dark round-shaped eyes with corners properly aligned, the way she interacted, the manner of her caring, and more wittily, the captivating way she draped her saree when she came on off-duty visits.

Likewise, Purnima did not hesitate to open up, saying, "I am from a very poor family and am the only child of my parents. Three of my younger siblings died in their infancy, mostly because of lack of care and medical attention. That is why I decided to become a nurse after finishing my high school education. That, too, was possible because of the love and care received from the pastor of local missionary outfit. My school education was almost free because of his support. This background infused in me an urge to love and live with people of various faiths and beliefs. I do not hesitate in uttering Bhagaban, Allah, and Christ with due reverence. Also, my family's poverty is one of the reasons why at this age of thirty, I am still unmarried."

Both, in their own domain, appeared to be relieved by stating what they had in mind. While Purnima lowered her face and focused on the ground with sublime facial mien, Josh Mohammad continued his unabated gazing of her. Absolute silence often enveloped the setting resonating eternal bliss.

In that moment typifying internal relief and subsumed pleasure of both, a staff from hospital administration showed up to hand over new assignment instructions. That stipulated that from week next, Purnima would be assigned as senior staff nurse in the newly commissioned orthopedic ward, while regular nurses would take care of Josh Mohammad. On subsequent query, the visiting doctor clarified that the services of Purnima were needed to attend to other critically needed patients. It was also said that normally attending nurses were rotated every week. In his case, that was a month-long assignment because of the language problem of Josh Mohammad. It was further said that four pending surgeries were mostly of routine type, and regular nurses would be able to handle that.

Being hospital staff, Purnima was aware of the essence of the instructions and was not surprised at all. The delay in communicating standard rotation practice was what she was thinking within herself all along. That initially was not the case with Josh Mohammad.

Sadness emanating from the contents of the order was both frustrating and disheartening for him. While having appreciation for all medical attention he was receiving, Josh Mohammad was certain that it was the care, attention, and compassion of Purnima that accelerated his healing process and inspired in him an urge to live. In spite of significant variance with the surroundings he grew up in, faith-related divergence, and unfamiliarity of language, it was Purnima—and Purnima alone—who allowed him to be at ease in a place far away from his root.

In that discouraging moment, he thought of requesting a temporary relaxation until his third surgery due in a few days but refrained from opening up to Purnima. He was very sad but, fortunately, only for a temporary period. Being from a structured army setup, Josh Mohammad was familiar with the requirements of institutional practices and processes and concluded that his feelings and needs had no relevance to institution's procedures. So he kept quiet. Purnima quietly finished her pending works and left silently with desolate facial expressions.

Purnima showed up the following day with a happy face. She did not waste any time and told Josh Mohammad, "I am a staff of the hospital and will always be around. The orthopedic ward, being a new one, is not that busy yet. It is located in proximity. I will visit you every now and then and will spend my leisure time with you. Do not think about it. Visiting old patients is a standard practice. I will monitor your treatment and recovery in consultation with nurses on duty. Most of them are juniors to me and would not mind my doing so."

Time passed, and so were the remaining days prior to the third surgery. Josh Mohammad did not miss openings during this period in having discourses with Purnima. While he was rather unwary occasionally, Purnima meticulously maintained the needed pause and mostly talked with him, looking at records or doing other errands to avoid attention of others. But the most enchanting feature of those discourses was that neither of them talked about feelings for each other in the shape of "I like you," "I love you," and so on. Both of them were maintaining a cover in hiding the real feelings.

The newly assigned nurse showed up on the last day; and Purnima briefed her about Josh Mohammad, the critical needs to prepare him for the upcoming surgery, and other related matters. As the nurse left, Purnima finished her remaining tasks but continued to change round his bed. It was emotionally arduous for her to say a formal goodbye notwithstanding all preparations. She was conscious of the fact that the conditions for informal discourse, to which both of them were used to unwittingly, would definitely be a constrained one notwithstanding the ability to visit occasionally. But she did not like to pass on that feeling. She soon inured herself, had a long and passionate look at him, bent her head toward right, dangled her long single-file braided hair, slid that near her chest, and through the movement of eyes, wanted to say goodbye, wearing an impish smile in an attempt to suppress her agony. She tried best to mask her passion.

Josh Mohammad was unduly subdued, had no physical response, and kept looking downward. Internally, he prepared himself very specifically and just was taking time in determining as to what to say and how much to say. His dilemma was premised on possible quandary related to their faith-linked conflict. He was certain about his ability to accommodate any other concern, but the faith-related one was beyond any possible compromise. He couldn't ask her for conversion. Neither could he marry her without conversion because of the inherent obligations to his forefathers and the essence of his own faith. He decided to postpone any faith-related discourse for the future.

As Purnima was about to leave the bedside, he drew her attention softly without looking at her. He picked up a piece of paper and pretended that he needed some clarification, a process he learned by observing the way Purnima talked to him most of the time.

Purnima turned back and eagerly waited to hear what Josh Mohammad had to say. Minutes passed, and he continued looking at the floor of the hospital ward as if he were trying to penetrate through it. In that standstill, he continued looking at the earlier piece of paper and just said without raising eyes, "I am not leaving Bengal after recovery. This would be my place and my rhizome even if I am alone. The days I spent so far with you will be my treasure in the future." After saying those words, he inclined on his bed, saying, "We will discuss further tomorrow."

Purnima returned to her room in the dorms meant for nurses' accommodation. Both during the walk back and while sitting on her bed in a lonely backcloth, she was excruciatingly immersed in thought as to what Josh Mohammad meant when he said "I am not leaving Bengal" and that the last one-and-a-half-month's association with her would be the treasure of his life.

Another recurrent thought was about herself and her own feelings. During the course of nursing education and during her working in the hospital, Purnima came into contact with many men; but no one had an imprint in her mind as was the case with Josh Mohammad. She had no commonality with Josh Mohammad in terms of faith, family background, language, and even race. Still, she often thought about him and harbored an indulgent sensitivity for him.

Being blessed with a strong sense of realistic vista—a by-product of growing up in a challenging setting—Purnima soon concluded that perhaps he most likely, because of language inadequacies, vented out his emotional paradigm in those desolate expressions. That made her happy. She likewise was chary about the imperative need to avoid any possible derelictions, considering her family background and faith-related impediments. Parking all impending subtleties in a corner of her mind, Purnima opted to enjoy the semblance of upbeat whiff from the earlier postulation. She had all the intent to pursue it in the coming days before giving serious thought about her possible relationship with Josh Mohammad.

During previous postoperation care and rehabilitation process, she tried to communicate with Josh Mohammad but in simple words and by body language. In the process, she mastered the art of communicating with him in a combination of Hindi, Bengali, English, and a few Pashtu words. Keeping that in mind, she decided to do two things. First was to help him in rehabilitation exercises in consultation with duty nurses. The apparent rationale was the language problem of Josh Mohammad and her familiarity with that to avoid any discomfort during the exercise regime. Second was to do a follow-on gradually to unearth inherent intents of words spoken before today's parting.

Purnima acted upon those loci three days after Josh Mohammad's third surgery. Her initial postsurgery visits were focused on recovery process. She used the intervening period to have a fresh look at Josh Mohammad as a person. Simultaneously, she rehearsed her own position to refresh and fine-tune them from her perspective.

Few days thereafter, it was time for Josh Mohammad to slowly walk to ensure and expedite his surgery-related recovery. She helped him in the process in and around the adjacent corridor of the hospital. Soon after first arrival in the corridor, Josh Mohammad succumbed to emotional pressure for talking, notwithstanding his usual handicap.

What he said on that day and the following days and what Purnima could make sense of after relating single or two words of each statement having different linguistic lineages was a very confusing one. To respond to such inadequacies, she often sought confirmation of understanding by saying what she understood. He would move his head up and down, confirming, or sidewise, disagreeing. In case of disagreement, he would repeat what he wanted to say by using other words. Thus, Purnima unexpectedly attained ability to partially communicate with Josh Mohammad.

Purnima was both surprised and happy, noting that Josh Mohammad picked up a few functional Bangla words while listening to routine discourses of hospital staff, and he would try some of them to impress her. What amused her was the mix and match of chaste Bangla spoken in Calcutta and around and that of colloquial Bangla being spoken in larger part of Bengal. Purnima encouraged him to try his few words of Bangla without either discouraging or correcting him. That had much unexpected outcome. Josh Mohammad's ability to understand simple Bangla words and expression improved dramatically.

Her general understanding was that Josh Mohammad grew up as an abandoned human species after losing his parents in infancy. As an orphan, Josh Mohammad rotated among doors and houses of his uncles, both for shelter and food. None of his close relatives, except Mariam *Khala* (maternal aunt), ever cared about him. It was because of her insistence and effort that he was sent to a local madrassa for education. Nobody loved him, cared about him, and expressed hopes and concerns about his growing up. All assumed that as he passed his childhood, he would be of value to them in carrying out household errands.

Time passed. Josh Mohammad grew up without any focus in life. His life took an unanticipated turn when the British government decided to raise additional battalions during the Second World War as a direct support in its military engagements in North African and the Asian fronts, primarily Burma. Specific rigid standards were relaxed. That paved the way for Josh Mohammad to join one of the Indian infantry divisions, which was deployed at the Burma front.

There was another helpful random source of information that enabled Purnima to know more about Josh Mohammad and his Burma chapter of engagement. His battalion would always communicate with him about their concern related to his well-being and his recovery, and keep him posted with recommendation for citation for valor and what options he had to retire and pecuniary benefits he could expect. As he was unable to read and understand, it was the onus of Purnima to convey to him the summation of those with additional responsibility to respond to his command in English as much as she could. Among others, such officially recognized need provided unhindered chances to both for spending more time together without inferences otherwise.

His Battalion was stationed in Mandalay, a city in central Burma. It was also famous for being the capital of the Kingdom of Burma for a brief period before British colonization. Its location by the bank of Irrawaddy River was of special significance.

At first sight, Josh Mohammad fell in love with Burma instantly. The frequent patches of low clouds in the sky, the greeneries all around, the frequent rains, the rivers—all were so different compared to his root. That instantly had immediate and permanent impression in his mind albeit the discomforting hot and humid conditions. He made up his mind for a permanent living in Burma if the war efforts culminated positively and he survived the horrendous brutality of the war.

Purnima had her impressions about him adequately framed during such walks, smidgen discourses and also during access to communications from his battalion. That helped an aerated sense of comfort and confidence, and she was in a bliss within herself. She had absolute clarity about the future of her relationship with Josh Mohammad and also how she would handle it from the perspective of her family.

Neither Purnima nor Josh Mohammad pronouncedly talked about love and marriage despite the obvious shared backdrop of nurturing a sublime desire for a possible relationship. Their longing to be together during the operations' follow-on recuperating phases was a distinct indication of feelings of their subsumed love. Both, though totally different persons by all criteria, exhibited an amazing match in handling that emotional paradigm. Even though they did not pronounce it in words, both were very clear about what they were talking about and where their discussions were heading to. In that setting, and to avoid future stress of any sort, Purnima had in mind two possible strains concerning their nascent relationship. She took the slow-walking regime subsequent to the fourth operation to convey those gradually.

Purnima quietly brought out the most delicate issue of variances in their faiths. In response, Josh Mohammad did not have verbal riposte but had a sympathetic look, manifesting a sense of reflection on his part too. While flexible on all other issues, he had no option but to request her conversion, as Islam does not permit marrying someone not believing in oneness of God and is not a follower of *Ahl al-Kitab* (divine books such as the Torah, the gospel, and the Avesta). Being a Hindu, Purnima was disqualified on both scores. He had no flexibility to compromise on those.

Josh Mohammad was reticent for quite a while, and Purnima continued gazing at him. Total taciturnity pervaded the locale of their walk of that day. She was aware of this impediment, thought about it for many nights, and raised it only after making up her mind. In reaching the desired inference, she was positively guided by what her late father told her about religions from time to time. Though a schoolteacher, her father was an avid reader. He would borrow books from the school library and other sources and would pass on his feelings and reactions on many social, cultural, and religious issues to his daughter.

Her father's chosen time for such discourses was both at the time of dinner and space available thereafter. Purnima was not able to absorb many issues she was told from time to time but listened to her father with due diligence. This habit of her father used to annoy her mother. She would often complain about it as many of the issues were beyond comprehension of a young girl of her age. But as she grew up and the father was no more there to talk to and guide her, many of the issues reverberated within her based on circumstances. As internal agony because of her unbounded love for Josh Mohammad and the conflict of radically divergent faiths caused insoluble confusion within her, she found solace and solution to her quagmire, recalling what her father used to tell about Hindu religions from time to time.

As was repeatedly told by her father, Hinduism had been an evolving devotion-oriented life philosophy, which has its premise on *dharanath dharma ucyate*, underscoring actions that sustain all species of life and help to support congruent rapport among them. That life philosophy has had been ascribed as *dharma* (religion) with the passage of time. This faith-related yearning is closely embedded in and with nature. In all its discourses, the philosophy attached foremost importance to conservation of nature. To propagate this, and to ensure sustenance, the emerging life philosophy emphasized worshiping of God in various forms and shapes as fire, water, air, sun, moon, and so on.

Notwithstanding its flourishing in and around India, there is lack of clarity as to the origin of Hinduism's first propagation. The common premise based on in-depth study indubitably concludes Hinduism as being a fusion of many earlier religions and philosophical motivations. It eventually transmuted into evolved beliefs of *dharanath dharma ucyate* in the surrounding areas of India, thousands of years back. That fusion of divergent dogmas and ideas subsequently resulted in allegedly having innumerable gods in the modern Hindu religion.

Her father used to emphasize one point: there is no particular founder of Hinduism. Neither it is premised on or associated with any revealed book like many other major religions. Some schools dispute this position. They believe that most of the Vedic and Rig Veda hymns are divinely divulged to the *rishis*, a class of saints with impeccable ability to hear and see. They were not the authors of those hymns.

The original inhabitants of India were at ease with the stream of people moving in from the West, North, and Central Asia. They moved in with their inherited life ideas, values, and practices; created their own interim settlements; and gradually got integrated with local beliefs and practices through both by contribution and by amalgamation.

As immigrants from the North and the West were absorbed by indigenous faith and embryonic philosophy, it reinforced the fruition process of *sanatan dharma* (evolved religion), having roots and flourishing for thousands of years in India. That subsequently turned into modern-day Hinduism. As a corollary to such phenomenon and the immediate upshot of Arab contacts, the original population believing in and aligning with *sanatan dharma* steadily came to be known as Hindu.

Hindu, being a non-native word, has no relationship with either Sanskrit or other native languages of the land. Being a nonreligious word, Hindu has no mention in the ancient Vedic (relating to the Veda or Vedas, an early form of Sanskrit originating in divine wisdom) scriptures.

Current research alludes that the word *Hindu* relates to Persians' reference to the mighty Sindhu (Indus) River of Western India where most of the earlier invasions from the West halted. Most of such invasions made by Persians and others were undertaken in summer because of climatic impulses. The Sindhu River, with snow melting in Himalayan and Hindu Kush Mountains, as well additional flows from merging other tributaries, was at its worst in terms of flow, force, and fury during summer. Thus, it was a deterrent to any invader.

The Persians were unable to pronounce *S*. They mispronounced it as *H*. Thus, the river Sindhu to them became Hindhu. The ancient Greeks and Armenians followed the earlier Persians' pronunciation; and thus, the word *Hindhu* was rooted with no link to any religion.

There is another reference as to the base of the word *Hindhu*. Celebrated Persian king Darius I's empire to the east extended up to the border of Indian subcontinent, and some parts of western India became part of his empire. Indians were also recruited in his army. They were referred to as Hindhus, being residents of areas around or east of Hindhu River. With passage of time and numerous spelling and intonation changes, the word *Hindhu* eventually came to be known as current word *Hindu*.

In essence, the word *Hindu* connotes neither any religion nor the identity of followers of any faith. It historically identified people living east of the River Sindhu and focused on the demographic identification independent of faith, philosophy, belief framework, and way of life.

The logical question is, What is the name of the religion being practiced by more than a billion people who follow the scriptures of the Vedic? The answer conceivably lies in its evolution process itself. Indubitably, the applicable identification would likely be *sanatan dharma*, i.e., evolved religion.

Reminiscing what her father told her, keeping them in view in apposite perspectives, and after many solo debates and self-argumentations, Purnima concluded that conversion to Islam was not in conflict with the root base of her religion as it is an extension of the concept of "contribution and amalgamation" practiced for thousands of years. To be time efficient and not to give her mother a shock, she wrote a letter with supportive stipulations that premised her own decision but had a second thought prior to posting that. She took an immediate decision to visit her home and discuss the issue face-to-face, enabling her to handle any startling antiphon. Purnima told Josh Mohammad about her unexpected dash home to see her ailing mother.

Her mother's instantaneous reaction to Purnima's unannounced presence had the usual mix of happiness and surprise. But as she looked at Purnima, her motherly instinct was wary about something grim. She maintained an uneasy quietness, recalling the late husband's advice for handling something unknown but likely to be ominous. Internally, with her heart thumping, she devoted praying to her *Ram* (God) for patience and guidance.

As Purnima opened up in a postdinner setting detailing her liking of and love for Josh Mohammad and her decision, subject to her avowal, to convert to Islam, her mother was aghast, shocked, and bewildered initially. She got her composure back, had a piercing look at Purnima, and closed her eyes. Her mother told Purnima that she would let her know the pertinent decision tomorrow morning as time was needed before articulating her stance.

With unexpected impulse, she exchanged a look with Purnima the following morning and very calmly said, "I thought through your postulation conveyed last night and sought guidance from God and your late father. I give you my unreserved consent to become a Muslim and marry the person you love."

As Purnima was about to respond, her mother further said, "You should know something we never discussed before. I come from a higher caste of Hindu religious structure than your father. It was unthinkable at our time for a Hindu girl of upper caste to marry one of lower caste. But I did so as I was in love with your father. My family forsook me and never had contact with us. But I had a fulfilling and contended life. If I could do that many years back, I have no reason to be an obstacle on the path of your love and life. You have my full and unqualified blessings."

As Purnima maintained her quietness more to give Josh Mohammad a window of opening after two days' gap, the usual walk of the evening following her return from home gradually lost its pace, the exchanges lost their warmth and spontaneity, and an unintended serenity permeated. She occasionally looked at him to gauge his body reflexes but focused more on the surrounding bushes and flowers with hidden emotional ease. Josh Mohammad was struggling within as how to tell her about his religious imperative and was more concerned about their relationship if the upshot was a negative one.

Time was running out. Purnima was in a state of wheedle and inveigle but equally was under leveraged exciting pressure to share the good news with him soonest. So without wasting any time, she impulsively held one of the hands of Josh Mohammad and asked him, "What happened? Why you are so quiet? Is something fretting you?" But before Josh Mohammad could respond, she just unburdened herself by saying, "I am going to convert to Islam." She focused her eyes on him and resorted to smiling covertly.

Josh Mohammad was equally relieved and exultant, but what he did to convey that made Purnima exuberant and embarrassed likewise. In an extemporaneous expression of his unbounded happiness, Josh Mohammad hugged her publicly on the walking trail of the park to the surprised amusement of bystanders. Their surprise and amusement were for two obvious reasons. One, it was not done publicly in a local setting. In a sense, it was also not encouraged. Second, there was the perceptible race difference between them.

As they walked back to the hospital, both of them were at ease with themselves. Purnima, with the articulation of small words, conveyed her mother's blessings to their future union. Josh Mohammad was relieved.

Each word had an inherent relieving implication besides providing an immense comfort. The resultant excitement and happiness were exorbitant in cases of both.

With the treatment making significant progress, time was there for Josh Mohammad to leave the hospital. In consultation with and assistance of Purnima, he rented a small accommodation at Balu Hok Kok lane and moved there. Besides spending time in the military establishment regularly during the initial phase to finalize his retirement and benefits, he used to visit the park adjacent to the hospital every day to meet Purnima.

Among others, they exchanged respective views about probable challenges and, in some cases, associated grumpiness both on account of visible variance in their very uncommon race factor and religious affiliations. The emerged common understanding was Purnima's conversion to Islam might minimize the issue over time. On the race issue, Josh Mohammad assured that nothing negative would unnerve him, either today or tomorrow; and he would take all steps to integrate with the local setting. He also stressed his voluntary first initiative to learn Bangla as quickly as he could. They also renewed their commitment to have a small family.

In the midst of the euphoria pertaining to the Allied forces' victory in the Second World War, the local conditions were ripe with tension due to incipient but determined political movement for faith-based division of India and independence from Great Britain. This caused follow-on rancorous communal rioting in both western and eastern parts of India.

Purnima and Josh Mohammad got married in that politically sensitive period, encountering disapproval and denigration of many of Purnima's colleagues and friends, while a few extended their encouragement. Purnima, with a surname of Khan subsequent to conversion and marriage, moved into the accommodation earlier rented by Josh Mohammad and started living there while continuing working in the hospital.

The eventuality happened after a while. India, as was so known for thousands of years and so under British colonial rule, was partitioned in 1947, crafting a new country for Muslims known as Pakistan, consisting of two wings (East Pakistan [now Bangladesh since 1971] and West Pakistan) separated by one thousand miles. A massive migration of population ensued.

Josh Mohammad and Purnima were a part of that migration process. They decided to move to East Pakistan. After some efforts and with the help of military establishment, they were allotted a temporary accommodation within the broader premise of the Dhaka cantonment. Subsequently, they were allotted a small plot by the office of the Military Land Cantonment Board. A small abode was built. Josh Mohammad also started a grocery shop nearby, which did exceptionally well under the supervision of Purnima and hard work of the former. Later on, Josh Mohammad acquired a space in the central cantonment area adjacent to the army CSD (central supply depot) store and relocated his business.

Soon the couple was blessed with a son. Josh Mohammad named him Sher Ali Afridi, an individual of his clan who became famous after assassinating Lord Mayo, Viceroy of India, during 1870s. The other reason, as he explained to Purnima for getting her consent, was his strong desire to carry the lineage of his roots though he readily abandoned the land of his origin.

The business flourished with the patronization of a solid clientele of the cantonment area. Sher Ali Afridi grew up and, in the process of growing up, exhibited special business acumen.

That made Areem's grandparents very happy. With the successive sudden demise of his grandparents, his father took over the business, expanded it further, and married his mother. Soon, they were blessed with a son whom they fondly named Areem Ahmed Shah Afridi as an effort to blend with the local naming pattern but retaining the family link.

When Areem was five years old, his mother suddenly died of an undiagnosed illness. His father was in a state of disarray. Because of the compelling need to have someone at home to take care of Areem, and encouraged by relatives and friends, his father married a second time. Areem's new mother, coming from a modest but socially respectable family, stepped into the house of affluence.

Areem, being a toddler, had not much reaction at the loss of his mother or the arrival of the new one. From childhood, he exhibited an unexpected proclivity of being nice, helpful, supportive, obedient, and somewhat submissive in actions and reactions. That made his father very happy.

Soon the new mother gave birth to a son to the joy of all. The close relatives of the new mother, particularly two elder brothers, started visiting her more frequently as the family of his own mother faded away in terms of immediacy and contact. His father was oblivious of these mundane matters. He was busy with his business and his new project of relocating the family in a spacious home in the periphery of upscale Banani, a model town of Dhaka.

The local setting was perfect for the play of intricate family politics. Respectable families that lost both affluence and influence have the uncanny quality of being suspicious with focus on protecting its immediate interests. So the brothers made it a point to alert their sister frequently about the challenge her own son would likely to face in future as Areem, being the eldest son, would gain control of the business in case anything happened to her husband.

Most of the time, such expression of sympathy and concern were predicated on requests for some money from the sister. Overtaken by such mien of commiseration, the sister would easily part away some fund.

Such concerns and empathy had a deep mark in the mind of the new mother, and she started to find fault with whatever Areem did. That accentuated with the family's relocation to their new home. It soon embedded in her thought that perhaps, being the eldest son, Areem would be the owner of this house too if anything happened to her husband. That entranced feeling, reinforced by frequent warning of her visiting brothers, made the new mother harbor an attitude of abhorrence toward Areem.

He sustained all these until he left for higher studies in Chittagong. This was the reason of his extended stay in the hostel as an option to minimize his presence in Dhaka, where he would be alone most of the time while Father being busy with business. That feeling was the outcome of subsumed torment Areem had been having from early childhood. As the time passed, that torment unwittingly was taking the shape of rage within the thought process of Areem.

RAGE

Areem continued sitting on his lone hostel chair as the cyclonic storm sustained its forceful lashing outside. The only other living thing in that lonely and dark setting was the dwindling half end of his candle with its flame dancing in different tracks based on flow of the wind that could penetrate through the narrow openings of the worn-out door and windows. What amazed him was the ability of the candle's flame to remain ignited notwithstanding the adverse conditions.

In those exceptional hostile situations, the candle remained unnervingly steady in trickling its brightness. The setting of wild storms outside and the struggle of the candle in his dark room to keep that illuminated had a mollifying impact on Areem's thinking. But that was a short-lived one. His thoughts once again started traveling through the track of his earlier agony. What wrong had he committed to have such a depressing childhood, which had been haunting him even in his early youth?

Areem accepted the divine will of taking his mother away in childhood. As he grew up, he came into contact with a few in his school who experienced the same. One of them was his class fellow Rukhsana. She often used to lament and weep, blaming her life and luck. Areem used to console her in various ways; one was: "Nothing remains the same in life. Time is the overpowering factor influencing reactions and responses. That is how life moves on. That is how one's will to make progression is shaped. Blaming oneself is neither the answer nor the solution."

Citing his own case, he frankly shared with her his life experiences and said, "In my short life, I have already been bitten thrice: once, in the untimely demise of Mother; second, in the cruelty being exhibited by new mother in spite of all positive intents and efforts by me; and third, in the distance that has been created in relationship with Father due to persistent negative feedback provided by new mother." He clarified further that new mother was persistent in her efforts to demean him in the eyes of Father. That was shrewdly accentuated by the sustained forewarnings of her brothers. The father, being captivated by the family rapport of his in-laws and relative youth of the new wife, trusted whatever he was told by her.

Events and incidents shading Areem's way of growing up were numerous. He unknowingly revisited them in that state of mind while still sitting on the chair with storms raging outside. Areem recalled a minor incident that, with careful fabrication on the part of new mother, became a major issue while she reported to Father.

It was noontime of a particular day. The new mother prepared milk for the infant brother, got that in a baby bottle, and put the nipple in the mouth of the baby. As she was needed to go out briefly to attend to some errands, the new mother placed a small pillow under the bottle to ensure that it remained in a stable position. She wanted to ensure easy flow of the bottled milk while the baby continued to suck. Areem, being about seven years old, was standing nearby, observing and enjoying the feeding process. He soon found that the nipple was out of the mouth of his baby brother. As an instant reflex, he was struggling to put that back; but the baby started crying. The new mother rushed in, noticed the stressed situation, and started shouting loudly, accusing Areem of trying to harm the infant. Areem was taken aback and left the room in a dumbfounded state of mind.

When the father came back, the new mother started crying while narrating what happened and simultaneously accusing Areem of having the intent to harm the newborn. His father's instant reaction was manifested in intense anger. His instantaneous action was a vociferous slapping of Areem. That was the first time that the father physically punished him. His father's second reaction was to go to their room and console his beloved wife.

That was the pattern of copious follow-on fake accusations of the new mother even pertaining to innocent, frisky happenings. Each of them was followed by louder accusations of the new mother accompanied by rebuke, slander, and vilification from the father. Spanking and slapping by Father became a regular feature of his growing-up years.

As Areem was growing up, he started exercising due care and caution in handling his younger brother. But the accusations of new mother, in one form or the other, continued unabated. His father's response, surprisingly, had a shadowy change. He minimized his conversation and contact with Areem as if they belonged to two different families. This waning of relationship between the father and son exalted the new mother. She was convinced that the father would eventually despise his eldest son and might deprive him from assets he was building up. The two brothers pursued their original strategy of cautioning their sister about unexpected eventualities. Her resultant complaints had a louder voice but less substance. In any case, money continued to flow from the sister to the brothers.

This sort of discourses between brothers and sister accentuated after the sister's family moved into their new home. On their first visit, the brothers concentrated on pampering their sister: underlining her capacity to run the family so nicely and acknowledging her taste and decisions in all related matters, from finesse in architectural design to finishing including the choice of drapers, and the control she had on her husband, being a Laxmi (something akin to luck and wealth as per Hindu mythology). That made the sister overwhelmed; and at her urging, they agreed to stay back that night to congratulate the brother-in-law too.

As the brothers were all set to leave the following morning, they, in their uncanny ability to pester their viewpoint, raised the issue of their perennial concern about what Areem could mean to her and her son in the future in a disparaging setting just at the time when Areem was approaching the stairs to go to the first floor. They were particularly referring to the new palatial home.

In their enthusiasm to make their point loud and clear, and for a very unguarded moment, they were placing their concerns in a high pitch to keep their sister alert. Areem listened to that minutely, refrained from acting in any adverse manner, took few steps backward, and carefully avoided any noise. Subsequently, he approached his new uncles with loud salutations and ostentatious humility, conveying his desire to take leave before going to school. They were evidently very happy, assuming that Areem did not hear anything.

That was a despondent day for him. Areem went to school but spent most of his time in a bizarre move around the school premises. He did only attend a few classes, moved from place to place, and spent quite a time in restaurant in the vicinity of the school. His understanding of his new mother's stroppy retorts to even small things was crystal clear to him.

Keeping that in view, Areem tilted into a deep trough but refrained either from surrendering to pressure, or exuding open displeasure, or reacting with occasional disdain. He argued with himself even at that tender age and decided to stymie his mind from seeding any raucous accusations about his new uncles. Even in significant emotional cessation, he was certain that attainment of his life objectives singularly lay in not reacting to such antique imperfections.

After due deliberations concerning his life so far and the quality of living he was experiencing, Areem, in his that early life, was convinced that there would be no gain point in exacerbating the situation. His honest cadging for redress from the Father would not mend the fissures in any way. Lack of contact and absence of support from his maternal side was another appalling impediment. All such negativities caused a nascent mind to think more prudently. Such enabling point is the cliché of the challenge having no direct bearing with age.

Areem thus concluded that the only way out was to ignore for the time being the peevishness of the new mother and disregard guileful maneuvering of the new uncles. His cogitated priority at that stage was to concentrate in studies, pursue greater goals with the financial help of his father, and then get out of this miserable surroundings to lead a life of his own with self-esteem, serenity, and dignity. He had no emotional penchant for property and money except those needed for pursuing his studies.

It was an easy thought but pained Areem very much. His love for his younger sibling was the main obstacle. He always had an ardent desire to cuddle his younger sibling, play with him, occasionally annoy him, and enjoy the fun emanating from that. But that was not to be because of the attitude and brashness of the new mother. That bothered him and likewise saddened him. He nevertheless carved a delicate way out by maintaining a visible isolation but padding and bribing the younger covertly with chocolates and other likable small treats. That vive of love and affection, notwithstanding the setting of dimness of his abode, was the reason for always having an impulsive desire to be at home. With that sort of feeling, he was at ease with himself with respect to issues that normally troubled him.

That tactic yielded some results. His father's demonstrated behavior pattern, premised on ignoring him for all practical purposes, gradually underwent an apparent decline in public shouting and abusing. That made Areem relieved. There was, however, a startling change in that behavior pattern premised on Areem's success in the board-conducted secondary school certificate examination. A subtle variation in father's approach and stance, reflective of some care and pride while observing teachers and neighbors coming in a stream to congratulate him on the outstanding achievement of his son in the board-conducted examination, was the most unexpected and equally welcome reaction that made Areem exultant too. Taking advantage of that supportive milieu, Areem floated the idea of his having higher study in Chittagong. The motive was to be far away from the present depressing setting.

Remarkably, the new mother endorsed the proposition with conjured additional justification that it would enable young Areem to groom himself up as an independent and equally confident person. Her concealed reason was that the resultant separation from daily encounter and contact with the son would minimize feelings and love while the budding second son would have unfettered opening to bond with the father more passionately.

Such thoughts, while he was still seated on his lone hostel chair in that stormy night, suddenly dispersed as Areem noticed the fading condition of the struggling candle. The lone candle of the room was at its kindling end. Areem was certain that it wouldn't last more than about fifteen minutes. He hurriedly looked for some eatables but did not find much except a small quantity of very old soggy *muri* (puffed rice) and a bit of drinking water in *kolshi* (water jar). Blaming himself for his stupidity, Areem unhesitatingly masticated those *muri* and drank the residue water to finish his eating for the night. After fixing his pillow, Areem drew a bedsheet to cover his body, blew off the candle to save the residue for emergency, and went to sleep while the nature outside was still at its worst in terms of wind velocity and rain volume.

The following morning was a late one for Areem. Surprisingly, even with dampening settings all around, including ostensible fear caused by storming, Areem had a sound and uninterrupted sleep until the past morning time. He had no clue as to when the storm abated. When he woke up, Areem's first action was to open the decrepit wooden window of his room. He was taken aback, seeing the clear blue sky, radiant sunshine, and vibe of calmness in contrast to the lambasting and lashing of last night. The marked evidence of that were broken branches and stems of trees and leaves on the ground and a number of shattered shops and houses nearby. Surprisingly, Kuddus Mia's fragile teashop was almost unaffected. He soon concluded that perhaps those aligned with the force and danced to its tune survived while the structures that put up resistance were smashed. Areem's erudite feeling was that adequate preparation and proper strategy are the sine quo non of survival in any engagement of life and living.

Days rolled by. It was time for Areem to leave the hostel and to be with his family in Dhaka to spend the remaining days of the summer vacation. He parked all his past experiences and current apprehensions temporarily and boarded the Dhaka-bound train only to realize that he was going without any goodies for his younger sibling. Being oblivious of all relevant consequences, and notwithstanding the imminent departure time, he jumped out of the train, rushed to a mini grocery cum stationery shop of the Chittagong railway station, grabbed a packet of Hashes chocolate, and without awaiting for the change due, started running toward the train, which slowly commenced its journey. He maneuvered himself, safely got into his compartment, and felt exultant. His fellow passengers were stunned, scared, and relieved at those moments of Areem's impulses.

The train was scheduled to reach Dhaka the following morning. For Areem, it was to be relatively earlier as he would disembark three stations ahead at the Banani Railway Station. His home, in the periphery of Banani Model Town, was comparatively a short distance from the station.

Areem happily reached home and was warmly welcomed by Father and younger sibling with the passive new mother being an onlooker. As it was time for his father to eat breakfast prior to going to his business office, he also asked both his sons to join him after they freshened up.

Areem's new mother, flaccid outside, was experiencing strenuous pressure within. She was taken aback witnessing the thrilling warmness shown by the father in welcoming the son and was more bothered by his asking Areem to join for breakfast. Her follow-on thoughts were disjointed ones, but she concluded that this attitude of warmness needed to be thrashed before it was too late. She also recalled her brothers' sustained warnings about what the presence of Areem could mean to her life in the future.

As an exceptional deviation from past practices, the Father inquired about his study, the quality of the faculty, and matters related to hostel life and food service. Areem took the opportunity to brief him about higher studies' openings in the USA without mentioning the cost because of the presence of new mother. The Father was enthralled, and to utter disdain of new mother who was serving Father additional breakfast eatables, quipped by saying, "You have all my blessings." While lamenting, he continued saying, "Though I value learning and knowledge, I did not have much interest during my growing-up years. Your grandfather's passion for business equally influenced me and shaped priorities of my life. That was accentuated by his relative early demise. I overwhelmingly got involved and expanded the inherited business. While I have money and influence, I can't go up anymore due to lack of education. Hence, you pursue your studies the way you consider and your teachers suggest to be the best."

That was too much for the new mother to endure. She retreated to kitchen area and asked herself what she did wrong this morning to be pestered by all this nonsense. Those supporting and encouraging words of the father belied her own earlier conviction, taking advantage of Areem's absence, in being able to influence her husband in articulating his decisions. But that was not the case this morning. She felt dismayed and distorted.

After finishing the breakfast, Areem took his leave to go to his room and, during the process, winked at the younger sibling, telling him to follow. The father was happy at seeing such bond between his two sons.

As Areem handed over the box of chocolate, the younger one was overjoyed and ran to his mother to show it. The new mother quickly capitalized the opportunity and started saying loudly, "Oh my god, why a box of chocolate? This is a vicious plan to harm our son in every imaginable way. What wrong our son has done to Areem?" She was persistently complaining and sobbing.

Sitting in the veranda, enjoying the puffing of his after-breakfast cigarette, Sher Ali Afridi was amused by the reaction of his wife. He considered it to be a transitory one based on unfounded apprehension. Recalling the relationship between two brothers just minutes back, he was certain that the tone and nature of the loud complaint were meant to convey her agony to him. He quietly stood up and took leisurely steps to his waiting car. Seeing that, the enraged wife was at a loss and started complaining to the lady household help. In fabricating the whole episode, she had all the furies but not the fire. Areem opted to ignore the new mother's obstructive reflexes and decided that taking a short nap was evidently a better option while the rambling in the kitchen continued unabated.

Areem educed his earlier resolve to park all negativities aside, ignore the new ones in the process, and have a relatively peaceful time until the end of the summer vacation. He happily enjoyed the father's genial welcome, queries about study and living conditions in Chittagong, and more significantly, his encouraging words about possible higher education in the USA. Areem's inclination for USA studies is predicated on his strong preference to pursue medicine as a future professional field as he was being unceasingly bothered by the premature and undiagnosed demise of his mother.

While spending most of the vacation time outside with old contacts and friends, Areem exercised required care and caution in interacting with his younger sibling. The former nevertheless continued to exhibit warmth and feeling as needed and as occasions warranted. That yielded expected dividends. Areem was having a relatively nice time (more during dinner) with father.

Something unexpected befuddled Areem and more devastatingly upset the new mother. Areem's baffled feeling was because of the sudden trust reposed in him against the backdrop of past experiences. The new mother's frustration was in observing that her unceasing raucous allegations were slowly losing relevance as those were having less impact on her beloved husband.

What the father alluded to was not the outcome of any serious contemplation on his part. As Areem was recounting his preparation for the TOEFL test, the Father impulsively suggested that the former devote some of his vacation time to coach younger sibling so that he could excel in studies in future as well. That was a simple stipulation.

Life, however, is not that simple. Even the most common and forthright stipulation may have varied upshots depending on the mind-set of the other person concerned. The resulting reflection can be both sweet and sour. That happened in this case too.

The younger sibling exchanged looks with the elder brother and winked with all glee he could muster in that setting. Areem was happy but was concerned about the possible antiphon of his new mother.

The consequential reaction of the new mother was a very erroneous one. The study related stipulation of husband caused immediate concern to her. The pressure was more as she was noting an apparent and increased trust her dear husband was reposing on Areem. The possible influence of Areem on her son with respect to the future she had in mind for the latter pertaining to business and property was the crushing factor. But more devastating was her anecdotal inability to comment on that openly. While keeping silence on the proposition, she decided to counteract it in the way she knew best. Her strategy was working through her son.

The new mother, following the advice of her visiting brothers, constantly bantered the proposition in the solitary presence of her son, emphasizing more that it was the age for him to play and enjoy life. On occasions, she also questioned the rationale of the proposition and was also candid in saying that there was no need for the boy to excel in studies as he would inherit in due course good assets and business.

That started yielding desired results from her end, while Areem was harboring a feeling of frustration. The more he was trying to bring his sibling within the purview of study regime, the greater was his drifting-away tendency, resulting in frequent complaints to mother and resultant constant rambling of the new mother.

His father, the proposer of that stipulation, was too busy with business- and property-related matters. He had no time to follow up on his proposal. Areem had no confidence to brief his father about the unsatisfying outcome of his efforts. The new mother was happy in that silence mode, counting the remaining days of Areem's vacation.

The preparation for TOEFL was not that challenging for Areem. Frequent alibis of his younger brother made unintended time spaced in. Areem thus had plenty of scope to ponder more seriously about his future in the family and possible relationship with his brother.

Areem frustratingly remained unclear on both the above counts. But he formed, unfounded though, impressions about the personality traits of his and the younger one's.

His patchy life so far in the environment of sustained negative attitude of the new mother bothered him the most. The constant hissing of her brothers made her pursue a strong resolve to ensure that the younger one inherit all or most of what her husband would eventually leave behind. As the time passed, she became more vocal.

Over time, Areem became used to it. He, however, was quite distraught, observing the unbridled demonstration of hypocrisy in the words and actions of the younger one, particularly when he talked to the mother. The new mother's vociferous commentaries were good enough for Areem to understand the twists and turns the words or events underwent in the relaying process. That was quite the opposite of the younger one's mannerism when talking to him or the father. Areem had no doubt that the younger was definitely growing up with the genes of the former's maternal side.

At that early growing-up period, the younger sibling was exhibiting a grasped acumen in interacting with elders of the family. He would be submissive in the presence of the father, polite before the brother, and obedient and responsive to his mother. He would do most of the things his brother wanted him to do but would fabricate events and actions as the mother would like to hear. That provided new mother needed opening to scream, to abuse, and then to apprise the husband upon his return home.

The human mind is the repository of a strange mix of response syndromes that often defy logic. A mature intellect could easily ignore relevant passing symptoms whereas a rather young one could very well be prone to pick up the inherent negativities. That alone makes a fundamental difference in how a life is patterned and pursued.

The mysterious musings of living shaped the essence of life that Areem negotiated subsequently for himself while neither the father's business success nor the mother's unbounded love could ensure a desired progression for their young son. That possibly is what life is all about.

Areem made two positive choices during the process. His first choice was to bear with the quirks of new mother so long as it was not impacting his relationship with others in the family and so long as they had no impediments in pursuing his studies. His second choice was to give benefit of doubt to his younger sibling, earnestly hoping that his father's influence and his own example in avoiding squabbles in the family would eventually have a positive imprint on his emerging personality.

In that thought process, Areem made a self-assessment about his personality traits, more to correct the course as needed. He had no memory of his mother and her death. He always accepted and respected the new mother even though her attitude and approach toward him were always scornful. He adroitly managed his relationship with his father, though many a time the father erroneously chided him based on the briefing of new mother. Based on the above and as no one from the family or the community commented otherwise, Areem concluded it to be prudent to stay in the present course, taking full advantage of the recent affability being shown by Father.

The joy of a joint evening meal, being experienced since his return home this time for summer vacation, was not an exception to Areem only. It was palpable from the comments and smiles of his father and incongruent twits of the younger one.

With the backdrop of that happy feeling, Areem, on being advised by household help and as per recent practice, walked to the dining table to have meal with father and sibling. But it was not like other evenings. They did not exchange looks. The father's usual welcoming smile was missing, the new mother was unusually quiet, and all the household help were tight and stiff. The only exception was the sibling, cogently being insensible to the happenings around. It so appeared that except Areem, all the other adults present had inkling of something portentous.

The new mother displayed unusual open concern supported by care-related comforting words. She repeatedly urged her husband to take care of himself during the period of stress and to have adequate dietary intake. From the few consoling words she uttered in the process, it was clear to Areem that the reason for the gloom was business related.

But that was not the lone night. The same milieu persisted in the subsequent evenings. Some problems were resolved, but new ones cropped up. The new mother was desperate to know the outcome, which, according to her judgment, ought to be in his favor. The saga continued.

Human response syndromes to anything negative in life have inescapable vent to unleash its grave feelings. Lamenting, on occasions publicly, is taken often as the sincere sharing of grief and exhibition of sadness. People seldom think of what else could have happened or more grievous experiences of others around.

That happened in the case of Areem and his family. Business-related glitches that were lingering during the last three days were taken to be the worst that could happen to the family. But no one had any clue of what could befall on the family from a totally unalike angle. That precisely ensued on the fourth day.

It was late afternoon of the day. The vibrant blue sky, affable sunshine, and unusual gentle and amiable temperature were featured in the setting. Areem was at the end of rather infrequent coaching of the younger sibling, more to share with father the progress they made so far. But his sibling, as always been, was inattentive and was frequently looking outside, commenting on the genial conditions outdoors. He was in a mood to flip and fluff the study focus the elder one painstakingly was aiming at.

As Areem tried to pull him back to an important lesson, the younger sibling unhesitatingly suggested going out and playing a friendly cricket game with the elder, unwaveringly asserting his expertise in the game. Cricket came into relevance as the last of five tricountry (Bangladesh,

Sri Lanka, and India) one-day-match series was going on in the cricket stadium of Dhaka.

With the objective of bonding with the sibling more assiduously and minimizing the influence of his maternal uncles, Areem readily agreed with the proposition. He even thought that acceding to such a wish would give the sibling a comfort zone of commonality, having favorable impact on their future relationship. Areem took a step forward and taunted his sibling by saying, "You are growing up. How long would you play cricket with a tennis ball?"

Unexpectedly, and contrary to the new mother's strict position forbidding playing with standard cricket ball with a hard surface, the younger one merrily showed up with the required gear of regular bat and ball. Both brothers enjoyed their rotation of bowling and batting.

It was the turn of Areem to bat. The younger made three nice successive deliveries, and Areem fumbled consecutively. Sober and even-tempered, Areem somehow lost his cool. He negotiated the following delivery with unanticipated professional zeal. Unfortunately, that return ball hit the end of younger sibling's left eyebrow, causing a cut and bleeding. That was enough for the new mother to explode.

She started yelling and crying, accusing Areem of harboring a creepy plan to harm her son. The sudden option to play with the normal hard-surfaced cricket ball against the decision to the contrary was the instantaneous confirmation of that motive, as she loudly and repeatedly stressed. The new mother's constant running and shouting got some reprieve as she saw the personal driver enter the house premises with the community doctor, who was also their family physician.

It was the turn of the driver to receive stormy assertions from the lady of the house. She accused him of lack of responsibility by not going to the business office of the master but for getting the physician. Everyone was dumbfounded, and so was the physician. The driver immediately left to fetch the master.

The physician, after finishing initial procedures, made three stitches on the cut portion of the left eyebrow and assured the mother that nothing serious had happened. He further said that the cut was neither too deep nor extensive to cause concern. He had stitched the wound more as a precaution. He further assured, saying, "Nothing has been damaged seriously, and eventually, there would be no mark of stitching on the face either."

The physician, being familiar with the response fetish of the house lady, made a passionate professional submission based on his expertise and experience. He further assured her, repeating the previous professional assessment of "no damage and no mark of the stitching eventually."

He was able to calm her down, and she felt at ease. Right at that moment, and coinciding with the finishing submission of the physician to the stirred mother, the driver showed up with the house master.

That, to the discomfiture of all present, was the beginning of the second and louder eruption of angst and agony on the part of new mother, emphasizing more the mean intention of Areem to harm her son. That indictment was reinforced by repeating the acquisition of playing with a regular cricket ball despite the strict prohibition.

Against the backdrop of continued loud accusations and repeated admonitions by new mother, Areem, for the moment, apparently lost his sureness and equanimity. He was standing speechless, leaning his physical frame against the wall of the home between the drawing room and the room where the younger sibling was temporarily being kept. Areem neither contested what the mother was saying repeatedly nor felt comfortable to pat his younger brother, assuring him of early and full recovery.

Mr. Sher Ali Affridi could neither enter the room to see his bruised son nor have discussions with the waiting physician because of the incessant sniveling of the wife. Stressed and exhausted because of the ongoing business problems as well as the pitch and tenor of the repeated accusations by his wife, the house master was dumbfounded. In a standstill position, he had a firm as well as a disconcerting look at Areem. The resultant anguish propelled his Pashtun blood to boil internally. He suddenly moved toward Areem and slammed a huge smacking on the latter's left jawline. Immediately thereafter, he moved toward the empty chair by the side of the physician and lolled without any verbal mien.

Everyone around was astounded. The family physician was discomfited, never seeing his favorite Afridi Shaheeb in such a rage. In the community setting, the latter was revered for his graciousness and amiability.

But the immediate impact of that was more visible on the new mother. She was quenched, realizing that her dear husband finally took notice of her sustained assertion about Areem having sinister motive to harm their young son. She calmed down while others slowly got engaged with respective chores. The family physician silently got up; went to check the boy in his reposing room, avoiding eye contact with Areem; and while leaving the premises, advised Sher Ali Afridi by saying, "He is okay. Nothing to worry. He will be all right in two to three days' time."

Areem continued standing in his earlier place, maintaining the same physical posture. Beleaguered hankerings heightened by self-loathing caused the same question to reenter his concentration repeatedly: What wrong had he done to warrant such a public humiliation at this young age? He recalled the earlier soft spanking of his father when he was a toddler in response to the made-up complaints of the new mother. His father stopped dispensing physical punishments a few years back, exercising the option of minimal contact with Areem. Things vibrantly transformed after Areem's brilliant performance in the last school examination.

Being in the middle of a consequential massive emotional rundown, Areem, revisiting response options, resolutely recalled that ostentatious humility with innate pliability would have featured elements of timidity; and that would only manifest admission of culpability. Such thought is a strange reality of life. A jerk or jolt experienced in life mostly has one physical expression but is always haunted by numerous and frequent emotional reflections of diverse enormities. It is very normal for one's thoughts at that time to rave around multitudes of options and consequences.

Areem's situation and consequential varied thought process were no exceptions. Consistent with his growing-up personality traits, his considered assessment was that both confrontation and boldness at this stage would cause unwarranted tiffs in the family, impacting immediately on his plan to pursue education eventually for an independent life and living. Areem saw little or no justification to stray from that course despite what happened and related thoughts otherwise. He decided to remain calm and quiet, giving space to his father to ponder and act, premised on the possible intuition of guilt for his most regurgitating act a few minutes back.

Thinking through choices and evaluating them, Areem also made occasional attempts to monitor his younger sibling from the position where he was. He decided not to be near his brother, or it might give an additional opportunity to new mother to identify afresh something spiteful and repeat her usual yelling.

Areem had irregular eye contacts with the younger one during the ordeal. What he identified in the process was most bewildering. When they had eye contact, the younger sibling would react with an impish smile. Contrarily, he would scream and complain of pain when the new mother was around. Areem was certain that notwithstanding the innocence of adolescence, the younger sibling was playing with the emotions of both mother and brother.

In that shattering realization, Areem opted to refocus his attention to his father, who was in a motionless condition. He remained seated, speechless, occupying the same chair in the same place. Snacks of different sorts and shapes, hurriedly prepared by new mother, apparently reflective of happiness for her dear husband's physical response upon return home, remained untouched. The glass full of water was intact. The hot tea became cold. The only refreshing thing in that setting was the sweet rendering of the call for Muslim's evening prayer (the *azaan* of the muezzin for *maghrib* prayer, as the Muslims call them) coming from the mosque nearby. Areem instantaneously felt sad for the father and miserable within, notwithstanding the anger that dominated his mind earlier. He quietly withdrew himself from that locale and returned to his room.

His return to his room was predicated by the conscientious reason of having a possible escape from the dismal state of standing posture all through since the late afternoon. But that was not to be. While his father's likely pacification was a matter of time, Areem was more haunted by the manipulative character traits being shown by his dear sibling. His deep thinking about that was disturbed by the unexpected presence of one of the household help with the dinner service. The household help placed that on the lone table and left. As room service of dinner was an exception to having food together since the arrival for summer vacation, Areem got the innate message and felt sad. Soon thereafter, he got lost in his thinking about the young brother and the future challenge he would have to face. His new mother's unceasing role and intrusions fraught him most.

Areem went back through his memory to reevaluate recent incidents and skirmishes that caused the new mother to complain often, though he, in most cases, could not make out the rationale. Most recent two were related to chocolate and teaching events. There was no earthly reason for the new mother to react violently on either of the cases unless the younger sibling twisted them otherwise to align the presentation and cause worry in the mind of new mother.

In thinking through those events while lying down on the bed, Areem concluded about the younger sibling having the gene of his maternal uncles: shrewd, manipulative, and self-serving. He also concluded that perhaps he was blessed by the genetic qualities of his grandfather: honest, sincere, straightforward, practical, and committed. That gave him much-needed happiness in those bleak hours of the despondent evening. He turned right, put the second pillow in between his legs, and unknowingly dozed off without having food.

Sher Ali Afridi was awaiting the usual service of his breakfast while glancing the Bangla daily newspaper, *Prothom Shongbad* (*First News*). As the houseboy started placing the breakfast auxiliary items, he lamented, saying, "*Bhaiya* [brother] has not eaten dinner last night." The father's instant reaction was asking the houseboy for breakfast service for Areem too and informing the latter about his awaiting in the dining table.

Areem came, took a seat on the chair opposite his father, and looking downward, just said, "Salai malai kum." It's a local way of saying the standard Muslim greeting "Assalamu alaikum." (Peace be upon you.) The father nodded. Both father and son avoided eye contact and oral communication.

The ostensive saying that nothing in life is permanent indubitably withstood all test of pliability. Human beings, somehow, are utterly oblivious of the other role time plays in life. Time is not only a great healer; it equally is a significant wader in helping life move on. That happened in this case of father–son rapport albeit evident limitations. The few exchanges predicated by tacit focus on pithiness were about the upcoming travel plan, next vacation, and plan to pursue postintermediate education with emphasis on location: whether he would continue in Chittagong or plan to move to Dhaka.

While the subsequent drill for breakfast and dinner together remained unchanged, the course of communication was slow and limited, the waves were infrequent, the words were few, and the warmth was always lacking. Such short discourses, however, were proved to be useful in lessening the burden of guilt on the part of the father and in minimizing the pressure of agony at the end of the son. They slowly became at ease with each other.

But that was not the case with the younger sibling. Whenever Areem encountered him, the similarities with and the canny qualities of his maternal uncles came to the former's alertness. Based on his assessment of a few past events, Areem clearly foresaw him growing up a flamboyant person with the ability to bilk and bungle at the same breath and having uncanny knack to ratchet up events and actions. He had absolute clarity about their future sibling track, decided to be vigilant, and opted to keep that private at this stage. He was thus cautious while interacting with him, maintaining nonetheless outward geniality.

It was time for Areem to leave for Chittagong at the end of the summer vacation. He was having his dinner with the father the night before his planned departure the following morning. The new mother's strategy to keep their son away from close contact with Areem resulted in his permanent absence from earlier practice of having dinner with father and brother.

Despite the passing of many days since that huge smacking, the dinner ambiance had the familiar constrained scenery. Like many dinners after that incident, this father–son dinner time exchanges were mostly limited to single-syllable questions and responses with occasional eye contact, elfin smiles, or nodding.

Any unexpected happening triggers inexplicable pleasure and gladness as well as shock and sadness, keeping in view its type—whether positive or negative. That precisely happened during the father–son dinner that night and, fortunately, from a positive stance. The father wanted to know more details about the process of getting enrolled in US schools, the likely field of Areem's study, and possible financial implications. Areem responded briefly based on his earlier research but remained unspecific about the finances. That was not by design as Areem himself was not certain about it. He, however, mentioned that to his understanding, US education was relatively expensive but more valued and better recognized with explicit remunerative advantage. His father nodded and concluded the brief discourse by saying, "Rest assured, I will finance your study to the best of my ability, and the recent happenings in the house would not have any bearing on my resolve."

Areem returned to his hostel the following evening. He was delighted to see his old hostel brushed with new paints and its tottering doors and windows likewise repaired and replaced. He did not have to ask anyone about such changes. His room boy carrying the luggage was the pungent source of all information: emergency cyclone rehabilitation fund made available by the government was prudently utilized by the college administration to fix the hostel, which was utterly needing restoration. The college authorities took that bypass approach as past periodical requests for repair were mostly turned down, mentioning paucity of resources as the reason. Come what might have caused it, Areem was happy to see unexpected improvements while contentedly enjoying the odor of the new paint.

Based on college policy, the hostel management reassigns rooms each year, with seniors having rooms on the first floor and juniors on the ground floor. Cognizant of this policy, Areem was directing the room boy toward the notice board.

The room boy's riposte amazed Areem. He casually said, "Sir, you have been assigned the same room that you stayed for ten days at the beginning of the vacation. That, of course, would be shared with Manzoor sir, and he did not show up as yet."

Manzoor was a student of the same year but of liberal arts course while Areem had science as field of study. Hence, they did not have much earlier interactions. Compared to shy and reclusive Areem, Manzoor was outgoing, omnipresent in all settings, and involved in varied activities. Because of these, his rather tall build and personal bearing more akin to someone higher, he attained the status of being senior among equals. That was why the room boy referred to him as *sir.*

Areem's delight was multifarious: the same room, a popular class fellow as a roommate, and the site of the room at southern end of the building.

As a firstcomer, Areem had the option to choose either of the two beds, which were standard Bangladeshi *chokis* (four-legged flat wooden bed without a headboard). Areem chose the one by the side of window with head ending with the partition wall. He leisurely opened his bed trappings, made the bed, and slowly reclined by twisting his pillows.

That was the idyllic moment and setting for one to relax, but it was not the case with Areem. His preceding experiences and thinking while with family in Dhaka started resurfacing and haunting him anew. Areem himself was surprised. His father's standoffish behavior since the last incident with cricket try-outs was something arduous for Areem to shake off. However, his equally kind and supporting commentary the night before made Areem try to wash away all negativities and grievances. With the change in context, Areem's real feelings and anguish started reemerging with pertinent queries: Is he, or will he be, treated as a real member of the Afridi family of Dhaka? Was his father's softness the preceding night predicated on his sense of guilt or real love for him? Will the new mother ever be congenial to him? Will the wealth and business of the family be a bond of or clash in the family once his father disappears from the vista? How would he be able to handle the capricious scheming of the two cunning maternal uncles of his younger sibling? There were many more besides the ever-fretting factor of incipient personality traits of his younger sibling.

Problems or frustrations in life do not wind up with broad unanswered questions or vital inquisitions. Once deliberations on broader reasoning pertaining to a specific matter are exhausted, the thought channel traverses through unknown but equally focused tangential inclines. That not only complicates life and living but equally takes away amity of the aggrieved party. That happened with Areem too. The more he was debating all these, the more he became exasperated and irate. His conclusions unvaryingly were trailing a negative track against all his will.

Areem felt miserable in being alone in this world, with no paternal lineage because of his grandfather leaving his roots when he responded to passion. The early childhood experiences of the grandfather precluded any sense of belonging either. Initial life was difficult and frustrating for him too. The later events—his decision to stay back in Bengal, his romantic attachment to Grandma, and the division of India in 1947—made ilife problematic and challenging.

In the case of Areem, the setting was different, but the features were conjoint though not identical. Areem was deprived of love and care of paternal lineage. On the maternal side, after the demise of his mother, he was recoiled permanently because of the influence and insolence of the new mother and her family. Being financially disadvantaged, they had neither the inclination nor the concern for Areem and his well-being. That essentially was a nonexistent part of his life.

Stressed inside and restless outside, Areem was overburdened by disquiets dominating his thought process. He got up, took a little stroll inside the room, and thought of eating but did not have the customary appetite. Positioning himself in a reclined position by twisting one of his two pillows vertically against the wall, he, against all intent, went deep in thoughts pertaining to peripheral issues.

Those issues and untidy muddled mind were both sequential and substantive from Areem's perspective. The more he wanted to distance from them, the acuter they became. One of such issues was the real feelings of his father for him. How much of that was love, and how much of that was obligation? Why did he always react with spanking or other forms of abuse just based on what the new mother told or reported? Why did he never question him or try to verify what actually happened? Had father been enamored by the warmth and charm of the new mother so much that he couldn't question her at all? What caused the apparent distancing from him during the period he needed paternal love and warmth the most, more so as he lost mother while still being infant? How could the father publicly spank him in his youth? Was the assurance of the preceding night's dinner more of a scape rather than a commitment likely to be reversed if new mother pursues that?

The fundamental question Areem had in mind was his standing in the family in future and the possible role of the two maternal uncles of the younger sibling. The future gamut of his relationship with the sibling and the nature of it, notwithstanding earlier lenient inclinations, became clear to Areem against the backdrop of recent experiences pertaining to cricket game, chocolate, and tutoring issues. He had no plausible reason to conclude otherwise, as he hoped earlier. It was more solidified as Areem recalled the absence of the sibling when he was leaving home this morning. Areem was convinced anew that under the misguided supervision of conspiratorial maternal uncles, in the eventual scenario of father's absence, there was a robust possibility of younger one's going rogue.

With that sort of feelings and thoughts coalesced with exhaustion because of travel and settlement, Areem fell asleep only to be awakened in the late hours of the morning as Manzoor showed up with bedding, a suitcase, and a new umbrella. The latter was an unintended addition because of the insistence of Manzoor's family in view of the last cyclonic storm that Areem experienced and what the former's clan came to know from radio and newspapers.

Manzoor's impression of Areem was limited to the latter's academic reputation, besides being known to be somewhat bookish and ardently introvert. But Areem had a broader casing of who Manzoor was: a good student, prominent student activist, polite communicator, and discernably respectful to all and sundries. Both were expressively happy to have each other as roommates for the year.

After customary exchange of pleasantries, Manzoor focused on early settling down in his new room. Finishing those chores, he opened a rudimentary packet and offered the contents to Areem without any hesitation, saying, "These are *pati shafta* [something similar to crepes with inside fillings of thickened milk with sugar] and *pua pitha* [medium-sized and deep-fried indigenous round product made of rice powder, sugar, and milk]."

The preferred ingredients for making various types of pithas in Bangladesh are unboiled rice, gur (molasses) or sugar, coconut, and oil, the latter for both preparing and frying based on need. The taste and aroma of pithas being taken as dessert usually are simply beyond description. It was more in the instant case as Areem was really hungry when Manzoor offered him pithas.

Manzoor continued, saying, "Mother fondly made these for me, having the anxiety of my feeling hungry. I said many times that there is no need, but she would not heed. Besides normal anxiety, she also alluded to glorious uncertainties during a journey and the delay often encountered. I could not decline anymore."

Parental anxieties for young children's living in unknown settings, more at a time without technologies in place, have had unalike manifestations. Some of those were perceived as embarrassing in front of other students, more those who are from relative urban setting and affluent background. Areem once again felt miserable for not having the destiny of being embarrassed like some others.

Areem gladly took one each of pati shafta and pua pitha and started mincing. Manzoor quietly placed two more in the former's plate. In the process, Areem said, "In eating these, I am enjoying the love and care of your mother. I do not have a mother. So I am deprived from all such feelings and care that make life beautiful." Manzoor was very touched.

But what made a permanent imprint in the mind of Areem was Manzoor's steadfastness and confidence. Typically, many youngsters are hesitant in offering mundane home products to one who is not close. But Manzoor did that without hesitation. Further, carrying and using an umbrella are being looked at as rural or old practice. Even then, Manzoor did not hesitate to carry the umbrella the family gave him out of its concern, though he would possibly never use it in Chittagong. These two subtle elements impressed Areem very much. He felt happy and relaxed, against all odds of last night's thinking, in having a genuine person as roommate.

With the passage of time, the rapport between the two not only strengthened but was also equally founded on trust and passion. While Areem, unlike in other circumstances, was forthright in divulging his past and current family details with candidness about what happened during the last vacation, Manzoor penned something quite opposite. Hailing from a respectable Muslim family of the locale, he had a congenial relationship with his parents as well as among the larger segments of the family. He had love and care from all concerned, focus on social good, and community well-being with emphasis on loftier issues of life.

They knew each other well in a relatively short time. Manzoor concluded that Areem's excessive engagement with books and study and his introvert personality were designed escapes from reality around. His acknowledged intellectual ability could be a factor but not the determining one. Other deficiencies in his life—including lack of empathy, love, care, understanding, and so on, besides the loss of his mother at an infantile age—compounded in a way that pushed him to the specific objective of academic excellence.

Manzoor further deduced that full blossoming of a potential life unknowingly being impacted upon by whims and caprices of others. He resolved to talk Areem out of that mind-set and encourage him to see and treat the world from a broader perspective, enabling him, like most others, to enjoy and live a life of purpose on his own terms. Anger and anguish are very much part of normal human living. But these in all cases should not be impediments in pursuing life. Rather, they, based on contexts, could be the source of strength to encounter all adversities.

Areem enjoyed sharing a room with Manzoor but was unhappy because of the frequent visits by many friends and well-wishers of the former. That impacted the way of life Areem used to and on his concentration. Gradually, and from Manzoor's frank admission, Areem came to know about the former's involvement in conservative students' organization known as Islami Chatra Shonmelon (ICS or Islamic Students Assembly). Manzoor also confessed that he and his good friends, many of them Areem knew by that time, were not only members of ICS but were in the lead roles of its college branch operations.

Without directly referring to Areem's veiled unhappiness, Manzoor volunteered to assure the former that what he was witnessing would not be the norm. Since it was the beginning of the session, the leadership needed frequent contact and consultation. He further assured that he would in the future step out while undertaking discussions with fellow comrades and workers.

Manzoor believed in the maxim that one either hides oneself or exposes fully. Half approach either way is neither conducive nor rewarding. So he decided to open up fully to Areem so that the former had clarity about who Manzoor was and what drove him instead of Areem learning it from hearsays.

From casual discourses with some visitors and other friends, Areem had sureness about Manzoor's open-mindedness in tandem with his intellectual prowess. Areem so far was very positive about his own intellectual ability and, in a remote corner of mind, was proud of that. Perhaps the said feeling experienced a jolt for the first time after interacting, knowing, and being familiar with Manzoor's sociopolitical activities, proactive engagements in edifying fields, and simultaneous excellence in academic pursuits. Areem unwaveringly concluded that what he achieved so far was the outcome of single-track priority, and he had not tested his true ability by concurrent engagements in other matters. Areem developed an innate interest in knowing Manzoor better and at a personal level.

Two young individuals from diverse locales presently sharing the same room had almost alike feelings for better bonding with each other notwithstanding distinctive nature of their rationales and objectives. They followed their designed courses in their own way. It took Areem no time to offload before Manzoor his frustration and anger pertaining to life as he experienced it so far. His last statement was an enthralling one: "I do not know anyone in this world who would understand my quandary concerning growing up in a family setting that is both insensitive and inimical. All my efforts to reverse this miserable tandem of life proved futile. I questioned myself many a time why this is so. Is it my destiny? Is it the divine dispensation for me? I am slowly inclined to the last one relating to the demise of my dear mother at an early age. I regret very much, and have a complaint to the divine, for not giving me a chance to address the one who carried me as part of herself for ten months and ten days, as Ma [mother], with love and passion."

Areem broke down by saying those words. He continued, saying, "I have had none in the family to share such feelings. I have had no shoulder to share this agony. I do not know what happened today. I am sorry to burden you with all my personal frustrations."

Manzoor shook his head as a physical demonstration of empathy, moved near the bed of Areem with a glass of water, and offered the same to the latter. Wiping plunging tears, Areem looked at Manzoor; smiled, which was more reflective of dejection; and gulped the water.

Sitting by Areem's side, Manzoor took time before saying, "Yes, I understand your exasperation. To have a burden is upsetting in itself. However, inability to share that burden is worse manifold. Though I do not have any direct experience, I learned about this and other similar matters from social settings that influenced my growing up. Unlike you, I was never in a cage. My congenial family allowed me to grow beyond the peripheral influence of the family per se. I was given freedom and flexibility more to grow as a son of the locale where I breathed, ran, swam, quarreled, played, and studied in the midst of seniors and juniors as well as friends and foes. That perhaps made me a replica of an elderly person at a young age."

After saying those words, Manzoor stood up and said, "I am thankful to you for opening up, though our familiarity with each other has yet to withstand the test of time and tribulation. We need to talk more. I owe you, because of your sincerity, to explain my life and its sustaining philosophy. Now let us pause for a while, take rest, and ponder about what we discussed so far in helping us on way forward." After saying those words with an unusual gracious tenor for a student activist, Manzoor quietly lay on his bed, keeping his eyes closed.

Manzoor took a sentient position not to press the sublime familiarization process with Areem. His unhurried approach was also comforting to Areem as he could devote to his academic pursuits. What surprised Areem was Manzoor's periodic focus on studies with amazing outcome excellence in regular class tests and examinations.

Availing an after-dinner relaxing condition, Areem made a related query to Manzoor about the motivation of his approach and secret of academic success.

It so appeared that Manzoor was eyeing for an opening like this so that what he had in mind to tell Areem would not seem to be an imposition but more seen as an innocent guidance and way forward. With an impish smile, Manzoor stated, "There is no specific design or approach. From early childhood, I was encouraged and practiced to learn and absorb from surroundings besides academic books. During the growing-up process, that dawned on me to be of immense significance and germaneness. Like current fad for multitasking, that proposition has immense relevance and positivity for multilearning. I also concluded that perhaps too much focus on a singular objective constrains the brain capacity and grooming of intellectual prowess, impacting on ability to outshine. So I always remained open to know the unknown from all sources and under varied situations. That has been paying unexpected dividends as I can increasingly handle diverse matters."

After articulating those words, Manzoor suggested going out to have a rather unusual late tea at a nearby wayside stall. While sipping tea, Manzoor opened up on an issue of immense significance from his perspective, more to caution Areem.

So he continued, saying, "In this process of openness and learning, I became interested in knowing the inherent traits that made al-Qaeda so appealing to many, especially Muslims, notwithstanding its militant focus and priorities. In the process, and it so appears, I have become a pawn of that philosophy myself.

"But there is a difference. I am not a radical individual. I, like you, am a Muslim and hail from a respectable family of our locality. I, however, respect all religions. I abhor terrorism, killing, and destruction. But still, I am interested to unearth the rationale for subsistence of al-Qaeda philosophy. I understand the justification for its emergence to begin with. Briefly, and as are known, they are history of injustice meted out to Muslims, experience of deprivation, intrigues relating territories involving rulers, exploitation of resources, sustenance of territorial control and influence ensuring trade routes, and, among others, abandoning of armed and trained mujahideen once USSR left Afghanistan.

"But what intrigued me is its sustained popularity notwithstanding continued emphasis on hate and destruction, deviating from genuine grievances. My simple reasoning is that perhaps being pushed to a defensive posture, the orientation deviated from genuine earlier issues to survival tactics focusing on radical alternatives. Increased negative coverage and enhanced internet technology made this an ugly force to reckon with globally. This is just an off-the-cuff assessment. So I want to go deep, understand operational priorities, evaluate the philosophy, and see whether this can be brought back to a movement that redresses some of the earlier grievances, with focus on local issues and local solutions.

"That encouraged me to enroll as a member of ICS when in the last year of school. Yes, I find many radicals in the ICS setting of Bangladesh, but there are a good number who, though sympathetic to causes, are opposed to death and destruction. I am presently trying to reshape ICS with focus on better learning, compassion, and social outreach for the greater good and sustained progression. So you see, a number of good students of our college have become ICS members.

"Even in a relatively short period, limited progress in reshaping ICS within our institution has been achieved. However, international influence of al-Qaeda, bolstered by the long-drawn war in Afghanistan, appears to be a detriment. I have read intensively about this war and reached an interim position that it possibly is the consequence of misdirected policy focus of Western superpowers, misguided military interventions, deep-rooted local mayhem, persistent territory-specific tribal animosities, conflicting interests of neighboring countries and Western superpowers, the traditional parochial preference for solving all problems through guns, emerging power of opium money, and so on.

"That has been aggravated by bringing Islam to the forefront of this conflict, both by Western superpowers and the media, and exigencies of local mullahs [religious leaders]. The present fight was projected, planned, and executed by the Western power blocs in the name of democracy and fighting religious fundamentalism to obliterate terrorism. Afghans have seen this as a fight to counter aggression against Islam as a religion, and most of the Muslim world's population ascribed to that. The latter has been aggravated in Bangladesh due to erroneous information blitz by half-literate local volunteers returning from Afghanistan and proliferation of madrassa-based education, in one form or the other, with liberal financing from some oil-rich Muslim countries.

"Because of such motley variances, I am often bemused. So I am thinking of joining al-Qaeda and go to Afghanistan for a year or so to have authenticated assessment of what is going on there and in what directions al-Qaeda is moving. This I consider relevant as al-Qaeda is having increasing presence in Bangladesh. We need clarity to address possible ingrained negativity. Rest assured, I am not planning to fight and die. I will endeavor to be a wonk to front people in the fight. I am working to ensure that.

"I know my life's objectives and will always keep that high in the agenda. However, being attuned to look at broader aspects of life and living from childhood, I am ready to sacrifice a year of my life, penetrate deep into al-Qaeda's objectives and operational priorities, and try to assess and understand its ability for operational momentum, maintaining stronghold on substantial territory of Afghanistan notwithstanding years of war with mighty military forces of the world. That may as well be the most rewarding time of mine."

On a specific observation from Areem, Manzoor clarified that his objective was not to reform al-Qaeda per se but to learn from field-level exposure and experiences to reorient ICS in Bangladesh. The inherent objective was to avoid future catastrophes in their own context. He emphasized that both time and objective were therefore limited.

Manzoor's predicament at that stage was what more to tell or how much to expose himself without having clarity as to antiphon of Areem. He thus plodded quietly, taking steady steps toward the hostel. So did Areem.

Both of them talked frequently about wrongly dyed religious attributes by powers and parties on contending sides of the conflict, resulting in the portrayal of Islam (meaning "peace") as the perceived desperado.

Before proceeding further and during a recent discussion, Manzoor made it clear that what he relayed as part of their current dialogue process were insights based on his limited knowledge, and Areem should always bear it in mind. They were not authenticated pronouncements but broadly reflective of that. However, that limited knowledge and information were not mere hearsays or fabricated opinions but based on documented facts, limited even though. These might vary in context and details but remained relevant in broader perspectives. Manzoor concluded this advice by saying, "Nevertheless, those influenced my positions, encouraging to look at the problem from a broader perspective. If opportunities so permit, Areem should research to know facts, faith, and philosophy before forming a definite opinion. My hunt to know more based on ground exposure is an effort in that direction, and that is the rationale for me to think about going to Afghanistan."

He continued, saying, "The focus of current civilized society is that Islam is a rancorous faith and philosophy unfit for modern world. Similarly, the embryonic disparate throngs of Muslim world, with varied identities but being primarily led by al-Qaeda, profess that most of the laws, values, and practices of non-Islamic world are repugnant to Quran and Sunnah. So it is incumbent on Muslims to fight and subjugate them, ensuring a way of life that Islamic injunctions provide.

"Both aforesaid positions are iniquitous. Seeking justice for unjust past decisions and actions are not in conflict with the modern value system. Contrarily, it is simplistic and naive to conclude that laws, practices, and values of the non-Islamic world are redundant and hence need to be replaced by Islamic ones. It is absolutely preposterous to conclude that about five billion non-Muslims are to be condemned just because about one and half billion Muslims believe it to be so. Such a position is untenable by any frame of reasoning.

"The more the Muslims are identified as barbaric folks, the greater is the defiance. The more the Muslim world disdains the systems and way of life of non-Muslims, the huger is its response from the other side. In such a process, the Muslim world becomes a breeding ground for indigenous groups who encourage a significant majority to sacrifice life and resources to counter this. On the other hand, it inadvertently causes prominence of conservative groups in the non-Islamic world to resist the Muslims. Both cause damage to larger world order."

Manzoor emphasized that he was not trying to influence Areem to buy what he said in the past. In a subsequent discussion, Manzoor requested Areem to read more, understand the gamut of the problem, and decide his future course of action, as deemed appropriate. Manzoor assured that he would be willing to help Areem in having access to required literature and publications while Areem had the freedom to access any other source.

This was followed by a period of lull in discussion with respect to the same subject while they discussed other matters of both academic and nonacademic interests. Manzoor was elated in noting Areem's engrossed reading on issues earlier discussed.

Time passed. It was a Friday evening after one of the periodic class examinations. Both were in a relaxed mood. Areem took Manzoor by surprise when he invited the latter for an after-dinner tea in the nearest wayside stall.

As they were sipping tea, Areem opened up, saying, "I have no skepticism about what you said in the past pertaining to historical and current contexts of conflict between Muslims and the rest of the modern world. Even though, and to my assessment, the information shared are of interim nature, they are acknowledged to be of relevance in the current context. Based on my past discussions with you and limited reading, I am convinced about the rationale of your thoughts and approaches. I fully subscribe that even though the larger issues that increasingly are pervading our society and the influence that al-Qaeda presently enjoys globally, we should at least try to do something locally to minimize its impact in Bangladesh, which has had lived peacefully for hundreds of years with other faiths. So I decided to join you, join ICS, and even travel to Afghanistan, if possible, with you. We will come back and try to refocus and reshape our social system, minimizing the impact of extremism and related focus on hatred."

What Areem voiced took Manzoor by surprise. He thought for a while, articulated his riposte, and slowly and calmly said, "I am thankful for what you said and what your proposal is all about. When I said all those things, it was not to get you by my side. As you unhesitatingly opened up before me, sharing depressing family complexities, I thought it appropriate to let you know who I am, my thinking, and my approach forward. I did so as a friend and a brother.

"I had no intention to derail you from your current emphasis on academic excellence. I fully respect your present objective to attain excellence in your current engagement and establish yourself as a respectful and independent individual not dependent on parental affluences.

"Every life is different. So are ours. I come from a large family setting and am the youngest one. My senior siblings have done everything to make our family a complete and happy one. So my parents took a liberal approach toward me. Because of that and the prudence I exhibited during the growing-up process, they have allowed me to act as I deem appropriate. Moreover, during preceding vacation, I alluded to them what I have in mind. Surprisingly, all in the family sort of consented as it is for the greater good, and some were surprisingly happy to see in me the element of a future politician. I, however, promised to them that I will not be looking for a combat role while, and if, I am in Afghanistan. Al-Qaeda's needs are many and varied. So I am working through ICS High Command to be there more as a wonk in helping them in policy matters. I will be seen and groomed as a future motivated agent in Bangladesh. That is my interest and priority.

"But your case is different. I would not encourage and not like to see that you are withdrawn from a minuscular family setting of yours to the likely dismay of your father. So I suggest that you think through it more guardedly before taking a decision."

Areem did not spend time to respond. He started by saying, "You have some idea about my family and my positioning in that. Whatever I do and wherever I am perhaps do not matter to my family. From early childhood, I was neglected, blamed, and abused notwithstanding all efforts to connect, love, and bond with everyone. My peace of mind and thinking have had been severely strained whenever I look back. I can't forget what I went through and am sure about what I will encounter once back to that milieu."

Having said so, Areem ordered a second service of hot chaya (tea) for both and kept quiet for a while. With the service of tea, which subtly worked as a booster, Areem resumed narrating his inner feelings. He said, "I am angry with my life. I am dismayed with what I experienced during growing –up phase. That for certain was contrary to all standard of normalcy in a child's life cycle that otherwise is to be the happiest period of his/her life. Among others, the trivial way I was treated by my father haunts me every moment of my life. He never ever held me, expressed love and affection, or hugged me either. Beyond him, I do not have any family nexus or a shoulder to share my frustration and anguish."

Areem, in detailing his parental roots in North West Frontier province of Pakistan and West Bengal State of India, continued saying, "Since my father was the only child, I don't have any paternal uncles and aunts. The sad demise of my late mother and the arrival of the new mother triggered a complete disconnect with my maternal side. Neither do I know them nor they have any idea about my growing up and living. I didn't have any bond with or obligation to anyone. I am alone in this world and will remain so in future. I am free to decide about my life."

Manzoor heeded passionately and refrained from making an immediate rejoinder. As they reached the hostel premises, he stopped for a while and just said candidly, "Your proposition has far-reaching implications for me. So I need to be absolutely certain about your intent and commitment. Please take time and ponder about it. Remember that there is no about turn. I will expect a decision either way by next Friday. Our preparatory time is short. In the event of an affirmative decision, we need to act quickly. I will think through the best way to include you in our group, which has four other members. They do not have academic excellence but are fully committed, even ready to sacrifice their lives for the sake of Islam. So think twice before conveying your affirmative decision."

The same and the following few nights passed without interactions on the subject. But two nights before the Friday deadline, Areem initiated the discussion on the same subject, conveying his irreversible decision on joining ICS and going to Afghanistan. He further said, "For the family, my existence is a source of unceasing discontent. The stipulated absence would not matter. Contrarily, it could as well be a source of happiness to a section. I am not exact about the probable feelings of my father. His grief, if that is so expressed, would be taken care of by my new mother and her cunning brothers' persuasive assertions, highlighting their conclusive earlier assessment about negative mind-set of mine and my inimical behavior to my younger sibling. They possibly would further highlight potential nasty things that I could do, including impacting the reputation of business and family's good standing. The obvious conclusion would be that my going away may be a blessing in disguise. It could be that in view of such goading, and after lapse of time, Father would reconcile with the reality."

Manzoor had a piercing look at Areem and cautioned him, saying, "At this moment, you are laden with emotions. The journey we have in mind has unforeseen deleterious implications. You should not feel sorry later on. You still have two days to ponder. Think once again. However, on my part, I will initiate the process for your possible inclusion in the group, more to work with me, thus keeping you away from combat engagements."

Areem's follow-on response took Manzoor by amazement. That was something quite unanticipated from one who normally had a sort of sedated personality with pronounced introvert proclivity. Without a second thought, Areem countered by saying, "The tragedy of my life is that I have no one who understands my inner frustration and anger, being uncared for and neglected from childhood. I may be reclusive and not societal in my daily comportments, but I have clarity about my dares, my priorities, and me. I am a frustrated individual but not a derailed one. My concentration for academic excellence, the way I sustained adversities for years, and my decision to move to Chittagong are ample evidence of what I am. All these testify about my ability to take a decision independent of emotions. Being unwelcome in the family, I would like to endeavor to be relevant to society at large. If I fail, so be it. I will not have any regret."

Areem paused, and what he uttered afterward not only took Manzoor by surprise but equally enabled him to identify a more thoughtful and unwavering individual sitting by his side. Areem's last comment was, "In my limited life and exposure, I have formed an impression: many people do not value the things they have. They mostly lament when those disappear from them. My father eminently represents such people. So by letting him know about my disappearance from his life, I want to send a signal of shock to cause pain and anguish in him. That will be my requite for all rages I have within me."

Manzoor did not prolong the discussion. He accepted the decision of Areem without reservation. During later discourse, Manzoor informed Areem about meeting with the agents of Chittagong ICS for their endorsement. That was acted upon in due course with the addition that besides being an aide to Manzoor, he would be recommended by ICS Chittagong to have training in computer technology under the supervision of internet experts of al-Qaeda and to give opportunity to work in organizational matters as independently as possible.

During a related discussion, Areem shared with Manzoor his game plan so far as the father was concerned. He stipulated, "Father is well aware of my preference and plan to have higher studies in the USA. I will request additional funds from time to time during the remaining period of the academic year as preparatory expenses related to that. This strategy will enable me to have some funds with me. I will let him know about going to Afghanistan and joining al-Qaeda once out of Bangladesh."

All subsequent actions were taken by Chittagong ICS and Manzoor to facilitate their joining al-Qaeda in Afghanistan by going to Pakistan first. Al-Qaeda had no organizational outfit of its own in Pakistan; they work and operate through Harkat-ul-Mujahideen (HUM), one of the strongest militant groups in Pakistan. HUM, a splinter of anti-Soviet militant group, was established in Pakistan in 1985 by Fazlur Rehman Khalil with focus on operations mainly in Indian-held Kashmir.

Though a splinter group with different focus, the bond between HUM and al-Qaeda was selfsame sonorous always. HUM was even allowed to share al-Qaeda–run training facilities in Afghanistan. The bond between al-Qaeda and HUM became more solid after 2001 when the USA-led coalition launched its war against the Islamic Government of Afghanistan. HUM substantially helped al-Qaeda and other Islamist groups to seek refuge in safe havens in tribal areas of Pakistan, more particularly in North Waziristan, South Waziristan, and Federally Administered Tribal Areas (FATA) bordering Afghanistan.

In the absence of an al-Qaeda structure, HUM worked as a facilitator for al-Qaeda matters concerning Indian subcontinent in general. Chittagong ICS's main contact point, both for al-Qaeda and Taliban matters, was HUM with sustained inflow and outflow of information. In a series of strictly confidential communications using mostly mutually agreed cypher expressions and words, Chittagong ICS advised HUM of the plan and scheduled for six mango baskets to arrive in Karachi by different flights but on the same date. Explanatory notes were communicated earlier about the discovery of a new mango who in the future would be valuable for the cause both al-Qaeda and HUM were pugnaciously engaged. It was also advised for more careful and cautious handling of this cargo, at least initially, with focus on language and culture. Things proceeded as planned.

QUEST

Manzoor and Areem arrived Karachi via Bangkok while four others reached it by direct flight from Dhaka. Areem mailed his final letter to his father at the Dhaka airport just before checking in for Bangkok flight.

Manzoor easily passed through immigration outpost of Karachi airport and was greeted by HUM agents with guarded warmth. That was not that smooth for Areem. The first unwary obstacle he faced was at the immigration point. The immigration official looked at Areem repeatedly, and glanced through his passport a number of times taking inordinate time before finally observeing, "Bangladeshi people have standard names ending with Ahmed, Rahman, Khan, Chowdhury, Ali, Hossain, etc. How come your name is Areem Ahmed Shah with Afridi as the surname?" That particular question relieved Areem instead of causing concern. He explained his background, tracing to his grandfather. He concluded his short statement by saying, "I have come to visit my roots."

The immigration officer was full of smiles and said, "Oh, you are our brother. Have a nice stay in Pakistan." He then stamped the passport and said, "Happy visit."

On walking out, Areem's immediate reaction was one of disdain mixed with irritation and concern. He was hoping for a big hug from the person receiving him. But it was an inconspicuous one. The predicament was worsened by language barrier. The English articulacy of host receptionist was less than of functional level. Areem did not have much knowledge of Urdu and other relevant languages like Punjabi, Pashtu, etc. All he knew were some words and expressions from popular Indian Hindi movies, but most of those were not of much relevance in the present context of Pakistan. Once, Hindi and Urdu had noteworthy elements of likeness.

But Hindi gradually moved to Bangla and Sanskrit while Urdu tilted more to Persian since the partition of India. In that backdrop, his worsening worries and related anguish multiplied, more due to not seeing Manzoor around.

Nevertheless, Areem's limited exposure to the tenor and tune of Hindi movies facilitated his restricted conversation with the agent receptionist, *Janab* (mister in English) Rashid Haqquani. That partial conversation was occasionally peppered by broken English expressions or, at the worst, nodding. While approaching the point of pickup, he whispered to Areem's ear, saying, "This place is full of government agents. So we cannot talk much. Once in your resting place, I will formally embrace to welcome you to Pakistan and to the fold of al-Qaeda."

They soon boarded a rusty pickup van being driven by a hefty person dressed in *shalwar* (baggy pajama) and *kameez* (long-flowing shirt) with a chador (akin to a shawl) dangling from both sides of neck and a local multicolored embroidered *tupi* (hat) with minute dull pieces of glass. That did not surprise Areem, but what unnerved him were the piercing eyes and overwhelming nature and size of mustache of the driver.

Sitting on the long front seat between the driver and Mr. Haqquani, Areem got engaged in looking around. The loud Pashtu song did not allow any discussion except a low-voice introduction of the driver by Mr. Haqquani, saying, "He is an Afghan refugee." Areem's thought about both the driver's physique and the rusty condition of the vehicle were soon overtaken by the unregulated speeding, sharp turning, risky overtaking, and continuous honking. Areem had no idea where he was being taken and what happened to Manzoor and others. Suddenly, it so appeared that Manzoor disappeared from his life. That made Areem nervous too. He was both edgy and chilled within but maintained a calm posture outwardly.

What drew Areem's attention was the frequency of police and paramilitary check posts reflective of law-and-order situation of Karachi. The driver soon started navigating through side roads and lanes until he reached the destination.

While disembarking, Mr. Haqquani said that this was the border between the main city and a relatively new settlement known as Federal Capital (FC) Area. They had a short walk, and Areem soon was ushered in a godown (warehouse) at the back of supposedly a big store. Mr. Haqquani drew Areem's attention to the lone *khatiya* (bucolic iron frames holding four legs with the top interwoven by broad cotton strips) and left the room by saying, "You sit here. I will be returning soon."

Mr. Haqquani returned, accompanied by a polished tall gentleman of about fifty years. He wore a starched white local outfit of a Muslim clergy and long-flowing henna-tinted orange beard. The additional elements of that ensemble were white cotton round cap with intricate hand embroidery covering his orange-colored hair, and tasbih (similar to rosary) in his hand. He embraced Areem with a broad smile, saying, "*Khosh Amadid*" (Welcome) and introduced himself, saying, "I am Mufti Quaser Ali, originally from northern portion of Punjab and now in Karachi for business purpose, and the front store is owned by me. But more importantly, I am here to serve the cause of Islam and to help propagate the movement for Islamic rule in Pakistan. My affiliation is with HUM, presently overseeing its activities in and around Karachi with other ten local leaders constituting Karachi *shura* [assembly] of HUM." Mufti Quaser Ali concluded his introductory remarks by saying, "I have all related details about you and, more pertinently, your excellence in academic pursuits, as well as your commitment to help al-Qaeda in Afghanistan. In you and some others like you, we see ruminant leaders of Islamic movement in Bangladesh. You may call it al-Qaeda or Taliban phenomenon."

As he finished those words, Haqquani reappeared with *kahwah* (local Pakistani word for "green tea") and some cookies. He was followed by apparently a very submissive person with hunchback posture, having a white tupi and ubiquitous white beard. He soon started taking Areem's wrought body measurements without any exchange of word and quietly left. Mufti Quaser Ali then indicated Haqquani to leave.

The service of kahwah and cookies ushered a sense congeniality in a strange place with a totally unknown elderly individual nurturing strong belief in Islamic rule in Pakistan even at the cost of life and assets. They, however, did not pursue discussions on issues related to Islamization, but Mufti Quaser Ali had a few words of caution and guidance.

While supping the hot kahwah, Mufti Quaser Ali voiced with all authority and decisiveness some critical aspects pertaining to Areem and his associates' journey to Afghanistan through Pakistan. Before articulating those, he, in order to make Areem comfortable and win over much-needed trust and commitment, said, "All important establishments and busy places in Pakistan are presently being swamped by government agents of different shades and facades. It is very difficult to be sure about one's real identity and certain about their motives. So we are exercising extreme care in planning and handling the journey of you and your companions all through Pakistan. The arrangements eventually worked out have earlier been clandestinely discussed and agreed with al-Qaeda and ICS through HUM contacts in Pakistan.

"Your reception at the Karachi airport was by design a low-key one, and each one of you is being handled separately following different routes through varied means of transportations. You all are likely to meet once in tribal areas. Present location of yours in this warehouse is for your safety, to buy time to brief you, and to ensure your semblance reflecting more of a local person. The elderly gentleman who took your measurement did so to help in getting a pair of local outfit for you. Haqquani has gone to market to buy *shalwar-kurta* [baggy pajama and loose top outfit] for you with supporting stuff such as *sindhi ajrak* [multicolored block-printed wrap with embroidery in selected cases and some small tainted round glass-like pieces] and *tupi*. Sindhi *tupis* have openings in front for visibility of forehead and made of intricate geometrical designs with small pieces of mirror sewed into it. Haqquani will also buy local footwear for you. Please bear in mind that both *ajrak* and Sindhi *tupi* are reflective of respect and adoration.

"Your present outfit has no place for a *mujahid*. Neither are your current belongings relevant, besides being a risk factor. Haqquani will give you a small pack containing bare essentials including a kambal [blanket]. That will be your belongings for the future.

"You are a *mujahid* and dedicated yourself to fight for the cause of Allah Rabbul Alamin [the Sustainer of the Worlds]. Your past, your comfort, your convenience are no more relevant. You are to sacrifice all earthly things and pleasures for the love of Allah. Hardships and inconveniences you encounter and dangers and challenges you face are your tests.

"After a day in this warehouse, you would be taken to a mosque known as Farzian-e-Matina, one of the largest mosques in Pakistan with a capacity exceeding twenty thousand. This is both a mosque and an Islamic education center. You would be given Urdu lessons and an orientation of Pakistan's Islamic history and culture to ensure that you are both groomed and at ease when interacting with local people. Your contact person in that mosque is Mr. Ansarul Hashmi, a person of *Muhajir* [refugee] origin and is well versed in Arabic, English, Urdu, and Sindhi languages. You will be impressed by his knowledge and understanding of the Holy Quran and *hadis* [the words, practices, advice, actions, and silent approvals of Prophet Muhammad (peace be upon him [PBUH])] besides his prowess concerning linguistic explicates and ability to communicate. As my person, Haqquani will accompany you until Janab Ansarul Hashmi takes charge of you.

"This has already been decided that from mosque Farzian-e-Matina, you would travel to Hyderabad on the following fourth morning by road. On the designated morning, Haqquani will escort you to a truck hub [popularly known as *adda*], and he would continue to accompany you until you are handed over to the known and designated person of Janab Abdur Muqtaqui Jatoi, HUM leader of Hyderabad and its periphery. He will be responsible for you during your stay in Hyderabad and journey unto Multan in Punjab Province. The place for meeting and handing over is Hyderabad truck adda. Once that is done, Haqquani will come back, and my responsibility would be over.

"Janab Jatoi is a young, vibrant, and influential local Taliban. He has enormous control and authority on areas beyond Hyderabad, by some account stretching up to midpoint between Multan and Bahawalpur, a few hundred miles. But he is also a jovial person and has the ability to make anyone feel at ease. So you will have a good time."

Areem, all through during the aforesaid extensive briefing, kept quiet and exhibited unimpeded attention and extreme concentration with a deep sense of absorbing what he was being told by Mufti Quaser Ali. To begin with, he accepted the stipulation about personal belongings but was determined to resist any proposition to abandon his carry-on bag. Having his grandmother's diary, wedding saree, and academic certificates, including TOEFL results, was of utmost priority and commitment as her grandmother's things were his identity and the academic records were the pieces of evidence for possible unknown options and opportunities in life.

Mufti Quaser Ali was having a tranquil posture after his long narration. He soon got engaged in refilling his indigenous cup with kahwah. Areem noted the opportunity and softly, showing full respect, raised the issue concerning his carry-on bag and made his point. He was determined that if it came to that stage, he would get out and get lost in huge Karachi metropolis with all the risks inherent. The cash he had was his reassuring safety bulb.

Areem dealt with his family background pertaining to his grandfather and his emotional attachment to things he was having in his carry-on.

Perceptively, he refrained from saying anything adverse if the decision was negative but placed more emphasis on getting Mufti Quaser Ali's sympathy and support by recalling, against personal inclination, his loss of mother and the treatment meted out by the new one without any prying of the father.

Mufti Quaser Ali assiduously listened to what Areem meticulously detailed. He continued to have a piercing look at Areem. It was something as if Mufti Quaser Ali was scanning someone for diagnostic purpose. Time passed, and that made Areem fretful. Flouting his focused look at Areem's face and eyes, Mufti Quaser Ali smiled a little and said, "Yes, I understand your emotional attachment. I am making an exception in allowing you to carry your carry-on. I will be giving you a written chit in this regard. You are authorized to show it to relevant persons of al-Qaeda and HUM, strictly based on need. But there is a condition: if circumstances warrant a choice between the belongings in the carry-on and greater cause for which you are dedicating your life, then the cause should take precedence over such belongings. You should not have any hesitation to abandon those at such a time."

Mufti Quaser Ali was pleased with himself for being able to make Areem happy and, in the process, cemented the latter's loyalty for the cause of Islamization. Areem, being relieved, kept quiet.

Observing that, Mufti Quaser Ali interjected, saying, "You are, as I observed, by nature a reserved person. Keep that up. Always bear in mind that the number one enemy in our dealings and actions with outsiders is our propensity to talk more than needed. Unguarded words in unknown settings are perilous, and we often forget that. So I am cautioning you. Also remember that in our journey and operations, there is no friend. A friend of today can be enemy tomorrow. The maxim is 'Never utter a word and share information beyond the needs.'" He then left, saying, "We would meet here again during dinnertime. We would have dinner together, and that would enable us to interact freely and know each other better."

As stipulated, Areem left the warehouse for mosque Farzian-e-Matina the following morning in the company of Mr. Haqquani and in the same vehicle that brought him from the airport. The only change was the driver, a Karachite fellow dressed in shirt and trousers. During the journey, the driver, in his desire to be friendly, said, "Everything related to vehicular road transportation has been monopolized by Afghan refugees, and he is a standby one. The regular Afghan driver failed to report for duty. So he is driving." Being of Muhajir background, he could communicate in Urdu well. Areem kept calm and only nodded. Mr. Haqquani maintained his assiduous silence.

Mr. Ansarul Hashmi greeted Areem very warmly at the doorsteps of Farzian-e-Matina. Mr. Hashmi was blessed with conspicuous somatic attributes. His slender medium-height body had exceptional skin tenor radiating brightness. His flowing beard was of decent length, indicative of occasional trimming contrary to prevalent Taliban practice. He had black beard and hair, deviating from preference for applying henna to have the piquancy of orange color. To Areem, his new host guide cum teacher was "one of us."

What amazed Areem was Mr. Hashmi's wearing a constant smooth smile in which all fasciae of his face had evocative involvement with a visible role of the eyes. All those features, including the surroundings of the mosque, had an immediate upbeat impact on Areem. The language proficiency of Mr. Hashmi was the added factor. Areem felt at ease instantly. They bonded easily.

The unbridled enthusiasm shown in learning Urdu, in-depth curiosity in knowing past Muslim history, unrestricted prying to know other languages and current Islamic ideologies in the shape of al-Qaeda and Taliban, and so on by Areem impressed Mr. Hashmi. He was delighted to have Areem as a Taliban under his direct supervision.

The designed Urdu rudimentary course of four days planned for Areem was finished in three days with the spirited guidance of Ustad (teacher) Ansarul Hashmi. Areem was happy, but more euphoric was Ustad Hashmi himself. During lunch break of the third day, Mr. Hashmi told his dear *Talib* (student), "I am very happy with your competence and committed efforts. Seldom do I have one like you. I have thought of an interesting but nonacademic test for you. But concentrate in finishing the designed course this afternoon. I plan to take you tomorrow to a local market popularly known as Bohri Bazar. I will encourage you to act alone, with me always behind you. You can talk and bargain as you like. You are to remember that Bohri is a huge congested bazaar with numerous shops in the heart of Karachi City. Most shops are basic in terms of structures and facade. One gets most of life's requirements there with bargaining being the dominant feature of most deals. Its customers are varied in terms of income, language, and ethnicity. Shopkeepers and salespersons are mostly Urdu speaking with some Afghanis. Few salespersons can also speak English. This will be an experience of your life and might help you, in one form or the other, in future."

The fourth morning was a relaxing one both for the *ustad* and *talib*. Their subject matters of that morning were not related to language enhancement but definitely pertinent to Areem's mission and related objectives.

Ustad Hashmi first dealt with Karachi's current standing, making it clear that what he would be saying might not be hundred percent correct but mostly reflective of facts as documented. He said, "Karachi had been famous for being a trading center and a friendly warm water port luxuriating in the cradle of the northern tip of Arabian Sea. That fame diminished with its being adored as the capital of the new largest Muslim country, Pakistan, showing gargantuan capacity to absorb peacefully hundreds of thousands of Muhajirs from partitioned India. This glory lasted for about thirteen years when the process of shifting the capital to absolutely new city up north, to be known as Islamabad and located between garrison city Rawalpindi and semicircular Margalla Hills, began.

"Karachi went into a limbo temporarily. It regained political prominence during Bhuttoism and its partisan slogan of *roti*, *kapra*, and *mokan* [bread, clothing, and housing] of late 1960s. It regained largely its past glory and earned the status of being a modern upcoming city of civility mostly during late 1970s to early 1980s. Beginning the later period, focus on Islamization by General Zia-ul-Haq and influx of Afghan refugees started to have marked influence on every segment of life.

"The increasing presence of Afghans in that backdrop and their involvement in daily activities impacted Karachi's life and living significantly. Though many refugee families returned to Afghanistan, a significant portion of more than three million are still in Pakistan and, for that matter in Karachi, with permanent footing. Among others, their presence in transportation sector is more perceptible.

"The aforesaid changes in the social fabric of Karachi were overtaken beginning mid- 1980s by a sudden escalation in manifestation, endeavor, and actions focusing on Islam all over Pakistan and the open political demand for justice system to be oriented in conformity with Quran and Sunnah. That got necessary boost from official Islamization policies of President General Zia-ul-Haq. Karachi perhaps had no option but to be a part of that politico-social reality of Pakistan.

"Karachi initially sheltered Afghans who, being loyal to monarchy, were inclined to conservative thinking, having visible hatred for communism. They mostly were classified as 'refugees' escaping chaos and confusion caused by coups and countercoups of late 1970s. Many of this group resettled themselves in Western Hemisphere, but a significant number remained in Karachi.

"Subsequent Soviet invasion of 1979 unnerved many Afghanis anew. It reinforced and triggered migration to Pakistan, besides Iran, once again. They mostly composed of ordinary Afghans of different tribes and varied locations. The remainder of the first group and some of the second group, being unexpectedly uprooted from their hearth and homes, rapidly aligned with al-Qaeda philosophy and Taliban phenomena. That also happened to those who were left behind in Afghanistan.

"In the aftermath of the 2001 US-led invasion of Afghanistan, extreme-rightist groups consisting of al-Qaeda followers, Taliban activists, and many indigenous Afghans moved to Pakistan. And most of them found their support and footing in Karachi, attracted by its economic buoyance and status. They were the third segment of refugees from Afghanistan.

"There had been a major swing in the pattern and objectives of infiltration since US invasion of 2001. Slowly moving out of FATA and adjacent areas—initial places of infiltration—al-Qaeda volunteers, Taliban activists, and some other Afghan refugees started penetrating urban areas and growth centers with the help and patronization of HUM. HUM not only helped them in having safe havens in cities and urban areas but also assisted in establishing them and in facilitating their getting new identities and new documents.

"Consequently, the open and pulsating city of Karachi fell prey to actions and policies of sporadic killing, murder, and destruction of critical national assets. Use of improvised explosive devices [IED] and the Molotov cocktails [bottles filled with gasoline], in a sense, became both random and routine. Suicide bombing also became an occasional feature.

"With a population of more than ten million, it provided both the unhindered space and depth for sustained terrorist activities. Many of the conservative followers started constituting varied groups to fight for Islam and against proxy occupation of Afghanistan by Western alliances. President Pervez Musharraf's open policy and material support for US-led alliances were taken by large segment of Pakistanis as a betrayal and heightened the determination to confront US on the ground, in the seas, and in the air. This emerging psyche made both al-Qaeda and the Taliban very ecstatic, and they did not miss any opportunity to use it.

"The worst impact of this was on the national fabric of Pakistan. Emergence of ever-increasing conservative organizational bases, focused propaganda through print and media, inflection of free madrassa education, inflow of unregulated fund from oil-rich Muslim countries of the Middle East, and open and brutal historical faith-related conflicts were some of the immediate outcomes disintegrating Pakistan's social fabric. And Karachi was very much a part of that process. That showed its ugly face when Sunni [majority sect] followers started killing Shia [main Muslim minority sect] followers, and vice versa, openly. Even the worshipers in mosques are not being spared. No one is safe now in Pakistan. Unfortunately, the rivalry between Saudi Arabia and Iran goaded quiescent internal conflicts within Pakistan, and both these countries inopportunely are using historical rudiments and practices of the same religion to achieve domination from respective perspective."

Ustad Hashmi concluded his narration about Pakistan in general and Karachi in particular by saying, "I know that your ultimate objective is to return to Bangladesh and work for Islam. So I thought it appropriate to put facts before you with advice that there is nothing wrong in working for Islam, but make sure that you do not repeat the mistakes we have committed in Pakistan. While in Pakistan, be careful in talking both to known and unknown persons, be always alert in all situations, and keep your mind and thoughts always open."

Areem had impressions about what Ustad Hashmi dealt with so far, though the depth was unclear to him before having the present discourse. As Areem was in the process of aligning his thoughts with life's objectives and current mission's motivation, Ustad Hashmi drew his attention and said that he would like to clarify an important matter for better appreciation and guidance in future. He started saying, "Though we commonly use al-Qaeda and Taliban in an overlapping sense, they are pointedly different. And you should have an idea about it."

Ustad Hashmi continued, saying, "Both of them are extreme Muslim conservative groups in terms of character and contents. Al-Qaeda and Taliban subscribe and propagate misinterpreted tenets of Islam advocating a violent agenda. Even then, they are different. Al-Qaeda is inclined to Sunni militant philosophy, known as Salafism. They pride themselves to be the real believers and accurate interpreters of the Holy Quran while considering others, including moderate Muslims, as infidels. Contrarily, the Taliban are identified as Sunni fundamentalists following the philosophy of Wahhabism, which propagates 'austere Islamic reform movement.'

"Al-Qaeda, founded between 1988 and 1990 by Osama bin Laden and Mohammed Atef, is an Islamist group with a global agenda. The Taliban, on the other hand, is a Sunni Islamist political movement and was founded by Mullah Mohammed Omar while fighting Russian and Northern Alliance forces.

"Mullah Omar's main support and strength were rooted in patronization by Inter-Service Intelligence [ISI], a very successful but equally infamous military intelligence outfit of Pakistan Army and numerous galvanized madrassa students all over Pakistan with dominant concentration in the province of NWFP and adjacent tribal areas. Most of such madrassas were sponsored and financed by oil-rich Muslim countries of the Middle East through sympathetic and religious political organizations in Pakistan. The Taliban [students] of such madrassas spearheaded the Taliban phenomenon in Afghanistan while actively supporting their political affiliates in Pakistan.

"Such political affiliates have had heavy Islamic orientation but insignificant political presence in Pakistan. Hence, madrassa students are being used as principal conduits for its field-level activities.

"The main party involved in such a game is a pronounced religio-political party predominantly influenced by thoughts and teachings of Deobandi school. The term *deobandi* is derived from the name of a town, Deoband, in the Saharanpur District of the state of Uttar Pradesh of present India where the Deobandi Islamic movement began around 1860s, originating in Darul Uloom Deoband [Darul Uloom Islamic School]. This Islamic school was oriented to teach revealed Islamic sciences according to Hanafi school of Islamic jurisprudence. It soon spread all over prepartition India and gave rise to strong Sunni philosophy and practices as a standard bearer of Islam.

"That political entity of Pakistan has the dominant power, influence, and role so far as the Taliban movement is concerned. To nurture this, the party focuses on recruiting activists from thousands of mosques and madrassas sponsored and financed by it. As a result, most such activists are from Deobandi mosques and madrassas in Pakistan. Its senior-level leaders are mostly madrassa-oriented theologians. The workers are those who have had training and association with religious schools and seminaries. Besides opposing progressive and liberal ideas, the party's protuberant political demand is the enforcement of Sharia law in the country.

"The theological base of al-Qaeda is enforcement of Sharia law all over the world with international emphasis for operations while adoring desired acuities of *jihad* [holy war] and *shahadat* [martyrdom]. The Taliban's favored ideology is a mix of Sharia law and Pashtun tribal codes cherishing elements of jihadi concepts with areas of operations limited to Afghanistan and Pakistan.

"The Taliban, under the leadership of Mullah Omar, ruled Afghanistan between 1996 and 2001 with full and total application of Islamic jurisprudence until it lost its power and control due to US invasion [dotingly code-named Operation Enduring Freedom]."

The historical perspectives and gainful discussions were of significant interest and relevance to Areem, and he was trying to internalize related details. Ustad Hashmi looked at his *talib* and was pleased to note the rampant attention with which Areem was trying to absorb all that Hashmi detailed.

The discussions, significantly facilitated by multilingual expertise of Ustad Hashmi, had to be called off to give time to prepare for *zuhr* (midday Muslim prayer), lunch, and rest. Before departing, it was agreed that both would meet at the same place around 4:00 p.m. for their visit to Bohri Bazar, as proposed and agreed earlier.

The visit to Bohri Bazar was a wonderful experience for Areem. Numerous shops of different sizes and shapes with merchandise of all types and qualities, noticeable varied identities of shoppers both in terms of ethnicity and dress-up, presence of modern ladies with make-up and attired in jewelry, mostly having hands full of glass bangles of different designs and shades, were of immense interest to Areem besides the most interesting presence of burka-clad women. The other phenomenon that amused him was the nature and type of numerous alleys, which literally had no beginning and end. Unless one knew them or was escorted by a known person, there was all possibility of one getting lost transitorily.

Areem moved freely in Bohri Bazar under the watchful eyes of Ustad Hashmi. He did not get involved in bargaining but observed intensely others doing so. Ustad Hashmi was happy observing Talib Areem's self-assurance and confidence while ordering *garam chaye* (hot tea) and mingling among crowds in the process of navigating his way through alleys of Bohri

Bazar. For Areem, the visit was a great opening for his future journey through Pakistan.

On the following morning, and as earlier indicated, the familiar face of Mr. Haqquani showed up with inescapable rickety vehicle to escort Areem to Hyderabad via the interprovince truck adda in the outskirts of Karachi. Areem took leave from all concerned of Farzian-e-Matina, but the same from Ustad Hashmi was more touching. It was equally emotional for both, and words were few. As Areem bent to touch the feet of Ustad Hashmi for performing salaam, the *ustad* held the *talib*'s two hands, lifted him up, embraced him warmly, and said, "Fee Amanillah." It meant "Be with the safety of Allah" and was more akin to English expression of goodbye. Areem then boarded the awaiting pickup van. He was positioned, like his travel from Karachi airport, at the middle of the horizontally laid-out single driver's seat in between the driver and Mr. Haqquani.

The drive from the mosque to truck adda in that early hours was more challenging than expected with traffic of different kinds and types trying to beat the morning rush hour. That was aggravated by congestion, honking, overtaking, and screaming with some pedestrians trying to cross roads haphazardly. For himself, Areem was engrossed with what Mr. Hashmi told him yesterday and was pondering about what the *ustad* wanted to tell but refrained from.

On reaching truck adda, they switched to a big truck loaded with goods being transported to Hyderabad. It was unusually big with significantly high-raised sideboards. The sitting arrangements were the same, with Areem in the middle.

As Mr. Haqquani accompanied the driver to settle arrangements for travel to Hyderabad, Areem, sitting alone, was gazing at the surroundings. Preponderance of trucks with intricate decorations on bodies intrigued Areem most. That feeling was jubilated, observing most trucks having multicolored all-encompassing floral patterns, calligraphy, paintings, and ornamental decor on their bodies with relative extensive focus on front and back. Some trucks mostly used mirror works as additional decor for the front and back of the trucks. The other noticeable feature were the dangling chains and pendants off the front bumpers of many, creating a jingling sound.

After switching on but before putting his feet on the accelerator, the truck driver exchanged looks with Areem and had a broad smile with a push of his shoulder, sort of indication conveying assurance of a worry-free journey.

Once on the highway, Areem was relieved, observing that his truck, like many others, was negotiating a spacious road snaking through the barren desert-like terrain being increasingly swollen by urban advances. In such unfamiliar setting without any semblance of either water or greeneries, a common feature of his life and living in Bangladesh, Areem was bemused, noting similarity in certain driving features. Overtaking chaotically, honking, and changing lanes frequently without signals were known to him from Bangladesh experiences. Unabated emission of black polluting smoke through exhaust pipes and persistent thudding noise were some other commonalities. But it was the speed and recklessness of the present driving that concerned and perturbed him most. However, jingling sounds of dangling chains and floating multicolored ribbons hanging from side-view mirror frame continued to amuse him. He was both scared and nervous but was trying desperately to fully absorb that smile and assurance of the driver. With accomplishment of every twist and turn, both while speeding and overtaking, the driver would look at Areem with a big smile, backing his driving performance and acumen.

Mr. Haqquani was mostly quiet without visible physical symptoms but always showed a sense of uneasiness whenever the truck had to stop at a security checkpoint. He would allow the driver to talk about cargo in the truck, posing himself as the buyer's representative. He would methodically extend his neck and head as a nonactive participant in the discussion. As it appeared later, it was a deliberate maneuvering to conceal Areem's sitting between the hefty Afghan driver and Mr. Haqquani and divert the attention of the security personnel.

The journey of about ninety miles was completed when the truck stopped at its designated adda. Areem was requested to be in his seat in the truck while the driver went to the public washroom to relieve himself, and Mr. Haqquani took measured steps outside the adda to locate Janab Jatoi's designated person.

As Areem was sipping local *garam chae* (hot tea served with a mix of full-cream buffalo milk and plenty of sugar) served in a small glass with all the warmth and love of an unknown driver, Mr. Haqquani reappeared in an auto-rickshaw, a motorized version of traditional pulled cycle rickshaw, in the company of Janab Jatoi's selected person.

Areem stepped out of the truck, responding to a gesture of Mr. Haqquani. He introduced Areem with the new person, just uttering the name Osman. Areem exchanged salaam with the new person and hugged the driver and Mr. Haqquani very warmly as if they were his kith and kin before taking his seat inside the auto-rickshaw, complying with the earlier instruction of Mr. Haqquani.

The auto-rickshaw driver, without wasting any time, started for the designated place he was evidently told about earlier. That was obvious as Mr. Osman did not say anything to the driver. While the auto-rickshaw was cruising with frequent jerks and breaks, both Osman and Areem were quiet inside, perhaps constrained by language ability. The only commonality between them were the Sindhi cap, droopy folded *ajrak* suspended from both sides of shoulder, and standard footwear, though with perceptible differences in terms of quality, design, and price.

The auto-rickshaw travel was not much different than the truck one, except its snail speed and frequent jams predicated by narrowness of the roads in some sections and discernible presence of camel-driven traffic transporting local cargoes. After tricky maneuvering resorting to occasional diversions and vociferous frustration released by the driver, the auto-rickshaw finally reached the Jatoi house in the periphery of Hirabad (town of diamonds), a prestigious residential area of prepartition India. While most of the Jatoi family moved to new residential areas being developed since middle eighties and also to Karachi, Mr. Abdur Muqtaqui Jatoi preferred to stay back in the old abode with all its elegance and vanity though diminished drastically.

Security personnel took a close look and, on being given indication by the escort, one of them opened the iron gate, sufficient enough for the auto to enter. He promptly closed the same. Evidently, that was demonstrative of security alertness of the house and of the surrounding setting.

Mr. Osman requested Areem to take a seat in the spacious receiving lounge and went to the inner courtyard. It was clear to Areem that the present structure, though large, was not part of the home but sort of a front structure for receiving guests and visitors, as well as the seat of office establishment overseeing landholding matters and administration of daily occurrence.

The lounge was very calm, with Areem being the only occupant at the moment. Though palpably a receiving area, access to it appears to be somewhat regulated. The staff of Mr. Jatoi, so it appeared, not only diligently avoided entry into the lounge but also did not casually wink to the interior of the lounge. To Areem, that appeared to be carry-over family practice or might be reflective of false sense of family prestige. In either case, it was immaterial to him. He stopped all this thinking and decided to relax as a preparation for meeting Mr. Jatoi, the feedback about whom so far being a mixed one: both implacable and jocund. What surprised Areem was a pleasantly comfortable feeling inside compared to the very hot weather outside.

Osman soon reappeared, and escorted Areem to an inner-side private room, which, by all nuance, was more akin to a study. The only marked difference was absence of books but abundance of skins of dead lions, tigers, crocodiles, and others, possibly reflecting the hunting trophies of his forefathers.

Both the entrance of and self-introduction by Janab Abdur Muqtaqui Jatoi were spontaneous, with no posturing of aristocracy, clout, and revengefulness—some of the traits Areem harbored so long about him. Mr. Jatoi took Areem by surprise when he apologized for keeping the latter waiting, saying, "I unexpectedly faced a very delicate family problem and excused myself from that discussion just to meet our brother once upon a time."

Uttering those five last words, Mr. Jatoi paused for a while as if he was in a trance. After a while, and recovering from the sudden gaffe, Mr. Jatoi soberly resumed his unfinished statement, saying, "I am referring to the pre-1971 position. My late father visited Bangladesh many a time, but I could not make it as yet. Incidentally, I was born on the day Sheikh Mujibur Rahman announced his six-point demand on behalf of the people of East Pakistan in a press conference in Lahore. My late father, among some other political luminaries of the time, was also present in that press conference on a noncommittal basis. I was jokingly addressed as six-*pointia* [something similar to six-point-related child] by close relations. It, I am told, stopped after the emergence of Bangladesh as an independent country in 1971. So when I was told by HUM High Command about you and my responsibility to ensure your safe journey to Multan, I was delighted. So take me as a brother.

"HUM assigned two responsibilities to me: first, your safe travel to Multan [in Punjab Province] and, second, giving you an orientation about Sindh, more specifically Hyderabad. I am certain of your in-depth familiarity with the first one by this time. The second one is pertinent as forged interim travel documents are being prepared identifying you as someone from my *taluk* [cluster of villages under the authority of a landlord]. So you need to have some broad impression about your supposed place of origin so long as you are in Pakistan. But more importantly, if you are in any incongruous situation threatening your security and life, Sindh will be the place of your refuge. You should try to be in Sindh territorial jurisdiction at the earliest and contact me. We will provide necessary cover to ensure your safety and security until we are united here.

"Presently, you are scheduled to leave Hyderabad for Multan night after tomorrow by an express train. One of my trusted men will accompany you until handing you over to the *pesh* imam [designated person to conduct prayers in a mosque] of famous Eid Gah Mosque located at the east of the old city. The *pesh* imam will take care of you until you reach Landi Kotal point of tribal areas."

Mr. Osman showed up and, ostensibly with a whispering attempt, told Mr. Jatoi rather audibly, "*Begum shaeba* sent her salaam," roughly meaning "The lady of the house has requested your return."

That triggered a sense of guilt in Mr. Jatoi's facial reaction. While dismissing Mr. Osman with a nod, Mr. Jatoi stated, "My uncle and aunt are in our place. They arrived about half an hour prior to your arrival. They have a major land-related problem with another set of my cousins and came to seek my mediation and help. I am in an emotionally challenged position as both the families are dear to me.

"Since it is impolite to keep them awaiting, I need to go. We will have dinner together here and then talk in a more slipshod scenery. In the meanwhile, the office manager of my *kachari* [office] will give you company and will accompany you in walk around my house complex, but please refrain from going out and talking any issue concerning the purpose of your visit and objective of your mission."

Mr. Jatoi then went out, and the office manager showed up in a twinkle of eye. He talked briefly with the manager standing at a respectable distance and then left for the inner house.

The manager took Areem out for a walk around the property but within the boundary walls. It was mostly a relaxing walk for Areem—breathing fresh, warm desert air—while the manager was engrossed in solo talk, occasionally highlighting his role and responsibility in managing the real estate of the Jatoi family. He traced back to his thirty-five years of service to Jatoi family and almost ventured to indicate that it was but for his acumen and effort that the Jatoi family is in such a good standing currently.

The follow-on dinner mirrored, in terms of variety and mix, a combination of food items; and the quantity was enormous. Chapati [pressed flat but thin bread made by hand individually], boiled rice, common vegetable preparations, chicken and lamb meat items of varied types, and lintels made the big rectangular dining table looked inadequate. As Areem was glancing, Mr. Jatoi underlined that his wife specially prepared fish curry, knowing that the guest of the night was from Bangladesh. He clarified that since she was late in knowing and starting preparation, the curry was still being cooked and would be served soon. He laughed and went to his designated chair with Areem sitting opposite of him. The ambiance had some resemblance of bygone aristocracy, but the sincerity and warmheartedness were both spontaneous and obsequious.

At the very outset, Areem recognized that Mr. Jatoi was different in many respects than other gentries of HUM he had encountered during the last few days. His showing up for dinner in a starched white *korta* (flowing long-sleeved shirt) and *shalwar* without the esteemed Sindhi cap and *ajrak*, his not having an all-pervading mustache common to most landlords, and his not having any *huqqua* (also spelled as hookah), a symbol of aristocratic culture and social prestige of Nawabs and other gentries, following him caught the attention of Areem.

The absence of all these had a comforting upshot on Areem's bearing during dinner service. Areem soon realized that Mr. Jatoi was a slow eater with evident liking for more munching before swallowing, and he had an elusive preference for soft exchanges in between.

After some detached inquisitions, Mr. Jatoi softly made one observation and two queries. The observation was related to Areem's clean-shaven face. He observed, "If you would like to be embraced by al-Qaeda and be one of them, then better stop shaving and grow beard." The pertinent two queries were related to the reason that motivated him to join the fight in Afghanistan and how much he knew about Pakistan. Areem mused for a while, agreed on the observation and responded on the first query, briefly detailing his life conditions in own family setting and frankly admitting that there was no ideological compulsion but more life-related frustrations that motivated him to join the fight in Afghanistan.

On the second query, he said, "My generation in Bangladesh does not know much about Pakistan. All we know is that once we were one country but had grievances. Thus, we fought a war with Pakistan Army but not its people, and won the independence. We know more about Pakistan in the context of cricket game, and there are many supporters of Pakistan's cricket team in Bangladesh. In sports, we are politics neutral."

It was obvious that Mr. Jatoi was at ease with Areem's agreeing with the observation and responses with respect to his two specific queries. He, however, was wondering about the future recourse of their dialogue, keeping in view the deep emotions preluding the first response and amiable annotations pertaining to the second one. Those frank elucidations carved a soft window in the mind and thoughts of Mr. Jatoi for the unknown young man from Bangladesh. He, however, decided not to deviate from the focus on dinner, which was prepared with a lot of effort and guidance of his wife.

The shushing sounds of slow steps of a household person holding one each of service plate and serving dish in a tray was a pleasing break in the quiet dinner partaking. Noticing his entrance, Mr. Jatoi was in a discernable joyful disposition. As the household help placed the service dishes on the table, he recommended his conversation, stating, "Bengalis are well-known for their liking of fish. Sindhis also like fish but prefer mostly fried ones. Some families also prepare fish curry. So both the types have been prepared for you. It is advisable that you concentrate on fish as meat will be the main intake during the rest of your stay in Pakistan and Afghanistan."

The very private dinner was over soon, and the household helps disappeared after serving kahwah in traditional teacups (cups without handles, more akin to Chinese ones). They left behind a big pot of kahwah with appropriate and delicately embroidered tea cozy (teapot warmer) covering it.

While sipping kahwah, Mr. Jatoi casually brought out his favorite cigarette pack of Three Castles—a surprise to Areem—and lit one. He then clarified that though not an ardent smoker, he mostly enjoyed occasional puffs after a nice dinner. He further said, "Not only was the dinner tonight nice but nicer was the company I had in your person."

There was an evident change in the tone of Mr. Jatoi. He concentrated more on puffing and avoided eye contact with Areem. It was evidently very discomforting for Areem in the private setting of that room. He was debating whether that was a reflection of burden of hosting him. But that thought soon disappeared as he revisited the warmth and friendliness with which he was being treated since arrival.

After finishing his second cigarette and sipping the kahwah, Mr. Jatoi serenely opened up. He started by saying, "Bengal's contribution in the creation of Pakistan is well recognized and known. But Sindh, among the western provinces of prepartition India, also played a significant role. It was because of Bengal and Sindh that the dream of Pakistan became a reality. However, when Pakistan came into existence, the power was arrogated by veiled interested groups. The genuine expectations and demands of Bengal [henceforth known as East Pakistan] were not only ignored but ironically looked at askance. Sindh has had its own problems with the federation and was always supportive of East Pakistan.

"That was not premised on the general idiom of 'The enemy's enemy is my friend.' It was mostly because of the long history of Sindh's involvement in and contribution to human civilization per se, the intellectual prowess Sindhi leaders had from time to time, the philosophical-political-literary exposes of Sindhis, both its Muslim and Hindu population, premised on the strong influence of Sufism, and probably, though remote, the influence of rivers and water in its territorial settings.

"Bengal is proud of its arts, culture, and literature. Sindh respects that reality. But Sindh, contrary to its present image, had historic relevance to human civilization and progression. Present Sindh was the southern tip of Soan Valley between the Indus and the Jhelum Rivers. Soan Valley is documented to be the place of earliest human settlement in India. Sindh and its contiguous territories bear the ruins of Indus Valley civilization, and the sites presently known as Mohenjo Daro and Harappa epitomize that. Mohenjo Daro and Harappa carry the evidence of town planning, brick-based construction, sewage and drainage systems, etc. thousands of years back. Even a writing skill was also developed on that site.

"Thousands of years after Indus Valley civilization, Sindh continued to play a pivotal role in human settlement and development in Asia, particularly India, under various backdrops and administrations. They included the Vedic chronicles, the Mauryan era, the Arab invasions, the Ghaznavids [a Persianate Muslim dynasty of Turkic origin ruling major parts of Central and mid-Asia extending up to northwest part of India) incursions, the Mughal administration, and eventually, the British conquest.

"Present Sindh, with nickname Mehran, and beginning the eighteenth century, was ruled for about one hundred years by Kalhora dynasty [a Sindh-based Shia Muslim dynasty of Baloch origin] with the capital in Khudabad. Due to repeated flooding, the Kalhora dynasty ruler of mid-eighteenth century decided to move the capital of his kingdom from Khudabad to the high plains of Neroon Kot. Neroon Kot was so named after the medieval Sindhi ruler Neroon. It is situated east of River Indus on a limestone ridge known as Ganjo [barren] Takkar [hill]. The city was adorned with its present name of Hyderabad in honor of the name of fourth Muslim caliph Hazrat Ali. When translated, it literally stands for Lion City, reflective of strength and valor Ali consistently exhibited in warfare. He was revered and known as Ali Hayder, roughly meaning Ali the Lionheart. The distinct words *Hayder*, standing for Ali, and *abad* meaning "settlement," constitute the subjective name of Hyderabad.

"Alluvial plains of the banks of mighty Indus River, a desert at its eastern border by the name Thar, a mountain at its western end known as Kirthar, arid plains bordering Punjab at its north, and the Arabian Sea in the south jaggedly expounds Sindh's landscape.

"Sindh's location is typified by hot desert climate with warm temperature for most part of the year and mild cold during winter. One noted feature of its weather characteristics is persistence of heat-relieving winds. The emerged local architectural style was reflective of this specific weather characteristic. The traditional structures mostly made of mud bricks keep them cool during summer and warm in limited winter by using heat-relieving winds. To capture and put them in use at no cost, most traditional structures have had triangular rooftops with opening to catch the breeze and channel the same into each home's living quarters.

"From medieval times, Sindhis [local populace of Sindh] excelled in artistic works. It simultaneously became a hub for trading, both inland and overseas, attracting artisans and traders from hinterland. Goldsmiths, silversmiths, leather tanners, and embroidery artisans mainly exported their products. Exports were made to places like Khorasan, Turkestan, Singapore, Japan, and inland India, while some exports were made to Egypt through Bombay. Imports were generally made from Varanasi, China, and Japan. In terms of fashion, design, and artistic excellence, Hyderabad excelled compared to many cities of India. Bengali Nobel laureate poet Rabindranath Tagore ascribed Hyderabad as the most fashionable city of India in early twentieth century.

"Besides common products like textile, cement, sugar, pottery, and paper, the handicraft industries of Sindh made marks in gold and silver work, lacquer ware, and silks with ornamental designs. Hyderabad alone produces most of the national market demands for glass bangles and glass inlays for jewelry. These are very popular among all types of female population of Pakistan. This handicraft industry alone employs about three hundred thousand people. Being surrounded by fertile alluvial plains, Hyderabad is the hub of major agricultural produce.

"Among other infrastructures contributing to Hyderabad's sustained economic progression, the famous Kotri Bridge of 1900, reconstructed in 1930, stands out prominently. It traverses the Indus with a length of 1,950 feet, having dual carriage of rail and road. Presently, Hyderabad is the center point of inter- and intraprovince road and railways communications. Its germaneness augmented manifold due to its connection with Karachi by the Indus and the national highways. Small cities like Kotri, Jamshoro, Hattri, and Husri around Hyderabad are emerging rapidly.

"Hyderabad's sociopolitical and religious life and history are one and the same with that of Sindh. Though a majority Hindu territory of undivided India, Sindh was greatly influenced by incoming Sufis moving from Midwest and Central Asia via Herat, Kandahar [also spelled as Qandhar], and Multan. Movement of Sufis from Midwest Asia was the normal outcome of spread for learning, exchange of cultures, and mixing with other faiths. That from Central Asia was primarily due to Mongol conquest and aggression.

"Some schools believe that the identity of Sufism is premised on their rejection of earthly things, adoption of simple living pattern, and wearing coarse garments. Sufis are in love with poverty and practice celibacy, focusing on strict self-control. The aim is a loss of self in quest for mystical union with God.

"The vastness of both arid and marshy lands with sparse population having creative qualities, Sindh is centered on the historic trade routes of India. Ironically, it remained economically poor but had shown unmatched tolerance for divergent faiths and believes, as well love for music. Because of these as well being rated as an area of mysticism, Sindh historically attracted an enormous number of saints and mystics. They were equally welcomed by local populace having the background of tolerance. The most famous and original torchbearer of Sufism in Sindh was the thirteenth-century Muslim saint Usman Marwandi, popularly known more as Lal

Shahbaz Qalandar. Besides being a Sufi saint of highest eminence, he was a religious poet revered enormously by followers of different faiths for preaching tolerance, especially among Muslims and Hindus. The territory of Sehwan, Shahbaz Qalandar's location in Sindh and presently more known as Sehwan Sharif, houses his shrine, which is visited by hundreds of thousands of devotees annually and by more than a million during annual urs [generally ascribing to prayers in celebrating deaths of saints and dear ones].

"Sindh and southern Punjab are inundated by hundreds of shrines and mausoleums of Sufi saints. Sufis travel from one to other shrines mostly to participate in festival of *urs* [Arabic word meaning 'marriage'], symbolizing union between Sufis and the divine. The essence of urs is difficult to explain and convey to others unless one himself is swamped by that. In the midst of sweltering heat and hot desert sands below in southern Pakistan with the scent of rose water overwhelming the locale along with garlands of fresh flowers, colorful coarse wrappings, smoke of incense and waft of hashish in the midst of pounding of drums, dances, and devotional singing with loud screams seeking invocations by all present both men and women and Hindus and Muslims, the urs take its own shape and rhythm, causing to ecstasy. It is just beyond explanation.

"The local people embraced some of the traits of Sufis while the latter also adopted some local rites. Such exchange took place without commotion and communal tensions. Unfortunately, that thousands-of-years-old social fabric has recently been thwarted by the advent Taliban phenomenon. But fortunately, that trend evidently has a weak link in Sindh. The Taliban presence in Sindh reflects current demographic divergence. Most Sindhi Taliban are from Urdu-speaking Muhajirs, Balochis, Pashtun, Punjabis, and Afghan refugees. Perhaps because of this phenomenon, Taliban has not been able to penetrate, though partially impacted upon, into the historic social fabric of Sindh premised on tolerance. While the Taliban occasionally causes disruption, dismay, and distress in Sindh's social structure, it has not been able to minimize the impact of Sufism among the major population segment, particularly those in rural areas. A cold war has been going on in Sindh between guns, cocktails, IEDs, grenades of the Taliban and the drums, dancing, music, poetry, and mystics of the Sufis. Demands, expectations, and frustrations of numerous subgroups compound this problem, ascribing Taliban influence to all incidents.

"Sufism, unlike sect-based identity of Sunnism and Shi'ism of broad Muslim faith, is not a religious cult. It represents the mystical side and spiritual aspects of Islam propagating ever-increasing sincerity in a quest of subtle and heuristic firsthand approach to reach Allah [the divine]. Sufism embraces both inner and outer aspects of Islam. It is classified as the path of gradual awakening of the heart.

"Sufism is neither coded nor an ideological doctrine. At no stage of its development were efforts made to give it a well-shaped identity, expressly articulated ideals, and formulated systems. It is practiced by a group of Muslims belonging to both Shia and Sunni sects. Sufism's ceremonial focus and practices are a combination of a number of sects, schools, and trends culminating in ecstasy for reaching out spiritual and intuitive cognition of the Divine. Sufis' practice of rejoicing in the form of chanting [*sama*]. An important element of Sama is *dhikr* comprising of listening and remembering. The *dhikr* [pronounced also as *zeikir*] consists of rituals including, among others, singing, dancing, instruments playing, reciting of poems, and saying of prayers. That listening aspect is called sama, and the remembering aspect is called *raka* [meaning "cycles of dancing"]. In practice, they are quietly divergent among Sufi fraternities. Because of singing, dancing, poetry recitation, etc., the philosophies of Persian poets like Rumi, Khayyam, Saadi, Hafeez, and others had deep marks on Sufism in general and its practices in Sindh in particular."

Areem earnestly tried to absorb those words of historical perspective detailed by Mr. Jatoi in his rather long oration concerning Hyderabad and Sindh. He was equally bemused in trying to understand the relevance of those in the context of his going to Afghanistan to work for al-Qaeda. That caused an agonizing whisper in Areem's thought with an intermittent soft but insistent buzz sporadically becoming a palpitant with arrhythmic pounding. Areem cautiously concealed his uneasiness and discomfort, taking note of the sober tone of Mr. Jatoi's expressions and his narration of related facts without emotional alienation to dogmatic bias for linking those with ultraconservative religious priorities.

An esoteric silence pervaded the setting. That quietness did not swarm and swamp Mr. Jatoi. Neither did it drag him down. He took note of the silence but remained truly empathetic both in facial expressions and exchange of looks. His follow-on sudden mild clapping amused Areem. Both of them exchanged smiles: one knowing the purpose and the other being totally oblivious. The instantaneous appearance of a household help took Areem by surprise. It became obvious to Areem that at no stage of that discourse were they alone. Mr. Jatoi, without oral exchange, indicated to an empty teapot and nodded. The household help lifted the teapot and went inside.

Mr. Jatoi than opened up candidly. He said, "When we receive mujahideen from outside, we always receive a brief about them. The brief about you stated that you are not a tested mujahid but an acknowledged academic who would be of significant relevance in propagating Taliban doctrine in Bangladesh in the future. So you, unlike your most other comrades, are not spare able and are an asset for the future. HUM management has therefore decided to train and expose you from that perspective. You will not ordinarily be engaged in combat operations but will help al-Qaeda in planning and executing those. Even then, it is considered apposite to expose you to field orientation in tandem with deep exposure to al-Qaeda doctrine, having link and roots with history.

"Your stay in Pakistan has been so planned to orient you first and then induct you in field work later. What you were told in Karachi and here relate to your orientation phase. Your induction will start once you reach Multan of Punjab, the stronghold of HUM in Pakistan.

"You are likely to have questions about time spent by me in telling you about socio-politico-religious aspects pertaining to Sindh and Hyderabad. That was premised on HUM's decision to arrange an identity for you as a Sindhi. It is considered very important as every future step of yours is susceptible to glorious uncertainty. HUM not only made me responsible for your complete orientation but also equally reposed responsibility in me for your overall security while in Pakistan. If you ever face a situation threatening your life and safety, you should use your Pakistani identity to be in Sindh territory at the earliest and try to contact me. I will give you a confidential direct telephone number and my address at the time of your leaving for Multan.

"For security reasons, I will put the information in a *taweez* [amulet]. Only in extreme condition are you to open that *taweez*, dial that number, and contact me. You are to use the address as needed. No one else should have access to those information."

While sipping kahwah, and in an ostensible lighter mood, Mr. Jatoi continued, "As explained earlier, Sindh historically is a tolerant place. Even though the Taliban phenomenon is presently overwhelming Pakistan, its base and impact in Sindh is relatively minimal. So once in Sindh territory,

77

you will comparatively be safe. Also, unlike other territories of Pakistan, Sindh is not burdened by tribalism. The social structure is more influenced by landholding. Thus, landlords are the dominant players in Sindh. As soon as I become aware of your presence, I can seek the help of fellow landlords of the area to ensure your safety. Among the landlords, we have strong bonds and are always helpful to one another. The primary premise of all these is our objective to ensure your safe return to Bangladesh for the greater cause you have committed yourself."

Though hesitant, Areem did not like to waste the opening Mr. Jatoi unwittingly provided. Putting his tone on a lenitive base, he civilly put his point, stating, "As I have listened to your brief but equally profound narration of Sindh's history and current situation, I have a feeling that you have had sort of a motley thought about your involvement in the Taliban movement and, later, HUM organization. I assume, may be erroneous, that you may presently be in a quandary with a feeling of being blurred about that involvement. More explicitly, do you have a feeling of remorse?"

Mr. Jatoi was neither miffed nor bolded by the depth and nature of Areem's query. Though apparently sounding simple, it had significant inherent implications pertaining to the philosophy of the Taliban movement, Mr. Jatoi's own association with HUM, and limited terms of reference he had concerning Areem's orientation. Nevertheless, Mr. Jatoi did not demur in tackling the same with honesty and separateness. He paused, almost similar to a daze; focused his thoughts acidly; and with blinkered optimism in tandem with determination to be truly emphatic, started saying, "The British administration had a lot of constructive traits pertaining to India's progression. Those were germane to Sindh also. But in my youth, I had misgivings about the suitability of the English judicial system in the context of Sindh. To my thinking of youth, Quranic code, with supplementation of Sufi philosophy, was more appropriate for the mystic land of Sindh and its thousands-of-years-old social structure. Islam, being the pillar of faith, coupled with Sufism's hypnotic rituals, primeval mysticism, and a trace of mystified psychosis could provide for a legal structure ensuring equity and justice. That could as well be sustainable by social backup of historic adherence to tolerance for which Sindh was renowned. Thus, I increasingly became inclined to judicial process as enunciated in the Holy Quran and Sunnah as I believe that it has more relevance in the context of Sindh's social structure. That was to be the response to British judicial system and a nonviolent antidote to conservative Islamic thinking. This motivated me in joining the Taliban movement.

"In that process, my family background and fame as well my rhetoric ability and enunciation competence became handy. I was impartial, honest, and occasionally ruthless. I was brutal only in extreme situations and resorted to that more as a last resort with openness and full justification. Soon my words and actions became sort of law in the periphery even outside Sindh. I did not join HUM officially. Rather, it engulfed me. Of course, I was a willing participant in the process, more due to its limited focus on Pakistan and its surroundings.

"But the Taliban rule of about four years in Afghanistan, the sustained ruthlessness of the administration encompassing every facet of individual life, the proclaimed brashness it demonstrated to other faiths and practices ignoring basic premise of tolerance, and the abhorrent interpretation of Islamic injunctions that systematically trekked to Pakistan totally frustrated me. But it was too late. I am, in short, now a reluctant HUM leader. There is no escape for me. As much as I value the original premise of my belief, my focus is now to minimize, being a part of it, the ultraconservative impact of the Taliban phenomenon in Sindh at least.

"So whenever there is an opportunity, I try to convey to promising young leaders the need to refrain from all those and adhere to Islam with room for Sufism, ensuring tolerance and coexistence. That is the only way out for me. And that is the reason I tried to allude the same to you. When you go back to Bangladesh, continue to be an active member of the Chittagong al-Qaeda but be always watchful so that fundamentalism and dogmatism do not override the basic principles of Islam and proclaimed values of Bangladesh's social system. I see a promising leader in you, and so I said all these to you."

Mr. Jatoi appeared to be exhausted by internal stress and said, "I will be closing this very private discussion after giving you a few additional advice. Those are not mandatory but for your thinking and future use. First, always remember that neither one is born as al-Qaeda and Taliban activist nor are all of them and all their leaders necessarily terrorists by implication. Second, most of these activists are frustrated and misguided young lot being alluded to rewards syndrome in the other world. Third, joining al-Qaeda and Taliban is voluntary, but leaving either is haunted by adversities of undetermined magnitude.

"Many of current activists would like to disassociate but are constrained by severity of punishment under strict and specified enforcement stipulations of the organization. Fourth, there are a lot to be achieved by aligning Islamic practices with modern-time imperatives. We need an open mind to achieve that. For example, having a beard and wearing a pajama above ankle are advisable but not a prerequisite for identification as a Muslim. But the Taliban misinterpreted and enforced them in Afghanistan. The same trend is visible in Pakistan too. I am drawing your attention to try, if you agree, and minimize the impact of such practices, which may be preferable but are not ordained by Allah. Making them a part of Islam may perhaps be repugnant to Islam.

"My last observation, not advice, relates to local focus. I am practicing it in the context of Sindh. Unduly enlarging one's agenda in terms of scope and coverage is self-defeating. Our resources and time do not permit it. The best is to strive to do what one can do better in the context of manageable setting. Keeping these in view, I will present you a book on Ahmad Shah Massoud, the legendary guerrilla leader and freedom fighter of Afghanistan. He was the only leader not to leave Afghanistan during Soviet occupancy, resisted the mighty Red Army, and compelled their retreat. You should, as time permits, read this book and try to absorb its contents. This book testifies what even an individual can do for the society and country."

Mr. Jatoi suddenly picked up another cigarette contrary to earlier indication of limited smoking. While puffing his cigarette, he advised Areem about their next meeting on the following morning at breakfast table. Areem was told that to ensure his safe travel within Pakistan, arrangements were made to prepare a fake passport identifying him as a Sindhi of Jatoi taluk. Officials concerned would need Areem's photograph as well as signature on the passport application form. That had been scheduled to be done after breakfast. Arrangements had also been finalized for Areem's scheduled travel to Multan by train.

He then stood up and clapped again. The trusted household help showed up promptly. He was told to escort Areem to the guest lodge adjacent to the *kachari* and ensure Areem's relaxed positioning on the bed. That was meticulously complied with.

While waiting for Mr. Jatoi in his private room for breakfast, Areem was amazed, observing incidentally the former in a very tranquil mood as he was viewing various flower beds in the sprawled garden between the front building and the homestead. It was a very private setting and not visible from outside. Perhaps it was meant for personal enjoyment and family use.

Mr. Jatoi was at ease and totally enamored in the setting of the garden with dry land and desert all around.

Slowly moving with a decorative walking stick in hand and stopping occasionally, Mr. Jatoi passionately looked at every flower bed and passed on instructions to the staff following him. Areem pleasantly noted a very relaxed Mr. Jatoi being at ease with whatever he was saying and doing. As apparent from his physical posture, he perhaps had light exchanges with the staff following him. That was definitely an exception as the staff continued to manifest uneasiness in their reactions. Mr. Jatoi was enjoying that.

The *kachari* manager showed up precipitously and whispered something. The facial expression of Mr. Jatoi changed rapidly. Areem, overlooking through his window, concluded that it was either very important or very ominous. But he soon became confused as Mr. Jatoi reverted to his previous relaxed posture after dismissing the *kachari* manager.

With the ambiance of earlier feeling, Mr. Jatoi came to his private room to have breakfast with Areem. Noting all those and keeping the cordiality and trust built up between the host and the guest over the last many hours, Areem wanted to float an idea that was in his mind since last night. He, however, could not raise the issue immediately notwithstanding the inner yearning.

He had another waggish impasse because of the breakfast service. The breakfast items ostensibly were more in number and different in varieties compared to the ones over dinner of last night and Areem's own experience of growing up in a well-to-do family with his father's penchant for good eating. Areem roughly concluded that all the items on the table were more than enough for their sumptuous breakfast and lunch. He was debating as to the proper item to start with. Mr. Jatoi came to his rescue. Both of them started enjoying their breakfast.

As it was ordained, Areem did not have to initiate discussion about his fake passport. Mr. Jatoi referred to background details for the decision to have a fake passport. In a nutshell, he said, "The government agents and agencies are very active now. If they find your Bangladeshi passport, then your plan to join al-Qaeda will just wither away, with your possible landing in jail. So the decision about the fake passport was taken."

In that very affable ambiance, Areem pointedly delineated his inside craving and proposed to Mr. Jatoi a change of surname, saying, "During most part of last night, a bizarre thinking troubled me. I asked myself that if I am to have a fake passport, then why can't I have a fake surname too? The surname I carry has no germaneness either for me or for the tribe it represents. As an alternative, the last name of Ahmad Shah Massoud, the war hero of Afghanistan, enchanted me amazingly. That also fits in well rhetorically with other components of my name: Areem Ahmed Shah."

Areem, keeping his proposition simple and brief, refocused his attention to breakfast. But that inquisition naively caused anguish for Mr. Jatoi. Within himself, Mr. Jatoi faced the traducement of morality in real-life setting. The innocent decision to arrange a fake passport for Areem was on the premise of saving someone who committed his life to the service of Islam from unforeseen challenges. Areem's proposition to change his surname based on the rationale predicating the decision for fake passport could either be a subtle intrusion on universal sense of morality or just a naive indication. After due contemplation, Mr. Jatoi opted for the second one. With an impish smile, having all elements of mendacity, he looked at Areem amusingly but refrained from uttering any word. He enjoyed very much the state of conundrum in which Areem was momentarily.

Mr. Jatoi broke the premeditated silence to the great curiosity of Areem, who was waiting to listen something concerning his earlier proposition. Areem, however, was totally downcast as the subject of Mr. Jatoi's much-awaited oration was far from that. Mr. Jatoi, politely exhibiting his sociopolitical eminence and clout, said, "I have just been informed that my designated person to accompany you to Multan has fallen sick. So we need to work out a new plan for your travel. This should be taken as a divine lesson for you. I am certain that you are constantly aware of the precarious track of life chosen being a volunteer al-Qaeda activist despite the warmth and fraternity of the last few days experienced in Karachi and Hyderabad.

"To be a successful mujahid, every step one takes or every action one is involved in should always have the elements of deception and puzzlement. So HUM planned your journey by a mix of truck and train modes until you reach Landi Kotal. The objective is to erase tinges of movement so as to confuse intelligence people. Because of the unexpected illness of my trusted person, your planned trip by train to Multan the night after tonight has been abandoned. You will nevertheless go as scheduled but in a truck being escorted by my designated person. We are working on it. You would have your new passport and my promised *taweez* at the time I bid you farewell."

Saying those words with all frostiness that he could muster, Mr. Jatoi stood up and extended his hand warmly toward Areem to say goodbye until they would meet again for dinner. Areem's response was reflective of his depressed mood, considering that Mr. Jatoi totally ignored his very sincere wish. A negative response would have been much better than no response as that would at least indicate some consideration.

Taking a few steps while holding the reluctant hand, Mr. Jatoi drew Areem close to his chest and smilingly whispered, saying, "Yes, you will have fake surname as desired. I will tell my staff accordingly. But to give that surname change a local tang, I will suggest to them to write it as Masud." After saying those gentle words, Mr. Jatoi left fleetingly; and Areem joyfully retired to his place of last night.

While waiting in his room, Areem remembered what Mufti Quaser Ali of Karachi told him about Mr. Jatoi as "a jovial person with ability to make anyone feel at ease." Areem's experience with his surname-change proposition and the way that was handled, among others, aptly validated the intrinsic qualities and abilities of Mr. Jatoi. Not only did Areem's respect for Mr. Jatoi burgeoned but, more pertinently, that also gave him an inner solace of having trust in Mr. Jatoi's pledges of readiness to help in handling unforeseen crunches.

During dinnertime discourse, Mr. Jatoi reconfirmed the scheduled truck travel arrangements and advised that Osman would accompany Areem until the latter was handed over to Janab Ahmed Khan Khakwani, the inherited *mutawalli* (trustee of a waqf, a trust established following Islamic religious injunctions) of Masjid (Mosque) Ali Amir Khan built around 1750s. It is located at the city center known as Chowk Bazaar and has unique architectural features.

To give an advance impression about his soon-to-be mentor, Mr. Jatoi said, "Janab Khakwani, of medium height and heavy built having relatively semidark skin tone by Punjab standard, wears a dense long dark beard with a delicately arranged multicolored scarf always adoring his head. His other outward feature is a heavy application of *surma* [powdered eyelash dye and cosmetic] on the eyes."

Mr. Jatoi further stated, "He is both a robust and determined HUM leader with responsibility to train and induct new al-Qaeda activists in a combat-ready status. Janab Khakwani, in carrying out that responsibility, has demonstrated singular focus on mission's objectives and neither entertained nor tolerated ever exceptions and excuses. So do never express any dissenting views on any of his directives. Obey him unconditionally until you are through the process of induction. Things could be a bit softer for you based on briefings, but it is Janab Khakwani's judgment and decision. You should keep this in view always."

With those grim avowals and specificity about his life and temporary living in Multan, Mr. Jatoi concentrated on eating. Downcast and relatively bewildered, Areem focused on eating too.

One is never certain about the human mind's thinking process. Its response is equally agape most of the time. For some odd reasons, it is sometimes prone to repudiate good options while many a time yield to negative positions. Areem briefly recapitulated his father's recurrent reactions, new mother's frequent interfaces, and young brother's manipulative responses contrary to facts or his positions. By visiting those and recalling jovial discourse during dinner of the previous night, Areem took time in assessing the sudden quietness engulfing the present dining scenery.

The waiting was relatively short, and the outcome was enormously sweet, both of which astounded and overwhelmed Areem. The subject of Mr. Jatoi's homily took him by total surprise. That had nothing to do with Islam-related anger, discord, backlash, response, and revenge, the hallmark of al-Qaeda mantra and gunpowder for elusive jihad.

Swapping from main dinner to dessert, Mr. Jatoi became somewhat emotional and philosophical in his follow-on premeditations. He said, "Youth is the budding phase of life when everything of choice and liking incontrovertibly appears to be normal with strong urge to possess irrespective of impracticalities and impediments in most cases. It often gives rise to determination, arrogance, and blinkered optimism resulting in frequent clatter, commotion, and cruelty."

As Areem was wearing a muddled look, Mr. Jatoi decided to elaborate on what he just had said. He therefore continued, saying, "I have measured qualm about mankind being the best among creations. The so-called best among creations has innate vulnerability and covert frailties. Various religions, holy books, and faith-based philosophies were propagated and intended to guard against ostensible susceptibilities. Still then, life is full of irritants, hatred, dislikes, suspicion, perfidy, and many more like these.

All these foster fickle friendships in social contacts with spikily feelings most of the times.

"There is an ostensible need to smoothen such negative traits within individuals' response impulses for an exultant, safe, and mutually supportive existence of mankind. People should have liking and love for other inspired elements of life beyond faith and philosophy. My life experience testifies that liking and love for music lessen stress and improves brain's power and heals pains; likewise, poetry expresses inner intuits from higher levels of feelings; and flowers enliven the soul and have an enormous impact in shaping responses in life. The impact of Sufism on its followers is a living testament. That encouraged followers of diametrically opposed religious faiths, Islam and Hinduism, to attend and participate in prayers at the shrine of Muslim saint Lal Shahbaz Qalandar of Sehwan Sharif located at Jamshoro civil district of Sindh and about sixty-five miles away from Hyderabad.

"As mentioned earlier, Lal Shahbaz Qalandar was a great poet besides being a saint and mystic. His poetry and associated music drew followers of diverse faiths to assemble in common prayer rituals while maintaining their respective religious affiliations. In my youth, and when I was at the zenith of enthusiasm to fight and die for Islam, I was at his shrine and spent a few days there. Something happened without my knowing. The rage and revenge within me premised on hatred slowly mislaid, and a sense of calm and peace prevailed upon me. Outwardly, and because of imperils omnipresent, I am an HUM leader. In my inner self, and in daily thinking and actions, I am being enthused by a sense of tolerance, peace, and amity. What you have seen so far is my outward self. In my inner self, which I want to keep private, I take refuge in music, poetry, and flowers, having tremendous bearings on my regular thinking and decision-making process.

"I have shared these with you with no particular objective or agenda. Neither have I ever thought of having such a discourse with one like you. However, frankly speaking, I have developed an enormous empathy for you in this short time. Your politeness, attentiveness, straightforwardness, and inquisitiveness, among others, impressed me most. Sharing of my life experiences with you is a manifestation of my earnest desire and prayer for a happy, safe, and fulfilling life for you in future. In that course of journey, and if ever, what I said to you or shared with you is of any help in pursuing your life's progression, I will be happy."

Saying those words, Mr. Jatoi came to his normal self and started talking about arrangements for travel to Multan on the following night. He mentioned, "Besides being a truck journey through desert setting and accompanying commercial merchandise, it would be a long fifteen to twenty hours with actual driving of ten to twelve hours, having stoppages in district towns of Nawabshah, Khairpur, and Bhawalpur."

Mr. Jatoi suddenly stopped and looked outside in the darkness of the night. He drew Areem to the window overlooking the inner garden full of flowers, which looked very mollifying and tranquil against the backdrop of moonlight.

Mr. Jatoi looked at the garden and looked at Areem, alternately wearing an appeasing smile but refraining from uttering any word. Silence perhaps conveyed all that he wanted to say.

While reversing to the previous position, Mr. Jatoi put his right hand on the shoulder of Areem and said, "I will be away from Hyderabad for two days and hence would not be able to say bon voyage to you during your scheduled departure. So this is *khuda hafiz* [generally meaning 'farewell' or 'May God be your defender']."

Saying those words, Mr. Jatoi clapped his hands, and his trusted household help appeared with small package. In handing over the same to Areem, Mr. Jatoi said, "This has both the *taweez* and fake passport I promised to you. The *taweez* has my address and confidential telephone number. Use them only in extreme situations. Do not forget to keep your Bangladeshi passport hidden carefully so long you are in Pakistan."

Having said those words, Mr. Jatoi promptly left for the inner courtyard without performing even the common ritual and courtesy demonstrated by exchange of hugs. Areem, looking at the departing Mr. Jatoi, was in a motionless, bewildered condition only to be alerted by the household help to proceed to his assigned room.

In an effort to find an escape from the emotion-laden farewell experienced recently, Areem took out the book on Ahmad Shah Massoud, which was fondly presented to him the night before last by Mr. Jatoi. The additional prying reason was Areem's realization that unspoken words and dilettante physical gestures of Mr. Jatoi often meant more than spoken words. He thus had the urge to read the book sooner so that he could understand the inner implications that predicated the presentation of that particular one among many other famous and popular books and publications.

All Areem did during that night and following day was reading the book and absorbing the contents with internal analysis of ever-changing situations. Each word, each line, and each paragraph testifies to what Mr. Jatoi alluded, relating to an individual's capacity to shape and create history. While going through the book, Areem recalled his own reading of numerous published materials pertaining to the Afghanistan war as made available by his friend Manzoor. That was the way Manzoor thought it best to help Areem in taking decision to join him in the Afghanistan mission, or not. Those publications of al-Qaeda mentioned many a time the names of post-Soviet president Sibghatullah Mojaddedi, President Burhanuddin Rabbani, President Mullah Omar, and guerilla leader and commander Gulbuddin Hekmatyar but minimally mentioned the heroic opposition and confrontation with the Soviets under the leadership of Ahmad Shah Massoud.

Areem was staggered in thinking at how a political leader and military commander of his eminence and determination, who confronted an enemy rated as the world's number two military power for about ten years without ever leaving the country like all other political and guerilla leaders, had not been given due recognition. Ahmad Shah Massoud's strategic prowess, military ingenuity, and tactical skill kept the mighty Soviet forces—with disproportionately superior war assets, manpower, mobility, and capability—out of Panjshir Valley all through. He exhibited the same competence in declining Taliban's unabated presence in Panjshir, and in tactically obliterating the Salang Tunnel while strategically retreating to Kulob of Tajikistan.

The Salang Tunnel provides a strategically needed shortest and most desired economic link between the north and rest of the country in the south—more importantly, Kabul. With the disintegration of the former USSR, it now gained greater relevance and importance in providing important strategic nexus between the warm waters of Indian Ocean and the many Central Asian republics of the north.

The tunnel was built by the Soviets in 1964 in a high, dry, barren, rocky, and jagged landscape with no plantation or shrub to be seen anywhere. More than two-and-half-kilometer-long tunnel is located at Salang Pass of Hindu Kush mountain range in an altitude of more than eleven thousand feet. This two-lane pothole-infested access tunnel reduced travel time between Kabul and Mazar-e-Sharif by sixty-two hours and shortened travel by about three hundred kilometers.

Ahmad Shah Massoud soon grasped that confronting and fighting a branded and superior enemy like the Soviets was much easier than interacting and negotiating with fellow impervious conservatives even though they, too, fought the common enemy. His repeated initiatives and efforts, while in power, for a mutually agreeable power-sharing arrangements, national election, and equitable participation of all fighting groups were thwarted repeatedly. Not only that, various initiatives, both in Kabul and outside, for national election failed to materialize.

Such misunderstanding had been the logical consequences of historically embedded caginess. The resultant animosity was undeniably the outcome of strong and much-cherished tribal identity of various segments of the population. But more crucially, it had been inflamed and reinforced by expressed interest, involvement, and interplay of immediate powerful neighbors and interested superpowers in the internal matters of Afghanistan. Consequently, the most critical policy decisions pertaining to the future of Afghanistan were either designed or taken outside.

The historical dictum that neither problem in general travels in isolation nor is an outcome of single factor was most discreetly repeated in Afghanistan. As if historic delusions, squabbles, deceit, deracinating, destruction, killing, and injuries were not enough, a new emotion-laden philosophy premised on religious justification crept into Afghanistan.

It trekked into Afghanistan by two discernible vestibules. The first one—and it is historical truth though denied by authorities in Pakistan—is conceptualizing, planning, training, and motivating thousands of madrassa students in an Islamic fundamentalist political melee. These students, later categorized as Talibans, enthused by encoring simple religious trepidation of "Islam is in danger," were committed to establish an Islamic republic in Afghanistan. Most of them, and at the behest of Pakistan defense agencies, penetrated into Afghanistan in a vacuum caused by the Soviet retreat and unswerving power struggle among political power stockbrokers.

That infighting was accentuated because of Tazik's hegemony under the leadership of Ahmad Shah Massoud. It was later essentially a confrontation between majority Pashtun strongly supported by Pakistan and northern power base of Tazik and Uzbek, which were expressly anti-Pakistan and more inclined to India. Pakistan could not accept this situation and augmented its multiple support for Pashtun military commander Gulbuddin Hekmatyar. Side by side, Pakistan fostered the Taliban movement in Afghanistan.

In about three years' time of President Rabbani's rule under the shadow of Ahmad Shah Massoud, the leaderships of Mullah Omar and the Taliban made major headway and were in dominant positions. Pakistan had to choose one between Taliban cum Mullah Omar versus Hekmatyar, and it decisively opted for the first one. The Taliban ruled Afghanistan between 1996 and 2001 under conformist interpretation of Islam until the US invasion following the 9/11 terrorist attack in New York.

The major conflict between Massoud and the Taliban was premised on the former's strong disagreement with fundamentalist interpretation of Islam as enunciated by the Taliban. Battered and beaten by sustained bombardment of Pakistan-supported Gulbuddin Hekmatyar, Massoud opted for complete pullout and took arms as an opposition. With the Taliban taking reign of the country, Ahmad Shah Massoud retreated to Kulob of Tajikistan. The book ended here with Massoud's optimism, in defeat even, about Afghanistan. He was quoted as saying, "Current animosity would certainly give in to peace. Much desired prosperity and progress in Afghanistan may take time but it will happen. When that happens, it is most likely to be fast and concerted with a bang."

Sitting in the truck between the driver and Mr. Osman in his maiden sojourn to Multan, Areem was overwhelmed by the recurring thought of reasons for Ahmad Shah Massoud's retreat to Tajikistan, which he did not do in his ten years of confrontation with the Soviets. The more he thought, the more bemused he was. It could be one or combinations of many reasons as prodigious resurgence of Islamic phobia; the toll that many years of relentless struggle entailed on the morale and support base among Taziks; the swiftness of success of Taliban, and so on. The retreat to a bordering place could be more meant to reflect and to reshape a strategic approach.

In that state of mind, and having a drive in the darkness of the night through the desolate setting of the southern Thar Desert, Areem involuntarily dozed off only to be awakened by the sudden brake applied by the truck driver. Mr. Osman immediately bended toward Areem and whispered, advising total quietness. He said that whatever it was, the driver would handle it. They were not to interact.

Areem panicked, seeing a few black-flowing-dress-clad, rustic individuals with alike wrapped headgear covering most part of the face besides the head, on horseback, dangling a rifle in one hand and the halter in the other. The only visible physical element, against the headlight of the truck, was their shivering eyes.

As the apparent leader approached the driver, others were encircling the truck. The driver politely told them, "This truck belongs to Jatoi *hujur* [sir respectfully] of Hyderabad, and the goods are meant for HUM to be delivered to Janab Khakwani of the mosque Ali Amir Khan located in Chowk Bazaar of Multan." The leader drew his horse close to the driver's door, had a penetrating look inside, and demanded some documents. When he scanned the documents with the help of another fellow abettor, questions were exchanged about the nature of goods, number of packages, etc. In handing over the papers, the leader said, "You are to be in a standstill position until you hear a gunshot, giving clearance to proceed." After he said those words, the group vanished into the desert as sleekly as they appeared.

In resuming the journey, Mr. Osman ventured to communicate with Areem in broken Urdu to lessen his plausible angst. He said, "This section of the road between Nawabshah and Khairpur is rated as a high-risk one for crime and kidnapping, mostly by nomads. Hence, trucks generally travel in a group. Isolated vehicles are prone to banditry and ransom payments. So what we encountered is not something exceptional. You should relax."

That road journey had a rather long break in the truck adda of Khairpur. Soon after the truck was parked in the same adda and the required offloading of nature's pressures was done away with in a hurry, the driver went out and brought, with the help of tea stall staff, *garam chai* (hot dark tea and *pani* [water]), some naans (rather large flat bread baked in rudimentary oven) and different types of kebabs (grilled meat items). The driver politely desired that both Mr. Osman and Areem share the food.

Areem was conjecturing to fathom the rationale of having food in a huddled setting of the truck's only seat instead of a large open locale of the eating place. The eating place in most addas is located at the entry point to avoid flowing dust as trucks negotiate the unpaved diversion access for stoppage and rest. These addas have very common and limited cooking facilities like a fire place for preparing tea and cooking lentils, rudimentary tandoori to make fresh naans, and coal-heated stall for making kebab under a thatched roof mostly of straws.

What enticed Areem's attention was the layout of adda and its sitting arrangements. There was no chair or table. Instead, it had numerous *charpoy* (traditional sleeping surface and more similar to *khatiya*), elegantly simple and lightweight in design. Charpoy was an open rectangular structure supported by four wooden legs that, when tightly woven by flat cotton tapes (stripes) or ropes, can hold body weights. Normally, the truck driver and his assistant sit at two ends of the charpoy; and food is served at the middle. The driver casually interjected, saying, "The charpoy is made available free for eating. But charpoys are also available for sleeping on payment of a modest rent." Areem was told that many drivers prefer to take a nap after a meal.

Areem was initiated to eating at the behest of Mr. Osman. After a few bites, Areem commented that the simple food had its unique taste. Mr. Osman stated that this food, though limited in selection, was very popular even among gentries, and Jatoi hujur would often stop to fetch some adda food to carry home.

As they finished eating, the driver yearned something to Mr. Osman, and the latter nodded. The driver took his Sindhi *ajrakh* chador, talked to a help of the adda, and lounged on an empty charpoy, covering his whole body with hand-carried chador. Mr. Usman reclined against the support provided by the driver's exit door and straightened his leg within the limited space. He likewise suggested that Areem relax himself by straightening his lower body.

The remaining journey to Multan, though a long one, was uneventful except for the occasional coughing of the driver, intermittent snoring by Mr. Osman, and the loud music of the radio. There were, however, a few brief breaks for varied needs and for tea.

On reaching Multan adda, Mr. Osman had some brief talk with the truck driver and signaled Areem to get down as well to get all his belongings.

JOLT

Checking in to a modest hostel-type accommodation at Multan downtown, Mr. Osman devoted his effort to make a telephone call. It was apparent from his facial bearing that he was under pressure. The reason of that duress was unknown, but its impact was obvious. In his apparent urgency to be prompt in contacting, Mr. Osman had a series of attempts because of a number of constraining factors such as getting dial tone busy, dialing a wrong number, breaking in line contact while dialing, and so on. With each such failed attempt, Mr. Osman was getting visibly shaky and nervous. Finally, he succeeded in contacting the person he was looking for.

Walking back to Areem waiting in the small lounge of the hostelry, Mr. Osman was discernibly relaxed and assured. He took his seat by the side of Areem and started saying, "I have precise instruction to hand you over to Janab Khakwani soon after arrival at the central district of Multan. This is an HUM-dominated place. Even then, one like you is not always safe. One is never sure about the real identity of a passerby. Local people are generally divided into HUM or al-Qaeda activists, or government agents in plain clothes looking for suspects.

"With your being from Bangladesh, even though wearing Sindhi outfit and symbolic untrimmed beard, and since al-Qaeda has a long-term plan focusing on Bangladesh, you are a prized asset. Hence, one can't waste time. Jatoi hujur told me about the need of secrecy and promptness in handling this journey. It was this background that we had food in the tiny space of driver's seat while in Khairpur and did not venture out unless compelled by pressing needs. It is my duty to hand you over to Janab Khakwani. That will signify the successful discharge of Jatoi hujur's responsibility."

Mr. Osman, who appeared to be a *garam chai* addict, got two cups of tea and resumed saying, "After repeated efforts, I could touch base with the trusted person of Janab Khakwani and reported our arrival and current location. My job is now over. I have been advised to stay put. He would personally come after *asr* [afternoon Muslim prayer], and escort us to the mosque Ali Amir Khan [locally known as Masjid Oli Khan] to meet Janab Khakwani. In the meanwhile, we will stay in this lounge. The hotel staff have been so advised by Mr. Khakwani's people."

Areem was escorted, along with Mr. Osman, to Masjid Oli Khan by Mr. Khakwani's designated person at the appointed time. It appeared to Areem that both Mr. Osman and the designated person knew each other very well; but surprisingly, they avoided addressing each other by name in public.

The mosque is located on a sprawled site even though it is in the city center. A longish structure is positioned in its immediate southern periphery. Known as *Musafer Khana* (accommodation for temporary visitors), it had a number of rooms with varied finishing and furnishing. Most of the rooms accommodated new al-Qaeda activists undergoing induction. Two upscale rooms were earmarked for visiting dignitaries, and another room was meant for meetings and briefings. It was sort of a consultation and command room. Areem and Mr. Osman were ushered in one of the vacant standard rooms while awaiting for the meeting with Janab Khakwani.

Areem was evidently tensed about his upcoming meeting with the most relevant person in pursuit of his current objective. On the other hand, Mr. Osman was relaxed, thinking about fulfilling his onerous obligation of handing over a new recruit from a foreign country to HUM Command, bypassing the ever-vigilant watch of the intelligence agencies of the government. The general milieu of the room was thus a calm and sort of hushed one.

Both of their attention was drawn outward, sensing some unexpected commotion outside. As they looked through the partially open door, they were startled not seeing anyone except hearing some sounds of quick footfalls. The sounds of commotion were as quick in vanishing as they were while surfacing. The pressure of thought was overpowering for both with variance in degree and the premise of angst.

After a while, the trusted man of Janab Khakwani showed up with three cups of *garam chaye* (hot tea) and three pieces of indigenous cookie.

He, wearing a broad smile and opening his mouth for the first time, introduced himself to Areem, saying, "I am Shakirullah Humdam, an associate of Janab Khakwani. *Bhai Shaheeb* [meaning Brother Osman] knows me very well from past interactions and dealings. Janab Khakwani unexpectedly got bogged down with an operational challenge. He would be delighted to meet you as soon as he is free. Thus, he instructed me to give you both company for the intervening period."

Areem nodded, signaling his understanding of what was conveyed. Mr. Osman was full of sense of security and happiness in the safe company of Mr. Humdam. All three concentrated on dipping cookies into the tea before sipping the same with pauses.

Mr. Humdam exhibited his special flair in conveying to Areem his status and position within the area of command of Janab Khakwani and Masjid Oli Khan, respectively, without any way mentioning specifics. He however alluded stating, "After the ensuing meeting with Janab Khakwani, it will be this ordinary self who will be responsible for all matters pertaining to your formal induction in al-Qaeda. Those include induction-process-related briefings, training in combat operations, handling of ammunitions, communications with fellow mujahideen and ordinary public, information gathering and sharing, and so on. We are to do all these in a tight schedule, and our different trainers are all well attuned and equipped. It all depends on you and your willingness and ability."

After a pause, Mr. Humdam continued, saying, "The relationship between al-Qaeda and HUM is mutually supportive one harboring almost similar objectives even though there are evident overlap between the two. The clarity about that divergence strengthened our relationship of mutual support and coordination. At the formative stage, al-Qaeda provided HUM access to its training facilities in Afghanistan. HUM, on the other hand, helped al-Qaeda in its retreat and settlement process temporarily in Pakistan with food, shelter, occupational engagements, fake identities, and so on after US military engagement of 2001, commonly termed as Operation Enduring Freedom, in Afghanistan. Since then, we are partners in supporting each other's movements.

"In that setting, this Oli Khan Masjid has special relevance so far HUM and al-Qaeda movements and coordination are concerned. This is the headquarters of that coordination arrangement under the wise guidance and leadership of Imam Khakwani. You are here as one of the outcomes of that process."

Areem was not only listening pedantically but also focused more explicitly in monitoring Mr. Humdam's changes in tones, expressions, subject matters, decision-making power, and authority without ever uttering "I am the second person in charge here." Mr. Humdam remained modest and composed all throughout while communicating his intent and delivering the content of the message.

A mild knock on the only door of the room drew everyone's attention. Mr. Humdam stood up, opened the one-side frame of the door, and extended his neck outward. The other person whispered something. Mr. Humdam returned to his previous place and happily informed that the much-awaited meeting would take place soon.

In his anxiety to finish the rest of his earlier deliberations, Mr. Humdam rewound his thoughts and started saying, "Consistent with role and responsibility of Imam Khakwani, this historical mosque has in place effective but equally indiscernible security aegis and drill. The rooms we have here are the inner shell of that with a defensive objective. Around the masjid, and surrounded by different residential houses, the second layer of offensive security plan has been designed to confront any intruder with the objective to cause harm to the masjid and the Imam. It is important for you to know this, and you will be exposed to it in due course. There are three more pertinent points about which you should always be sensitive. Their compliance is mandatory. First, you should always wear *shalwar* above your ankle. Second, you should never miss namaz. Third, you should never have negation on any instruction."

After saying those words, Mr. Humdam left the room with only Mr. Osman in Areem's company. Mr. Osman had all along been passive with no communication at all, as if he were under some sort of sedative in the presence of Mr. Humdam. He continued to remain so as if Areem was not known to him.

Soon Mr. Humdam reappeared, escorted both Areem and Mr. Osman, and ushered them in the room where Janab Khakwani was sitting. On being introduced, Areem bent slightly and said with due reverence, "Assalamu alaikum." (Peace be upon you.) In acknowledging the salaam, Imam Khakwani exchanged looks with all three and, by gesture, showed the empty chairs to sit.

Total taciturnity prevailed in that room. Areem was trying to match the brief description of Mr. Jatoi about Imam Khakwani and was impressed very much by the similarity of that description with the reality. The only element that Mr. Jatoi did not mention was Imam Khakwani's overbearing physical and communiqué miens within the HUM structure in general and setup of Masjid Oli Khan in particular.

Imam Khakwani exchanged looks with Mr. Humdam, who nodded. Taking note of that indication, Imam Khakwani softly said, "Whatever Humdam said earlier are my words, and I will expect total compliance with those. In our induction process, there is no excuse or exception. However, you being from the brotherly country of Bangladesh and considering the overall objectives of using your mettle in spreading al-Qaeda movement in Bangladesh, some relaxations will be made. In spite of that, you will have to go through the basics of al-Qaeda induction process, which, among others, would include usage of basic arms, mixing of ammunitions, making of IEDs, participation in operation, and other related tasks and responsibilities."

Imam Khakwani repositioned himself on his special chair and continued, saying, "As the people in different communities have variances in their approach and understanding of issues and objects, so there are divergences in their opinions and views. Al-Qaeda, and for that matter HUM, is not immune from that. Al-Qaeda has strict principles and guidelines concerning the focus and objective of its movement. Al-Qaeda explicitly recognizes that in many respects, it is straightforward to fight a known and specific enemy rather than fight enemies hidden within."

He continued his avowal by saying, "Present Muslim *umma* [supranational community with a shared history] is suffering from this. This is Islam's major ailment currently. Muslims presently have divisions like Sunni, Shiite, Ahmadiyya, Qadiani, Sufis, Bahá'ís, Alawis, moderate Muslims, and so on. Keeping all these elements in view and to have a unified religious identity and position, al-Qaeda firmly subscribes to Salafism, a Sunni philosophy that considers itself as true believer and guardian of the Islamic faith and authentic interpreter of the Holy Quran. Consequently, the followers of Salafism like al-Qaeda and HUM consider all other sects of Islam and cohorts of other religions as infidels. Premised on that assertion, the philosophy considers it as an obligatory responsibility to oppose all other sects and beliefs, fight them as needed, and destroy them where necessary. Those who do not subscribe to this doctrine are all non-Muslims."

The meeting was drawn to a close with that unequivocal assertion, leaving no room for accommodation. As they left the meeting place, Mr.

Osman embraced both Mr. Humdam and Areem while whispering to the latter in a low voice, "Remember Mr. Jatoi always. He is there for you in case of any extreme need. I will report back to him."

As Mr. Osman was leaving the premises of Masjid Oli Khan, Areem stood by the side of Janab Humdam and continued to look at the departing figure. The feeling within Areem was a unique one. The departing skeleton of a person whom he barely knew for about three days and seldom talked to unexpectedly caused an emotional backlash as if someone very dear was leaving. Areem was unable to rationalize that feeling.

At the behest of Janab Humdam, Areem followed him to an unspecified direction, though earlier indications were that all initial movements would be within the periphery of the masjid. It turned out to be exactly so but following a different route with a shorter walk through an unlit alley, bypassing the longish structure. During that walk, Janab Humdam said, "I am not aware of your background. But all necessary things here such as food, water, bedding, clothing, rest, etc. are, by design and as part of induction, very limited. You will have to live with those."

He did barely finish that discourse when Janab Humdam entered a poorly lit residential property. As Areem entered the main room, he was surprised to see an elementary eating arrangement with about ten young men being engrossed in eating. Noticing the presence of Janab Humdam, all of them stopped eating, while some others stood up as a sign of respect. Without wasting any time, Janab Humdam desired that they continue eating while he introduced Areem, mentioning his name and nationality. One by one, others introduced themselves, identifying their names and nationalities. Among them, and besides four Pakistanis, there were one each from Libya and India and two each from Somalia and Iraq.

Janab Humdam soon left, leaving behind a marked impression of his status and authority within the Masjid Oli Khan and the induction process of al-Qaeda's new recruits.

The group welcomed Areem. One of the Pakistanis, by the name Azmal, was from Karachi. He, having an extrovert personality due possibly to Karachi upbringing, easily bonded with Areem. The other supporting factors were Areem's coming from Sindh and his origin of Bangladesh from where Azmal's parents moved to Karachi during turbulent period of 1971 war in East Pakistan.

With a mix of both excitement and frustration, Areem meticulously underwent his induction drills with enthusiastic cooperation and encouragement of fellow recruits. Janab Humdam was happy, and he reported to Imam Khakwani the extraordinary commitment and ability of Areem.

That exultant feedback and resultant feeling got an unexpected jolt when Areem, part of a select team, was told about his upcoming participation in an operation centering a Shiite mosque in one of Multan's suburbs. The very proposition of planned confrontation in a mosque unnerved him. When he was told about the mission's objective of opening a quick salvo on the Shia devotees coming out of the mosque after saying *fajr* (early morning prayer of the Muslims), Areem's impulses were not only calcified. He was on the verge of open revolt. Janab Humdam had a quick thought observing the physical reflexes of Areem but opted to remain prudent as he would not like to lose a would-be capable leader of al-Qaeda based on one incident.

Janab Humdam deliberated on Areem's evident reactions but wanted to divert that from the attention of others. He concentrated on spelling out the plan and assigning responsibilities to each of the team members. When it came to Areem's involvement, Janab Humdam took an unusual step in explaining the reason of his participation. He stated, "As you all know, the induction process has mandatory requirements, and there are no ifs and buts. Everyone needs to complete the regimen."

Though Areem's induction had a different orientation, he, too, needed to complete this. That was the premise of his participation. However, Areem's area of responsibility, and that being equally important, related to the rear to monitor civilian movement and alert the team about vulnerable pointers. The critical task of efficient pullback of the front members after every such operation greatly depended on the efficiency and effectiveness of the rear guard. Areem would not have the chance to pull the trigger but would be responsible solely for time-efficient withdrawal avoiding public notice.

What the team was told and the inherent essence of the mission's objectives disturbed Areem very much. The burden was onerous. The pressure was irrefutable. The high moral ground that motivated him to join al-Qaeda received a major jolt. Areem was frustrated and baffled. He had difficulty in reconciling with the pronounced focus and could not swallow food that night. Areem had equal strain in falling asleep. The more he thought about it, the more tensed he became.

Each pronouncement and each word of Imam Khakwani about different sects of Islam and his assertion of them being non-Muslims justifying annihilation pinched Areem's feelings and reflections. The self-evoking question Areem faced on that thought process was: Who was Imam Khakwani, and for that matter al-Qaeda leadership, to decide who was a Muslim or not? What righteous values could authorize obliteration of one person just because he belonged to different faith or held different views? Is that the cause that motivated his joining of al-Qaeda?

His inner responses to all these and other related pressing questions had all been persistently negative in different scenarios. The option of leaving al-Qaeda secretly and going back to Bangladesh, possibly with the help of Mr. Jatoi, to resume his student life winked in his thinking. That took him to the possibility Mr. Jatoi alluded to during their last discourse. He also recalled Mr. Jatoi's profound statement: "Joining al-Qaeda and HUM is voluntary, but leaving either is haunted by adversities of undetermined magnitude."

As a recourse in that dark setting of the night, he took possession of the book on Ahmad Shah Massoud given to him by Mr. Jatoi and held that in his hands more as a symbol of being reclusive. Areem's understanding and appreciation of the moral and ethical premise and rationale of Ahmad Shah Massoud to break away from supporting al-Qaeda and his determination to fight them were beyond any shadow of qualm.

With the internal debates throughout that bleak, dark night and his inability to share his feeling and concern with anyone, Areem had sudden yearning for meeting Ahmad Shah Massoud, who had since become so near to him. That motivated him to continue with al-Qaeda and finish all its requirements until he met Ahmad Shah Massoud and got his guidance. Areem also decided to put to rest his thinking about actions and decisions pertaining to his future life.

That very cogitated stance experienced its first major tremor when Areem was participating in the operation code-named *Hukumet-e-Sunnah*. As he observed from his rear position the people going to the Shia mosque, his reflexes were quivering by the thought that possibly all or many of them would return to their homes as dead bodies. Areem continued to be steady and committed as he would like to unearth the ultimate.

Very strangely, all related anxieties and quandary of Areem mislaid as soon as Operation Sunnah was launched. The fulfilling and smiling faces of forerunner devotees coming out of the mosque after saying *fajr* were greeted by a resounding brush fire of automatic weapons. Those who were behind crawled and rushed back to take refuge within the mosque. It was a brief operation to convey the message of HUM presence and strength. The additional objective was of efficient retreat before anybody could identify them.

The success of the operation with symbolic carnage made the team happy and Janab Humdam happier. When they were together, Areem was one among others sharing that euphoria but had a very muddled and exasperated feeling when he was alone. Areem was unsure whether such a diametrically opposite syndrome was the outcome of coercion or castigation.

That ostensibly had its physical toll. As Areem was about to have his lunch with comrades who took part in the operation, the falling figure of a young man of his age, who was at the forefront, flashed before his eyes. Areem had an abrupt feeling of gagging and choking, with his mouth full of saliva, while lunch eatables were being served. To his utter mortification, Areem vomited instantly in that semi-bent-over position, spoiling food items that were served. His friends lifted him, washed his face, asked him to freshen up, and took him to his room for rest. Soon thereafter, Areem went to sleep.

On hearing the full details, Janab Humdam observed, "It was frenzy physical response to something he was not used to. Gradually, he would get accustomed to it. Tell him that he would be resting for the next two days."

Areem spent his unanticipated rest period more by pondering on the objectives and modus operandi of al-Qaeda movement. The more he thought, the stronger was his alienation. While pondering about his future course of action, Areem started discreetly revisiting relevant portions of the book on Ahmad Shah Massoud. He could not do that always as the setting was an anti-Massoud one.

With diligence in approach, genuineness in compliance, and expressed obedience, Areem accomplished his induction process to the satisfaction of Janab Humdam and the pleasure of Imam Khakwani. In their recommendation to al-Qaeda in Afghanistan, Imam Khakwani emphasized Areem's standing as a valued asset, stressing his persuasion knacks, negotiation capacities, and communication skills.

Areem's transformation from being an apprentice of al-Qaeda to that of al-Qaeda Mujahideen had some theological imperatives and a few outward sequels. The implied dominant requirements of unflinching loyalty to al-Qaeda movement and its leadership, adherence to simple living, compliance with performing five-times daily prayers under all duress, as well as willingness for unbridled growth of beard stood out prominently. Many of these were reemphasized and practiced vigorously just prior to induction period and during the induction process.

Areem's formal induction and receiving of blessings from Imam Khakwani had standard ceremonial features besides others concerning outward attires. The latter was undertaken under the meticulous supervision of Janab Humdam, while the ceremonial event had its own standards and specifics.

In place of pajama and kurta given in Karachi by Mufti Quaser Ali to ensure Areem's assimilation, Mr. Humdam's similar action for effective integration consisted of outfits more common among Pashtun citizenry inhabiting both Khyber Pakhtunkhwa Province (KPP),or former NWFP, of Pakistan and Afghanistan.

In general, Afghan men's wears consist of a knee-length long-sleeved shirt having a front slit in the chest, the top with or without collars, and a real baggy white *shalwar*. It is normal to belt the shirt at waist level, giving the lower portion of the shirt a skirt effect. A sleeveless waistcoat, most of the time having embroidery patterns, is worn at the top of the shirt. Such a waistcoat is made of wool, but some are made of silk and cotton too.

The *shalwar* consists of a pair of trousers joined at the upper end of the thigh, with a broad loose-fitting top. Traditionally, the *shalwar* trousers are tailored to be long and loose fitting with broad hems above the ankles that are stitched to look like manacles.

The other casual item of men's dress is the footwear whose designs and materials mostly depends on local terrain and climatic conditions and differ significantly among regions. A pair of footwear is locally called *paizar* and is generally of different designs and types. The most popular *paizar* is known as *chapli*, worn in KPP of Pakistan and southern part of Afghanistan. These are generally made from soft leather that's dark red or heavy brown and black tan and sewn onto the rubber tire sole. They are handmade. *Chaplis* made in Charsharda Township of KPP are most famous.

But the features and implications of the last item of men's wear, as narrated by Janab Humdam, took Areem by incredulity. That related to *pagree* (turban).

Areem knew that Afghans in general and Pashtuns in particular always put on turban as a headgear. He, however, was totally unaware of its varieties, types, colors, materials, length, tying features, and more significantly, importance attached to its upkeep, and respectability associated with its possession.

Janab Humdam explained that under local culture, the turban is not only an identity but, more importantly, a symbol of prestige. It is a sign of respect and is a keepsake (*amanat*); hence, special importance is attached to its maintenance and safekeeping.

As briefly mentioned by Janab Humdam, turban is the most prominent among various types of headgear. Afghani turbans are made by wrapping a fairly long flaccid material skillfully draped around different base hats with a longish tail end down the back. There are many varieties of turbans; and the chief variations are known as the *lungee*, *patka*, *shamla*, and *qola*. Each variant has its tribe identity. It is therefore possible to identify the tribal root of Afghans in general and Pashtuns in particular by the type of turbans they wear.

With passage of time, and in some areas, the traditional turbans have been swapped for relatively more convenient head tops. The most noteworthy, popular, and one-sized replacement is known as *pakol*. It is a soft and round-topped men's head cover made of woolen materials. The sides needed to be rolled up after putting it on. The rolling-up process generally ensures a flexible fit without the need of stitching. This results in the formation of a thick band, which helps the top to remain steady as a head cover, more similar to a beret or cap.

Pakol gained prominence during the Afghan war against Russian occupancy between 1979 and 1989. With each photograph of Tajik political leader cum military commander and war hero Ahmed Shah Massoud wearing the *pakol*, as carried by print media and flashed by numerous and frequent coverages in various TV channels, it was made trendier.

Indications were perceptible about possible culmination of Areem's induction process. That was evident when Areem was presented a pair of Charsharda *chapli* by Janab Humdam as a demonstration of his admiration and affection. It was done in an informal gathering of the group of mujahids.

While presenting those, Janab Humdam detailed the relevant features of *chaplis*. *Paizar*'s description, make, and other details pertaining to its societal significance and use beguiled Areem.

But Areem was more bemused by the background information about the turban detailed by Janab Humdam earlier. He continued wondering whether he would have any role in choosing the type of one for him. Availing a lighter moment of discourse with Janab Humdam in that gathering, Areem carefully articulated an unspecific query as to how the types of turbans are assigned to each mujahid.

It so appeared that Janab Humdam liked the inquiry. He very cordially took Areem out, leaving others in the room. Putting a hand on Areem's shoulder, Janab Humdam said, "You are a special mujahid, and as advised earlier, al-Qaeda expects long-term returns from you. Hence, your training and induction process have specific features and variations. One of them was shortened duration. Because of that and while your colleagues of the last many days are yet to spend time on training, HUM has decided to have a special investiture ceremony for you this afternoon following *asr*."

Janab Humdam paused for a while and then continued, saying, "Imam Khakwani will preside over the brief ceremony, and he would make decision at that time as to assigning the type of turban for you. The investiture ceremony would come to an end with Imam Khakwani putting the turban on your head. I will soon take you to his room where you will see different types of turbans for decision by him. In the case of Afghans and other Pashtuns, the process is easy as they have their families' traditional ones. In case of mujahideen like you from other countries, it is the prerogative of Imam Khakwani to choose one. So no one knows."

He further said, "HUM exercises strict confidentiality about the movements and commitments of higher echelons of its leaderships. So no one among your associates knows about the ensuing investiture ceremony. Precisely because of that, I brought you out before responding to your query. This is also a part of your training. The essence is people, however trustworthy, are not to be trusted. I told them that a mock session of investiture process would be enacted to make all familiar with the process. Upon our return to the room, you should act in a way as if you do not know anything."

On returning to the room, Janab Humdam said that he would like to make a statement but prior to that would allow ten minutes' time for attendees to go out and attend to personal needs, including nature's call. He, however, would like everyone to return after finishing ablution as per norms of Islam as no one would be allowed to step out until about 6:00 p.m.

With everyone back as per timing stipulated, Janab Humdam was candid in informing all about a special investiture ceremony already planned for Areem. He also made clear the rationale for secrecy, and that was to ensure security and safety. He further desired that fellow associates help Areem to dress up as per requirement. It was also made clear that the turban would be chosen by Imam Khakwani, and he would place that on Areem's head. That would be the culmination of the event.

As Janab Humdam got engaged in finalizing the details pertaining to the investiture event, the ever-curious and equally smart Azmal, Areem's fellow comrade from Karachi, quipped, drawing attention about a missing item in the outfit mentioned by the latter that was also an essential ingredient of male Afghan dressing up. Azmal referred to the inescapable kambal that all Pashtuns and most adult Afghans carry generally on their left shoulder.

Known as Afghan *patu*, this shawl is made of pure wool and is worn in the Pakistan-Afghanistan mountainous regions where cold seasons and cold nights are very common even during summer. Responding to the need of such natural climatic traits, the *patu* can double as a blanket during cold nights.

Instead of being flustered by the inquiry, Janab Humdam, with an impish smile full of confidence and admiration, responded by saying, "I have not mentioned that intentionally. *Shawal* is more for comfort but not in any way reflective of faith, identity, or commitment. Because of that, we deliberately kept that out of ceremonial requirements. This matter and the additional one, a long and stout walking stick, will be handled by Imam Khakwani. In drawing his attention, I will identify you as the one who wondered for not keeping those as part of ceremonial requirements."

No doubt, Janab Humdam tackled the issue with grace and conviction. At the same time, he achieved a balance between regimentation for which al-Qaeda structure is known and a sense of openness and participation for sustained better commitment of its recruits to its philosophy and association within.

As ceremony-related mundane activities were being carried out within the room where everyone was huddled, there was a sudden hush-hush all around. Janab Humdam winked outside momentarily through partially opened door and confirmed the arrival of Imam Khakwani.

That ceremony was completed meticulously in ten minutes' time as per the drill earlier with less talk and more actions. The only notable exception was a low-voiced brief conversation between Imam Khakwani and Janab Humdam. In his still-shorter sermon, Imam Khakwani emphasized the danger Islam is facing both from inside and outside, the imperative need to confront those, the pious objectives of the movement of al-Qaeda and HUM, and the need of the hour to address them with fire and fury, emphasizing that the time of dialogue was over; and he reiterated the reward in case of *shahadat*.

In concluding his brief oration, Imam Khakwani casually touched base with issues of the *patu* and long walking stick. He said both of these items are necessities but has nothing to do with al-Qaeda's philosophy and local identity. It is therefore left to individual decision of each mujahid.

After saying those words, he exchanged some words with Janab Humdam, went nearer the table where different turbans were placed, picked up a *pakol*, placed it lovingly on the head of Areem, and embraced him avidly. This action of embracing was then repeated in an orderly manner starting from Janab Humdam and unexpectedly ending with Areem's closest friend in the camp, Azmal.

The successful completion of the special investiture ceremony made everyone happy, more so Janab Humdam. In a relaxed mood and voluntarily, he said, "Imam Khakwani is really a very wise man with sagacious attributes concerning life and living. In his fleeting talk with me prior to choosing a *pakol* for Areem, the imam mentioned the rationale for his selection. Considering Areem's lack of tradition and exposure to turban as headgear, he selected a *pakol* that is easy and handy, and Areem would not have a problem in handling that with respect due."

Prior to breaking away from that assembly, Janab Humdam told Areem to meet him just before dinner in the same room they were before. As Areem showed up, Janab Humdam greeted him warmly once again, requested his taking seat, and started saying, "Whatever we were to do with respect to you, we have done that. You are now a full-fledged al-Qaeda mujahid, responsible for your decisions and actions."

In continuation, Janab Humdam touched base with Areem's upcoming travel plan to Landi Kotal, a historic and equally thriving smuggling place located in tribal areas of PKK on the way to Kabul. He said, "On your way to Landi Kotal via Peshawar, you will travel up to Peshawar by train and then will have escorted road travel to your destination. That road travel would be through tribal areas where Pakistan's civil and criminal laws are not applicable. The distance between Peshawar and Landi Kotal is about thirty miles, but because of the foregoing, that could as well be overly perilous."

Janab Humdam opted for a diversion to ensure that Areem had full understanding of the significance of what he had just said and would be saying soon. So he briefly dealt with the historical backdrop of what the tribal area was and currently connotes. He started saying, "A strip of variable fifty dry, hilly, and mountainous miles of landmass to the northeast of Afghanistan, and bordering the NWFP-Balochistan provinces of Pakistan, was recognized as tribal areas during British rule. It has since been continued by Pakistan. This landmass starts at the northern tip of NWFP and runs to the south covering about two-thirds of the Balochistan Province's western border. The demarcation line between NWFP-Balochistan provinces of Pakistan and Afghanistan is internationally known as the Durand Line.

"After recurrent wars with Afghanistan at the beginning of its rule of India, the British government, as a strategic military option, worked out an administrative arrangement with fiery and independent-minded tribes inhabiting the border areas with Afghanistan, allowing them maximum concessions in lieu of territorial integrity vis-à-vis Afghan incursions and allegiance to British rule. Almost a similar type of arrangement is in place since the creation of Pakistan. The president of Pakistan is administering such tribal areas with the governor of NWFP serving as his agent and through an administrative structure known as FATA [federally administered tribal areas]. FATA basically works through *mallicks* and *sardars* [local tribal chiefs]. Each band of land under the control of a *mallick* or *sardar* has its own laws and rules. Thus, al-Qaeda or HUM always makes it sure to have escorted travel in FATA. Such escort travel witnesses escort changes with the change in jurisdiction of the respective *mallick/sardar.*"

Saying those words, Janab Humdam reverted back to discussion pertaining to Areem's travel arrangements. He said, "From now on, you will mostly travel alone, but HUM has a present for you. Your Multan-Peshawar rail itinerary has two days' break in Lahore as HUM would like you to get adequately familiarized with relevant important places. Lahore—being a historical place of political, military, economic significance—was the obvious choice. HUM will take care of you from reception at Lahore railway station to departure through the same station. A representative of Peshawar al-Qaeda will receive you in the railway station named Peshawar

City. Local al-Qaeda will make all necessary arrangements for your road travel to Landi Kotal. You will travel by train christened as Tezgam Express coming daily from Karachi and going to Rawalpindi via Lahore and vice versa. Your travel is scheduled for day after tomorrow. The train leaves around afternoon as per the time table, and you will be given a train ticket up to Lahore. The ticket for the remaining travel will be handled by Lahore HUM. Your friends will bid you farewell as you board the train. You can explore Multan tomorrow and can take Azmal with you."

Areem's associates were delighted in knowing his departure details and other stipulations related to that during the dinner, but Azmal had his reservations about taking around Areem tomorrow to explore Multan. In an anguish, reflective of both happiness and desolation because of the success and imminent separation of a dear one for whom he developed a special liking, Azmal opined, "I barely know Multan. My familiarity with Multan is limited to two specifics. First, it is the place bearing testimony of presence of numerous Muslim saints and their shrines. Second, it is the birthplace of Pakistan's famous test cricketer Inzamam-ul-Haq. Because of aforesaid limitations, we would not have much option but to often make uncoordinated inquiries, possibly drawing attention of the government's anti-terrorist field agents.

"So the better choice will be to approach Janab Humdam, propose his approval of substituting tomorrow for next Friday [being the usual weekend], and allow all of us to mingle with Areem in a relaxed mood and leisurely setting before we get separated."

The group agreed with the proposition, met Janab Humdam briefly after dinner, and got his approval. All present were very happy for the outcome, but all were happier for Janab Humdam's subtle comment, saying, "The group's concern about security impressed me most. I am happy to see that our training is having an impact in shaping all your thinking and action."

The following day was spent by Areem reading the book on Ahmad Shah Massoud as the time permitted. Areem spent the designated Friday with friends while strolling the roads and alleys, shrines and mosques, and bazaars and malls of Multan, in casually reverting to respective social setting, family life, and way-forward vision.

One thing in such improvised discourse took Areem by surprise. That pertained to the lack of clear assertion by anyone of explicit choice to become al-Qaeda mujahid for the cause of Islam. Among the four

Pakistanis, two were encouraged to join al-Qaeda because of allurement of specific benefits to the family. The other two, including Azmal, were pressured by respective fathers to join. The one from India was the victim of Indian intelligence agency and decided to escape by joining al-Qaeda. The rest five from Somalia, Libya, and Iraq joined al-Qaeda to take revenge, in their own way, for the atrocities committed by the United States in their respective countries. Areem was also clear that his own involvement was a product of uncharted coincidences and had nothing to do with Islam per se.

This realization and resultant feeling caused immense internal stress within Areem about the whole rationale of him being there. But being a person endowed with sobriety and serenity, Areem opted himself out of any hasty conclusion and preferred to use this opening to go deep and comprehend the real truth—and the whole truth—about the motivation that had been propelling the movement all over the Islamic world.

All preparations were afoot on the scheduled day for the much-awaited journey of Areem for Lahore as being an al-Qaeda mujahid. His temporary friends of the training camp in the complex of Masjid Oli Khan were both excited and dejected. The visible one was Azmal.

In his final exchanges with Areem, the emotion-laden Azmal said, "I do not know why I feel so sad for your departing us. Possibly, I still have in my blood the influence of the air and rain of Bangladesh. My parents had to leave East Pakistan for Karachi unexpectedly. That was definitely a traumatic one under hostile conditions. They had to leave behind a well-established business and a hilltop house in Chittagong. Notwithstanding that horrifying experience of midlife, and unlike some others, they always had nostalgic words about their living there and about the people of Bangladesh.

"My parents always prefaced their comments on Bangladesh with expressed sympathy for grievances being voiced. Many of the related statements of my parents always charmed me. But the summation was more interesting. They used to say that Bangladeshis individually are calm, quiet, and submissive ones with strong pride in their beliefs, culture, and way of life. On common issues of religion, language, and identity, their reflexes are quick, their apprehensions are spontaneous, and their emotional surge is both collective and vociferous."

Azmal continued, saying, "I did not have any inkling of what that meant but always had a fond hope to visit Bangladesh. That possibility is now remote after joining al-Qaeda. But I am happy to have the chance of meeting you and having exchanges with you. I now tend to understand what my parents meant by those expressions and words. I may not meet you in future. But if you are in Karachi ever and you need any help, or even otherwise feel like, you are most welcome to visit our home. I will inform my parents about you."

After saying those sentimental words, Azmal handed over his Karachi address to Areem, hugged him warmly, and bid farewell, expressing his inability to be at the railway station because of urgent other commitments.

During this discourse, Areem hardly talked but rather concentrated, mostly observing Azmal and digesting his words and expressions. After Azmal left, Areem moved from his bed, occupied the lone chair, and continued looking the way Azmal walked out. Areem had his impish smile when he concluded that it was avoiding a public emotional backlash rather than urgent commitment that would cause the absence of Azmal at the Multan railway station.

As a final act prior to commencing his maiden journey as al-Qaeda mujahid, Areem went to salaam Janab Humdam and to get his blessings. As most of the times, Janab Humdam was very polite and to the point at this encounter too. Instead of repeating earlier guidance and advice, he gave the only advice to Areem, which was to take note of the names of passing railway stations. That would give anyone like him an idea of the topography and directional identity being negotiated by his train. That could as well be of some undetermined relevance in future, especially in Areem's case.

Areem reached the Multan Railway Station in the company of two associates. The rest, excluding Azmal, joined him casually and left quickly to project the impression of a normal journey by a common friend. This sort of strategy was often resorted to by HUM to avoid suspicion of field agents of government intelligence outfits. As an additional safety measure, Areem was given by HUM a luggage that befitted the features of people traveling locally. That was, of course, in addition to his backpack having his dearest belongings.

Taking a seat positioned parallel to the platform, Areem was exchanging looks with friends whom he would probably never see again, but refrained from talking. The public address system's announcement alerted all about the imminent departure of the Tezgam Express for Lahore. With nippy air bust, dainty rattles, complex metal scrapes, and cranking sound of the wheels, Tezgam commenced journey, gaining speed quickly while waving hands of friends vanished speedily.

Soon after leaving the Multan Railway Station, Tezgam Express started cruising through relatively flat plains of the Punjab Province. The intermittent greeneries in the backdrop of dry and dusty top soil was indicative, to Areem's evident ignorance, of a speedy transition from desert-type topography of northern Sindh to fertile green landscape of southern Punjab.

Being blessed by an inquisitive and alert mind, Areem soon noticed the related changes and started enjoying it. The vastness of farming panorama, proliferation of mechanized equipment in agriculture activities, visible absence of traveling public, and frequent surfacing of camel-drawn carts, among others, amused Areem. Most of the aforesaid features were nonexistent in Bangladesh but cogently enthralling for the eyes of a person of Areem's background.

There were other palpable but related trifling factors contributing to the related conations. They were the short nature of his current travel and the fact that someone from HUM would meet and escort him out in an unknown and historically significant place like Lahore. The very fact that he was still being conducted and taken care of provided peace of mind, giving assurance concerning his safety and security. That was a significant solace to him in the context of uncertainty that featured Areem's current life.

Another reason that hugely contributed to Areem's ephemeral relaxation and enjoyment even in a challenging journey involving unfamiliar route and uncertain destiny emanated from the fact that the next stop of Tezgam, being an express train and as was told by friends of Masjid of Oli Khan, was Lahore. So there was no chance of getting deluded.

The equanimity of familiarization process, extensiveness of induction coverage within the time constraints, efficiency and timeliness of related actions, and cordiality extended with high degree of religious emphasis during the short spell of stay at Masjid Oli Khan of Multan overwhelmed Areem. All these were testaments to the effectiveness and efficiency of HUM as an organization.

Such feelings were contrary to his earlier experiences, assessments, and conclusions that intermittently made him a disillusioned al-Qaeda activist. Among the disconcerting messages of different sermons, the grueling scene of massacre of innocent worshipers coming out of the holy place of

Muslim prayer, in which he was a participant to, flashed before his eyes with perceptible opposing inferences.

Coming out of temporary disillusionment, Areem quickly concluded that those two assessments were premised on totally different perspectives. The first positivity was related to physical arrangements and attributes, while the second negative one was anchored in moral principles and ethical values as well as greater sense of justice in social setting. They are neither concurrent nor harmonious. He, however, concluded that even a bad cause could be augmented by having an efficient and effective physical support at ground level. Notwithstanding this type of internal inferences, Areem saw little option but to acquiescent that a bad augury like faith-related intolerance of al-Qaeda, in spite of cruelty, nourished its progression perhaps because of the efficiency of physical attributes at the ground level.

As Tezgam Express started approaching and finally stopped at the Lahore railway station, Areem became nervous. As a consequential antiphon, and to supposedly expedite the process, nervous Areem physically pushed upward the frame of glass window and partially extended his head through the open frame, looking for someone ostensibly holding a placard with his name. Right at that moment, a sweet and euphonious greeting from the back said, "Assalamu alaikum, brother." It startled an already anxious Areem momentarily.

Looking back with a spontaneous Muslim response ("Wa alaykumu s-salam") to such greeting, Areem was awed and surprised to face a person beyond his contemplation. There was a clean-shaven young man of slim physique with back-brushed straight black hair and a multicolored tie befitting his tugged-in long-sleeved dress shirt. He projected all features of likely amiable attributes and behooving disposition of a modern person. Every element of the person facing him was at significant variance compared to what Areem was exposed to in the recent past and had in mind. Areem rapidly concluded that the person could as well be an intelligence guy with a trap to befool him. With that sort of reflection overpowering his thought process, and to buy time, Areem resorted to slow down in retrieving his belongings.

The gentleman, keeping in view Areem's personal profile as reflected in the briefing note and his present assessment of physical disposition, decided to act first and direct. To warm up the setting, the gentleman extended his hand for a handshake with Areem, who complied coldly. After shaking hands, he said, "I am Amjad Hussain Naqvi, an urban mujahid of Lahore al-Qaeda, deputed to receive and take care of you. We need to get down quickly as stop time is very limited. Once on the platform, we can talk in more detail." That was acted upon without any thinking to the contrary.

The Tezgam Express left the Lahore station soon after Amjad and Areem disembarked. The bustling platform suddenly had an unintended quietness. Amjad was in a hurry to leave a public place like the railway station with a companion who had no similarity with him. He physically came closer to Areem but kept his focus on the railway track of the departing Tezgam going north. Amjad, in a style of talking in solitude, murmured, "I am a professor of sociology in one of the government colleges of Lahore. People and media talk more about al-Qaeda activists in terms of jihadis. But there are scores like us belonging to civil society who constitute the inner frame of the organization. We are the people who, from behind, ensure the organization's effectiveness and sustainability in good and bad times. I am here today performing that sort of role to hoodwink field agents of intelligence outfits. Another apposite point that you should remember is that from now on, you are my pen pal from Hyderabad and that you're going to Islamabad to attend organizational meeting of your political party. You are on a short visit to Lahore at my insistence and would be staying with my family. The rest we will talk about when we reach our home."

Saying those words, Amjad picked up a portion of Areem's baggage and moved out of the railway station on his way to *tanga* (single-horse-driven traditional transport) cluster point just outside the main building. Areem quietly followed him with the rest of the luggage even though his nervousness compounded with each step as he thought more about the true identity of Amjad. The question that haunted him time and again was whether Amjad himself was a government agent. Areem premised such concern based on the halfhearted responses of Amajad pertaining to his own identity. In that thought process, he recalled the brief nature of introductory exchanges at the railway station platform, which was kept incomplete. Areem continued to remain bemused until he became conscious of the sitting features of the tanga he was about to ride.

A tanga is a two-wheeled horse-drawn transport normally pulled by one horse. The wheels are relatively big, featuring riveted heavy-duty construction holding a mini quadrangular-framed structure providing seating capacity for four, including the coachman. It has a solid pedestal. The horizontal seat, often padded, has usually a padded divider, with the coachman and one passenger sharing the front section and the other two sharing the back portion but facing the back view. For Areem, the tanga was not a surprise as it was mostly reflective of *ghorar gari* (horse-driven transport) of Bangladesh. But what amused him was the openness of the design with the back seat arrangement and placing of the noseband, covering the nose and jaw of the horse. The tanga is very common in the Punjab Province of Pakistan with a dominant presence in Lahore.

Amjad negotiated with the coachman of one of the awaiting tanga and guided Areem to share the back seat with him, while placing the luggage in the front by the side of the coachman. To test the coachman, Amjad started having a chitchat with him. The more Amjad tried to be friendlier and divert the discourse to political issues, the greater was the efforts of the coachman to say how proud he was in successfully carrying the family legacy in spite of overwhelming competition. Not only that. The coachman, to demonstrate expertise and efficiency in steering his tanga, started playing with the reins, conveying subtle commands or cues for varying speeds, turns, halts, or rein backs. Amjad convinced himself that the coachman had no link with any intelligence agency of the government. He took a quiet look at Areem who, besides being amused, was enjoying the rhythmic sound emanating from galloping of the horse on the cemented road surface leading to, as he heard, a settlement known as Model Town.

Slightly leaning toward Areem with follow-on mild coughing, Amjad established eye contact with the former. He then started saying, "I briefly mentioned earlier about involvement of unnoticed campaigners in al-Qaeda activities notwithstanding their totally neutral fascia. There are scores of people like me from most areas of civil and defense occupations, and it is us who constitute the midstructure of the al-Qaeda organization. The front structure comprised of jihadis who by action or sacrifice project the public face of the movement. We play a critical role in carrying out sensitive activities and missions, camouflaging the main organization as needed. Another important work we do is to impartially monitor reaction and support among intelligentsia class of our actions for reporting to higher echelons. By design and inevitability, we mostly remain outside the customary publicity radar. Teachers of madrassas, imams of mosques, field-level workers of conservative political parties, and like-minded NGO establishments comprise the third structure or layer, propagating the idea and steering the movement forward. Immersion of some is spontaneous, while others are being bought out based on their relevance and competence.

All these tiers are relevant and important in their own perspectives and contribute equally to attain the objectives of HUM and, for that matter, of al-Qaeda.

"Lahore HUM shura, on receiving brief about you, decided to keep you out of the ostensible domain of al-Qaeda during your brief sojourn in Lahore. This decision is premised on the fact that you had your orientation already. The imperative need is to make you familiar with some historical aspects of Muslim rule in India as it was before 1947 and to imbibe in you a feeling and conviction as to what a Muslim rule again could deliver. Lahore eminently fits in for such showcasing while the planned exposition would be relevant to your future role and responsibility in Bangladesh.

"Keeping that in view, I have been assigned the responsibility to take care of you during your stay in Lahore. I have planned your stay in Lahore accordingly more to expose you to the glories of earlier Muslim rule while simultaneously keeping the perspective of tourism in view. The whole objective is to renew in yourself a pride for the grandeurs of earlier Islamic prominence and, secondarily, to have a feel of the city so that you can identify yourself easily with Lahore even though your stay is brief one. You will be staying with my family, and one senior HUM person would visit our home hours before you are to leave with latest instructions and your railway ticket to Peshawar."

As the tanga took a sudden turn off the Multan road and entered a congested settlement, it had to slow down; and the galloping of the horse was substituted for something similar to pogoing.

Areem could sense that they were near Amjad's home because of frequent exchanges of salaam with bystanders. Based on similar practices in Bangladesh, this trend instinctively conveyed to Areem the eminence Amjad and the prominence his family enjoyed in the neighborhood.

Amjad was preoccupied in wishing both friends and associates, and even unknown elderly individuals, more, making an effort to create a sustainable political capital for the future. Areem had no doubt that he was in the model township referred to in the discussion in Multan.

Lahore, being the principal city of undivided Punjab, attracted greater importance and attention as the most important city of the newly crafted country, Pakistan. Concerted decision was made to expand Lahore City in a planned manner. Envisioned as a planned urban settlement, the designated area was given a futuristic name of Model Town. But that was the victim of an unintended prey because of the rush of people from hinterland sensing emerging economic opportunities and immigration of Muslims from East Punjab and the rest of India. Thus, the concept of being a model town was lost even before it could perhaps start.

Areem was innocently baffled while observing the proliferation of unplanned structures, facilities, passages and walkways resembling haphazard growth, random encroachments, man-made congestion, and societal obstinacy, which was probably reflective of some upshots of muscle power and political patronage. Most grippingly, the chaotic end result is self-evident in a place that was to resonate as being a model settlement.

Ecstatically, the scene changed with a left turn of the tanga to a subsidiary road casing a respectable piece of land with what seemed to be a big housing complex from the outside. On indication by Amjad, the coachman stopped the tanga in front of the house. Amjad promptly got down and settled the bill. Areem followed him silently.

Within those ephemeral moments, two household helps rushed toward the tanga, got hold of the luggage, and went inside. Areem had no doubt that household staffs were briefed adequately earlier. A similar scene on an identical occasion in his Dhaka home flashed back in Areem's mind momentarily.

Standing in front with abundant open space to breathe fresh air, Amjad said, "We are originally from East Punjab, now a part of India. After partition, and utilizing my father's prepartition business relationships and contacts, a mutual exchange of properties between the owner of this house and that of ours was acted upon. We have been living in this area since the partition of 1947, which soon thereafter became a part of an ambitious urban planning, and our area was named as Model Town. Now you can gauge what type of model we have."

Before proceeding to the main entrance of the house, Amjad looked at the magnificent structure in front and started saying, "Perhaps, you know, this type of traditional townhouse or mansion is known as *haveli*. Apart from the size and grandeur of the property, mostly made popular in India by Mughals, the principal design attraction of a *haveli* is its chowk [center courtyard] having multipurpose ceremonial use. You will notice an altar at the middle of the chowk with almost a dying plant. That is sacred tulsi plant revered by the previous owner. That family, as is common to most Hindu families, used to worship it daily, perhaps to bring prosperity to the *haveli*. It was the previous owner's earnest request to my father, and in a sense a part of the deal, to allow the tulsi plant to remain at its assigned place until it dies. After so many years, we are still waiting for that day. Over the period, my father has got emotionally attached to it. All our expressed requests for its removal were ignored by him, sometimes politely and on some other occasions assertively."

Amjad and Areem set foot at the chowk, sharing a common feeling of informality and conviviality. That was most conspicuous when Areem met Amjad's father, reclining in an easy chair with the decorated pipe of his hookah in his left hand even though its top vessel, supposed to be ablaze with burning tobacco cake, was latent. Seeing Areem by the side of Amjad, the father had no doubt who he was. Smiling broadly in reciprocating the usual Muslim greeting of Areem, the father said, "Beta, take it as your home and be at ease. We were bonded by common nationality until 1971. That has politically been snapped, but our faith-related bond remains as strong and as viable as any bond could be. Amjad will take care of you."

The vacant guestroom adjacent to the main entry point of the residential quarters of the *haveli* was assigned and prepared for the temporary stay of Areem. Entering the room, Areem could sense meticulous preparation of the room for his stay and noted a glass jug full of water and a glass by the side of the bed. Both of them had hand-embroidered knitted covers. That touched Areem very much, and he concluded about two days' enjoyable stay in this *haveli*. Amjad soon reappeared with a copy of an English daily newspaper for Areem. He was followed by a male household help carrying an over-filled tray with snacks. After finishing the ritual of welcoming tea and snacks, Amjad excused himself, asking Areem to take rest.

Areem had minimum interactions with members of Amjad's home since his arrival. He reconciled with it as being the offshoot of discreet stay in the assigned room as a precaution exercised by host. But Areem remained surprised having not heard any female voice, forget about seeing anyone moving. Except the two assigned houseboys, he had not exchanged words with any other person of the house. So Areem was taken aback when Amjad advised him on the early evening of the first night about having dinner in the main section of the house in the company of his father. That most unexpected indication overwhelmed him. The word *beta* uttered by Amjad's father during the first encounter accompanied by mien of unhesitating fondness, unrestrained love, and unqualified warmth flashed back to Areem's mind. He also recalled having never been so addressed by his father. Areem unwaveringly concluded that while blood is relevant in linking segments of family, it is the warmth of expressions and depth of care that matter more in cementing any relationship.

Traveling through the track of early thinking, Areem joined the father and son for dinner, waiting for the service. Amjad's father, more to create an informal ambience, started saying, "Beta, so far, I know your visit to Lahore has permeating preference for familiarization with the citadel of history, civilization, and culture of the subcontinent. This is a golden opportunity. Take full advantage of it. Your preferred focus should be to see and assimilate with queries rather than waiting to hear or being told.

"As legend goes, this city was founded and named after Prince Lava or Loh, the son of Hindu deity Rama. Since then, it witnessed a series of changes in patronage involving Jain, Hindu, Buddhist, Greek, Muslim, Mughal, Afghan, Sikh, and the British. Lahore, as a city—with protuberant tombs and mosques, museums and miniatures, palaces and fortresses, gardens and greens—both survived and flourished through its long run of bittersweet history. As the second largest city of Pakistan, it has become the beacon of history, both absorbing and preserving variations in culture, literature, and architecture."

That dinner had no other mentionable rendition except eating quietly as per local tradition. Amjad soon retired to get up early the following morning.

Contrary to the orthodox approach and confronting attitude towards other faiths as well as the interpretation and practices of Islamic beliefs and values for which al-Qaeda is universally known, the Lahore shura planned Areem's orientation with a surprisingly secular focus. The orientation commenced with a visit to a historical garden currently listed as one of the UNESCO World Heritage sites. It was known as the Shalimar.

When they positioned themselves at the entrance gate, Amjad took a step back and made a brief overview about the gardens for the benefit of Areem. He said, "It was designed as a Persian-style garden with a focus on harmonious existence between humans and nature. Its development was also influenced by regions like Central Asia and Kashmir as well as architecture preferences of Delhi Sultanate. Constructed between 1641 and 1642 during the reign of the Mughal emperor Shah Jahan, the gardens cover an area of about sixteen hectares, has three levels of terraces with each one thirteen to fifteen feet higher than the earlier one; contains 450 fountains in total, which, along with designed dense foliage, keeps the gardens cooler, a significant environmental planning keeping in view the blistering summer of Lahore. The gardens are distinguished to have an amazing oblong parallelogram shape with brick wall all around having exquisite intricate fretwork."

Once inside, it was the turn of Areem to ask questions of interest to him and for Amjad to respond based on what he knew about it. That was just not Shalimar Gardens specific. It was the designed pattern of discourse during that familiarization strolling in and around Lahore within the framework of Amjad's plan for this brief visit.

Amjad clarified that the center of focus of this visit was on and around the Walled (Old) City of Lahore. The old city dates back more than thousands of years and so named as being fortified by a mud wall during medieval time. It is around the Walled City that most of the historical monuments and structures of prominence, including those of Mughal era, are located with close proximity, some not even a mile.

He further clarified, "The garden itself is only a few miles away from the Walled City, but most other structures to be visited are around that city." While visiting the Lahore Fort, Amjad told Areem, "The site of the present Lahore Fort was historically the location of a fortified structure, known as a mud-brick fort, and dates back to eleventh century. The modern fort was built on that site during the reign of Moghul emperor Akber. It is located at the periphery of Lahore's Walled City. Lahorites fondly call it *Shahi Qila*, and UNESCO recognized it as one of its World Heritage sites."

Identical was the introductory premise of the Badshahi Mosque. Amjad stated, "The mosque, located roughly west of Lahore Fort on the outskirts of the Walled City, is ranked as the most iconic landmark of the city and is designated, to my current knowledge, as UNESCO World Heritage site. The architecture is a mix of regional features and Persian style. Apart from structural minutiae of the main section, the entrance gate itself is an amazing one. The relative, and more imaginative and striking, feature is the spacious sandstone-paved courtyard. That covered approximately an area of about 275,000 square feet with capacity to accommodate about one hundred thousand devotees. The mosque was commissioned by Mughal emperor Aurangzeb in 1671."

During the impromptu walk, Amjad diligently resorted to small variations and experiences to keep Areem's interest active and alive. Small breaks in shades and occasional sipping of local drinks like sugarcane and pomegranate juices featured this unusual visit. On possible opportunities, he would draw Areem to the Walled City area as most historical things and practices were around it. In one such venture, Amjad offered him an ice cream, locally called *kulfa* and named as Benazir. Areem enjoyed that both for the current political prominence of the name and its traditional taste.

In one of such breaks, Amjad told Areem that for both better focus and familiarization, he preferred the program of today to end with a walk from about the Assembly Building at the center of the city's main boulevard to famous Anarkali Bazaar and the Punjab University area end. He also opined that tomorrow morning would be a better time and setting for absorbing the uniqueness of the bazaar though the glare of light and the presence of families would be missing. Areem's option was limited to listening and agreeing, and he did that.

The main boulevard of Lahore was known as the Mall, and that generally ran northeast to southwest and lay at the periphery of the historical Old City. It was roughly the symbolic demarcation between the old, and emblematic identity of new Victorian Lahore. The Mall, with its uniqueness in notion, priority for spacious design having up-and-down reverse roads, provision of a broad divider with trees and flower beds, and forethoughts pertaining to wide promenade captivated many; and Areem was no exception. But what attracted Areem the most was the existence of a controlled irrigation system placed in the divider for periodic irrigation of the plants and trees. Likewise, having sections of walkways shaded by trees and tree-shaded plots along the boulevard pleased Areem very much as it did others.

Promenading along the Mall of the Victorian Lahore, from its Assembly Building end, was as casual as it could be with Amjad keeping quiet and Areem gazing. After finishing the casual strolling, Amjad stopped at the other end of the Mall. That end had a few specific milestones of the time. One was the main General Post Office, commonly known by its acronym GPO. The others were the museum and the beginning of the campus of Punjab University. However, most popular and much-talked about and frequented place of common interest was the bazaar known as Anarkali.

In introducing Areem with that bazaar, Amjad stated that it has two entrances: one from inside old Lahore and is known as Lahori Gate. The other one is around the location where the Mall ends around bygone days aristocratic store known as Tollinton Market. This is known as Tollinton Market Gate.

Giving historical perspective of the bazaar, Areem clarified that it is so known after the name of a courtesan of the court of Mughal emperor Akbar. History, however, has no uniform position on this. Her other identities in history are wife, lovebird, professional dancer, and so on, depending on the source one relies. Each one of them seems to be relevant against the backdrop of the supporting story, and most of them are commonly accepted.

The name Anarkali consists of two words. *Anar* is the Persian word for "pomegranate," and *koli* stands for "blossom." So the beautiful performing girl was adoringly named Anarkali in recognition of her gorgeousness. The market was so named as some sources believe that the courtesan was buried there alive at the order of Emperor Akbar, who could not accept her romantic relationship with his son, Prince Salim.

But a run-down coffee shop in close proximity of Tollinton entrance gate of the Mall presently outshines the historically dreamy epic. Named Coffee House, it was the favored place for intellectuals, journalists, writers, professors, and a host of young activists to frequent. They spent hours together, debating social, political, and economic issues, palpably with not much of eventual common understanding. Thus, this coffee shop is both popular and relevant to the society. Amjad suggested and Areem agreed to have a cup of coffee in that shop before returning home with the understanding that they would visit Anarkali Bazaar the following morning.

As they entered the Anarkali Bazar around noontime the following day, small shops and tiny empty spaces were all overflowing, exhibiting various brass, copper, leather products, jewelry items of different types and designs, and cheap silks and prints besides ready-made garments and make-up accessories of ladies' preference. Areem's pronounced but equally reserved response to commercial preponderance of Anarkali Bazaar initially muddled Amjad. However, he soon regained his focus as he observed Areem minutely looking at small tables full of old books on varied subjects. There were hips of old books in the available spaces of the alley side.

These books were selling between quarters of a dollar to a dollar at most. Areem was enthralled by seeing a book on Taxila archeology being offered for sale at equivalent of $0.75. He spent most of his time reviewing the books, glancing casually to other merchandise, and admiring the aggressive overture to sell the products. But his last proposition took Amjad by surprise. At Areem's preference, both of them went to a rudimentary tea stall, enjoyed local tea, and at the insistence of Areem, Amjad agreed to allow the former to pay the bill. That made both happy, obviously for different reasons.

It was past noontime of the day. Areem was to depart for Peshawar. Communication with Amjad was minimal since returning from orientation outing of the earlier morning cum noontime. He appeared to be preoccupied with precipitous confronts.

After arranging his belongings and luggage for his imminent departure, Areem was in a deep exclusive mood, pondering about his stay in Lahore, more in the abode of a totally unknown family. The love and care extended and the quantity, quality, and variety of food fondly served during the last two and a half days were beyond expectations. He never enjoyed these even in his Dhaka house.

The procrastination of Areem related to his ensuing journey came to an end when Amjad showed up and advised about the presence of a designated representative of the Punjab al-Qaeda. Both of them went to meet the gentleman.

The gentleman, Ahmed Khar Mustafa, was a typical Taliban cum al-Qaeda senior leader by all physical attributes and dress-up, including flowing unregulated beard and colorful headgear. His body was wrapped by a chador (dark robe worn by devotee Muslims). The only missing attribute was a tasbih (prayer bead) normally carried by many Muslims as a demonstration of their faith, commitment, and practice. After exchanging the ritual Muslim greetings of salaam, Janab Ahmed Khar Mustafa welcomed Areem and wished him all well in his journey to mainstream al-Qaeda in Afghanistan. He prayed with his two palms lifted up to his chest level seeking Allah's mercy to condition Areem with heightened dedication and effort in pursuing the broad objectives of al-Qaeda in Bangladesh.

After saying so, Janab Mustafa took a small break to put a *pan* (a traditionally prepared betel leaf with lime, nut, and ingredients emanating flavor) in his mouth. Areem kept on observing him. What impressed him the most was the softness of his rendering. It was devoid of arrogance and ultimatum normally expected from a person of his status and bearing.

Exchanging looks with Areem and Amjad, Janab Mustafa resumed his avowal, saying, "We planned your travel to Peshawar by Awam Express train tomorrow morning. More common people usually journey by this train, and the fact that it travels from Karachi to Peshawar unlike Tezgam, which terminates its journey at Rawalpindi, premised the decision on the use of this express. You should continue to be careful until you cross

Rawalpindi. Once you cross Rawalpindi, your anxiety of being an al-Qaeda activist should wither away. The more you proceed toward Peshawar, the greater will be your comfort and exaltation.

"Bear in mind that there are two railway stations by the names of Peshawar City and Peshawar Cant. The latter one is the terminal station. But you will get down in Peshawar City station. Our designated al-Qaeda compatriot will receive you. You need not look for him. The compatriot would have all details about you. He would locate you and greet you by saying, 'Peshawar is so beautiful.' That would testify genuineness of the person and link with al-Qaeda."

After delivering the instructions, Janab Mustafa handed over to Areem the Awam Express ticket and some Pakistani rupees for unforeseen needs. After that, he left Amjad's house hurriedly. What surprised Areem was his noncompliance with standard practice of meeting the elder of the house in case of such a social visit by another senior person. Areem kept quiet. Amjad volunteered to tell Areem that he would accompany him to the railway station tomorrow morning and oversee Areem's safe and secure departure.

Taking his assigned seat in the designated compartment of the Awam Express after bidding sublime farewell to Amjad with multiple hugs and shaking of hands, a sudden mixed thought concerning his involvement in al-Qaeda and present uncertain journey started haunting Areem anew. The brutality experienced in Multan, not for religious differences but for practices within a religion, shook his high moral grounds that motivated Areem to join al-Qaeda. He could not reconcile with using any religious belief for killing, destroying, and sustaining hatred among mankind. Overemphasis on religion and justification for all heinous actions in the name of religion—and that, too, from a particular perspective—became insupportable to Areem. He ironically concluded that when one individual kills another, that is called murder and is abhorred by society and its legal system; however, when a group of people kills another group, that is ascribed as eventuality for a cause and tolerated by society. What an irony!

In that lonely backdrop both within and outside the train with fellow passengers and outside onlookers having significantly distinctive physical features, different languages, noticeable variations in cultural practices and expressions, Areem's confused status of self-groping received a shake with the sound of steam chuffs and follow-on rail clatter as wheels of Awam Express started rotating.

The stable mind-set of Areem of late started showing its tendency to justify and question his choice and decision to join al-Qaeda. It mostly had off-and-on reflections based on current experiences and thinking. That happened during his journey from Lahore to Peshawar too.

Consistent with that mind-set and contrary to hitherto nurtured agonizing reflections, Areem surprisingly started cherishing sort of a positive feeling about al-Qaeda. Lahore al-Qaeda's focus and approach in planning and executing his present visit overwhelmed him. The selection of Amjad for the task was undoubtedly the hallmark. The planning and execution of his familiarization expedition were indubitably superlative from all perspectives. The most pertinent point for Areem was that neither during numerous discourses nor during follow-on exchanges relating to familiarization visits did Amjad ever refer to the past Islamic glory or current al-Qaeda focus. Areem learned a lot from this experience. The essence was that one can promote a cause or pursue an objective by not echoing or emphasizing the same often.

Traversing through associated thoughts, Areem unknowingly swiveled through musings of his life and living so far and the uncertainty that beholds the future. Suddenly, he started feeling despondent. Areem wanted to shake that off reasoning. That instant predomination of depressing thought could have been a by-product of the lonely setting in the compartment of the train, which was releasing occasional chuffs as it was gaining speed after passing each of the designated stations. He rebounded himself with determination not to look back and never to nurture a feeling of debasement.

There was no doubt in Areem's mind that once in a game, one needs to play it fully for one's own interest. Since becoming a member of al-Qaeda was a voluntary decision, he should not have frequent dilemmas until he experiences the whole gamut, either to appreciate it fully or take other courses without remorse.

Enjoying the fast-receding panoramas, Areem was in the mood of having some positive contemplation about the future outcome of his present venture. A likely prospect of being in touch or contact with Ahmed Shah Massoud made him momentarily content.

Areem's fleeting gladness was distracted by the evident reduction in speed of the train. In the midst of unfamiliar (mostly spoken in local version of Punjabi) language-specific exchanges and queries as well as marked anxieties among fellow passengers, the express unexpectedly stopped before reaching an important junction known as Lala Musa. No one had any idea of the reason that caused it. A fellow passenger sitting behind his seat, appearing to be a young student, was making summary statements about possible causes; and that traversed a number of common ones. But he kept adjacent passengers glued to his statements and off-the-cuff jokes.

Areem could not make any sense of many of those. He nevertheless paid full attention to what was being told by that wannabe learned young man. In the process, he could comprehend a joke concerning Lala Musa. The fellow student—with a mix of English, Urdu, and Punjabi—referred to a general hypothesis having ramifications on history, story, humor, satire, and taunt depending on how one took it. That, however, had all the intent to convey hushed assertions of his presumed intellect and related prowess.

The young man said, "Bhai Shaheb [revered brothers], the real reason is that the soul of our *Lala* [brother] Musa [name] was not happy in naming a minor station, even though a small junction, after him against the backdrop of his actions and sacrifices. Acknowledgment of noble work done by any illustrious person and society's response to recognize it adequately and in a timely manner is sine qua non for orderly process. That was not done in the case of beloved Lala. His noble soul continues to be in a timorous stage. This is the reason why Lala Musa railway station has had occasional unforeseen problems. Today's one may be one of them. Let us see how that is responded to today."

The Awam Express was stationary for an unusually long time in the midst of nowhere. The agility of the people in speculating reasons mellowed, and a nebulous anxiety overawed many. The talkative pseudo-young man appeared to be exhausted as he reclined his head against the window frame, keeping his eyes closed. Some, however, stepped out of their compartments to get relief from heat and chattering, among others, shrieks of small children. But people at large experienced thirst and some hunger too. Areem was no exception. It was worse for him as he was not supposed to overexpose himself. By compulsion, he thus stayed glued to his seat and followed the practice of the young man, opting for a reclined posture with closed eyes.

In the midst of chaos and confusion, Areem unwittingly dozed off. He woke up sensing some commotion around. On hearing about an oncoming track inspection trolley (wheeled cart pushed by hand), the young man from the back seat jumped out and started moving toward the locomotive in haste and expectation. He came back soon with an ominous news that the unexpected delay was because of an inadvertent local situation, having the tint of communal tension that unwittingly prodded chaos at Lala Musa train station. It took time to bring things under control. The train would leave for Lala Musa any moment now.

Those words momentarily unnerved Areem, but he soon overcame that as the spurting of the locomotive and the rattle of the compartment were matched by the most desired movement of the train. He categorically concluded that there should not be frequent negative procrastination and jerks, as was being experienced all throughout his thought process since joining al-Qaeda. Good or bad, it came as a package; and he would have to live with that.

The train reached Lala Musa junction about two hours later than the schedule with significant rotation of outgoing and incoming passengers. Fortunately for Areem, the new passenger sitting by his side was a professor of a local college and could communicate in various languages.

Looking at Areem, the professor perhaps suspected his un-familiarity with the local setting. He volunteered to narrate, mostly in Urdu, the incident that caused the most unlikely communal commotion and started saying, "Lala Musa was a trivial settlement within the deserted area of District Gujarat and located about 145 kilometers south of Islamabad. It came into celebrity around late nineteenth century when the colonial British government constructed the now-famous railway junction. The living pattern, cultural orientation, and religious harmony got a boost with the settlement of many English families who mingled with Hindu and Sikh majorities and Muslim minority. With mass migration of 1947, the Sikhs and Hindus had become minorities, and the Muslims attained the status of majority.

"Though Pakistan is known as a land inimical to other faiths, Lala Musa is known for its communal harmony. Contrary to the whole country, Lala Musa residents always enjoyed religious freedom. The presence of a small English graveyard, a functioning church, and a temple are ample proof of continuing amiable setting. The Sikh and Hindu minorities have pervasive religious freedom and are treated as equal citizens.

"In this background, a third-year undergrad Muslim student of a local college developed romantic feelings for a freshman Hindu girl student. The response was sentient. Initially, it was overlooked as a very natural manifestation of emotional feelings of youth. But the time passed coated that feeling to cause anxiety to both families, more to the family of the beloved. They hurriedly arranged a marriage for the daughter with a groom from Gujar Khan area of Rawalpindi District, who was a promising contractor.

"Gujar Khan, located about fifty kilometers from Islamabad, is a bustling tehsil of Rawalpindi District having ancient links with Hinduism and appositely deep-rooted contacts with Sikhism. Even after massive migration of 1947, there is, like Lala Musa, a notable presence of Hindu and Sikh population in Gujar Khan with functional Hindu temples and Sikh Gurdwaras.

"The beloved young girl initially resisted and then gave in before the command and expectation of parents and community. All follow-up events concerning that wedding were carried out smoothly. But the young man, at the behest of his close associates, could never take it easily. His anger and frustration were aroused by the constant challenge of losing his love to minority Hindu society's pressure, and that was equated as a slur on Muslim marital traditions in an Islamic country like Pakistan and his youthful surge of love.

"Even though positioning love against the backdrop of religion could seemingly be a subject of emotional intensity, in totality, it is too trivial to influence the cherished outcomes that the society upholds from faith related identity. Often the same is metaphysically conflicting too. In that background, the wedding was done smoothly with the participation of the local Hindu society, Muslim and Sikh gentries, and tiny representation by the dwindling Catholic segment.

"The happy bridal party was waiting at the Lala Musa junction's passenger waiting room for the incoming local train to go to Gujar Khan. As they stepped out in the midst of loud music by the local band to board the train, a short-lived burst of gunfire from both sides of the waiting room sent people competing for safe shelter. The paramour and his associates quickly withdrew from the scene. Train operation was suspended immediately.

"Within minutes, the news spread like wildfire with multiple versions of what happened, creating confrontational reactions among the segments of the society. Communal tension was built up spontaneously. Muslim anger pertains to the audacity of Hindu minority to confront the overwhelming majority. The Hindu rage is premised on sheer survival trepidation in a country they nurtured as their own for generations. The other minority communities sided with Hindus' fear due to precipitous common interest. This was rather exception for a place like Lala Musa, which traditionally enjoyed the reputation for being a place of amity, forbearance, and mutual deference.

"Eruption of most expected communal atrocities was jammed due to prompt action by the law-and-order authorities, including sustained public announcements by mobile loud speakers informing the public about the unfortunate rash firing by miscreants at the railway station and side-by-side highlighting that no one was injured or killed.

"Taking advantage of this, and living up to tradition, the majority Muslim civic and political leaders sent urgent message for a protest assembly by all at the station, the venue of firing. Responding to that call, prominent Hindu, Sikh, and Catholic community leaders also showed up with their fellow civic leaders. In his thought-provoking rendering conveying the feelings and the sentiments of the most vulnerable segments of the society, the local Hindu leader said, 'The utmost dismaying act of hours back is not Lala Musian. The onus is on current generation to uphold the previous tradition of tolerance, amity, and mutual respect. Pursuing uncorroborated motivations would only aggravate the present conflict. Revenge would result in reasons for regrets. Irrespective of variable reasons, we, the minority but equally loyal Pakistanis, would like to consider the whole episode as an isolated incident. We thus propose to move on by bidding a befitting farewell to our daughter in her journey to new home.'

"That was acted upon with applause, and Lala Musa rediscovered itself in traditional tranquil setting for which it is famous."

Areem listened to what the professor was detailing in his professorial mood. His unceasing alertness and unspoken curiosity impressed the professor. The professor had a direct exchange with Areem and pointedly asked whether the setting of the incident was clear to the latter. Areem nodded and meekly said *shukria* (thanks). Scared of further intimacy and personal queries, and as a diversion, Areem focused his attention to the fast-receding panorama. Polite coolness of Areem did the trick. The professor concentrated talking to fellow other passengers, mostly in local dialect.

For some arcane reasons, the narrative pertaining to Lala Musa incident, as detailed by the accompanying professor, bemused Areem. Even in an extreme situation where shoots were aimed to their daughter- and son-in-law, the local Hindu-Muslim leaderships chose the wise and pragmatic option of peace and amity, instantly defusing a volatile situation. The question that haunted Areem once again was if local Hindu-Muslim communities could take such a calm decision against the backdrop of hundreds of years of enmity, then why are Shia and Sunni sects of Islam, with many common elements of the same faith, killing one another, and why such a harmonious approach is not getting needed inspiration?

On leaving Lala Musa, the Awami Express maintained its scheduled momentum. Rawalpindi train station—being the service station for Pakistan's military headquarters and notoriously famous for snooping their version of anti-state elements, about which Areem was cautioned earlier in Lahore—passed unnoticed.

The Awami Express made a shrill whistle before entering the train station named Taxila. On noticing the name on the railway's cement-concrete standpost, Areem spontaneously came out of his stupor. He recalled his reading about Taxila, along with Mohenjo Daro and Harappa, in his high school history book while reading about the Maurya dynasty.

Taxila, as written in English, was mostly spelled and pronounced as Taksasila in Bangla and Hindi. Since the Maurya Empire (322–185 BCE) had its roots in Bengal and its adjoining territories, the spelling above is taken as more reliable. It was an eminent center of Buddhism, the distinguished center of learning and culture, the place of Gandhara sculpture, and presently the home of world-renowned archaeological sites. It likewise has been famous for having Emperor Chandragupta Maurya's chief advisor and prime minister, Kautilya, as a member of its faculty. Kautilya became famous as a statesman and philosopher by popular name of Chanakya, the founding father of modern-day tricks and turns of diplomacy.

As the train stopped, Areem edgily maneuvered to take out his head through the window of the rail compartment as if he was certain to enrich his intellectual prowess by inhaling the air of Taxila with the attributes and eminence that are thousands of years old but prominently related to both Chanakya and the center of learning located there.

The next station was Hasan Abdal, and the stop was a brief one. But it enabled easing of suffocating congestion in the compartment ever since Areem boarded the train in Lahore. Surprisingly, more passengers disembarked related to incoming ones, and the reason remained unclear to Areem. He did not bother about it either as a new contemplation kept him preoccupied. Involuntary ruminations of historical details pertaining to the kingdom of Magadha and documented thousands-of-years-old eminence of Taxila, Mohenjo Daro, and Nalanda caused within the thinking of Areem an internal inquiry about his identity. He was debating whether all these should portray the uniqueness of his identity or whether the faith revealed in the desert of Arabia should be the overpowering one, or both. He was puzzled. The more he thought about it, the more he got confused.

In that muddled mood, Areem was oblivious about the train's movement and passing stations. Compared to his earlier travels from the mosque Farzian-e-Matina of Karachi to Multan via Hyderabad, Areem's subsequent journey involving a distance of about 250 miles by train from Multan to Peshawar of KPP (North-West Frontier Province) via Lahore happened to be stress free but not necessarily uneventful. There was no escort to accompany, no caution about hiding identity of being an al-Qaeda mujahid, and no restraint on conversations with others made Areem feel as one just being liberated. He was enjoying his recent freedom but never ever forgot all those told to him earlier during the orientation phase. Though not regulated, he followed them meticulously all through and was mostly by himself.

A soft assalamu alaikum from behind brought Areem out of the unusual bafflement. He looked back to find a lanky young guy. Without wasting time, the young man said, "Peshawar is so beautiful. I am Zakaullah. Al-Qaeda of Landi Kotal deputed me to escort you safely. We need to go down as it will be time soon for this train to leave for its terminal station."

Saying those few words, Zakaullah helped Areem with his luggage, got down promptly, and, after a short walk, checked in a *sharaikhana*, a mix of ordinary tea stall with limited boarding facility at the back. Zakaullah appeared to be not only soft-spoken but also less talkative. To some initial queries of Areem, his responses were mostly in single syllable unless otherwise needed. The only elaborate statement he made was, "It is not advisable to travel at night. So we are staying here. We plan to leave tomorrow around early noon after your travel arrangement is finalized."

STEPS

It was very early dawn of the following morning. Areem had a very uncomfortable and equally sleepless night, more thinking about the remaining journey about which he heard different stories from multiple sources. In the setting of tribal areas, administration and justice dispensation have unspecified mix of insolence, varied command arrays, rudimentary ways of decision taking, and spontaneity of actions. By the time Zakaullah showed up to escort him to *jamaat* (assembly) of *fajr* namaz, numerous *azaans* started simultaneous rattling from all neighboring mosques. Zakaullah sort of scanned Areem and was markedly pleased to see him all prepared to go to prayer. He only asked him to lift the lower part of *shalwar* about three inches above the ankle in line with what the Taliban practiced as a more Islamic way of wearing it.

During breakfast, an arrangement of service on the *khatiya*, like the one Areem slept over last night, Zakaullah told latter to keep waiting for him as he would soon be going out to finalize their escorted journey to Landi Kotal. As they were having breakfast, Zakaullah was looking at his wristwatch frequently with disquiet beholding him. After some time, a tarnished pickup van with mud marks around its body slowly came and parked in front of the *sharaikhana*. No audible signal was passed. No one came out from the van to meet Zakaullah. The only visible sign was an expression of glee in the reaction of Zakaullah as if the presence of the van removed a great anxiety that was bothering him.

In the midst of munching clay-oven-hot naan and *chapli* kebab (made of ground beef or mutton with a variety of spices and shaped as a patty) and occasionally sipping *garam chae*, Zakaullah perhaps lost track of time momentarily. Looking at his wristwatch, he realized he was getting late for his scheduled commitment. He then stopped eating breakfast, stood up impulsively, wiped his mouth with the tail end of his *pagree*, and boarded the parked van without exchanging any word either with Areem or with the manager of the restaurant.

Though fleetingly baffled, Areem soon recouped. His inevitable conclusion wrapped itself to matters related to their forthcoming travel through the notoriously famous FATA region.

Areem vividly recalled what Janab Humdam of Multan explained about this briefly in one of his discourses. The parcel of land now called FATA is divided into seven tribal areas from north to south with each one being called an agency. These agencies are linked to six parallel frontier regions of Khyber Pakhtunkhwa (erstwhile Frontier Province), again from north to south.

Ability to recall all such details based on one discussion took Areem himself by surprise. He realized the premise for teachers and students in Bangladesh always acknowledging and admiring his memory and ability in varied academic and nonacademic pursuits. For a moment, he felt sad and disjointed. He had the feeling that by pursuing a normal academic life in Bangladesh even with predictable limitations, he could possibly do or achieve something that socially and economically could benefit humanity at large.

But such thought could not prolong. Areem evoked his earlier promise to himself not to be distracted by new thoughts and to pursue his present course. The future was not closed for him. He would not be an al-Qaeda frontline fighter. So he might have opportunities to pursue greater and larger goals in life. With that thought, he was at peace with himself instantly.

Sitting alone with his mini luggage by the side, Areem, being unable to communicate in Pashtu, kept quiet and concentrated, looking outside. This was the first occasion for him to see and have a microfeel about Peshawar. He recalled reading about Peshawar in school history books.

In that short duration of sitting, a number of elements amused Areem beyond expectations. That encouraged him to take a leisurely walk in the periphery. While walking, Areem noticed a number of attributes specific to his location but might have commonality across Peshawar. Uniform trends and types of men's dress amused him very much. It is very difficult to distinguish social strata of men by dress. Most men have uniformity in terms of physical build, head cover (either a cap or *pagree*), flowing beard, vest on the top of men's long-flowing shirt, and some sort of a weapon in hand or cartridges arranged visibly in a leather belt across the chest.

Other characteristics were the discernable presence of men on the streets, and few women visible were all uniformly covered by burka (an outer cover on the top of garments worn by ladies to cover their body and face). There was predominance of small stores mostly tendering kahwah, cigarettes, dried fruits, copper products, and glass cum colored metal bangles. Passersby seldom greeted one another, but those who met known persons embraced one another while standing in the middle of the road, oblivious of the haphazard traffic maneuvering. The dump of garbage on the roadside quickly reminded him of Dhaka. Areem returned after a while, got engaged in sipping a regular cup of tea, and kept on waiting for Zakaullah.

After some time, Zakaullah showed up on foot while wiping sweat around his neck by the tail end of his revered *pagree*. That was quite amusing to observe as the most revered headgear, symbol of pride and prestige, was being used frequently for all mundane purposes, e.g., wiping washed hands or sponging secretions in face and neck areas.

Zakaullah sat by the side of Areem and said, "The driver has gone to fetch fuel for our journey. There will also be a change of vehicle as the earlier one was not in a good condition. All other arrangements have been worked out, and we will leave as soon as the driver returns."

To make Areem feel relaxed, Zakaullah continued, saying, "I feel bad that I could not show you much of this historic city. Peshawar—one of the oldest living cities of Asia and the winter capital of Durrani dynasty of Afghanistan [of Ahmad Shah Durrani], birthplace of famous luminaries like Indian film actor Dilip Kumar [a.k.a. Yusuf Khan] and multiple-times squash world title holders Jehangir Khan and Jansher Khan—manifests itself in color, variance, vitality, and deep-rooted traditions in varied settings. Besides interesting sites like the university, Gandhara museum, etc., the most interesting place of Peshawar is known as Qissa Khawani Bazaar.

"Immortalized by the English poet Kipling as the Street of the Storytellers, this is a must-visit place of Peshawar to have its real ambiance. Pedestrians, bicycles, motorcycles, vans, auto-rickshaws, and automobiles all swerve around horse-drawn buggies and scurrying camels in its narrow passages dotted by outlets involved intensely in various trades and eateries."

Zakaullah only stopped seeing the vehicle approaching the *sharaikhana*. It made him more relaxed and happier than ordinarily could be conceived. Areem noted all these beginning with Zakaullah's narration of Peshawar's history and snapping of that narration with the sudden summation noting the arrival of the driver with new vehicle.

The experiential journey commenced at a time roughly indicated earlier. But it halted soon before an outpost. Zakaullah went inside and came out shortly with a piece of paper. He dangled it excitedly, handed that over to the driver, and then took his seat within the vehicle, instructing the driver to commence the journey without further delay. As the vehicle started, Zakaullah became more open and friendlier. He started talking freely in contrast to his very reserved posture of last evening and this morning. Areem could not make any sense of such a sudden twist but nevertheless enjoyed the variation. Unexpectedly, he himself started feeling relaxed.

In that backdrop, Zakaullah maintained a smiling bearing in his facial expression with ease and started looking at Areem frequently. In one of such looks, Zakaullah winked for a while and then drew Areem's attention to the pickup van behind. Areem knew from Janab Humdam about escorted travel requirement between Peshawar and Landi Kotal but always had impression that the escort would be from military or paramilitary outfits. But what he saw astounded him: two bulky locals with usual tribal outfits including headgear and unregulated flowing beard positioning themselves behind the trailing vehicle's driver seat, holding AK-47s (as told by Zakaullah) with their fingers on respective trigger.

As the vehicle's speed and maneuvering were at the mercy of the persons taking seats behind the steering in a partly dirt road with many bends, Areem felt instant nervousness. A simple mistake or uncontrolled reflex could be fatal for both of them as the follow-on pickup van was driving very close to Areem's pickup. That uneasiness worsened as he observed a change in follow-on vehicles after a while. Zakaullah explained that as per standard requirement and practice, their pickup would be escorted by a vehicle of each tribal chief within his area of command. There were likely to be four such changes in escorts until they reached Landi Kotal. So Areem needed to relax.

Zakaullah noticed the instant nervousness of Areem. In order to make Areem feel at ease, Zakaullah took possession of one of Areem's hands and drew attention to the passing barren mountains. He continued to explain their strategic relevance in the life and fighting efficacy of the tribal people.

But continuous holding of his hand by Zakaullah caused inexplicable uneasiness to Areem. He was aware of the fondness of the Frontier males for sort of same-sex relationships, and that made Areem felt puzzled. Pretending that he needed the clasped hand to scratch a part of his body, Areem, without conveying any sign of discomfort, slowly got his hand disengaged. Zakaullah maintained his ease and smiling bearing.

To divert Areem from apparent discomfort, Zakaullah introduced a new topic of conversation. He said, "I would like you to know more about tribal phenomena since you are in this area. The term *tribal* as used with respect to FATA has no ethnical or faith-related overtone. The inhabitants are of the same ethnical roots, follow the same religion, and practice identical rituals as others of Pakhtunkhwa Province. Though branded as 'tribal,' they are unlike varied tribal groups of other areas. They are so patented because of their ardent desire to lead their lives as per their customs and traditions as well to enable the British administration of undivided India with a quite Western front. In conducting life according to cherished values and ensuring security of the inhabitants living in the most unfriendly and rough terrains clustered by hills and mountains, the people acquired specific fighting aptitude and capability. That enabled them to resist equally the mighty forces of the British Empire, to fight against Soviet occupation, and to confront current colossal US military might. Except these, they are the same people."

The ease with which Zakaullah narrated the specifics of Peshawar earlier in the morning and explained the tribal phenomena in FATA context while sitting in the vehicle and the succinct ways of those articulations convinced Areem that he was not an ordinary al-Qaeda fellow. For the first time, Areem took positive interest to know the person and looked at him pryingly. Against the practice of being noncommunicative except responding to specific queries, mostly by nodding, Areem framed a kowtowing attitude, boosting the dialogue between two strangers who behaved like that for so long.

The resultant exchanges were positive. Areem assiduously opened up himself to harbor a sense of trust within the thinking of Zakaullah. In the process, Areem pithily told elements of his life and journey so far, indicating clearly that he was being groomed as more of a field motivator stimulating the objectives of al-Qaeda and building up commitment among youth and ordinary folks to be mujahideen. In the process, he unwittingly confessed that he had no desire to embrace *shahadat* in the process.

The inadvertent candor on the part of Areem did the trick in stimulating identical response from Zakaullah, and they had affable conversations devoid of caution and care exhibited earlier. Areem cogitated on that intermittently and eventually could not hide it anymore. He bluntly asked Zakaullah the reason for his being so reserved while in Peshawar and being so open once they stepped in FATA.

Zakaullah was not startled by the tenor of the question but evidently was taking his time to react. His first reaction was to deflect eye contact with Areem and keep mum for some time, focusing on the lower end of the front seats. The solo occupant in the front seat was the driver enjoying favorite Pashtun songs by playing a CD. He was mostly noncommunicative except drawing the attention to rear vehicle occupants with a broad smile every time a change took place in escort vehicle based on territorial jurisdiction.

Areem was convinced that his blunt openness was perhaps causing an epiphany within Zakaullah. Taking out gently a piece of paper from the pocket of his traditional overflowing shirt, Zakaullah sliced it in a way to have a small rectangular piece, took out a pen from his vest, and started writing as Areem kept on overseeing. Zakaullah wrote, "I am an Indian Muslim from Mysore State, graduated from Mysore University, never got a job perhaps because of religious background. Opted for al-Qaeda out of pressure and frustration. Peshawar is full of intelligence and counterintelligence agents, both national and international. India has strong intelligence presence too. You can't trust anyone in Peshawar. So I am always scared if sent on assignment outside FATA and more so in Peshawar."

That diligent frankness overwhelmed Areem, but the subsequent action of Zakaullah stunned him. It was something he could neither think nor act at any time.

Zakaullah, maintaining exceptional societal upbeat, continued talking more about Afghan-Pakistan territorial dispute and the history of the Durand Line. He also briefly touched base with the historical backdrop and relevance of Landi Kotal being the sole gateway of smuggling earlier.

Zakaullah concluded this stint of discourse by observing that the Afghan war dating back to Russian occupation of late seventies had numerous imports of incredible repercussions. Faith-based conservatism had been brought to the forefront of statecraft in many countries, destabilizing peace, harmony, and democracy. Frontal animosity between Afghanistan and Pakistan was partly neutralized because of the latter's hidden but strong inherent support against foreign occupations and forces despite threats, sanctions, and abhorrence from superpowers. Others included Pakistan's secret willingness in providing secure sanctuaries for training of mujahideen and launching surprise intermittent attacks in Afghanistan by al-Qaeda against titular authorities; easing the flow of resources, arms, ammunitions; offering strategic information to al-Qaeda bases in Pakistan, etc. The most germane benefit for Pakistan, however, was gaining the confidence and trust of Pashtuns in general as true torchbearers of Islam in the southwest Asian region, minimizing the controversy centering Durand Line as being the international border between Pakistan and Afghanistan.

Zakaullah, with an impish smile, then made a thought-provoking observation, saying, "Still then, peace between the two counties is far away. Tribal inhabitants of northern Afghanistan like Tajiks and Uzbeks continue to be anti-Pakistan. Neither the government of Afghanistan nor major foreign powers trying to stabilize Afghanistan trust Pakistan. Conversely, al-Qaeda penetrated within critical establishments of Pakistan and has many hideouts and camps in the mountainous northern region. Consequently, areas like Landi Kotal as smuggling havens multiplied in other border areas too. Some, with the name *bara*, are operating very much within Pakistan, and authorities cannot enforce any rule or law. The classic example is *bara* in the periphery of Peshawar itself, a replication of Landi Kotal in the administrative heart of Pakistan."

All these talking by Zakaullah had its inherent objective of buying time to soften quietly the texture of the piece of paper on which he earlier scribbled his background. During his authoritative discourse on Pakistan-Afghanistan relationship, Zakaullah, holding the tiny rectangular paper in the palm of his left hand, continued to softly press it by the thumb of the right hand, keeping focus and attention on his deliberations. As the subject matter was of immense interest to Areem, he, too, was oblivious of what Zakaullah's left palm and right thumb were engaged to.

With sustained pressing, the tinny rectangular piece of paper curled into a shape of standard vitamin tablet. Without any hesitation, Zakaullah put that in his mouth and swallowed it to utter surprise and shock of Areem.

Zakaullah did not like to give time to Areem to question him. He therefore initiated his own statement, indirectly responding to what Areem possibly could have in mind. Premising with an observation pertaining to closeness of Landi Kotal and the likely end of their journey soon, Zakaullah said, "We will be apart soon after reaching Landi Kotal, and it is most likely that we would not meet again. In your journey of life, do remember two very mundane but predominantly relevant axioms: do not sign any paper unless you are certain, and more importantly, never ever leave behind written sensitive things, facts, or opinions."

Listening to all these with spasmodic symmetry, Areem had no doubt that this short journey in a pickup van with a lone companion was more rewarding and stress free compared to his earlier travels from Farzian-e-Matina in Karachi to Peshawar by trucks and trains involving a long distance.

With him being in FATA soil, the feeling of persistent suspicion evaporated with spontaneity. There was no need to exercise sustained caution about hiding one's identity of being an al-Qaeda activist and carefully choosing words and expressions. Areem suddenly felt relaxed.

That euphoria was a short-lived one because of a jolt from the sudden application of brakes by the music-loving driver of the van. Evidently, the application of sudden brake was symbolic mien of the end of the journey. No specific parking was involved. No word was exchanged between Zakaullah and the driver. The driver, who was very quiet so far, took position by the side door of the van nearest to Areem in a casual manner. Avoiding any direct eye contact, he outwardly exhibited all casual traits and was apparently engaged in taking out his *pan* residue by carefully applying a toothpick in between his tooth.

Looking around from a stationary position, Areem first noted the barren and gradient mountainous landscape in its totality. The nearby landscape, as far as eyes could see, had the same rudiments of similar dust and stones. The surrounding structures were of dreary nature. Groups of people having identical physical features and outfits were occupying the empty spaces while scores of loaded trucks were waiting their turn for commencing journey. Surprisingly, Areem did not see any visible presence of guns but was amused noticing a big colorful billboard of Coca-Cola significantly dirtied by dust. Everything was so different from Bangladesh that Areem suddenly felt a yearning for his homeland. That feeling, however, was a short-lived one as he could feel the presence of his grandfather in the dust and rough terrains of Landi Kotal, some features likely to be similar to Kohat. Areem was lost momentarily in passionate thoughts pertaining to his grandfather and his own roots.

In the midst of all these, he did not notice when Zakaullah stepped out of the van and entered the run-down structure just opposite the parked van. He came to know about it when the driver of the van communicated with Areem by signs from outside.

As the time passed, Areem's discomfort for being inside the van with the vehicle's ignition switched off worsened. That was aggravated further by the overhead bright sun, warm polluted air in the surroundings, and increased level of thirst exacerbated by the dirty presence of a Coca-Cola billboard nearby.

After a long lonely waiting, Areem was evidently ecstatic about seeing Zakaullah finally come out of that dreary structure, enter the van, and take a seat by his side—exactly the way they traveled in a very pleasant vein a few minutes earlier. But it was not the same happy, relaxed, and open Zakaullah that Areem increasingly came to know when they started the pickup-van journey. It was more Zakaullah of Peshawar rail station: firm, reserved, and emotionless. It struck Areem, but it had not much impact on him as he was clear in understanding that all such occurrences were transitory by nature until he reached his endpoint. But Areem had one thought, and it possibly could be a relevant one: Zakaullah did not like others to be aware of his casual discussions and ephemeral friendly relationship with Areem during the travel from Peshawar. This could as well be Zakaullah's compliance with confidentiality and privacy adhered to by al-Qaeda.

Areem was told by Zakaullah that his travel arrangements for Kabul had been reconfirmed. He was advised to report to the local committee of al-Qaeda shura, pointing to the shabby structure where Zakaullah went and came out. The latter took the opportunity to brief Areem about the protocol that was expected to be followed on first introduction. He was also asked to take his belongings as both Zakaullah and the van driver were relieved of their current responsibilities.

The departure of Zakaullah and the driver had all the apathetic mood one could think of. Notwithstanding earlier validations for such impolite comportment, Areem could not avoid having the nauseating feeling of specificity against the backdrop of basic social niceties he was used to.

Disheartened and disjointed, Areem slowly picked up his baggage, took small steps with apprehension, and entered the obvious structure.

After taking a few steps in a hazy setting even at daytime, Areem was encumbered by negative feelings. As the access turned right, he was amazed in encountering a multicolored one-piece silk door curtain in front. Peeping through the narrow opening, Areem saw five men sitting on the floor in a semicircle. He was startled at having the glance of affluence within compared to the shabby outside fascia. The sudden glimpse of bright-colored carpet and refined silk cover of side pillows startled him. Slightly placing the curtain to a side and disengaging his footwear, Areem set his feet inside, saying with all veneration, "Assalamu alaikum." The response was warm and blissful.

Areem was advised to keep his belongings near the entrance and come forward to join the group. That was complied with due diligence and expression of respect. Subsequently, he took position in kneeled-down fashion within the semicircle and complied with the unwritten requirement of shaking hands with each one, holding their respective hand in his two hands and lifting the hand of each one of them to kiss. That evidently made the gentries very happy. The semicircle was enlarged slightly to create space for Areem, which made him very much at par with others; and that pleased Areem too. The feeling of being equal among seniors as well as unknowns was quite thrilling. But what puzzled him was his inability to identify their ranks and positions by sitting arrangements or dress or physical mien. Most of them looked alike in terms of age and build, headgear, dressing-up, flowing beard, and tasbih in their hands with fingers continuously rotating the beads, while their respective chador was on the carpet but mostly under the thigh.

As the very reticent and succinct welcome statements were completed, a Taliban-type al-Qaeda mujahid entered with cups filled with kahwah and some dried fruits in a large round copper plate: a mix of almonds, raisins, pistachios, pine nuts, walnuts, and cashews. The young mujahid placed cups filled with kahwah in front of the attendees including Areem and kept the service plate of dried fruits at the center. Somewhat quiet and reserved, the relatively younger participant sitting next to Areem exchanged looks with him, dragged the plate of dried fruits, and invited Areem to initiate the sharing process. Areem took it as an honor and did not fail to convey his gratefulness to the shura committee as a whole. The amiable disposition and respectful physical overtures shown by Areem in such a short stint impressed the leaders present as was evident from their facial expressions and eye contacts.

Areem kept on observing the interactions among the participants to understand them and form a notion about the leader among them. It soon was evident to him that the shura committee functioned on equality with the young person sitting next to him apparently being more equal than others. However, what amazed him was their practice of not addressing others by name. They practiced indirect address as *janab* with alternatives *shahib* or *huzoor*.

In the midst of such curious setting of public discourse, Areem enjoyed repetitive and equally varied reference to Allah predicating most avowals and evolvements. Some of them were inshallah (if Allah wills it), mashallah (what Allah wanted has happened), *alhamdulillah* (praise be to Allah, more lucidly expressing gratitude for Allah's goodness), and *subhanallah* (all praise be to Allah). Though Areem was familiar with them from his time in Bangladesh, their frequent repetition in every statement was an enigma to him. He absorbed it without outward reaction. The scope for that was nonexistent also as the discourse was being conducted in Pashtu language.

After some intense discussion, the young participant by his side told Areem, "We are glad to have you as a guest. We are very impressed by your demeanor and wish you luck, by the grace of Allah, both in your stay in Afghanistan and later-on activities in Bangladesh. The setting in Bangladesh is quite different. So we need intelligent people like you to propagate the message of al-Qaeda.

"Our current worry pertains to your limited communication skill and exposure to Pashtu. So we have decided to keep you here for additional one day and engage an instructor conversant with English, Urdu, and Pashtu to help you in memorizing and pronouncing correctly about fifty Pashtu words and expressions critically needed to handle and overcome challenges. So you are leaving for Kabul day after tomorrow in the company of some other mujahideen. The instructor will escort you to the truck that would carry you all including supplies to be delivered in Kabul. For the time being, you will stay in the next space, and the volunteer who served us tea will take care of you during your stay here and in every respect."

After he uttered those words, all five participants performed traditional handshakes, holding both hands of one another. They exchanged embraces and left the venue. Soon thereafter, the young man who earlier served kahwah showed up as if synchronized by someone from a remote location.

This time, he was jovial and relaxed. Picking up the luggage, he conveyed to Areem by body language to follow him. Following the young man briefly, Areem landed in a similar setting as the meeting place except its smallness in size. The bright carpet was there. So were the side pillows. The young man advised him by gesture to take rest.

Looking around, Areem was amazed in identifying three adjacent tents under the shady cover of an outwardly dilapidated structure as he saw from the vehicle. The one he was ushered in first was the bigger one. The one under which he was lounging was the second largest one. The third, both in size and reference, was the one used as a temporary place of the young man. It had an elementary cooking facility. This was possibly a unique masquerading tactic to circumvent public prominence. Keeping this assessment in view, Areem concluded that not addressing anyone by name as practiced by the al-Qaeda committee could as well be a deliberate resolution not to open up before one about whose trust and commitment they are yet to be certain. Simultaneously, this could be a strategy to impede future evidence and reference under unfavorable situation or by opposing parties. This was more than a caution, one of the important operating procedures of al-Qaeda.

The evening was setting in. Early night hours from inside the tent appeared to be darker than usual. The quietness was trembling. Something audible was limited to occasional gunshots and their vibration through isolated mountains. The loneliness was overwhelming. Right in the midst of that feeling, the young man resurfaced with an indigenous lamp. Placing the lamp by the side of Areem, he hurriedly left and returned soon with some naans wrapped in old Pashtu newspaper, kebabs in an aluminum service bowl, and a handy container full of water. He placed them on the carpet. Bearing a full-blown smile, the young man, by physical gesture, suggested Areem take the food, which he brought with so much love.

Though not a single word was uttered, Areem got the message and started eating. In the process of chomping food, Areem recalled a saying that his father repeated many a time in support of his zeal in urging the guests to take more food even if the latter would not like to. He was proud in saying, "I am son of a Pathan, famous for entertaining guests." He often would recall that a Pathan would even feed his enemy before pressing the trigger on him.

The exchanges between the young man and Areem gradually attained some regularity though limited to physical expressions and a few limited words like *shukria*, *umda* ("tasty"), *meherbani* ("kind of you"), and so on. Though primarily Urdu words with some commonality with Farsi, these are generally understood even by Pashtun-speaking people. The young man took Areem by surprise when the former was retiring from the tent at night, saying "Shab ba khair." (Good night.) That was a sophisticated Urdu salutation Areem learned from Mr. Jatoi of Hyderabad. He was certain that some proficiency in Urdu language was necessary to say that meaningfully. Areem was stumped, thinking that even the ordinary guy like the young fellow, consisting with al-Qaeda policy, concealed his ability to undertake functional discourse in Urdu. Areem learned a lot from this experience and retired for the night.

The following day had a busy schedule beginning the time of *fajr* involving introduction to the instructor, clarification concerning the objective of limited language focus envisaged, and carrying out the process of functional Pashtu learning.

The instructor, Khuda Baksh Janjeeb, was a young person of apparent strong will; and it so appeared that he was not enthusiastic about the task and did not like Areem from the beginning. The reason was not Areem. Janjeeb's uncle, while volunteering to fight for alleged saving of Islam in East Pakistan (now Bangladesh), died in 1971 at Akhahura sector. From then on, he developed a general feeling of mistrust and enmity toward Bangladesh and had a firm view that most Bangladeshis are non-Muslims based on local media highlights. That appeared to be the reason for Janjeeb's primary response.

The teaching-learning exercise scheduled for the day made quick progress after initial exchanges between Areem and Khuda Baksh Janjeeb. The latter was amazed by Areem's knowledge of Quran and Sunna; historical details of Islam; Khulafa-e-Rashideen (thirty years' reign by the first four caliphs, successors of Prophet Mohammad [PBUH]); Muslim conquests; and rule of India. These and other similar types of feedback, primarily in English and a little by Urdu, caused the most unexpected change in Janjeeb's initial brashness and approach. The progress was beyond anticipation because of the use of some common Urdu expressions, focus on functionality, and intelligence of Areem.

The day following, Areem was met by Janjeeb in the company of the young man of the tent. He was handed over a gun for his use and was escorted to a truck almost loaded fully with provisions. The young man carried Areem's luggage as he himself was struggling in finding out a proper way to carry the new toy. He was told that the remaining al-Qaeda mujahideen would join him at the nearby border post of Torkham.

Sitting among the loads of provisions and necessities, Areem positioned himself against a huge bag instead of wooden body frame of the truck. That was done deliberately to absorb jerks and jars of travel in a vehicle with apparent poor suspension and presumed dilapidated road conditions. The choice of sitting was predicated on other considerations of Areem, including avoidance of possible bumping against the body of unknown fellow comrades, as the truck likely would maneuver suddenly because of road conditions or giving space to others. Most of the strategic roads were repaired and upgraded during Soviet occupation. However, more-than-expected volume of traffic, trucks and military vehicles with axle loads exceeding the limit, constant war and guerilla fights, and lack of regular maintenance affected the road conditions, with vehicular traffic increasing every day.

All these came to Areem's mind, recalling his travel experiences from Peshawar and envisaging the one to Kabul he was about to commence. The former was in a shiny Japanese pickup van in tip-top condition for a travel of about 35 miles. The latter one would be in a rickety overloaded truck for a travel of about 170 miles. While the former was a drive sitting in the cushioned seat, the latter was going to be drive on the top of loaded luggage with few unknown fellows.

Another unforeseen thought startlingly crept in Areem's mind. That was one of personal reflection. Since he landed in Karachi airport, it was he who was at the center of attention and action. Now, and once on the top of the truck, he was about to be in a setting of many following the general direction with multiple diversions. He would be lost among many. It was to be him alone to take care of all challenges facing and pitfalls encountered in order to make progression. The journey between Karachi to Landi Kotal was guided, assured, and comfort oriented; thus, it was a soft one. The upcoming one was to be a real-life situation where he alone would be responsible for the outcome. His only solace was the *taweez* given by Mr. Jatoi of Hyderabad in case of any life-threatening situation. He touched his luggage once more to assure himself that he had everything with him. That was like a double check.

Other activists joined him at Torkham. They differed in ethnicities, nationalities, languages, and physical expressions though dressed uniformly as Afghans. The communication among them were both brief and needs related. Most, as a diversion, were checking and rechecking their respective arms as if those were the most precious possessions of their lives. Areem's attention was on his accompanying luggage because of valuable personal belongings of great relevance for his life and journey forward.

Areem very much wished that Manzoor and others would have been in the same truck to make the journey a bit more enjoyable in spite of jerks and bumps that would cause inevitable body ache. Learning from al-Qaeda norms and practices, which he was trying to internalize both by observing and listening, Areem refrained inquiring about Manzoor and others at any stage though he missed them all.

The journey entailed whisking of the truck because of the frequent maneuvering in negotiating barren country sides and hilly slopes with common features of sands, dust, boulders, coupled with unpredictable frequent bends. It made the journey a tremulous one with mayhem all around. As the journey deepened, Areem was muddied noting visible lack of priority of the authority in maintaining already-damaged infrastructure. He was convinced that it was the obvious outcome of magnified focus of a fundamentalist, and retrograde autocratic government's singular emphasis primarily on faith and practices.

Areem had no idea that an unfertile and sterile landscape featuring sand and exposed hilly areas could be so eye-catching. He was amazed in perceiving the raw silk and barley beige-shaded ground with stripes of occasional lush greeneries. This setting was magnified by the equally green presence of rated fruit orchards. From the truck and because of the moving landscape, it was difficult for Areem to judge which one of the two features made the totality so enchanting.

The silver lining of this journey was a modest break in Jalalabad, a city of historical eminence, about forty miles from Torkham border post of Pakistan. Fortunately, local commander of the Taliban was present at the point the human luggage like Areem was taking the first break. The commander was educated, quite knowledgeable, and ardently hospitable. He entertained the group with a huge basket of mixed fruits. His occasional references to various characteristics of Jalalabad were refreshing to someone like Areem. Some of the points made by him were, "Jalalabad is strategically the gateway to two important eastern valleys: Laghman and Kunar. Its importance multiplies due to proximate situation to Khyber Pass of Pakistan. It is the most important trading center in the context of trade with Pakistan and India. Its trading profile has been enriched by being near the confluence of Kabul and Kunar Rivers as well as being home to a variety of citrus fruits like orange, tangerine, grapefruit, lemon, lime, pomegranate, and mulberry, besides sugarcane."

The group of mujahideen not only enjoyed the fruits but, at the insistence of the commander, also took some with them for a travel of ninety-five miles to Kabul.

This lap had similar mood and setting except being nearer to Kabul, one can easily notice the evidence of a war-ravaged country with dwindling infrastructure, unrepaired and uncared-for buildings and other structures, resemblance of lack of law and order, and omnipresent apprehension on the faces of people around. But as the truck slowed down near Kabul, the presence of limbless, uncared-for people was dominant.

The arrival reception in Kabul was mostly officious, formality oriented, and noticeably cool. That was not expected; but Areem, resorting to his intelligence, identified a semblance of friction between higher echelons of al-Qaeda and the Taliban. Areem prudently concluded that both parties successfully kept it confined within higher levels, and field-level operations were not being impeded in any way.

All accompanying mujahideen were individually briefed, assigned, and sent to respective commands except Areem. He was sitting near the reception desk awaiting needed communication. Soon a call came for him to see the local Taliban chief in his office.

Areem was escorted to his audience and ushered in a sprawling room without any formal furnishings. He was surprised to see a young Taliban leader sitting on the carpet with the posture and expressions of an elderly person. That manifestation was all the more obvious because of his donning of *surma*, a traditional preparation for cosmetic purposes by applying the powder to the inner surface of the eyelid. His leaning against a back pillow with spread-out side pillows was reflective of traditional shura or other Islamic committee meetings. Burning incense placed on a copper plate between two side pillows, placement of *attardan* (perfume container and tray) stowing an essence oil derived from botanical sources and processed as concentrated perfume, and a decorative kahwah service arrangement with dates in a silver plate near him were all additional decors reflective of his position and command authority even at a young age.

Initial exchanges of greetings were remarkably suave. As the escort left the room, the Taliban leader, in chaste English, told Areem to close the door and to take a seat near him.

Areem was both relieved and happy. He was relieved because of the congenial ambiance. He was happy as he found himself once again in a setting where individuality was acknowledged.

As Areem took his seat, he was formally offered on the backside of his right-hand palm a brush of small cotton piece soaked in *attardan*. That was a noble Muslim practice of welcoming an alien as "one of us."

In offering kahwah and date, the Taliban leader tenderly said, "As you are aware, the basic purpose of having you and others are diametrically opposite. Unlike others, your mission is not to kill or get killed for Islam. You are being groomed, because of your intellect and acumen, to propagate the al-Qaeda doctrine in challenging settings."

He continued, saying, "Though about three years in power, Taliban administration is still in its infancy. We are yet to demarcate clearly functions between the movement and administration. Our capital is Kabul. But the head of our administration is in Kandahar, and so is the location of our movement. Considering all these, it has been decided to send you to principal al-Qaeda authority based in Kandahar. They would decide the focus of your assignment and field of your work. You would leave day after tomorrow, and proper arrangement for your travel is being worked out."

That statement was followed by mild clapping by the leader. The Taliban apparently in charge of security of the leader surfaced promptly. The leader gave instructions in Pashtu while the Taliban nodded. Nothing was understandable to Areem except the word *guesthouse*. Subsequent physical expressions and actions made it clear that the leader talked about dos and don'ts concerning Areem and his stay in the guesthouse.

As Areem stepped forward to accompany the Taliban, the leader called him back and said, "I have a friend in the History Department of Kabul University. I am trying to get him to take you around Kabul City tomorrow. He is very well versed and fluent in English. If I can get him, you would enjoy his company and discourse. If things work out, he would show up by 9:00 a.m. He is known as Professor Golam Ahmed Rabbani." Saying those words, the leader retreated.

Brevity in conversation, protection of identities, and focus on main objective without unnecessary information sharing were some of the traits noted by Areem that were specific to this interaction. He tried to internalize those.

Professor Rabbani showed up at the appointed time. The sojourn, undertaken mostly by foot and on occasions by yellow taxi, focused on standard interesting places like downtown, commercial and residential areas, educational institutions, government buildings including the presidential palace, abandoned house of King Zahir Shah, etc.

What drew the attention and interest of Areem were the presence of numerous yellow cabs almost looking like a flower garden in spots of concentration and absence of other means of public transport, damaged road conditions, frequency of marred and abandoned military assets on the roadside, bullet-ridden buildings, and on the top of all these, scary presence of arms in the hands of folks roaming around. But learning from al-Qaeda practices, Areem restrained himself and kept on waiting for moments and methods of unleashing some such thoughts for a meaningful response.

However, what amused Areem was seeing a number of Soviet-style civilian blocks of housing supported by basic education, health and recreational facilities, and protected by barbed wire and tanks during Soviet occupation. Such housing complex was known as *mikrorayon (microraion)* and emblematically reflected a classical clash with Afghanistan's strong tribal way of life and heritage.

As strolling and yellow cab rides covered about a major part of their sojourn, Professor Rabbani proposed a break and invited Areem for lunch. They entered a reasonable eatery, and the professor promptly ordered food of his choice but obviously of general acceptance as was evident when served. The food items were naan, chicken tikka (grilled chicken), and chicken tikka masala (bite-sized boned breast pieces in gravy). As a traditional preference, he also ordered *anar* juice. Areem liked the choices made and the simplicity followed by the professor in ordering food.

But his professorial attributes came out when, while waiting for food as well as maintaining conscious eagerness to conserve the friendliness developed so far, he had a responsive and warm look at Areem. As immediate reflex, Areem sipped the *anar* juice, appreciated the choice, and made a neutral observation about countless bullet-ridden buildings along the roads and pathways of Kabul. To make his points clear, Areem stated, "What I observed stood opposite to Soviet claim about peace and order in Kabul, their command center, as well most of the country. Though the Soviets had left a long time back, the current setting is equally very depressing. It is difficult for one to reconcile perception with reality in the context of Kabul."

Professor Rabbani appreciated the inquiring mind of Areem and his eagerness to know facts. In response he said, "It is a fact that Soviet claim per se had inherent propaganda attributes. Notwithstanding that it is reality that what you see now is mostly the offshoot of about three years fighting between Pashtuns and Tajiks after the Soviet withdrawal." He continued saying, "I have had double mind in burdening you with background information about Afghanistan. To my judgment, that is very relevant to understand the present in its proper context. The needed exposé would be very relevant for your future work too. Keeping your query in view, I am certain that you have the mind and aptitude to understand the current mind-set of Afghans, focusing primarily on intrigues and guns against the backdrop of the long history of their being the bastion in engaging philosophies for intellectual attainment. You have the intellectual aptitude to digest details. I will try to do that as succinctly as I can."

The professor continued, saying, "Afghanistan evolved over thousands of years. It was identified as a country thousands of years back. Kabul, a historic place of relevance, is located at high altitude of about six thousand feet above the sea level in a narrow valley between Hindu Kush Mountains with the curving Kabul River flowing by its side. Though the exact origin is still uncertain, Kabul River and Kubha settlement, as Kabul was known about 3,500 years back, were mentioned in the Hindu Rigveda and the primary collection pertaining to Zoroastrianism known as Avesta. Some historians ascribe to modern-day Kabul with Sanskrit name of ancient township Kamboja in Hindu scripts.

"Described as a 'bowl surrounded by mountains,' Kabul had been famous for being located along the trade routes of Central, South, and Western Asia and as the learning center of Zoroastrianism, followed by Buddhism and Hinduism. Being legendary for its gardens, quaint bazaars, and palaces, Kabul attracted tribes and races who wielded power. Kabul was ruled by powerhouses like Mauryans, Samanids, Khaljis, Timurids, Mughals, Ghaznavids, Ghurids, Durranis, etc. from Central and East Asia. Whoever came to rule and subdued subsequently by others left some of their people behind to give rise to tribal culture of modern Afghanistan.

"One Hindustan [Indian] poet, Mirza Muhammad Haidar Dughlat, after visiting Kabul, wrote, 'Dine and drink in Kabul. It is mountain, desert, city, river and all else.'

"People visiting Kabul fell in instant love with it due to friendly inhabitants, enchanting location, and gorgeous weather. So was Babur, the founder of Mughal Empire in India. He was buried in Kabul as per his wish with his tomb containing the famous Persian couplet: 'If there is a paradise on earth, it is this, it is this, it is this.'

"Becoming the capital of modern-times Afghanistan in 1776, Kabul had been symbolic witness to varied and periodical power struggles, conspiracies, intrigues, assassinations, coups, and rebellions, coupled with changes of dynasties. That has been aggravated by power play of Western muscles, overwhelming political and strategic pressures of the authoritative big neighbor USSR, Indian hegemony, Iranian influence, Saudi Arabia's meddling, and Pakistan's alternate policy of trust and mistrust.

"In its volatile, intriguing, conflicting history—stretching over thousands of years, harboring divergent faiths and practices, and being on the crossroads of evolving religions—modern-times Afghanistan finds itself engrossed in a controversy pertaining to practice-related variances within Islam, positioning simultaneously in conflict with itself and at war with Western powers on Islamic beliefs and values. That precisely is the situation you are in here. You may not bear arms but have the potential and the capacity to achieve more than guns. You are a very relevant part of one of our twin objectives: arms struggle and pursuance of convincing persuasion.

"Armed confrontation is the public face of Islam's current struggle. You have observed and noted that. These are symptoms. Through this, and various related manifestations, the world is kept on notice for fair play and justice in resolving conflicts. The objective of persuasion is to alert Muslims at large and condition themselves to fight and sacrifice for the faith.

"The present scenery within Afghanistan is both disheartening and ubiquitously frightening. The backdrop is in its prolonged history of divergent races, ethnicities, and faiths. Resultant tribal affiliations are both pride and problem for Afghanistan, which originally was known as Aryana, subsequently as Khorasan prior to its present identity.

"Whatever the history is, the tribe affiliation continues to be the raison d'état in identifying inhabitants with language closely linked to it. That precisely is the reason why—with Pashtun being spoken by 42 percent and Tajik by another 27 percent, both with close link to Persian—Afghanistan could not have a national language.

"In a chronicle of long history, the twin elements of ethnicity and language could not be compromised for higher objectives of forging national unity and the need for developing a uniform national language.

People continue to be identified, both in war and peace, based on tribal roots and the language they speak. They are Afghans only for international travels and transactions. This is the root of the current problem.

"The situation is goaded by yearning for power and jurisdiction. And that pertains not only to territory but also to means of income. Thus, commerce in arms, and opium production and trade, in a geographical landscape featuring sand, stone, and snow with mostly barren surface, have taken prominent role in usurping power and authority.

"Other hidden elements are relative competence and personality adoration. Pashtuns, being shrewd and more exposed in dealing with varied brokers due to recurrence of earlier invasions, are better negotiators and politicians. They traditionally occupy high political positions in the government. Contrarily, Tajiks, with Russian links and heritage, are better educated and occupy important administrative positions. Such specific competence variances create mistrust and accentuates intrigue.

"In some situations, personalities become paramount in taking decisions of national relevance. The classic example is what happened in 1992 with the fall of Soviet-backed government of President Najibullah. After about four coups and countercoups, fighting mujahideen groups assembled and agreed on the formation of a national government. The same, known as Peshawar Accord, or 'a peace and power sharing agreement,' was considered a definite relief, signaling final hope for peace in a war-ravaged country. Professor Burhanuddin Rabbani, a long-time Islamist mujahideen and a Tajik, took over as the president with Ahmad Shah Massoud—another Tajik and commonly known as Lion of Panjshir for his heroic resistance against Soviets—as the defense minister. Gulbuddin Hekmatyar, a notable mujahid military leader of Pashtun origin, refused to sign the accord and started bombing Kabul. The fight continued for about three years. Minister Massoud ordered a total retreat from Kabul.

"During this period, and with active support and patronization of Pakistan, a radical and ultraconservative Islam-based phobia swept Afghan refugee camps and Pashtun-inhabited province of Pakistan. It soon became a formidable movement sweeping from south and east to north and west of Afghanistan. The size and seizure of areas, the speed and specter of success, and the motivation and mass participation took ground people by shock and surprise, mixed with happiness. It created an incredible enthusiasm among many. Its momentum was ensured by steady and generous flow of resources and war assets from Pakistan.

"A dedicated and conservative Muslim clergy, Mohammad Omar by name, who hailed from a very poor family of rural Kandahar and studied orthodox Sunni Muslim edicts in Jamia Uloom [renowned Islamic religious school] of Karachi, participated actively in the war with Soviets. He was wounded four times in that war. An exploding shrapnel from a Soviet tank wrecked his right eye in 1987. But he continued in frontal engagements with the Soviets until they left. He, however, did not participate in the armed fight after the Soviets withdrew.

"Mohammad Omar established a minor madrassa in a village near Kandahar with himself involved in teaching there. Subsequently, he taught in other madrassas of Afghanistan and in Pakistan. Mohammad Omar—being dismayed and disgusted with rampant corruption and inconceivable social injustices, including raping of young girls by the rich and powerful—established first formal group of fifty Talibans [students in Pashtu] in 1994. They were armed to confront opposition. Cases of rape and other forms of injustices brought to the group's notice were promptly dealt with in public, and punishment, including hanging, was administered openly. Omar's name and fame spread like fire, and the title of mullah, prefixed to his name Omar, was on the lips of everyone in Afghanistan. The Taliban movement gained overnight momentum and spread all over the country and adjacent regions.

"The new wave was floating and flying on the crescent symbol of Islamic moon, a perceived pictogram of equity and social justice. The better-educated Massoud foresaw the futility of confronting such a popular and religion-based move. It was no more a fight with Pashtuns under the command of power-hungry Gulbuddin Hekmatyar. With options limited in the wake of newly emerged Taliban's onslaught and advance, he decided on a total retreat from Kabul and went back to Panjshir. Gulbuddin Hekmatyar vanished from prominence and was no more relevant.

"Ahmed Shah Massoud's perseverance and patience withered away soon after observing atrocities committed all around in the name of Islam by half-lettered Talibans. He found many of the interpretations of the dictums of the Holy Quran and various edicts irreconcilable with the tenets of Islam and hence unacceptable. He took up arms against the Taliban government of Mullah Omar, started losing, and for the first time in his life, sought refuge in the foreign soil of Kulob, Tajikistan, while his followers continued resisting Taliban advance in his stronghold, Panjshir. Then, the USA ushered in with land forces and aerial bombing.

The outward damages of the facade of structures and buildings are the consequences of all these."

As Professor Rabbani was talking and both of them were meandering, they visited a few other places having similar features. Areem suggested and Professor Rabbani agreed to call it a day. Wishing Areem the best of everything in his future assignment and before saying a formal goodbye, the professor took the hand of Areem as a gesture for shaking hand and kept on holding it as if he were in a daze. After a while, the professor drew Areem closer and slowly said, "I have purposely touched base with some details of our past and current history and politico-social nuances. This is just to broaden your base so that you can take proper decisions in future, not just relying on what you experience now but relating them to the past, as necessary.

"Also, remember, our Afghan society historically has two segments: poor cum rural people and rich, educated urban folks. Most of the rich and educated people took refuge to safe havens like the USA and Europe during the last twenty years. The present demographic composition has all the negativity associated with unlettered social setting. Most people are either illiterate or half lettered. Their commitment to life circles around religion as portrayed by mullahs.

"So in your future work, you should endeavor to relate issues to the perspective of religion and then articulate the discourse so that the person listening has the impression that whatever you are saying has the sanction of the religion."

Saying those few words, he hugged Areem and left immediately. The vacuum around Areem was filled by melodious call for Muslim afternoon prayer from a nearby mosque. Areem slowly walked toward the mosque to participate in the prayer, exchanging as many salaam with fellow pedestrians as he could.

The journey to Kandahar, a distance of about three hundred miles, commenced the following morning as per arrangements articulated earlier by the leader and subsequently updated through the manager of the guesthouse. The manager also informed Areem about an overnight break in the journey at Ghazni, after about one hundred miles, with arrangements for a stay in a similar guesthouse. He also advised that Areem would share the horizontal driving seat with the driver, and the assistant would place himself on the top of the merchandise being carried.

Areem's fleeting sympathy for the driver's assistant disappeared as soon as he remembered his school days' history assignments relating to Emperor Sultan Mahmud Ghazni's conquest and rule of India between 1001, his accession, and his death in about 1030. A son of a slave mother, he rose to occupy the throne of his father's kingdom of Ghazni and established Ghaznavid dynasty to rule Ghaznavid Empire spread over most of modern-day Eastern Iran, Afghanistan, and Pakistan. His invasion of India seventeen times for acquiring riches and wealth, with the plundering of Somnath temple of Kathiawar State being the hallmark, continues to be a pertinent historical reference point.

That feeling and that recollection were overwhelming for Areem against the backdrop of the assistant's being on the top of the merchandise.

As the truck made its way toward Ghazni, the road, other infrastructures, and private houses all bore evidence of the brutal latest fight between forces of President Rabbani's government and the Pashtun insurgents under the leadership of Gulbuddin Hekmatyar. But those did not have any immediate impact on Areem. Neither time nor the distance was a matter of anguish for him. He was mostly in the ambiance of his history class in school. Areem was deliberately looking forward to set his foot on the soil of Ghazni not for pride but for its own peculiar feeling.

Ghazni, both as a historical place of eminence and as for its present strategic importance being on Highway 1 connecting Kabul with Kandahar, fell much short of Areem's expectations. Visible lack of Urdu-and/or English-speaking people hampered much-desired conversation. His conversation with the truck driver during the journey was through body language all throughout, supplemented by single-syllable Urdu and Pashtu words. Once he was in Ghazni, conversation was carried out through the manager of the guesthouse. It pertained to rest, dinner arrangement, and departure in the following morning. In the presence of Areem and with supplementation in Urdu, the manager advised the driver to leave early morning in view of distance involved. That was agreed.

Areem's unbridled expectation was the cause of his paramount frustration. While resting in the guesthouse, he eventually came to the same realization and graciously reconciled with what was reality.

The journey resumed the following morning as per schedule agreed the night before, and the manager was gracious enough to be present to say *khuda hafiz*. As miles after miles were being negotiated in the quest of a target of two hundred miles by sunset, both the speed of the truck and edginess on the face of the driver were remarkably conspicuous. None of the negative attributes of the road as damaged by IED, abandoned burnt vehicles and tires, potholes, and broken asphalts could deter the driver. Areem tried to draw the attention of the driver a number of times, but that did not work. The only time of communication was when he, through delicate maneuvering, overtook another vehicle. He would then look at Areem with a broad smile on his face.

There were exceptions too. Possibly because of a very early start, the driver would frequently take breaks in truck addas. The assistant would jump down, rush to the serving place, and get two cups of *garam chai* for the boss and the guest. Then he would sip his tea with embarrassing shyness.

But the next stop was not like that. It was apparently a gathering of numerous males. Both the driver and his assistant jumped out and rushed to the gathering very happily without knowing what it was about. Scores of people were in and around a field, shouting loudly, reacting with happiness, and expressing resultant pleasure with others present. Areem was baffled as, to his knowledge, such assembly and merrymaking were features of *buzkashi* (goat-carcass-pulling game of Central Asian origin), since outlawed by the new Taliban government.

After having exchanges with some present, the driver gleefully returned to the truck and invited Areem by gesture to get down and participate in the happy celebration.

Areem heeded. Standing among the boisterous people, he froze upon knowing the reason of such public celebration. The lady positioned at the midfield and tied to a wooden post was accused of committing *zina* (an Islamic legal term dealing with unlawful sexual intercourse, including adultery or illegal sex by married people and fornication or sex by unmarried). It has broadened applications in cases of rape, prostitution, and bestiality.

In order to prove *zina*, it is needed that the act of penetration or a confession should be repeated four times and witnessed by four persons. More significantly, under Islamic jurisprudence, *zina* belongs to class of *hudud* (crimes) for which punishments are Quranically specified.

The accused lady not only denied committing *zina* but also simultaneously pleaded for sparing her life, having given birth to a baby boy a few days back. Most of the assembled people roared against such plea and demanded public punishment.

After brief deliberations in the midst of roaring by the crowd, the Taliban leaders and *kazi* (a magistrate or judge in a Sharia court) present pronounced the lady guilty and sentenced her to twelve public lashings by a man. Absence of accused, recent delivery, and some deficiencies in evidence produced were some of the reasons fostering a lenient verdict. People nevertheless were very happy and enthusiastic as Sharia law was being applied.

With each preparatory maneuvering for lashing, the crowd roared. The fragile young lady screamed after each one. The assembled people were jubilant as if with each lash, Islam as a religion advanced.

Areem felt dejected, distressed, and disgusted, both by verdict and by the people's response. The accused woman in each adultery case was being treated as goat carcass like in *buzkashi*. He felt like vomiting and started experiencing pain at his lower abdomen. Areem smiled at the driver to conceal his real feeling and walked back toward the truck, keeping his head down.

After taking a lonely walk and sitting alone in the truck significantly far away from the maddening crowd, Areem had a serious internal debate about efficacy of the Taliban objective of establishing a pure Islamic society and the relevance of unqualified Sharia dictums, which are about 1,500 years old. The more he thought through, the more exasperated Areem became. His internal thought and debate drew him closer to the position of Ahmad Shah Massoud. His yearning for a meeting with Ahmad Shah Massoud grew stronger.

The lashing was nearing its end. The driver and his assistant rushed toward the truck to recommence the journey, avoiding chaos and obstruction when all would start for their respective journeys. From their body language, it was apparent that they were recharged and exultant, having the chance of witnessing the event premised on full Islamic tint. The speed of the truck, in its recommenced journey, was an ample proof of that.

Areem remained engrossed in his thought about the Taliban objective and al-Qaeda focus. The more he thought, the more aggravated was his general concern. He accepted the position that the Quran, being the fountainhead of divine guidance for Muslims, contains the words of Allah and hence can't be changed or altered. But what agonized Areem was almost the similar but unspoken position pertaining to hadith or words, advice, and practices of Muhammad (PBUH).

According to Sunni Islam, hadith also embodies words, advice, and guidance of the Prophet's close associates. However, Shia Islam maintains that hadith is a collection of words, advice, and practices of the Prophet and his family. The hadith is the source of Islamic jurisprudence known as Sharia.

Sharia, in essence, is based on three specific sources: words of Muhammad (PBUH) called hadith; his actions called Sunna, and the Holy Quran, which was dictated by him. Within the premise of restrictions concerning alteration, Sharia's interpretation is given some latitude, and it is called *fiqh*. In reality, *fiqh* is rarely availed of. The present divergences in the Islamic society discourage this and definitely are an impediment. Interpretations are thus premised on tracing the path of negativity, encouraging pronouncements of retrograde fatwas (religious edicts), particularly with gender bias. Policies and instructions confining women inside homes, closing of girls' schools, and seizing of radios and cassettes are some examples of what are interpreted as being un-Islamic. Retrograde ones are like restrictions on women working outside, barring women to be alone in the presence of or talking with a man not a blood relative after attaining puberty, compulsory wearing of burkas when outside, banning of music, prohibition pertaining to keeping of pigeons, banning of kite flying, and so on. These are some examples of Taliban government's policy restrictions on citizenry, particularly women, based on Quran and Sunna.

The journey continued. The evening sun was halfway in its setting situation in the western horizon. The traffic was becoming less. The truck accelerated. Cracks and potholes were increasingly becoming more indistinct. Devastations of wayside structures were pervasive all throughout.

In the midst of thinking, Areem was swamped suddenly by another most unlikely premise: Do Afghans, with inheritance tangled with war and weapons for thousands of years, enjoy acrimony, chaos, and destruction as a way of life? This ingathered in his mind, observing easiness with which Afghans were treating disturbing evidence of obliteration in general. They are not tormented by all-pervading damages. Contrarily, they find exhilaration in publicly dishonoring a lady for an alleged crime in which a man too was involved. In the midst of impositions and prohibitions, they need something for exhilarations. It does not matter whether it is the carcass of a goat in a *buzkashi* game or a vulnerable female victim under Sharia law, which has no provision for appeal. Areem was dejected, feeling that generations back, this place was the center of enlightenment, dealing with broader policies and philosophical tangent of famous ancient faiths and religions like Zoroastrianism, Buddhism, and Hinduism. Now, in modern times, instead of being enlightened by the most egalitarian religion, Islam, the same people degenerated to a psyche wedded to fighting, killing, revenge and abuse, and merrymaking at the cost of powerless and vulnerable segments of its populace. He felt both sad and bad.

Even though it was early hours of the night, the darkness all around carried with it the ominous feeling of loneliness, fright, and anxiety. The speedometer mark of the truck was as before; but the sound of the engine, because of emptiness all around, gave the impression of roaring with desert wind blowing speedily through the openings on both ends of the driver's horizontal seat. That nevertheless created a smooth feeling. Areem, with all anxieties in mind, somehow dozed off and for some time was oblivious of his surroundings and movement. The driver, sympathizing with Areem's exhaustion, sighed and gleefully increased the volume of music with the hope that the noise would help him to remain alert and awake, enabling driving without incident.

That objective was served except the need for application of brakes suddenly on reaching the destination. Areem woke up and was embarrassed. The driver beamed because of his accomplishment in reaching the destination slightly ahead of time.

Their late arrival by local standard did not cause any problem in Kandahar. Based on experience, Kandahar al-Qaeda projected their arrival hours after sunset. So as the truck came to a halt, an elderly al-Qaeda official, accompanied by a young mujahideen, his obvious escort, approached and guided Areem to a rest house near the main office of al-Qaeda in Kandahar. They scheduled their briefing, among others, tomorrow. That was followed by a standard Afghani dinner, but he ate alone. The physical exhaustion overtook his mind. Areem fell asleep soon after retiring to bed.

The following morning started a bit late. He was escorted to the venue of al-Qaeda's regular *majlish* (a meeting or a sitting venue of an assembly) and advised to wait outside until his subject comes for discussion.

The clock ticked. The time passed. The waiting lingered. Finally, a senior gentleman came out of the *majlish* gathering. Keeping his head down and in the midst of fixing the outer cover of his traditional loose outfit, he approached Areem, introducing himself as Mollah Gajan Baksh. Apologizing for keeping Areem waiting so long, Mollah Baksh said, "The objective of your presence was clear to the *majlish*. Your competence and commitment were evidenced by various field reports. So those were not the issues. We bogged down in discussions pertaining to your location for activities from which both al-Qaeda in Afghanistan currently and future work in Bangladesh would be benefited. So a decision was taken to send you to northern province of Panjshir. We do not have a proper base there. Fighting is still going on with elements of Tajiks. So we need to have a solid presence. Your official position is assistant postmaster. Your implied duty is to neutralize the feeling of animosity focusing on the *talib* and other youths and elders, being yourself as an embodiment of honesty, sincerity, decency, and kindness. That would be a wonderful contribution."

As Mollah Baksh was explaining the focus and objectives, the call for *zuhr namaz* was being pronounced. He hurriedly finished, saying, "Panjshir area command of al-Qaeda is being advised about your assignment with directive to look after you, help in initial settlement, and monitor you from a distance. Your duty is to project yourself as an ordinary civil servant not particularly aligned with al-Qaeda. Your perceived neutrality is important for accessing people and having dialogue with them about al-Qaeda philosophy. Nothing adverse is to be said about Tajiks and their culture."

He further said, "You would have no guidelines relating to work, and there will be no supervisor to monitor you. It would always be your commitment and your genuineness. However, you would have a periodic reporting obligation about what you did and what you plan to do. The timing and the structure of that would be conveyed to you later on."

Mollah Baksh continued, saying, "We have a convoy going to Panjshir via Kabul two days from now. You will accompany the convoy and will be in the lead truck. The driver of the lead truck is of Yemeni origin, speaks functional English, and knows the route very well. So you will not be uncomfortable. The driver will be in touch with you soon to work out pickup arrangements. In the meantime, enjoy Kandahar, the ancient capital of Afghanistan."

After finishing the discourse, both of them took steps toward the mosque but seldom talked further.

On return, Areem got involved in evaluating his Kandahar experiences so far. He understood why he was not a part of deliberations of the *majlish* concerning his work and responsibility. But one reality hit him point-blank. Being seat of both the establishment and the movement, everyone around was preoccupied about agenda close to him. So there was no time to be nice to others or have a personal rapport with one unknown. It was common in case of one not belonging to the powerbase or connected with that.

Areem was surprised to see a pamphlet-type publication on Kandahar in the drawer of the table of his room. Perhaps someone who had curiosity in knowing the details about this historic place intentionally or unwittingly left that. He immediately concentrated to read it and was astounded by the information detailed in that ordinary publication. That was very helpful to Areem, and he absorbed most of the information in knowing Afghanistan better.

As the tale goes, Alexander the Great founded the city in 330 BC. It became known as *Iskandar*, the way Alexander was locally pronounced. The city, according to another ancient etymology, came to be known as Kandahar, having root in Persian and Pashtu words of *kand* or *qand*, meaning, "candy." Kandahar and its adjacent areas are famous for high-quality grapes, apricots, melons, pomegranates, and other sweet fruits. The name Kandahar, or its twisted version of Candahar, possibly stands for "candy area."

Irrespective of such historical derivatives and deviations related to its founding and naming, Kandahar played a dominant role in the history of Afghanistan for thousands of years and more recently from 1747 when Ahmad Shah Durrani, founder of Durrani dynasty, made Kandahar the capital of his empire, known as Afghan Empire. It continues to be prominent as being a major trading center located at the crossroads of various trade routes. It enjoys the enigmatic reputation of being a distribution point of marijuana and hashish to Central Asia and Europe. The prominence during Taliban rule, of course, related to its being the headquarters of the Taliban movement and de facto capital of Afghanistan.

While having late breakfast the following morning, Areem wanted to be chummy with his assigned escort. Discussion did not make much progress, primarily because of language constraint. The staff in charge of that guest house was sitting in the cashier's chair and overheard Areem's queries. He voluntarily came, introduced himself, and said in Urdu that there was not much to see around. Areem was surprised to know that, considering Kandahar's thousands-of-years-old existence. He passed the following two days monitoring people's movements and way of discourse. Everyone appeared to be busy and in a rush. Areem spent time strolling in the vicinity often in the company of his escort.

SCENE

The planned convoy consisted of five trucks. Areem was seated in the front one, comfortably sharing the seat with the driver. The Yemeni driver, Jabel Hamed, spent some time in Karachi too and so was relatively familiar with functional Urdu. He went to Panjshir a number of times before. That made the journey more enjoyable even in the backdrop of deteriorating road conditions.

Areem was mostly familiar to sceneries in that long course as he had seen those while going only recently. The inevitable was omnipresent. Everywhere, and in every band of this enchanting and breathtaking country, the ugly remnants of death and destruction were observable. A war of about a quarter century circled around repeatedly on itself, leaving damage and death anew. The relatively common features were preponderance of wayside vehicle repair shops and intermittent truck or bus addas and rudimentary gas stations in the barren surroundings featured by sand and dust.

So most of the discourses with the driver related to listening to his family details and his spending time in Karachi looking for work. The only exception was the presence of numerous men in an abandoned football stadium. Upon inquiry of Areem, the driver made a brief break in convoy's planned journey, went out, and came back soon with the news that a lady and her male accomplice were being stoned to death for a crime related to sex. The driver curiously asked Areem whether he would like to see how Islamic Sharia was being implemented. Areem said no, and the journey resumed.

The travel after Kabul was different and of interest too to Areem. The destination Panjshir is located about hundred miles northeast of Kabul.

The landscape was undergoing noticeable changes as one entered and negotiated Parwan Province. Roads, in relatively good condition with portions being two-way tarred, had many bends. Tips of enchanting mountain ranges were visible, some naked and others capped by snow. The mountain surface was initially brown but subsequently turned grayish. Human settlements in that terrain on varied laps of rising landscape had their own characteristics. It was difficult to gauge that fully from a moving truck, though the convoy slowed down considerably because of the shaking old trucks in front and very usual maniacal driving of Afghans. Yet Areem tried to observe and absorb as many features as he could.

Both houses and settlements were spread out but following no particular pattern; a few were along the spread-out roadside stores for essentials, and most others were in negotiable laps of adjoining mountains. After some distance, Areem, during his journey up high and down, was excited to see breathtaking views of the enthralling valley. That was magnified many times by the flowing of the parallel river, Panjshir, which runs through the Panjshir Province from north to south, dividing it into half.

As an unanticipated and equally pleasurable change, Areem was excited to notice identified spots for picnic and rest, coupled with some wayside eateries selling kebabs and freshly caught local fish roasted on the spot, mostly near riverbanks. Jabel Hamed, the driver, based on past experiences, was telling Areem about the special aroma of kebab made here and the taste of freshly roasted fish.

Being himself from Yemen and having lived in Karachi for some time, Jabel Hamed had liking for fish. He was certain that Areem, because of his overt facial responses, would like to have some fish. So he proposed; and Areem readily agreed, volunteering to host other accompanying drivers too. That made the proposition merrier. Locating a suitable site, Jabel Hamed positioned his truck and advised others to do so.

The eatery owner, getting some supplementary supplies from nearby ones, responded to the orders, which had preference of kebab for others and fish for Areem and Hamed.

With the first fish bite after so many days, Areem not only appreciated the flavor and taste of Panjshir fish but also redeemed his native preference for fish. He expressed that to both Hamed and the eatery owner by physical expressions.

The ingenuous driver made the eating more enjoyable by occasionally twisting facts and features of the local setting. He mentioned, among

161

others, about the cleanliness of river water, which has the tint of turquoise; its fittingness for swimming for most part of the year except winter; and the variances in water flow based on depth, surface, and season. He also mentioned, based on hearsay and as the folklore states, that the naming of the area as Panjshir, meaning Valley of Five Lions, has had its origin to the mystical presence of five Walis (literally meaning "protectors") or spiritual brothers in the valley.

As the trucks approached the central Panjshir Valley, the first and the most pungent sight was the remnants of war-damaged Russian military assets including numerous tanks and heavy carriers. That was also the evidence of Ahmad Shah Massoud's military ingenuity, which forestalled outright victory and occupation of Panjshir Valley by the Soviets during occupation of the rest of the country for about ten years and subsequent about four years' armed confrontation with the Taliban.

The drive continued, passing a cluster of derelict adobe homes (structures of earthen blocks comprising of mud, farm runoffs, and sewage). Proliferation of riverside kebab eateries and *chaikhana* dominated. Most of such structures were temporary by design as Panjshiris were apprehensive of another round of confrontation with adversaries.

More people were visible on the road as the journey to the north continued. So were the traffic, stores, and shops on both sides of the road, indicating an urban touch to the surroundings. Jabel Hamed looked at Areem and said, "We are approaching the main city of Panjshir Valley known as Bazarak [traditionally spelled as Baazaarak]. That is the destination of our convoy. We will park in our assigned place, and I will then escort you to the makeshift command post of the government. Everything else will be done by them."

During the follow-on meeting, the regional administrative official informed Areem, saying, "You will formally be welcomed after the coming *jumu'ah*, and our local post office will start functioning from Saturday next. Selected few local gentries would be present too. We kept the meeting size small for security reasons."

He continued, saying, "The local madrassa for boys lacks optimum enrollment at this point in time. It is not likely to change soon. So the administration decided to house the local post office in the westernmost vacant room of the madrassa. The room's location is ideal from access point of view. The assigned staff of roving post office setup, who served the locality so long on a two-day tour of weekly duty, will train you for two days prior to Friday. The convoy has brought all supplies, and that will be delivered tomorrow. We consider the functioning of the post office very important as that would prove bringing needed services at the doorstep of local population. That would definitely augur well for all."

He further said, "You can use the room temporarily as your place to stay. We have put a charpoy, one almirah, two tables, and two chairs in the room already. You are to arrange them with the help of our staff being deputed, but make sure that the room has the semblance of office during operational hours. Tonight, you will be our guest along with fellow truck operators, and from tomorrow, you can get food from eateries outside."

On being escorted to the assigned classroom to be converted into a post office, Areem was amazed, noting the preparations taken for his settlement and office setting. A moderate mattress, a blanket, one pillow, two aluminum plates, two glasses, and a water jug with the supplement of two serving spoons were placed respectively on the charpoy and table in a corner, while the other table with chairs facing each other and almirah at the back were nicely placed at the entry section of the room.

From his arrival in Karachi to his travel up to Bazarak in Panjshir, one thing always impressed Areem: the organizational focus, efficiency, thoroughness, competence, and farsightedness in planning activities and in linking those with needed support system, keeping the objectives clear. That made the process of his journey both comfortable and enjoyable against apparent odds. Areem's adoration for al-Qaeda multiplied. But that did not last long.

It soon became awry, reflecting on incongruous, misguided, and misplaced interpretations of the Holy Quran and Sunnah, which agitated his mind and thinking. The coldblooded killing of fellow Muslims in the periphery of Multan, the public lashing of a new mother he witnessed while approaching Kandahar, and the story related to stoning of a lady and her male accomplice on his travel back to Kabul were fresh in Areem's mind. Though details were short for his total assessment, Areem was certain that most of these were based on hazy accusations, deficient charge sheets, misinterpreted stipulations of Islamic laws premised on a justice system with no appeal recourse. The process encourages abuse and afflictions at the dispensation of fairness and human dignity. His anxiety and thought circled around unresolved inquiries within him: What sort of Islam it is projected to be; and What type of interpretations in the name of a faith they amount to? He never got out of that.

But a new inquiry pervaded his mind and thought. He wondered how such an amorphous formation could be so effective. Areem recalled his own journey from Chittagong to Panjshir and marveled in concluding about its total efficiency. He lamented that but for ultraconservative religious focus and brutality, it could be a model organization for any decent purpose. He trusted his assessment and promised to himself to replicate it in Bangladesh without repeating mistakes evident and experienced, once he returns.

The inauguration of the post office and his induction as assistant postmaster were carried out as smoothly as planned. Service regularity, efficiency, and delivery became Areem's topmost priority. As a lone-man operation, Areem was performing all functions from receiving to stamping, sorting, and distributing. It soon dawned on Areem that the post office operation might be small in volume but had major social repercussions, particularly in keeping the establishment's objective of efficient services at the ground level.

Areem soon identified that people around were less enthusiastic about incoming postal mails. They demonstrated some preference for sending postal mails, but their main focus was on receipt of money orders. Most incoming postal mails were thus handed over to recipients or neighbors during their visits. Areem's lack of knowledge about the community made such deliveries often difficult and time-consuming. There was always sort of pressure on Sunday, Tuesday, and Thursday—the days of incoming mails from central systems based in Kabul and Kandahar.

Areem also found the identification of the correct recipient in administering money orders to be a significant problem, especially with him being a non-native. Keeping these in view, he met the government functionaries, seeking help, and could obtain services of two local staff for fixed period of mail incoming three days: one to help with incoming money order matters and the second to manage crowd. Post office operation improved significantly, and everybody was happy.

In handling matters concerning a one-man post office operation, Areem noted the occasional presence of a middle-aged person. He was tall and slim, dressed up in traditional bright-colored outfit, with a face having the signs of stress and strains typical of a nomadic tough living in the mix of extreme climatic conditions. It mostly, as Areem was told, had all the elements of dry surface, snow-clad mountains, unpredictable snowstorms, occasional heavy rains, and uncertain floods with significant daily and seasonal ranges in temperature—very hot days with surprisingly cool nights.

The look of the gentleman, like many others in Bazarak, could easily be read in the absence of bushy beard, which was so common outside Panjshir. Areem was surprisingly pleased to note that even the use of varied and frequent references to Allah such as inshallah, mashallah, *alhamdulillah*, and *subhanallah*—so high in most parts of Afghanistan—were significantly low in the periphery of Panjshir.

The gentleman would come, take a seat on the borrowed school bench near the wall, keep quiet, and observe him working. Because of the frequent visits and his queries about incoming mails, Areem came to know that he was from a location between Bazarak and Baadqol, about thirty minutes away. It is the second prominent city housing the largest health-care facility known as Changaram Hospital. It appeared to Areem that most people knew the gentleman by his name, Shahram Tajik, but would refrain to talk about him. He was wondering how a popular man like him could be single-mindedly so standoffish and reclusive!

Areem's interest for knowing the person swelled. On a subsequent occasion, Areem greeted Shahram Tajik with a broad smile, besides his usual exchange of salaam, and by physical gesture invited him to be seated in the lone chair gracing the opposite side of the only office table. Shahram was pleased and responded with another broad smile supplemented by the soft saying of *shukria*. That took Areem by surprise as he thought all along that the visitor's spoken skill was limited to Tajik language. But he kept his surprise within himself.

Of the two part-time assistants Areem had from the administration, the one helping him in "money order" matters could speak relatively good Urdu, being a *talib* of Darul Uloom Khusbu, an Islamic religious school in Khyber Pakhtunkhwa Province of Pakistan propagating ultraconservative Islamic views and interpretations. That happened when he crossed the border as a refugee soon after the Soviet invasion of December 1979 and returned after three years to fight the Soviets. He picked up Urdu while being a *talib* in Pakistan but did not finish much of its education even though he was heavily influenced by Darul Uloom's philosophies and policies.

Areem, without exposing himself, motivated the chosen assistant to talk about the visitor. What he detailed slowly was, "Both Ahmad Shah Massoud and Shahram Tajik are from the Jangalak village of Bazarak

District. This possibly is the only commonality between the two. Massoud's father was a colonel in the Afghan Royal Army, and thus, he spent most of his childhood in many places of Afghanistan while living with the parents. He was recognized as a gifted student and went to Kabul University to study engineering. At this point in time, he was exposed to politics and took up arms against Soviet aggression.

"Contrarily, Shahram Tajik had little interest in formal learning, took exceptional pride in Tajik history and culture, exhibited brilliance in analyzing and assessing local issues of conflict, and demonstrated an uncanny ability in negotiations. So he was very popular locally.

"Though from the same area and almost of the same age, they grew up with different personality traits. Their early casual relationship had all the bearings of informality but manifestly lacked cordiality. That significantly changed when Ahmad Shah Massoud took up arms against Soviet forces. In that sudden warring situation, their informality bonded to cordiality and trust, giving it a new twist of strategic relationship soon to be transformed into one of strategic contact and alliance. Ahmad Shah Massoud was overwhelmed by Shahram's incredible ability to gather both civil and military information and analyze them for operational considerations.

"Ahmad Shah Massoud discovered a real gem and positioned Shahram as in charge of civil and military affairs concerning areas in and around Bazarak. While Commander Massoud strategically moved from position to position to throttle Soviet advances, Shahram had always been in and around Bazarak area as the most trustworthy man of Massoud and a fighter to be reckoned with. He soon attained the name and fame for singlehandedly killing five members of the Red Army in an ambush near Changaram Hospital. Shahram's acknowledged triumph sustained the defense of Massoud's core base, while advance and retreat became common phenomena of the latter's war efforts."

The assistant continued, saying, "Like many others, Shahram's family too went to Pakistan as an earlier batch of refugees. In between warring situations, Shahram would visit Karachi to spend time with family. He had a relatively long stay in Karachi after the Soviet Army pulled out, and Massoud took charge of the government with Janab Burhanuddin Rabbani as the president. Fighting initiated by Gulbuddin Hekmatyar against the new government shattered the temporary peace achieved. The surge by and onslaught of Pakistan-based and armed Taliban touted the

Rabbani government. Ahmad Shah Massoud came back to Panjshir and subsequently retreated to the border area of Tajikistan.

"During the course, Shahram brought back his family. They were one of the first to leave and one of the first to return. The family settled surprisingly easily, returning after about twelve years. Shahram appeared to be very happy and permitted the son to join the fight against the Taliban. Then the most unforeseen tragedy shattered his life. The son who joined the Taliban resistance force was killed in an ambush near the hospital where he was born. That shattered the family. Outwardly, Shahram would say that it is the will of Allahpak [decision of the Lord], and he embraced *shahadat* while fighting for the right cause. Internally, he underwent a significant change and slowly became reclusive."

He concluded by saying, "Possibly, in you, he finds some commonality with his late son. That probably brings him to the post office more often."

Areem subsequently was both correct and cordial in handling and addressing Shahram. It was around late morning of a Wednesday, a day of less pressure, that Areem was preparing to treat himself with a typical subcontinental chai when Shahram showed up. At the proposition of Areem, Shahram consented to have chai too. They enjoyed the chai together. Since it was Wednesday, as usual, the traffic was very slow. They were only two souls in the room sipping chai.

Areem's eagerness to have a discussion with Shahram suddenly ratcheted. He politely said, "Your Urdu pronunciation is very good. The ease with which you said *shukria* that day impressed me most."

Impulsively, it unwrapped the encumbrance of pretense and isolation. He laughed inaudibly, sipped his tea, looked around, and softly said, "Yes, I do understand functional Urdu and can also speak reasonably. But I can't read or write. This is the upshot of my family's long stay in Karachi as refugees and my frequent stay and working there. My wife had limited options as she spent most of her time in the camp. My daughter is better in speaking Urdu as she attended public schools though within the periphery of camp. My son and I acquired proficiency in understanding and speaking as we spent most of our time outside the camp. Possibly, as a family, we are blessed with the knack of picking up language."

Taking a pause, he said with a neutral stance, "Nobody here knows that I can understand and speak Urdu. This is a strategy to pick up information when the Taliban speak with one another. This and my reclusive persona are the two strategies I have adopted at the suggestion of Commander Ahmad Shah Massoud. So you should never talk to me in Urdu in public."

Areem was most understanding and suggested, "Unless you have pressing matters, you should come on Monday, Wednesday, and Saturday when we can talk in Urdu and sip chai."

Shahram readily agreed. Areem was the one most delighted by this outcome. Reference to Ahmad Shah Massoud by Shahram and the closeness of the latter with the commander as alluded made Areem very happy. He concluded within himself that the entire episode involving his coming to Panjshir was possibly ordained by Allahpak to fulfill his most heartfelt desire.

Areem promptly decided to cultivate his relationship with Shahram more with a tint of emotional focus. His firm conviction was that he could not let this opportunity go in vain. Areem decided to center future discourses to family background with windows kept open to know specifics, in a step-by-step information sharing, having focus on his childhood and the assassinated son of the former. He consciously opted to postpone any request pertaining to his desire for meeting Ahmad Shah Massoud.

JOLLITY

The chai meeting was more frequent than expected. The emotion-laden discussions were more recurrent and in greater detail than earlier envisaged. Areem's fundamental reasoning for unqualified opening up before Shahram was that if Ahmad Shah Massoud could trust him, why couldn't he! But Areem was quite oblivious of the fact that back at Shahram's home, it became a routine to talk about what Areem had said; and thus, two additional compassionate souls were laden with apprehensions about him.

Such friendly discourse, however, had two mentionable features: Shahram continued to sit in the bench near the wall of the post office as he previously used to and refrained talking to Areem in the presence of others except through physical gesture.

Otherwise, they bonded with each other warmly, and Shahram would focus most of the time on his son in an apparent effort to unburden himself.

In a series of unplanned and unstructured information sharing, Shahram detailed his family life from his marriage to his son's unforeseen demise. The outcome was as follows: "I was married in 1977 with one Gul Bahar and was blessed with a son the following year. Fondly named him Bazrak Tajik, a derivation from the name of the town Bazarak.

"Gul Bahar's brother, who had a very flourishing restaurant business in Kabul and Kandahar and had connections with important functionaries, left hearth and home with immediate family members soon after Soviet occupation for a refugee life in Karachi. At the behest of my brother-in-law, I agreed to follow suit. I stayed in Karachi for some time and helped the family to settle in an Afghan refugee camp. Being adequately motivated by news coverage and social discourses, I returned to Panjshir as a mujahid fighting the Soviet Army. This was the time and occasion when I bonded

169

with Massoud deeply. Even in the midst of a raging war, I made it a point to visit Karachi occasionally to be with the family. I was blessed with a daughter in 1982 and fondly named her Gul Meher, following the name of her mother.

"I was very happy about seeing Soviets out of Afghanistan, being of meaningful help to my brother-in-law in expanding his business operation in Karachi, and seeing the family growing up. But my chief anxiety centered around the perceived lack of pride in my son's persona as being a Tajik. I opened up and discussed my concern with my very understanding brother-in-law cum sentinel, who happens to be a very wise and farsighted individual. The brother-in-law concurred with my anxiety and suggested that the son be relocated to Panjshir temporarily to rejuvenate his dormant pride of being a Tajik. But he suggested so with one observation. The brother-in-law observed, saying, 'I am certain about the deteriorating law-and-order situation in Afghanistan even though the Soviets have left.'

"Recalling the inexplicable coup that sent King Zahir Shah to ingenious exile and the brutal overthrow and murder of successive presidents in a span of about two years, the brother-in-law had a very negative insight about the future of Afghanistan. He stated, 'My connections with some of the elites of the time of King Zahir Shah's reign who were temporarily residing in Karachi and a few members of diplomatic corps encouraged me to apply for US immigration. The US government relaxed its requirements for immigration of Afghans after Soviet incursion, and that lenient policy is still being continued, taking cognizance of deteriorating social and political imperatives consequent to the Soviet invasion.'

"Having said that, the brother-in-law paused for a while and then said, 'After examining pros and cons, I have decided to apply. Subject to your assent, I would also like to include Gul Bahar and Gul Meher as my dependents, you being involved in the fight with the Soviets. Once they are approved, Gul Bahar can apply for you. You can decide to go to the USA or bring them back to Panjshir after their having US passports. The advantage is in case of an unforeseen deteriorating situation in future, they would not have to become refugees again.'

"He continued, saying, 'Gul Bahar is my only sister and so the sole link to my late parents. I need not say much about my feelings and love for her. Our three sons make us happy, but both of us lament for not having a daughter. I give you my solemn word that so long as Gul Meher will be with us, we will take full care of her and would treat her as our daughter.'

He took a long break and concluded his proposition by saying, 'At no stage in life will we force anything on Gul Bahar and Gul Meher. Please consider my proposition and feel free to talk to me when you are comfortable. I still have slight time to decide on the list for US immigration.'"

Detailing that backdrop, Shahram continued, saying, "It was an absorptive proposition about the future of my family. I gave due thought and consideration to the proposal against the imperatives of current and future prospects of living. I discussed with Gul Bahar intensely. Both of us agreed to concur since it was premised on open options of coming back to Panjshir once they have their US passports. Our principal worry pertained to the future of our son.

"With that impediment in mind, both Gul Bahar and I met the brother-in-law and conveyed our concurrence, highlighting nevertheless the perceived worry about the future of our only son. There was a protracted silence with the brother-in-law in deep thoughts. I myself was in a stumped mind-set, and Gul Bahar infrequently looked at her father-like brother, who not only loved her but also guided and took care of her all throughout with positive judgment and futuristic outlook since their parents died in an earthquake.

"To the relief of both, the brother-in-law untied himself from the agonizing silence and started saying, 'Thanks for the positive decision. Both of your concern about the son is well-founded. I have also thought through it before talking to you. Even if I apply now, it is likely to take at least some time before we get endorsement. By that time, my nephew will be more than eighteen years old and would have to apply as an individual. Once we are there, and if it is so needed, we can at that time look for other options, one of them being getting him married to an immigrant Afghan girl who can sponsor him as a spouse. That is the shortest course we have. But now let us proceed as I proposed earlier.'

"He continued, saying, 'The current arrangement has another innate advantage. It will allow him to spend time in Panjshir in the formative period of manhood. He can connect with his roots and absorb the pride of being a Tajik. After that period and experience, his place of stay and living would not be consequential. He would always remain a Tajik.

"That appeared to be a win-win outcome in the present context and the prospect the future held. Both Gul Bahar and I expressed our profound thanks for the guidance of the brother.

"As we were about to leave, the brother-in-law, by physical gesture, desired our presence for some more time. He opened up, saying, 'My earlier suggestion to relocate our nephew at Panjshir equally applies to Gul Meher. She was born in Karachi, grew up here, and goes to Pakistani school. As she is growing up, Gul Meher is slowly losing the traits of a typical Tajik woman. It will be advisable and helpful also for her to be relocated in Panjshir until the US immigration process is finalized. In view of the impending US life, it would be helpful for her to preserve the flavor of a Tajik woman. Since the Soviets have withdrawn, I suggest you think of relocating the whole family now at Panjshir. First, when you live as a family in your own locale, the family bonding is ensured and strengthened. And more importantly, the warmth and the feeling of the father would bless the daughter. Second, it would offset any negative repercussions in the thinking and way of life of the family consequent to immigration.

"He further said, 'Please do not bear in mind that I am proposing the resettlement for financial consideration. I believe in what I said. On my part, I will continue to remit some money to you on a monthly basis, besides visiting you often. So rest assured, it is a good gesture by which I am trying to repay some of my debt to my parents.'"

Shahram resumed his oration, saying, "With relocation arrangements in place, I brought back the family to Panjshir. Gul Bahar was happy to be back to her accustomed and known habitat and to have her identity back. Surprisingly, both son, Bazrak Tajik, and daughter, Gul Meher, embraced Panjshir without dithering and got acclimatized in no time.

"The first action of Bazrak was to lift the gun of his father—weaponry he had no access to in the refugee camp—and fired blank shots in the sky as part of his assimilation process. That made me happy.

"For Gul Meher, the open and clear blue sky against piercing gorges' tips with sporadic snow, spread-out green trees in the valley, and the Panjshir River rolling with its melodic sounds of water flow were elements of nature totally different from what she had in and around the refugee camp and with what she grew up . She spent most of her initial time outside home, walking from one strip of land to another. Gul Meher soon noticed the absence of girls of her age outside the home and the reluctance of grown boys to talk to her. That was so different from her Karachi life.

"She could not help but raise the issue with her mother. Gul Meher was told that this was the norm, and she should as well try to adhere to that as otherwise her father would be ridiculed by the society. Gul Meher yielded to social requirements with shock and sadness at an enormous emotional cost.

"During the process of acclimatization, Bazrak spent most of his time outside with a gun discernibly dangling from his left shoulder, cultivating new friends, and establishing new contacts. His stories of Karachi life were like fairy tales to many of the young local fellows. He was an instant hit in a war-torn environment and soon became a celebrity to many local youths. On his part, he also heard stories of fighting the mighty Russians and increasingly became aware of war efforts of Ahmad Shah Massoud and contributions of his father that brought appellation for him and the family."

The loss of power and consequential withdrawal to Panjshir were major setbacks for Northern Alliance, comprising mostly of Tajiks and Uzbeks. It was particularly exasperating for Massoud. The inimical interactions continued unabated as the Taliban wanted total control of Afghanistan including Panjshir, while Tajik followers under the leadership of Massoud were adamant to deny that at any cost. Shahram played a vital and equally proactive role, wearing the camouflage of a nonaligned individual. He floated and nursed the idea of further negotiations with the Taliban.

That contact and dialogue with the Taliban, however, did not last long. The initial tactical exchanges soon took the shape of armed confrontation as major differences emerged between the two groups concerning faith-related practices. The followers of Ahmad Shah Massoud in particular and Tajiks in general opposed the Taliban's interpretation of Islamic principles and policies . Tajiks, being more educated and more secular, were generally opposed to orthodox application of Sharia law in varied situations, including girl's education, women's freedom to work, and of movement. But a small section of Tajiks was influenced by the Taliban policies. So the struggle continued. Armed confrontation with the Taliban flamed afresh with renewed orthodoxy and new ferocity. Shahram Tajik was playing his undercover role, keeping close contact with Ahmad Shah Massoud.

The Taliban entered Panjshir with a lot of gunpower and troops. Their physical presence was pervasive, but they did not have full control of the territory at any time. They continued to be resisted at every point by Tajik followers of Massoud.

At this point in time, and in keeping the advice of Shahram in view, Ahmad Shah Massoud decided a strategic relocation in Tulub of Tajikistan, a location near the border of Afghanistan and Tajikistan. The game plan was that while Tajiks would continue to resist Taliban rule, Ahmad Shah Massoud would lead that from the temporary safe haven of Tulub.

The bond between Massoud and Shahram, which stood the test of time, became rock solid at this stage with field-level support and advice from Shahram in confronting and fighting the menace of Taliban onslaught and rule.

Shahram did not participate in any frontal confrontation with Taliban forces and followers anymore. That was a tactical decision to ensure his unimpeded access to information pertaining to Taliban approach and strategy. Because of such stratagem, Shahram was wearing the camouflage of a nonaligned civilian, projecting himself as someone having lost interest in terms of ambitions, actions, and pursuits of life demonstrated so glaringly during Soviet occupation.

While the father seemingly retired from active engagements, the son, Bazrak, in consultation with his father, became a member of Tajik resistance force and had some sporadic encounters with the forces of Taliban. He quickly earned the name and acclaimed status as being valiant, aggressive, and preemptive with special prowess and gifted alertness in undertaking reconnaissance assignments. Part of this was due to his youth, Karachi upbringing, and ability to understand Urdu language being spoken in Panjshir by the Taliban only. Startling leniency shown by Father Shahram to cultivate within the mind-set of the son "the pride of being a Tajik" also played a role. He increasingly became carefree and nonchalant.

Bazrak made it a point to return home before sunset. If required to stay in the town, he would tell his mother upfront or send a messenger to inform home well ahead of time. Refugee camp living in Karachi taught him this. On a particular day, Bazrak's return to home was delayed; but he still decided to go as it was just after sunset, and he was being escorted by one of the fellow Tajik fighters of neighboring settlement. As they crossed the periphery of Rajaram Hospital of the town, Bazrak and his fellow companion were ambushed and killed.

In narrating all these, the solid and stable persona of Shahram broke down a number of times. He cried incessantly and experienced glitches frequently. Areem served him water a number of times for drinking and suggested that they discuss the remaining facets some other day when he felt comfortable. Also, just as a caution and not to send any wrong signal, Areem always kept personal discussions short with the assurance of further sharing next time. Shahram took that in good grace.

But he promptly showed up on the following Wednesday, took his seat and, as observed by Areem, was somewhat restless, as if he were under pressure to offload some burden. After an exchange of desirable salutations and pleasantries, Areem went to prepare chai for both. He took his seat on the bench by the side of his visitor after serving chai. Shahram was embarrassed but equally happy.

Upon the initiation of Areem, Shahram opened up, saying, "I have one burden and one inquisitiveness to share with you. First, even though I take Bazrak's death as Allah's will, I cannot escape my guilt for bringing him in Panjshir to ensure that his mind-set is fully conditioned by Tajik heritage and pride. That burden disturbs me a lot, especially when I look at Gul Bahar. Second, on hearing about the sad demise of Bazrak, dear Commander visited Panjshir stealthily and asked me to see him. When we were together, he held both my hands and tears rolled down his cheeks silently without a word. That was all through about five minutes we were together. It was a surprise not only for me but for all others present. Commander killed hundreds of people. He had seen hundreds and thousands dying in the battlefield. But nobody ever saw him crying. I fail to understand that emotional recourse."

Areem took note of those and responded respectfully, saying, "In life, there often are experiences for which reason does not work. I lost my mother while being an infant. What crime did I commit at that stage to be deprived of heavenly love and care of a mother? I also experienced a miserable childhood due to that. I do not have an answer, but I get solace in parking it at His court. So I suggest you do that, identifying Bazrak with every bit of sand and snow nurturing Tajik heritage and pride. You may not get the answer to your frustration but will certainly be blessed with peace of mind. This is the beauty of believing in Allah. The Almighty takes care of you in varied ways.

"To understand the commander's reaction on meeting you, we need to remember that in all strong structures, there are elements of pliability. They are neither visible nor active normally. They respond only in case of intense feeling. Those tears obviously reflected that the commander was as sad as you are for losing your only young son. It may also additionally reflect his very emotive feeling for you."

One of the offshoots of Areem's discernment was that the chai making often provided necessary space to both of them to relax and muse. So he resorted to that often while having discourse with Shahram, keeping the quantity medium compared to standard service size.

Against the backdrop of emotionally laden current discourse, Areem opted to make additional chais, giving space for the setting to warm up.

While making chai, Areem came to a conclusion about a poised bond and trust with Shahram. He decided to open up but as a caution decided a two-stage approach. The first one was to test the genuineness of Shahram's feelings for him. The second one would be to share his cherished desire for an audience with Ahmad Shah Massoud.

Having developed confidence pertaining to the bond and trust of their relationship, Areem sought the help of Shahram in finding a modest accommodation as he felt embarrassed in staying in the office for so long. He also elaborated that unfamiliarity with the place and people and the language problem had been his major impediments in searching for an accommodation. So, he made the request.

While Shahram took note of the request affirmatively, Areem decided to defer raising the second issue. He firmly believed that a favor to be sought or request to be made should have interlude so that the importance of each one was not mitigated. The other tested positive aspect was his belief that such discourse should be undertaken cautiously so that the other party had no reason for being motivated to draw a withering inference.

Two days later, Shahram showed up with a smiling face and an outbound letter in hand. He said, "You are like my son, and your request carries a lot weight with me. I have an innate obligation to help you. But I am also conscious of the reality that it is almost impossible in Panjshir to have an accommodation for a bachelor, more so when he is a non-Tajik.

"Gul Bahar's parental home is located at a short distance from Bazarak Township and to its north. With her only brother mostly living now in Karachi for business purposes and Gul Bahar being married to me, that house generally remains empty. That family abode has a self-contained small but separate accommodation bordering the periphery of the main road going north. That is an adobe home. It is not comparable with houses in cities but a reasonably functional one, especially keeping in view your need and related limitations of you being single. That came to my mind instinctively soon after you made the request. I discussed the proposition of renting it out to you with Gul Bahar, in the presence of Gul Meher. Both of them agreed with Gul Bahar lamenting for you having lost your mother while still infant.

"I was taken aback when Gul Meher handed over the unsealed envelope this morning to me for mailing to her uncle. At my request, she read out the letter. I was amazed by her reasoning on our behalf, including the probable better security of the house as the prospective tenant is a government functionary who earned a good standing in the society in a short time. I was so happy to note that our little daughter has grown up and can think independently. This happiness is marred when I thought of her marriage and the related challenge in finding a suitable groom to match her intellect. I, however, have come today to mail the letter promptly at the bidding of my family."

That was done happily. Usual chai was served. Shahram joked while sipping chai, saying, "I was never addicted to tea. Panjsharians are not at all familiar with your type of tea. But my frequent stay in Karachi made me accustomed to this type of tea preparation. Now if I do not have your chai, I feel somewhat lazy and unprepared for the day. I told my wife and Gul Meher about the way you make tea. They were both curious and mirthful."

Then, suddenly his mood changed. He breathed long and heavily. Areem was taken aback but preferred to be noninterfering. After some time, Shahram revealed himself, saying, "My earlier expression that you are like my son was not a premeditated one. It was spontaneous and without any schema. The fact is that the first day I saw you sitting in this chair and stamping outgoing letters, in my mind and thought, it was Bazrak sitting there. Because of his Karachi upbringing and education, I always had the feeling that one day he would be a government functionary, and my social identity would be 'the father of Mr. Bazrak, so-and-so of the government.' That was my fondest hope, and I refrained from open confrontation with the Taliban to make sure that Bazrak's chance of getting a government job was not impaired. Since then, every day I came and sat on this bench, it was not you but Bazrak occupying the chair. Momentarily, I felt joy and happiness. That was the reason that I was drawn close to you."

He continued, saying, "Initially, Gul Bahar discouraged my visits to the post office and sitting there without any seeming chore. Slowly, she not only relented but also started taking interest in knowing about you: your look, personality, behavior, sincerity, and so on. After some time, reporting back every day became a routine for me. On most occasions, Gul Meher would be sitting by the side of Mother, and she would lengthen her head cover to conceal embarrassment for awkward queries about you."

The axiomatic consent of the brother-in-law reached home from Karachi in no time. The good news was shared with joy and happiness. Areem's happiness was premised on his finally having the choice of vacating the office, which he used partly as his living space with embarrassment evident. The joy of Shahram and the family was grounded on being able to respond to Areem's request.

But Areem, being a farsighted person, though in his youth, wanted to play correct and safe. He first informed the regional administrative official who chaired the opening of the post office about the moving out. He also decided to have a conversation with Shahram to avoid any likely fallout as many people had seen him in his office regularly. Areem, by this time, also became familiar with trend and type of local sociopolitical relationship frequently complicated and marred by jealousy, hate, clique, and conspiracy.

As Shahram stood up to leave after sharing the good news, Areem requested him to stay as he had important matters to discuss before the move. So Areem said, "I have by now a fair idea about the local relationship. Keeping that in view, I would suggest that you keep yourself at a distance from all visible actions relating to my move to your brother-in-law's adobe home. In essence, you should outwardly behave like a landlord and treat me just like a tenant. I plan to go to your place with my two part-time assistants managing and handling my belongings. You will formally hand over the key to me in their presence. Once that is done and they are gone, we can revert back to our usual relationship, but it would always be advisable to exercise care and caution. I hope that you do not misunderstand me. Please bear in mind that back home you have a marriageable daughter too."

That quivered Shahram's wonky mind. He kept his head down for some time and then thanked Areem to remind him about the social reality and efforts needed to protect the good name he had earned.

Both left the office cum residence of Areem jointly and got separated near the main marketplace. Areem felt relaxed at having been able to tell Shahram what he had in mind. The message that Areem conveyed to Shahram got ratcheted in Shahram's mind initially; but eventually, and after deep thought, he saw merit in what Areem articulated. He returned home, happily informing the family about formalizing the renting arrangement.

During dinner, Shahram told Gul Bahar, "My assessment that Afghanis are good with guns but Bangladeshis are undeniably good in games has once again been proven to be true today. They may relatively be shorter in height but travels further in intellect." Then he narrated his discourse with Areem and reiterated what Areem desired as to the public face of mutual relationship. Gul Bahar was very happy and assured. But Gul Meher was thwarted, and lengthened her head cover to conceal her frustration, a response syndrome most Asian Muslim girls resort to concealing both happiness and sadness in matters of feelings, especially in the presence of seniors.

A mystified lull engulfed the setting. It was Gul Bahar who raised a very apposite issue, having a slight element of taunting in her observation. She said, "You are obviously happy in finding an accommodation for the postmaster [as Areem was known in the locality]. But have you thought about how and who will cook for him?"

Shahram brushed aside the query, saying, "We are not responsible for all his needs. He is a smart guy and will solve his problems the way he thinks best. Also, there are eateries in the town. He can continue to do what he was doing so long. My happiness pertains to our ability to respond to his specific request. Let us now observe his progression."

Inexplicable sensitivity within herself was always prying Gul Meher. She riveted the words, facts, and events related to the postmaster even though had neither seen him in the past nor had hoped of a possibility in the future. She, for unspecified motivations, was very attentive to current discussions of her parents concerning the postmaster and had an arcane and thwarting feeling about the tone and texture of the said discussions. While rearranging her head cover, and contrary to normal behavior pattern, she observed, "Regular partaking of restaurant food could both be boring and unhealthy. Father can occasionally drop wrapped food from our house, avoiding the eyes of others. By nature, the pack will be small, and carrying that under the shawl would not be a problem. Even if there is a bulge, people would normally think that to be the butt of gun Father normally carries." Saying those words with all firmness within the veil of respect and family values, Gul Meher quietly vacated the place.

To the parents, the sudden departure of Gul Meher almost amounted to be the frame of decision to be taken with no room for further discussion. To lighten the disposition, Shahram commented, "Whatever you say, our daughter has not her mother's sunny disposition." On hearing this and concluding negatively, Gul Bahar also stood up and unceremoniously left the room. Shahram had a sorcerous laugh at himself, thinking about mankind's general incompetence in accepting even unbiased comments in good grace.

Responding to Areem's earlier subtle indication, and based on family discussion, Shahram reduced his visits to the post office. That caused an unnecessary mayhem. The few times Shahram went, he stayed for a relatively short time, still envisaging Bazrak in the chair of the postmaster. Fellow Bazarakians, who were generally familiar with this mind-set of Shahram, were sympathetic and caring.

The issue of significantly reduced visits came up for discussion one night suddenly as Shahram was unable to respond to Gul Bahar's routine query about how the postmaster was doing. In the midst of statements and explanations, Gul Meher intercepted, saying, "What the father is doing perhaps is correct but not perceptibly sensible. Father's noticeable absence may give rise to hearsays and speculations in the society. To my mind, Father should resume visiting the post office, but it could be intermittent, say, mostly on lean days. This will have all positive impressions both socially and personally as people in general may have a sympathetic conclusion as that being reflective of grief and sadness of a father of a deceased young son."

It was three days after the family's discussions about what they could do to ensure a comfortable living for the postmaster and the day following the discussions about Shahram's reduced visit to the post office. Shahram told Gul Bahar about his chance meeting with Janab Mudaressi (owner of a locally popular *chaikhana*). Prior to returning to Bazarak, Mr. Mudaressi used to work for the brother-in-law in Karachi. They maintained business relations, and Mr. Mudaressi visited Karachi often. This time, he carried information about an important mail from the brother-in-law in immediate future, requesting Shahram to monitor its arrival and receipt.

Shahram told Gul Bahar of his plan to go to the post office the following morning to inquire about the important incoming mail from brother-in-law. "That could as well be related to your and Gul Meher's possible immigration to the USA as his dependents. I am not sure, but Mr. Mudaresssi repeated that as being very important."

That instantly caused a reflective as well as a germane emotion within Gul Meher. The more Gul Meher wanted to shrug off any starry-eyed feeling for that indiscernible person sitting on a chair at the post office and stamping outgoing mails, the more she was drawn to him in terms of well-being, comfort, love, and care. Her father's sustained approbation of the postmaster, partly premised on his seeing deceased son in him, might have contributed to it. But she had her own part too.

She was fully conscious of the fact that parking reason and blame on another court is perhaps a convenient way out in disparaging situations, but it is never the end of the path. That only causes a detour until the truth finds its own way.

Being born in Karachi and growing up in a hybrid social setup of the refugee camp in the urban setting of the metropolitan, Gul Meher nurtured and cherished an interactive relationship with minimum gender factor. When she returned to Bazarak, that underwent a radical change. The visibility of grown-up boys was minimal in the vicinity of her house and, for that matter, in most parts of Afghanistan as Gul Meher picked up from occasional conversations of parents. Some stayed back in Pakistan temporarily if not already settled abroad; some died in the prolonged war. Most of the local youths were involved in fights and confrontations within. In that backdrop, the first love of most young Afghanis was their gun. Wives or female companions were for fun and enjoyment at their will and for a limited time.

Having cognizance of related laconic idea of the above inevitability, Gul Meher noted a significant shift in her mother's words, advice, and conduct ever since their return home. She kept in mind the inevitable and her mother's regular pronouncements that centered around what to expect from marriage: total submission to husband and in-law's family, childbirth, and competence in cooking and house management. So Gul Meher got preoccupied in acquiring all those attributes.

It was only when her parents started talking about the postmaster, his mother's early death, and how he reminded Shahram of Bazrak did she start to have interest in him. That involuntarily created a trivial window in her mind that slowly caused tending of a compassionate feeling. She eagerly looked forward to know more.

Areem moved to his new accommodation following the first visit along with his assistants. Life made its standard progression in the midst of turgid milieus. His reliance on local eateries became absolute even though a gradual aversion to repetitive meat-based local food was skulking in. Being a Bangladeshi, Areem's acquired food taste was premised on fish, vegetable, meat, and lentils supplemented by variety of spice mixes. Most of them were totally absent in local culinary. Though fish had occasional presence, the recipe was totally different with fish being grilled as a food item unlike the gravy-based preparation in Bangladesh. Even though he missed the food he had grown up with, Areem reconciled with the reality based on his previous mental preparation.

Areem and Shahram discussed various issues in their reduced faddy discourses dominated mostly by reminiscing of Shahram about the time and reign of King Zahir Shah, refugee life in Karachi, combat against the Soviets, valiant fight of Ahmad Shah Massoud, current political divide, frequent slide in tenets and conduct, and so on. The discussion pertaining to his deceased son was normal but was neither common nor in detail. Seldom had Shahram talked about his daughter Gul Meher except lamenting the absence of a good young man in the local setting to match her competence and intelligence.

Shahram was neither as docile nor as dumb as some people would normally imagine after observing him sitting in the post office bench for long hours, seldom exchanging words. He was known and understood by limited people whom he liked and trusted but was respected enormously by most Tajiks as a valiant mujahid. Among leaders fighting shoulder to shoulder with him against Russians and involved in tactical maneuvering with the Taliban later on, Ahmad Shah Massoud was one of them. His confidence in Shahram's judgment was immense. The former trusted Shahram, respected his opinions, and valued his suggestions. Massoud's retreat to Tulub was mostly at Shahram's bidding.

Shahram had a mix of politeness and arrogance in his social facade. Thus, people had different perceptions about him even though everyone was candid in concluding about his vigor, valor, and virtuousness in upholding Tajik identity and traditions. Most esteemed was the way he handled the sudden demise of the only son.

Because of cultural inhibitions, Gul Meher never had enjoyed a profile of excellence in social discourses even though her ability to read and write, as an offshoot of Karachi living and growing up, helped many unlettered ladies of the area in having communications with husbands, sons, and other family members outside Bazarak. Even in some special circumstances, elderly ones would come seeking her help, maintaining the requirements of *parda* (modesty). Her ability to preserve delicate family information was acknowledged by all and sundry. She was never the talk of the mail-dominated social system. On his part, Shahram thanked Allahpak for blessing him with such an intelligent and responsible daughter.

Following the earlier implicit observation of Gul Meher, Shahram decided to visit the post office more regularly than in the immediate past and thoughtfully opted to do so on lean days of operation. The next morning, as he alluded to Gul Bahar earlier in the context of tracking urgent letter from her brother, was such a lean day.

Shahram was getting ready to go to town the following morning. Gul Meher came with shy steps and handed over a packet of lunch for Areem.

Shahram winked at Gul Bahar, who was standing by his side, and said, "We often complain of things happening in our life without having any notion about the end game. Allah alone knows the reason and the consequence. Our daughter is not only growing up but also attaining ideas and wisdom. Our refugee life in Karachi might have many glitches, but exposure to a metropolitan setting and good education have had interminable impact on our children."

Perhaps the plan of the father to go to town that morning was an ordained one and a response to what Gul Meher had proposed earlier when discussing what the family could and should do to assist the postmaster. As the time passed, the uncaring sensitivity started gaining ground within the fidgety, mystic mind of Gul Meher. Her feeling for the postmaster deepened with each discussion, and she felt closer to him.

Seeing Shahram stepping in after a gap, Areem was relieved and happy. Shahram took his usual seat but soon proceeded toward the table, pretending that he had some things there to attend to. He quietly left the food packet between two sets of folders. No exchange of word took place between the two. The aroma of food was sufficient indication. Areem looked around and quietly put the packet in the drawer and closed it. Soon, it became the norm.

In having that food on that day as his lunch in the solitary setting of the post office, Areem not only enjoyed the flavor and taste of home-cooked food but also had an intuitive feeling of the touch, though not mentioned, of Gul Meher in preparing that. The same feeling about the uniqueness of that culinary excellence was innate in Areem's frequent later observations.

That sort of repeated kudos by Areem was sufficient to provoke a major break in Shahram's closely held Tajik value of not discussing openly the life and activities of family's female members. Areem soon realized that normal human feelings are the same all over although impaired principally by imposed stipulations and restrictions of societies with variances in type, content, focus, and implication. Once that social barrier was broken, there was nothing to stop Shahram. Like any proud father, he was stirring in talking about the qualities of Gul Meher, so closely held so long. Shahram dealt with, among others, Gul Meher's character, commitment, confidence, intelligence, pragmatism, and a host of other attributes in a series of follow-on discussions spread over many days with each session ending with two common indications: one, "Will discuss the rest later", and two, "I am anguished by the lack of a prospective and match-worthy groom for her."

Sharman always tried to exercise prudence and diligence in underscoring upbeat attributes of his daughter in isolation. He would only underline the relevant points in tandem with issues or persons in discussion. Areem developed a habit of revisiting that feature when he would remember the discussions after every such meeting. That sort of thinking on his part was obviously pungent as he had nothing else to do. But truthfully, it was also reflective of his own innate desire to know more about Gul Meher.

Areem slowly nurtured more open exchanges in matters of his active desire with Shahram carefully avoiding any direct reference to Gul Meher. Following the topic and trend of recent discussions, Areem obliquely made reference about the taste and quality of food of Shahram's home as he was eating of late but intermittently. He observed, saying, "I had some food from two homes: one from the restaurant owner where I had frequent meals and the other one from one of my trusted assistants. Those bear more of a typical palate, but yours always had a different flavor and penchant. Is cooking in your house a reflection of a routine preparation of local food or an exception to that?"

Shahram was evidently pleased to receive kudos about cooking in his home and opened up unwaveringly, even with some faulty expressions, saying, "Partly, it is due to the inquisitive mind of my daughter, Gul Meher, and partly premised on the family's long living in the refugee camp. Structured on a block design, the camp housed more than a thousand of refugees of varied linguistic identities, regions, and tribes of Afghanistan. Born and brought up in that setting of the camp, Gul Meher had no idea or experience of tribe-based culture and traditions. Because of linguistic variances and attending schools run by the local administration, most children took solace in learning some Urdu even though thoroughly discouraged by parents. We tried our best to orient our children to traditional living and way of life in Bazarak, but the end result was very limited.

"Gul Meher grew up as a very social person and likewise was adored by many female residents of our block. She used to visit some houses of her liking, talk or listen to the ladies, and observe their way of cooking and living. Thus, she acquired a culinary expertise reflecting various regions and tribes.

"Implausibly, there was a culinary contribution from a very unexpected quarter too. In the northern periphery of our block, there were three empty quarters, and the block *sardar* decided to rent those under clandestine arrangements with strict instructions both to residents and the tenants: for the first group not to talk about it and for the second group to keep a low profile. The common objective was to finance the running of a Quran reading class for small children of the block.

"Most of the tenants were short-duration ones looking for temporary shelter, being illegal residents. The refugee camp was outside the direct and regular police vigilance, monitoring, and meddling. And hence the three-room accommodation soon earned a name for its safety and security.

"That was a safe transient place for most newly arrived illegal Bangladeshis until they establish local contacts and find livable surroundings of their choice and confidence. Prior to 1971, Karachi had a sizable Bangladeshi population. The familiarity, current job opportunities as cooks and ready-made-garment workers, and frequent abandonment of prospective overseas workers who were on their supposed way to Middle East destinations constituted the bulk of illegal Bangladeshis.

"One afternoon, Gul Meher was returning from school, taking a temporary entry point of the northern camp boundary. She was struck seeing a mid-sized brown-skinned lady wrapped in one-piece long material. She had long straight black hair and beautiful dark eyes with flowing eyelids. She came out of one of the rented accommodation.

"Gul Meher was unmoving momentarily. Noticing her in that static position, the lady smiled and requested her to come near. Gul Meher unhesitatingly responded. She introduced herself as Rizia from Bangladesh. They bonded easily, exchanging a few single-syllable Urdu words with which Rizia was familiar. She came from a place known as Saidpur in Bangladesh, which had a strong Urdu linguistic influence until the emergence of Bangladesh.

"Asking her to wait, Rizia went inside her tiny accommodation and came out soon with a toasted biscuit and a glass of water. Requesting her to take that, she said, 'You are my first guest in about one month. So please honor me by taking this small eating item.' Gul Meher complied but really enjoyed having those.

"Gul Meher continued visiting Rizia mostly in the late afternoon time when the latter used to prepare fresh curry for her husband. She was amazed while observing Rizia using and mixing various spices in making different items of fish and vegetable, mostly having gravy. Occasionally, Gul Meher would taste a bit at the request of Rizia but initially did not like it due to the strong presence of red chili in the preparation. Nevertheless, she enjoyed observing Bangladeshi cooking and its mix and match of spices, and Rizia was enthralled, mostly recalling her younger sister back home.

"Gul Meher told her mother about visiting Rizia. She was happy for Gul Meher having found an elderly friend but was not at all interested in knowing about Bangladeshi curry preparation.

"That bond and relationship between an innocent and outgoing Tajik youngster and a soft and sweet Bangladeshi lady soon came to an abrupt end as the Bangladeshi couple decided to relocate. But the culinary specialties Gul Meher so keenly observed and internalized stayed with her with no opportunity to try it.

"Since our resettlement in Bazarak, Gul Bahar concentrated in shaping up our daughter as an ideal Tajik young girl in all respects including cooking. So most foods in our home are now being prepared by Gul Meher under the watchful eyes of her mother.

In spite of that, she continued trying out various mixes of spices she learned in the camp, but of course, she never had the chance to try out Bangladeshi curry preparation. Whatever you were intermittently eating during the past few days were all prepared by our daughter."

Shahram concluded his rather long narration with expected gaps and splits but was nevertheless able to convey fully what he wanted to. He did not fail to lament about the dearth of good young local men to trust with the hand of his daughter.

Areem was happy for unknown reasons. He was delighted because of his arcane expectations. He enjoyed the contents of conversation without explicit element of feeling and care. But the summation of all these for Areem was that Gul Meher knew something about Bangladesh. Neither the five and a half yards of unstitched draping material (*saree*) nor the mix and match of spices were foreign to her. Areem was resolutely reluctant to be concerned about the end result least he spoils the present good feeling.

He was in his own self and enjoyed the present without the pretentious outcome of the future.

Shahram showed up two days after that long talk about Gul Meher, but there was no food parcel. That took Areem by surprise, particularly in the context of his all-positive feelings about having a closer relationship with the family, which could result in a possible intimate association with Gul Meher. In the context of emanating negativity in the process, Areem always argued with himself that if his grandfather from Afridi tribe of the Frontier Province could fall in love with a Hindu girl of Bengal, then what could possibly negate his having a bond with a Tajik girl of the same faith?

While mingling with related reasons, justifications, and expectations, Areem stood up to prepare his usual chai—one thing he knew and mastered over the days in entertaining Shahram. Out of blue, and for the first time, Shahram stopped him and whispered, saying, "You do not order food for lunch tomorrow. I will bring food of Gul Meher's choice and preparation, and we would eat together in your place, the day being a weekend." Saying those words, he hurriedly left the room. That was a straight statement of fact. There was no sensitivity involved. There was no one in the post office at the time to warrant whispering. Still, Shahram was edgy and insecure. It was difficult for Areem to comprehend that mind-set.

Instead of getting bogged down with the latest impulse of Shahram, Areem opted, keeping in view the proposition of home cooked foods, to look forward and guess as to what it would hold for him. Such a gesture was an exception in his life. During the entire process of growing up, Areem had high priority and explicit emphasis on keeping new mother and the father happy. Even in that scenario, Areem never thought of the end result, or self-interest, except in academic pursuits. But this appeared to be an exception.

Being in the post office alone during afternoon of a lean day, Areem leisurely lifted his two legs and put them on his office table while relaxingly positioning himself on the chair. He opted to close his eyes for a while.

His mind and thought at that exceptional moment of feeling were dominated by all positivity: eatable items being chosen and prepared by Gul Meher, sharing of the same food with Shahram in his rented place, and the sort of conversation the family might have around all these. Areem was certain that even though he had not been physically seen or formally introduced, he had sort of a steady presence in that family's periodical discourses. That made him happy. When he closed his eyes again, Areem for the first time tried to visualize Gul Meher as a person and an intelligent young lady. Shahram's earlier frequent references helped him in that regard.

With that positive and happy outlook, Areem slowly brought down his legs, stood up, and got involved in making chai to entertain himself against expectations of progression. His pragmatic mind, however, recognized the imperative tableau of reality against the backdrop of smooth sailing so far. Contacts, interactions, and bond with Shahram, and his family through him, with all limitations were pleasantly rated as suave even in most unfamiliar environment and the predicament of social interactions. Pragmatically, that relationship remained vulnerable to unknown uncertainties and unpredictable time. Areem was intelligent enough to take note of that.

Recounting indirect inferences during past conversations alluding to Shahram's close relationship with Ahmad Shah Massoud, Areem decided to open up before the former, seeking his immediate help in having an utmost desired audience with the Leader. He also concluded that ensuing lunch event would likely be the best setting and occasion to make that request.

With all such stirring and enthralling emotions playing within, Areem moved promptly to close the post office on time, made a detour of the market to buy a drinking glass and a teacup, hurried to his residence with minimal social interactions on the way, and fixed his room to look nice and neat. That was consistent with his habit of doing or fixing things well ahead of time.

No time was specified by Shahram for his arrival at Areem's place with food, but obviously, it was to be early noontime. As the assumed time ticked and there was no trace of Shahram, Areem became restive, being oblivious for the moment that adherence to time in the valley area had no direct link with commitment either for meeting or for action. It was always to be variable one, and local practices had no qualm with that. It was difficult to plan everything in the valley with relation to sun even as it was visible very late than usual and eclipses very early than normal due to high-rise mountain peaks all around.

Finally, there was the cracking coughing sound outside the hanging dry-vegetable-made curtain creating privacy within. Areem opened the door, went out, lifted the curtain, exchanged salaam, and gracefully ushered in his august visitor. Shahram was requested to be seated on the lone charpoy. Areem took his seat on the lone low square chair with backrest and woven thong seat with firm base ensured by even lower curved legs with round posts.

This noon, Shahram was different from the one who met Areem on the preceding day at office. The riled body expressions of the previous noon were swapped by a surprisingly unflappable bearing and cherubic smile gracing taciturn expressions. Areem was pleasantly bemused.

To make him at ease and comfortable, Shahram offloaded two cotton hanging bags from his two shoulders, which he carried so long under his traditional shawl. Placing them at one end of the charpoy, he lifted both his feet and took a cross-legged sitting position at his end of the charpoy. Requesting Areem to place his only piece of other furniture, one vintage chest of cedar wood, by the side of the bed, Shahram started taking out food items carried by him and partly placed them on the flat top of the chest. The flavor of the first two items was both beguiling and familiar to Areem. He had been eating regularly meat and fish kebab since the arrival in Peshawar, Pakistan. And the other follow-on item, naan, had its presence in all local food intakes. But the separate salad preparation amazed Areem.

Shahram paused after having a look at Areem. With expressions having the mix of embarrassment and happiness, Areem started saying, "I am so thankful to you and your family. Based on your past avowals and witnessing what you are unfolding now, I am all the more certain about the contribution of the lady of the house in making you such a complete person. And—"

Before Areem could finish what he wanted to say, Shahram stopped him. He thought it to be opportune for him to shorten formal discussions so they could partake the food when it was still warm. Gazing at just unwrapped food items, Shahram said, "I have been instructed by Gul Meher to eat what you are seeing but to offer you a very special preparation she painstakingly made recalling how Rizia of refugee camp occasionally used to cook. If you like it, then she will have her dinner with the leftovers of that preparation. She also categorically said that if the taste is not good, it would be okay with her too as she does not claim to have any expertise in preparing such food. In that event, you are to have your full meal with naan and kebab, and back home, she too will have it once I report back. Whatever you will see is her effort. I am happy to have whatever she cooks for me occasionally."

Saying those words, Shahram took out from the other bag filled with two aluminum containers, one having rice and the other Bangladeshi-style fish curry with a lot of gravy. Areem was speechless and almost in a static position with his eyes visibly soaked with tears.

Without spoiling time on further niceties and rituals, Areem took his plate and started having his fish curry and rice in Bangladeshi style of eating by hand. With successive self-service of rice cum fish intakes, Areem finally said, "It could not be better. I relished eating those. I enjoyed it thoroughly. No one in my life did a similar thing for me. I am really grateful to you all, particularly to Gul Meher." Continuing, he said, "Please tell Gul Meher that her surprise befuddled me. I have decided to keep half of rice and fish for tomorrow and would supplement tonight's dinner by keeping leftover naan and kebab after you finish eating."

Shahram, amused initially by the solo eating of Areem, followed him in eating his naan and kebab. At a later point, they shared the said items too, with Areem eating the fish kebab.

The thrill on the part of Areem for having most startling fish curry in the unlikely scenery of Panjshir and the glee ubiquitous in the facial lexes of Shahram for his daughter's ability to cook something that she never before did or tasted gave that moment and backdrop a distinctive connotation in respective thinking. Beguiled, Areem, in spite of his indubitable aptitude for clear thinking, could not decide about the appropriateness of raising his personal agenda at that trice. Shahram's exhilaration looped around all that sprouted centering eating, including patchy mentioning of Gul Meher's openness, liking, and ability. Suddenly, it dawned on him that perhaps he committed a gaffe by mentioning, in a quotation form, what Gul Meher told him about partaking of fish curry when he left the house with food. He felt embarrassed and promptly decided to correct it.

While sharing postlunch chai, Shahram unwrapped his pressing thoughts by saying, "We do not know much about each other though I have shared our refugee living in Karachi with germane flank aspects. Even with that constraint, we have taken you as one of our own, especially seeing in you our lost son. My family has not met you, but they know every bit of our interactions. So as a person, you are quite familiar and close to them. Gul Meher, being a simple Tajik girl with perceptive intelligence, made frank avowal about fish preparation and eating inclinations. I was not supposed to relate that to you in verbatim. So please don't conjure anything. I am sorry for that."

After a brief break, Shahram continued providing further erudite rationale, saying, "We live in about a hundred-mile-long valley having all features surrounded by high and majestic peaks of Himalayas and Hindukush ranges separating Central Asia from its southern portion. We are at ease in breathing fresh air of the lush green valley meadows asymmetrical to well-designed carpets, enriched likewise by soothing but equally surging glacial melted water. Similarly, we are at ease in having enchanted and magnificent mountain peaks often shrouded by stationary cum damped white miasmas. The first imbues within us a sense of simplicity and straightforwardness. We mean what we say. We do not play with the twists and turns of words to say something meaning something else as most people of Karachi and similar urban places do. The second teaches us to remain ever vigilant against obstacles and adversities as mountain peaks denote. So we are equally kind but ferocious too."

Momentary silence was broken by Areem when he said, "I understand what you said. I respect respective contents and intents. So far as the statement of Gul Meher is concerned, let us agree that neither have you said anything nor have I heard anything and seal it for the future. I give you my word of not admitting otherwise under all probable situations."

Assuring Shahram with respect to his apparent prime concern, Areem continued, saying, "I am under oath not to divulge anything about my roots and purpose of being here. But I have decided to the contrary to reveal myself before you, come what would be the consequences. Losing my mother at infancy, I survived notwithstanding the hate of my new mother engulfing my growing-up years, the indifference of my father, and the cleverly concealed dislike of my younger brother in spite of all efforts of mine to the contrary." In detailing his life's progression, Areem also referred to his frustration based on his field experience after joining al-Qaeda. He stated that his continuing with al-Qaeda so far was premised on the sole objective of meeting the Leader Ahmad Shah Massoud. That definitely was a well-thought-out longing and an offshoot of reading his biography.

"I have had the feeling that I can get deserved guidance and direction from him. My retaining link with al-Qaeda is a calculated step toward that pursuit of mine. I did not join al-Qaeda to kill anyone and to embrace *shahadat* in the name of religion. In my hostel life of initial college education, I had a roomie, Manzoor by name, who was a very bright student and equally committed member of extreme conservative political outfit of Bangladesh. He provided me occasionally with publications and literatures pertaining to al-Qaeda movement and Afghanistan's war against the Soviets. There, I first read about the Leader but did not form any views about his role and actions. Perhaps because those were al-Qaeda documents, Ahmad Shah Massoud's leadership, role, and contributions were by design camouflaged.

"Though minimal, that was sufficient enough to create an inner interest within me to know more about him. But it is very clear that I opted to join al-Qaeda as an easy and immediate conduit initially to escape my family, with larger objective of knowing the rationale of the movement and its core focus, and to assess the suitability of the philosophy in the context of Bangladesh.

"A copy of the biography of Ahmad Shah Massoud was incidentally presented to me by Taliban leader Janab Jatoi of Sindh, Pakistan, as an informal input in the orientation process. The more I read that book, the more I was enchanted by the views and valor of the Leader in pursuing both political and military objectives.

"I read the biography immediately and partially reread it after participating in the tragic operation in Multan where Shia devotees were brutally killed while coming out of a mosque. That was a very unnerving experience for me, and I almost decided to leave the movement without caring for consequences. But as I reread the book partially, my decision was reversed. My inclination to meet the Leader burgeoned many a time when I came to know his disagreement with al-Qaeda with respect to interpretations of edicts of Islam. I also find al-Qaeda's implementation of Quranic pronouncements as abhorrent. I still opted to continue and embarked on an unmapped journey to meet the Leader while outwardly having the identity of al-Qaeda. I took all chances and faced all challenges. Finally, destiny brought me to Bazarak as an assistant postmaster.

"I had no specific input in the process of my uncharted journey. It appeared to me that the whole journey was an ordained one, including your developing affection for me in the context of tragic demise of your only son."

Consistent with his upbringing, Areem straightway sought the help of Shahram in having an audience with the Leader so that he would be benefited by the Leader's opinion and guidance. It could ensure a more resilient future journey in life, fulfilling the commitment he had made to himself. He revisited his sole determination of doing something good for the people of Bangladesh. It was also considered critical because of the emerging ground presence of al-Qaeda in Bangladesh.

The locus of discussion was an eye-opener for Shahram as he had better and clearer appreciation of the traits and hidden objectives of the young man whom he had mostly known as a government functionary. From the beginning, Shahram took fancy on him; his family, even in the absence of contact, similarly liked him; and the community by and large loved him. The genesis of all these was predicated on Areem's amiable disposition and running the most critical postal system efficiently, ensuring much improved communication and inflow of funds.

Shahram made no effort to look either behind or beyond Areem's demonstrated public intent and accepted him as he was. That was the rationale for his being oblivious of predicaments concerning qualms, risks, and vulnerabilities of trust in having open contact with Areem. Though it was contrary to Shahram's significant guerrilla war background, he nevertheless was at ease in having regular contacts with Areem. The other reason was his getting tired of fast-deteriorating social values in and around Panjshir. That was significantly being impacted upon by increasing prevalence of animosity, nasty manipulations, grandstanding in projecting oneself, and mischaracterization including defamatory innuendo in every bend of life. It never mattered whether the scenery pertained to social, political, military, and religious conduits. It always occurred, and every succeeding one was nastier than the earlier one.

Because of these, the sudden death of his only son, and his honest quest for a peaceful life, Shahram opted to remain loyal to Ahmad Shah Massoud for a relatively unassuming role in conflict with the Taliban, providing nevertheless ground-level intelligence from time to time on critical matters. His life pattern was analogous to that of a roaring tiger in the forest resting after a wild chase of its prey, nonetheless monitoring the surroundings with quenching eyes. In the process, he found solace and peace in the company of Areem and his personal traits, and always felt happy in sharing mutual lonely times.

Shahram did not take much time to assess the request of Areem and to be convinced of its genuineness in the background of immediate past experience. Shahram pleasantly recounted all that but still remained noncommittal.

He took the dinnertime to fully brief the family about lunch, liking of food by Areem, especially the fish preparation, as well as his keeping a portion of each fish curry and rice for the next day. Areem particularly requested him to convey to *betty* (daughter) Gul Meher his heartfelt thanks, saying, "No one in his life has done such an amazing thing for him with so much thought and care." Hearing the related observation, Gul Meher instinctively stood up, covered most parts of her face by the *dupatta* (material worn as a scarf or head covering), and left the dinner setting momentarily. That reaction was as per Central and South Asian tradition on hearing that someone unknown referred to her by name. It was also a demonstration of modesty. After a little while, Gul Meher returned with the leftover fish curry and continued eating.

With the dinner over and associated cutlery items put back in respective places, the family was in a lightened mood with Gul Meher rotating her tasbih beads, invoking Allah's blessings for long life of the father, a practice she followed during after-dinner discourse of every evening.

They sat together when Shahram was indulging in his usual limited smoke craving. Gul Bahar observed that Shahram's smoking was not like other days. A sense of disquiet and diffidence visibly was overriding his normal self. As a wife, that did not elude Gul Bahar's eyes.

Commissioning all respects and invoking all humility on her part as the social and traditional dictums require, Gul Bahar inquired politely whether there was anything that was troubling him. Breaking her usual practice of listening only, and in an emotion-choked voice, she said, "Most part of our married life was dominated by war and conflict. I never questioned your decisions and actions as I was certain that the related forays were motivated by duty and not ambition. We had intermittent family living in Karachi, far away from the scene of conflict. Ever since we resettled in our own place, we rediscovered ourselves and started enjoying our family life though suddenly our loving son fell prey. With all sorrow and distress overwhelming our lives, I got happiness in observing that you never hankered for rewards and of late in having a simple family life, sharing with us your time and company with most of our relatives still in the refugee camp. However, it appears to be different this evening. I am concerned and worried."

Saying those words, the assumed-simpleton Gul Bahar took some rest and concluded her avowal by saying, "I have never talked to you in that fashion. Zubaida Khala of the refugee camp always told me to talk to you frankly about family matters. Betty Gul Meher always insisted that I have more frank conversations with you. So I voiced my concern to know what is going on within you. I might not have articulated it properly but hope you got the message."

Gul Meher, who was standing nearby rotating her tasbih beads, was very happy. She sat down by the side of her mother and put her hand on her shoulder, signifying happiness and support.

Enthralled, Shahram had a mix of seriousness in his facial expression but burst with hilarity, saying, "Look, Gul Meher, your mother can talk and even on serious family matters contrary to my understanding. I had no earlier idea but valued her present concern, noted anew her self-confidence, and enjoyed her assertion. I have something in my mind since today's lunch event but cannot find a way out. But before I unfold that agitating matter, I would like to have a service of chai. The postmaster has spoiled me."

Both mother and daughter left to prepare chai, but Gul Meher returned soon, while the mother was preparing the chai. She was most concerned, thinking that the post master might have committed an error to annoy her father, and it could have a possible impact on future relationship.

With that agonizing backdrop, Gul Meher slowly stepped in and sat by the side of her father, respectfully placing her tasbih in the open palm of Father without saying anything. She continued looking at the mother engaged in the cooking area.

Gul Bahar returned to her place by the other side of Shahram and served the chai. But pervasive wavering of her was manifest in expressions, more looking at Gul Meher. The touch and influence of Zubaida Khala were largely casual in the setting of the refugee camp but palpably had an indelible mark in influencing Gul Bahar's thinking even in the remote location of Jangalak village of Bazarak.

She could not be quiet anymore, just waiting for Shahram to open his mouth. Breaking the age-old tradition of just listening to what a husband would say, Gul Bahar almost demanded to know promptly what he had up in his sleeves. She even said, "Your play with suspense is killing us. Look at the face of dear Gul Meher, agonized and fretted beyond all comprehension."

Seeing life in various perspectives in war and peace as well influenced by the Leader, Shahram gracefully responded to that assertion of Gul Bahar. He asked both of them to take seats opposite to him, a proposition to read their minds and reactions better. That, however, caused unexpected loaded pressures in the minds of both mother and daughter, but they complied without dithering.

After finishing the long and the last sip with sounds of escape, Shahram jovially said, "It is nothing about us or anything said or indicated by the postmaster. However, the subject of the last part of our postlunch discussion was such that both of us are emotionally tangled." That statement alone relieved the two ladies present, particularly Gul Meher as glee emitting from her eyes and facial reactions were testifying.

Shahram then detailed all those said by Areem and touched upon his most chanciest and equally undefined journey endeavor to meet the Leader. He then said, "Being aware of my access to and close relationship with the Leader, he almost begged of me for help to fulfill his most harbored yearning since destiny has brought him to the doorstep of final encounter." He concluded by saying, "I am at a fix now. What to do? I am convinced that Areem is a good person, but that is not enough from security perspectives. We cannot take a chance. But equally to disappoint a nice and committed person like Areem is ethically incongruous. In the melee of such thought, I, against my will, remained noncommittal but assured him of due help. That was the reason why I was laden the whole evening and very much wanted to seek your view. Now, the ball is in your court. Help me in taking a proper decision, which should be both practical and prudent."

Gul Bahar, consistent with her personal traits and traditional behaviors, was prompt in saying, "You have a better idea about the inherent implications. You have all along been loyal to the Leader. You know the postmaster better. So you are the best person to assess various options. We will always be supportive of whatever you decide."

But that was not the case with Gul Meher. She thought a while and looked at her father straight, observing, "While returning from school one day in the periphery of the refugee camp, serving both the camp and adjacent community's children, I saw a small gathering of ladies exchanging loud words on some alleged lumpy behavior of two identified young fellows. As rage was steaming up, Rizia Khala suggested, 'Instead of taking decision based on hearsays, it would be better to determine facts first regarding what was said, what words were used, whether this was a first-time occurrence, and so on. Only then can the concerned party take a good decision. Emotional backlash of apparent pugnacious decision may as well be the reason for capricious ramifications subsequently.'"

Gul Meher continued, saying, "That was an eye-opener for me even at that stage of life. I always, in my own limited field, practiced seeking inkling from other angles before coming to a conclusion with respect to the main issue and silently thanked Rizia Khala for those words and guidance."

Having said so, she exchanged looks with her parents to assess their reactions to what she alluded so far even if not directly relevant. Gul Bahar's reaction was a shallow one as she was not used to this type of discourse. She noticeably did not like having such a lecture from her daughter.

Shahram nonetheless was amused by the tenor of Gul Meher's initiations and was expectantly waiting as to what she had to say in response to his dilemma on the matter.

Without wasting time, she straightway told her father that to help in taking a decision, he should have clarity about the motive of the postmaster. In elaborating her point, Gul Meher said "You should revisit your interactions and conversations with the postmaster over the preceding months and identify answers to pertinent questions such as whether he ever made direct or indirect queries about the Leader, his disagreements with the Taliban, what you do and your role in current confrontation, or any other matter that would give indication of a hidden agenda. If the answers to most or all such questions are negative, then you can mostly conclude about his innocence."

Shahram was pleasantly surprised by that thought-provoking response and was very happy. He called Gul Meher to be by his side and blessed her by putting his hand on her head, still holding the tasbih that was given by her a while back. He blessed her, keeping his eyes closed, a conventional way of conveying love, good wishes, and invocations.

In subsequent meetings, Shahram guardedly advised Areem about his affirmative decision and likely efforts, keeping other matters like possible date, venue, arrangements, etc. imprecise.

Areem was doing his routine office work, expecting Shahram to show up soonest with positive news. But he was not there to be while two mails for his household remained undelivered. As it never happened in the past, Areem became apprehensive. He decided to visit Shahram's house, about whose location he had good impression as identified by Shahram to him while visiting one of his ailing support colleague in the Changaram Hospital. His justification for the planned visit was premised on ostensible excuse for the delivery of pending mails.

That thought was acted upon the following Friday at late noontime when the surroundings tend to be quiet being a weekend, especially after pious *jumu'ah* congregation.

Similar to many houses of the area, Shahram's house too had a modest mud wall, ensuring privacy within. The only entry had a usual hanging-type curtain made of indigenous dry vegetation.

Areem, feeling somewhat embarrassed, positioned himself near the entry point, making himself partly visible within the norm of decency. He started calling the name Shahram Tajik loudly.

After repeated calls, an assured female voice responded in a language with possible mix of Tajik and Dari, but Areem was unclear about the substance of the response. To introduce himself, Areem just started saying, "I am the postmaster of Bazarak." He could hardly finish what he wanted to say when a surprised and thrilled Gul Meher, forgetting all sense of propriety, came out spontaneously as if she were waiting for him. Traditional local burden of diffidence soon overtook that sudden burst of startling response, and she partially covered her face. She quickly took a few steps back and positioned herself behind the makeshift curtain even though she was still partly visible.

Areem, in little Urdu and broken Dari, resumed saying, "Your house has two mails, but Janab Shahram Tajik did not visit me for many days. So I am here to deliver the letters as well as to check on his well-being."

With ease and directness, to the incredulity of Areem, Gul Meher said, "My father, a very considerate individual, has the habit of being away from home occasionally without indication, and he would seldom open his mouth either to apologize or to explain the reason. My mother is used to it, and I am slowly getting acquainted."

Saying those words, Gul Meher speedily realized that perhaps she was talking more than required. Premising on that realization, Gul Meher extended her hand beyond the vegetable curtain for the letters. That perhaps was too much for Areem. The innocuous hand gesture by Gul Meher added a punch to the ingenuity of Areem.

The skin tone of the hand, the semblance of faded henna, the shape and size of fingers with flawless manicuring even in the rural setting of Jangalak village made Areem stationary for a while.

Taking advantage of the momentary motionless mien of Areem, Gul Meher had a full look at him through the worn-out openings of the vegetable curtain. She was happy for having the opportunity to see the person who was the center of discussion in her father's recent discourses with the family.

It surprisingly had an involuntary dent in the mind of Gul Meher too. She was pleased with what she had seen and started liking his manners and way of talking in that limited time.

In order to get out of that rousing but equally awkward locale, Gul Meher had twin reflexes: she stirred her already extended hand, simultaneously saying, "Letters, please." Areem promptly handed over the letters, having inadvertently touched the palm of Gul Meher. Embarrassed, he hastily left the venue, equally feeling happy for the touch.

Observing the prompt retreat of a panicky person, the poised and confident Gul Meher maneuvered the dry vegetable curtain to move that aside and had a full look at the departing figure. She laughed loudly and then ran to tell the mother about the sudden visit by the postmaster to deliver letters as Father did not visit him for quite a few days.

At her mother's behest, Gul Meher started reading the letters from her uncle audibly, and her excitement bounced with each additional sentence she encountered. In substance, the letters carried positive news of her uncle's application for his extended family's immigration to the USA. The US immigration requirements were relaxed in this case as the family was closely identified with past governments having pro-US tint and their continued living in Afghanistan was susceptible to unforeseen risks and associated perils. That, of course, included Gul Meher and her mother too as dependents.

On his part and once out of the sight, Areem decelerated his walking speed and started evoking with a mystic feeling the sudden touch experienced with Gul Meher's hand while handing over the letters. He repeatedly put his left hand on the inner side of his right palm as if he were trying to hold the touch there. He was likewise thrilled by the limited exposure of Gul Meher while awaiting the delivery of the letters. That was overwhelming enough to disturb his sleep the following two nights.

Areem's engrossed thoughts centering around Gul Meher—her attitude, aptitude, mannerism, likes and dislikes, and more about her feelings for him, if any—kept him awake at night. His only recourse in that aloneness was a reference book on Afghanistan he recently bought from an old bookstore. But he lacked both interest and eagerness to read it as he had the impression that he knew most pertinent things about the country. Undoubtedly, his thoughts and phantasm concerning Gul Meher were other impediments.

In that mind-set, he was flipping the pages of the book to pass time when his attention was drawn to a section of writing detailing authoritatively that Afghanistan was the root and origin of various faiths, philosophies, and practices before Islam's presence beginning about the seventh century. He was astounded to know that various segments of Afghanistan were the sediments of Zoroastrianism as was in the northeast, paganism in the south and the east, Buddhism in the southeast, and Hinduism dominating in and around Kabul or Logar.

Areem was amazed in visualizing Afghans having the bearings of a preacher, walking through the villages and settlements of this rugged terrain, carrying the message of peace, conservation, sustenance, justice, and so on compared to their current profile characterized by carrying of arms and penchant for revenge, intolerance, and social injustices including gender disparity, most of which are in the name of religion.

Shahram reappeared in his family milieu on the third day of Areem's visit and was visibly happy. Following past practice, he refrained from talking about his absence. The family, seeing him happy and healthy, did not have any specific query, knowing that he would open up in due course. The family had emotional pressure to share the contents of letters delivered by the postmaster but refrained, taking time first to know where he had been so long.

Gul Meher, in consultation with her mother, decided to wait for typical postdinner relaxing dialogue and concentrated in making a feast both as a reflection of Shahram's safe return and the good news contained in Karachi letters.

That was acted upon. As Gul Meher jovially was approaching her father with his night chai, Shahram amusingly commented, "What happened during my absence to make our daughter so happy?" At this point, Gul Bahar interjected, saying, "Since the day of your banishment without any indication, we used to have an argument each day concerning you. In response to my agony and trepidation, our daughter would always maintain that you, by the grace of Allahpak, were safe and must be engaged in doing something sensible and virtuous. She is taunting me with respect to that avowal since your return."

She continued, saying, "There were two letters from *bhaijan* [dear brother]. As you were not visiting the postmaster, he was concerned and came to our place three days back to check on you and hand over the mails.

As read out by our daughter, both the letters relate to our immigration to the USA along with *bhaijan*'s immediate family."

Gul Meher supplemented, "Our dependent status has also been approved. So the main obstacle is behind us."

Shahram suddenly became tense and serious. He said, "Betty, you were born in Karachi and mostly grew up there. So your attachment to Bazarak—and, for that matter, in greater context Panjshir—is obviously peripheral. I understand that. However, the pervasive rain, sleet, snow, slush, and ice together with periodical blue sky, snow-clad mountaintops, and enchanting greeneries of the valley for me are what I am and where I belong to. So while I am happy for your immigration possibility with occasional visits either way, I would prefer to stay back to serve this land."

For a less-loquacious individual like Shahram, that was a long and thought-laden statement. He always expressed his views in bare-minimum words while giving rapt attention to what all others were saying. Shahram was like a wonk inhabiting Afghanistan thousands of years back. A combination of these perhaps was the reason why Ahmad Shah Massoud liked and trusted him so much.

That does not mean that Shahram was a standoffish person. In the private setting of the family, he never failed to applaud his loving daughter. Likewise, he seldom missed an opportunity to tease and needle his wife, of course devoid of any malice. In the close circuit of friends and political workers, he was rated highly for his genuineness and candor.

The above backdrop even compelled an acquiescent wife like Gul Bahar to voice her own position for the first time. Scaling out of her usual reposed attitude, she opened up, saying, "For this world and the world hereafter, you are my identity, my life, my band, and my destiny. You can't just say that I should be in the USA and you would be here by yourself. I did not initially object as I wanted the process to make progression. So when time comes, I will talk to *bhaijan*. You do not worry about that."

Gul Meher was pleased not for what the mother had just said but for the poised way she asserted her position. Shahram wondered how and to what extent a mixed exposure could change and enhance the personality of an individual. Years of living in Karachi refugee camp among divergent tribes and groups shaped up Gul Bahar in a way totally unfamiliar to him. Of course, it could be the other way around too. Fortunately, that did not happen.

Shahram avoided rooting about positive feelings concerning what Gul Bahar had just said. He thought it prudent not to prolong this specific conversation as time was needed at the end of all involved to assess available choices and decide accordingly. He just thought it to be opportune to share with the family the positive news he was yearning to share.

Shahram recounted the reason of his sudden absence, saying, "The Leader has decided to give a video interview to a news media in Europe and, for that matter, planned a visit to Panjshir and, more particularly, an unidentified location in and around Bazarak. Our field-level intelligence is dubious about this and strongly suggests that we should convey the related assessment to the Leader with request to cancel the interview. That was the reason I had to leave for Kulob immediately.

"I met him on the evening of the second day. The focus, after an exchange of initial pleasantries, was about on-the-ground situation and status pertaining to resisting the Taliban. I took the immediate opportunity and apprised him about field-level intelligence assessment concerning the proposed video interview.

"He listened carefully and desired to have time to ponder about it. So I had to stay longer than normal. I was called in on the following fourth day and met the Leader alone. He was very calm and pensive at that moment. After contemplating for minutes, laden with apparent deep thought, the Leader, devoid of his usual martial tone, said, 'I have always valued your opinions and mostly acted on your suggestions. However, the present one is causing a dilemma within me. While I respect your assessment, which motivated your unscheduled travel to Kulob, I am sorry to say that perhaps the time is too short to cancel such an important interview, already scheduled for next Sunday, without adverse international media reaction. However, taking serious note of conclusions of local intelligence and your concerns, I will change the venue of the interview to an unidentified place in northeastern Takhar Province to forestall any sabotage. From there, I will come back to Kulob and will briefly visit Bazarak on Friday of the following week."

Getting a clue of the Leader's possible visit to Bazarak soon, Shahram, with all modesty, enunciated the proposal for granting an audience to Areem, predicating his background, objectives, focus, and effort, highlighting the major objective to meet the Leader and get guidance for the future. The Leader trusted whatever Shahram articulated but nonetheless made specific queries from the perspective of security, confidentiality, and commitment.

"In the end, the Leader denoted lunch together after *jumu'ah* of that Friday, to be followed by one hour natter between himself and Areem. The Leader also suggested I should keep a close watch on the movements of Areem from now onward, and the date, time, and venue would never be shared with him in advance.

"I readily agreed and, in showing my gratefulness, bent down, held the hands of the Leader, and kissed them with passion.

"This is beyond my expectation. I am so happy for the outcome. I am engrossed with the thinking of a seemly venue for meeting the postmaster and the apposite way of communicating the good news in view of the nature of the security labyrinth."

There was a momentary lull. Gul Bahar's position was a standard one—something akin to "whatever you think best." Gul Meher had a mixed feeling, inhibited by increasing emotional attachment she was feeling for the postmaster within the restraints of local customs and traditions. To escape from that woofing mood, Gul Meher left the scene, making another cup of chai for the father. That proved to be quite consequential for relaxed thinking.

In blithely handing over the new cup of chai to his father, Gul Meher straightway said, "I think there is a way out complying both with security parameters and local customs. As there can't be any better secure place than this home, and since during his first visit, we did not offer him anything contrary to local tradition that a first-time visitor must have something to eat, you can invite him for dinner at our place tomorrow to outweigh that shortcoming. That responds to both concerns, and you would have solid ground to defend your action if it is so raised in the future."

Shahram was both relieved and happy, but his overarching thought predicating the future of this intelligent daughter perturbed him most. With a half smile vouchsafing his concealed pride and outward happiness, Shahram stood up, took slow steps toward Gul Meher, placed his right hand on her head, and passionately said, "I am unsure about your mother's final decision. But I give you full and unqualified consent to migrate to the USA with only a request that wherever I may be, please keep in touch with Panjshir as much as possible." Shahram then went inside and reclined in his *khatiya* as a prelude to falling asleep.

Gul Meher spent a restless night obsessed by the disjointed thinking about arrangements, menu, service, and so on pertaining to the dinner tomorrow. The unqualified consent of Father for her migration to the USA was nowhere near her thought process.

Areem was surprised to see Shahram relatively early in the morning in the post office. On first available opportunity, Shahram approached Areem to quietly tell him, "Please do not buy your dinner tonight. We will have it together in my house. I will be back in the afternoon to escort you."

As he looked at the fading figure of Shahram, awry thoughts got muddled within Areem. He wanted to assess the reason for inviting him for dinner soon after arrival. But the very fact that it would as well be an occasion to see and exchange looks, more than a thousand words, with Gul Meher bolstered his feelings. He concentrated on his official work to finish that on time.

At about the chosen time, Shahram showed up, took his usual seat in the post office, and kept on waiting unwearyingly. Areem said salaam and endeavored to make chai, the regular single-item entertainment for Shahram, which the former had pleasure in preparing and latter had the enjoyment of sipping as a treat.

But that was not the case that afternoon. Seeing Areem standing up to make chai, Shahram softly said, "No tea now. Let us go. We will have chai at our place." That startled Areem. He was entranced by his competing thoughts of why the invitation was so soon after Shahram's return, what motivated Shahram to invite him in his house while he always demonstrated a cautious approach to avoid public antiphon, and what was the hurry to say no to chai, which Shahram always enjoyed.

Once out of post office, both started for the same direction with Shahram taking the lead followed by Areem but maintaining a distance. That was reflective of outwardly low-key relationship in the eyes of others.

As they took the required diversion to get out of the main road, both of them started talking amiably, maintaining the same pace. On reaching the homestead, Areem stopped near the mud wall entrance, which had the usual indigenous dry foliage curtain.

Surprisingly, Shahram did not say anything and just went inside. That made Areem more uneasy. Soon Shahram reappeared and invited Areem inside the mud wall, saying, "My family had no idea when we will show up. So I went first inside in a haste to see the state of preparedness. Gul Meher has done everything so diligently that my concern was totally redundant."

Both of them sat at the two ends of the same charpoy kept in the courtyard with their feet dangling. The only other furniture item was a service table in between them. Few yards away, Gul Bahar and Gul Meher were busy in giving finishing touches to the dinner to be served. While the mother was preparing for the dinner service, the daughter, sitting opposite an emblazed clay stove, was apparently in charge of cooking.

There were many perceptible commonalities between the two: type, design, and preferences for clothing; sitting stances; and eluding any form of eye exchanges. But there was a noticeable deviation.

To Areem's incredulity, the mother, cognizant of liking of both the guest and host, approached the charpoy reservedly, holding a rustic tray with two shaking cups of chai. Shahram introduced her as "my wife." Her immediate reaction was to lengthen her head scarf as a sign of modesty.

And after a follow-on silence, Shahram, surprisingly though, pointed to the other and said, "She is Gul Meher, our daughter and the only child presently after the sad demise of our son, Bazrak."

On hearing her name, Gul Meher turned her head to position her face toward the father, lengthened a little her dupatta, and raised her right palm a little, signifying a formal way of conveying salaam in silence.

That openness was ignored by Shahram but caused equal delight and agony to Areem. He was happy in having a facial view of the young lady whose identity for him so far was the name except for a glimpse during his earlier visit to deliver the letters. With the instant experience, he now could relate the name with the person. That was his delight.

Since Gul Meher was sitting a long time facing the emblazed clay stove fired by dry wood in the midst of shifting valley winds, the skin tone of her face became visibly reddish with a tint of pink; an obvious emblem of stress and hotness was visible. Within himself, he felt embarrassed.

The chai-sipping milieu provided a much-desired opportunity for Shahram to detail what he wanted, while Areem was a bit confused and apprehensive. On his first point, Shahram was frank and upright. He said, "You must be wondering about our decision to invite you home so soon after my return. During my absence, you visited our home but had to leave without partaking in any sweet or food. That was contrary to our culture. Betty Gul Meher felt ashamed. So I decided to invite you immediately to mend that slide."

He took another sip, holding casually the chai service bowl with both hands, while Areem impishly exchanged an emotion-laden inquisitive eye contact with Gul Meher. He was mostly oblivious of the background being explained by Shahram. Two focuses of Areem at that moment were to have as much glimpse of Gul Meher as possible within acceptable propriety and to reenact in thinking his grandfather's first encounter with Grandma Purnima in the civil hospital of Calcutta. It was just not excitement but in-depth passion reminiscing the feelings of his grandpa. For a moment, Areem could identify himself with his grandpa; all he learned about him was from the diary of Grandma. Momentarily, though, Areem was in a different world.

That deviated but basically affable mood was soon shaken upon hearing the name of Ahmad Shah Massoud in the follow-on singular utterance of Shahram. That was not intentional on the part of Shahram. In confusion predicating the appropriate window for the introduction of the hidden objective, Shahram just jumbled. Uttering the name of Ahmad Shah Massoud without link or reference was the outcome of that quagmire. Areem continued to look at Shahram with all twinkle.

Shahram closed his eyes, both to escape and to create a space for renewed thinking. He then repeated what he told Gul Bahar and Gul Meher earlier in explaining his unexpected absence.

Areem was dumbfounded by the turn of events. It was so sudden, so positive, and so rewarding. In expressing gratitude, he was in tears.

Shahram had no second thoughts about the sincerity of Areem. The spontaneous tears were another proof of his earnestness. He placed his fatherly hand on the shoulder of Areem and said, "It is okay."

As Gul Bahar delicately placed the dinner items on the rudimentary service table, both Shahram and Areem repositioned themselves at the opposite rear ends of the charpoy with their feet folded.

Continuing his narrative, Shahram said, "The Leader has reposed his trust and faith in me. The turn is mine now to live up to inherent responsibility and trust. I will not tell you in advance where and when our meeting would take place. For the sake of flexibility and to avoid suspicion, I have arranged it on any upcoming Fridays, and you are to be always prepared to accompany me at a short notice. Meanwhile, you are not to talk about this with anyone including myself. I will minimize my contact with you after tonight but will keep a close watch on you. You will never be out of my sight until we meet the Leader."

Gul Meher noticed the excitement within and the ostensive impact of that on food intake of Areem, even though from a distance. She whispered something to her mother.

In serving a freshly baked tandoori naan, Gul Bahar noisily said, "You are not allowing the beta to eat. Please concentrate on eating, and you can talk later on."

Shahram was embarrassed. He devoted subsequent time and made specific efforts to ensure that Areem ate properly.

For Areem, eating had become secondary in the looming possibility of meeting the Leader. His hunger suddenly withered away. The only factor that enabled him to visibly swallow food was the person engrossed with cooking. Areem, even in the midst of serious talking, exchanged acquiescing glints with Gul Meher; and that carried him through the evening gleefully.

A clearer sight of the physical profile of Gul Meher, exchanges of casual glances with her, and his eating in the family space of the homestead made the evening an enchanting one; and the imminent prospect of meeting the Leader, a much-esteemed yearning of him, was the icing on the cake. But that was too copious to absorb in one go and in his situation. The delight of that evening turned into a happy anxiety at night for Areem.

Pressing thoughts of divergent nature, bewilderments, and tenuous expectations marred the peace of mind initially, triggering strange postures in the bed. Much-desired sleep with expectations of sweet dreams was tenuous. As the night progressed, his eyes were wide open, causing more disjointed reflections.

Areem determinedly tried to brush such stray thoughts temporarily under the rug. He concluded that the subjects and tone of his proposed meeting with the Leader would entirely depend on him. His own role would be that of a genuine listener with needed clarifications sought during the process. Areem also cautioned himself in not trying to read too many things pertaining to the dinner tonight, which unpredictably provided an opportunity to meet the family of Shahram.

To take him out of the current scenery, Areem decided to think of his grandpa's initial dilemma in harnessing sensitivity toward his grandma. A casual approach from out of sheer desperation yielded positive upshots. Similarities dazed Areem.

In acting on his thought, Areem closed his eyes and revisited the pertinent words and lines of Grandma's related notations in her diary. Since he read that diary many a time to absorb what were written and what were implied, most of the contents were fresh in memory.

Based on recollections, Areem recalled his grandpa's life journey some of which were: isolated childhood; no real link with and pressure from the family for excellence; similarity of Bengal with Burma in terms of topography, which he liked on the first sight; and care, sincerity, and evident expression of love for Purnima grandma. The negatives—such as race, language, and faith-related identity—serious in terms of repercussions, were overcome because of the sheer commitment of both for a loving conjugal life.

Grandma penned the following in detailing rationale for her decision to get converted to Islam without any pressure from Grandpa. She observed, "One needs to premise his or her love based on obvious limitations. Then, decide whether you are in or out. Love, in essence, is a one-way traffic. Rarely, it can be mutual. You love one as he or she is irrespective of positive or negative qualities. It is unfitting to delink love from emotion and view that as a commodity. To do that way is barter, not love."

Relating himself with his grandpa's conditions against the backdrop of his grandma's assertion, Areem made a resilient conclusion, backing a very blissful future relationship with Gul Meher. After many hours, he was in a relaxed mood. He straightened his feet and played with his hands blithely.

Moments later, and quite unexpectedly, a thought smacked him, damping his short-lived happiness. That particular condition was not relevant in his grandparents' decision-making process. But it definitely was being seen as a major impediment in Areem's case. Grandpa's pension from the British Army and grandma's professional competence as a trained nurse assured them of steady income. But that was absent in his case, besides being too young and being in a state of swinging academic objectives and pursuits. The issue is how he would sustain the family.

The exuberant but poignantly composed Areem soon felt frozen and fidgety in that lonely accommodation. He continued to focus on the container with leftover food through shades of light. That was prepared by Gul Meher at the end of the dinner and passed on to him via Shahram with an exchange of looks full of alertness and attachment.

Areem thought through the unexpected events that shaped his life and impacted its journey during past few months. To his utter surprise, Areem concluded of being a pawn maneuvered by some invisible hands. Few months back, he had no idea about leaving Bangladesh; and had no inkling about the place called Panjshir. He definitely had theological preferences but never excoriated any other faith or way of life; and he never thought of working in a place like Panjshir where Muslims were fighting Muslims.

During such process of self-examination, Areem started talking to himself, more for poise and mental peace. He maintained, "I had no hand in the decision to be located in Bazarak. The son of Shahram died much before my arrival on the scene. Shahram's visible fondness for me was not a goaded one. Gul Meher's ostensible pliability is perhaps the most logical outcome for one born and brought up in an urban setting and now trapped in a limited sphere of a resettlement in Bazarak." He went further in thinking and instituting an outward similarity among the framework of events that decided the course of life of his grandpa and that, as it appeared, was going to chart the way of his life.

For a moment, a bemused thought crept in mind, *Is it Grandpa?*

That thought came to a predictable halt with the traveling dulcet *azaan*, the religious call for Muslims to get up and say early morning prayer known as *fajr*.

Areem got up out of sheer desperation caused by not having any sleep and opened one of his windows. He continued standing in the same position, enjoying each bit of early morning inflow of subtle, sweet, and fresh breeze. Areem had no idea that flow of such air had a fragrance of its own. He was enjoying that experience in a standstill position.

Soon his attention was calibrated to visible snow-capped mountain crests slowly unfolding themselves with the plodding vaporization of morning mist. That became all the more enchanting with the dancing rays of early morning sunlight making its emergence through the copious peaks in the eastern horizon.

In that unique serene setting premised on the sweet and melodious vibrating sound of *azaan* and enthralling shifting sunrays conforming static posture of numerous mountain peaks, Areem quickly made a resolution about his life. He promised to himself that come what may, he would take charge of his life from now on. Respecting the divinity involved in the process, he would no more be a pawn but a party in deciding his life's journey.

Areem also concluded that his appreciation for Gul Meher had been predicated by Shahram's frequent mentioning about her. He unknowingly developed an attachment for her. He slowly became interested in her, gently harboring feelings for her and, after having a cursory glance to her physical self, started liking her. All these seemed to be ordained. Now he would take command of that irrespective of challenges. By gestures and actions, he would convey his love for her as Grandpa did. And this position would be irreversible, whatever the future glitches and challenges would be. He made a solemn promise in this regard, keeping the early morning dew, the snow-clad mountain peaks, and the rising sun as watchers. Areem felt at ease, retired to bed, and had a comforting morning nap before going to work.

Shahram showed up as usual in the post office. While serving chai to his honored guest, Areem whispered, saying, "Last night's food was very good. I had defaulted in conveying my honest and sincere appreciation to your wife and Gul Meher. So I will be going to your place this evening after office hours, will have a cup of chai, and will take the opportunity to thank them for last night's dinner and their taking care of me." Shahram kept quiet with no discernible antiphon. He finished the chai and quietly left. That confused Areem very much.

After closing the office in the afternoon, Areem went to market and bought a very trendy dupatta of golden-yellow shade to make Gul Meher's red-pinkish complexion more vivacious. To deflect attention of others, he also bought two local hand towels, soap, matches, etc. and returned to the office to store the additional items. He then nicely packed the dupatta and carried it discreetly under his chador while walking toward Shahram's house.

From a distance, Areem could identify Shahram as having a slow walk in the periphery of his home. Areem writhed an unpredictable jolt, and the resultant negativity engulfed him again. He started questioning himself: Was Shahram's leaving the post office this morning without a word after he proposed the instant visit—or his sort of being around the house presently—a sign of reluctance to receive him? He paused a while. Recalling last night's thoughts and solemn promise, Areem resolutely decided to pursue the course to see for certain where and how it would end.

Being near Shahram with dithering, Areem was taken aback. Shahram took steps to welcome him with a broad smile and two extended hands for warm embrace as per local customs. After the embrace, Shahram unleashed himself, saying, "Both Gul Meher and her mother chided me for not responding to your proposition and leaving the workplace silently. I was thus unsure whether you would come at all. My sense of desperation brought me here with probable chance to face the reality upfront."

Shahram further said, "My visiting your office this morning had a specific objective. On receipt of an early morning message as to schedule your meeting with the Leader, I could not wait. So I went to the post office to invite you to our place this afternoon for a one-on-one discussion. However, when you indicated your plan to be in our place around the time I had in mind, I was confused. I had all along been thinking: How you could know the timing I had in mind? Are you working through another intermediary? Similar questions and possibilities winked in my mind. To me, the matter is of trust, and any breach of that has insuperable insinuations. Panjshirian values and traditions are very firm about it. So I was flummoxed. It was betty Gul Meher who prevailed upon me for confidence and patience. She said that if the postmaster shows up in the afternoon, then nothing is to be worried about, and prevalent notions and disquiets would be proven to be wrong. I agreed with her assertion and proposition. As time was not passing, I was in a restless state of mind. In that backdrop, I am here as if my standing outside will hasten your arrival." He laughed atypically.

Areem held Shahram's right hand with due reverence, a symbolic act assuring him about his continued credulity. Once inside, they were seated on the charpoy, while Gul Bahar took her usual place between the charpoy and the kitchen area. Gul Meher was sitting with full pause and alertness as if guarding and safekeeping the lone clay stove were her pivotal responsibility. Seeing them taking respective sitting positions on the charpoy, Gul Meher, who kept a kettle ready with water, engaged herself in repeated efforts to emblaze the indigenous wood strips as a prelude to making water hot and preparing chai. She neither felt embarrassed for taking a long time in igniting the clay stove nor looked back unpretentiously as she did last evening. The latter made Areem dejected.

He was trying to analyze that change internally while outwardly explaining reasons for present visit to Shahram. In a voice of sufficient high pitch, Areem said, "Last afternoon, and in your home, I defaulted on two counts. That caused a lot of disquiet as well as wakefulness last night. So I planned to be in your home once again to redress those failings. First, it is customary in Bangladesh that whenever one eats in another's abode, special thanks are needed to be conveyed to the lady of the house before leaving. I did not do it to your wife. That was against the teachings and noble traditions with which I grew up. Second, when someone special like Gul Meher prepares food, a matching gift needs to be given to her as per our family practices. I could not do that as I was not prepared. That was the cause of anguish within me. Before coming today, I went to the market and bought a fancy dupatta for her. If it is okay with you, I want to present it to her as copious expression of thanks."

As Areem was about to continue the oration, he was taken aback upon seeing Gul Meher walking confidently toward them with chai in a tray. That mien had no semblance of dithering shown by mother last evening. She first offered the chai to her father and then to Areem with ease and pause as normally as it could be. She kept on waiting to be sure that the preparation was okay in terms of mix and match of milk and sugar. During the entire process, she wore a partial head cover with a portion of her sinuous dupatta covering a part of her face as a gesture of modesty. This she delicately maintained by holding a segment of the dupatta's flowing borderline between her lips.

What Areem narrated evidently relieved Shahram. Taking advantage of that genial reaction, Areem said with all politeness in his grasp, "If you are agreeable, I would like to present it to Gul Meher for excellence in cooking. I have no one in life to give a present. So please consider that."

Shahram congenially nodded and conveyed to Gul Meher by physical sign that she could take it. Gul Meher, placing the tray on the charpoy, instantly extended her hand but quickly withdrew them out of coyness. She then almost snatched the package from Areem's hand, held it near her chest with two hands in crossed position, and ran to the inner quarters. Observing that innocent response, Shahram commented, "Notwithstanding her intelligence and alertness, she still remains a child within." Areem, being extremely pleased with the turn of events, made a supporting comment, "Let her be what she is. That will bring happiness in life."

After that stress-relieving discourse, Shahram started detailing pressing matters he had in mind. Moving himself closer to Areem to ensure secrecy, he said, "Your date and time for meeting the Leader have all been finalized. The Leader will now have his TV interview on next Tuesday, and he would meet you after *jumu'ah* on the following Friday. The place and other logistic arrangements are not to be discussed. I will come to your place around noon of the ensuing Friday, and both of us will have our travel to the destined location. This is what I wanted to convey to you, and that was the reason why I was in your place this morning."

The news of scheduled meeting and much-desired audience with the Leader so soon were beyond expectation of Areem. He stood up impulsively, bent his head, held the right hand of Shahram by his two hands, and kissed it with due veneration after raising it diligently. All Areem did was to express his gratefulness and fidelity. Excitement for him was so pungent that he even found it difficult to sit. Shahram was impressed beyond doubt about the commitment and sincerity of the young fellow from Bangladesh.

Once out of sight, and being positioned in the cozy setting of the inner court, Gul Meher started gently cuddling the dupatta. She was having a feel of indirect contact of the person whom she not only adored but also longed to see. She sensed a link, an attachment, a contact. That, to her, had the moods of embracing Areem in absentia. The reaction pertaining to the gift was more intense than usual. Being born and growing up in a refugee camp, she never had a gift from anyone except the father.

Gul Meher controlled the sudden burst of amazing feelings. She calmed down and took guarded steps outside, being unsure about others' reaction to her snatching of dupatta and running away.

Stepping out, she was taken aback by the sudden serenity of the setting, which was full of exuberance a while back. Seeing Areem in a standing position, Gul Meher concluded that he was about to leave. Deviating from traditional practices and norms, she drew the attention of her mother loudly to reach each all sets of ears, saying, "*Ammi* [mother], why don't you request him to have dinner with us? Whatever we have, much better than what he has at his home, we will share. Also, we, on our part, forgot to serve dessert of kalkool-e-fuqara [milk and almond pudding] last night, which we especially prepared for him. We should also have a chance to redress that."

There was no further conversation on the proposition of Gul Meher. To the utter delight of Areem, that demonstrated the sway this young girl had over her family, more importantly on her father, a jihadi of good standing and repute. Areem really liked that sort of command and communication even though he himself lacked that.

Her mother moved to help Gul Meher in dinner-related chores. Shahram slightly reclined on the charpoy while discussing about external perceptions concerning policies and priorities of the Taliban government. Areem very blithely responded by taking his seat. He was feeling elated at being considered one of the family and was euphoric because of the directness and congeniality of Gul Meher. None of these he ever had in his life in Bangladesh. Areem's inclination to bond with this family and with Panjshir started growing stronger.

The ensuing night, after the unexpected positivity on all scores of the afternoon, was a perfect setting for a sound sleep; but Areem experienced difficulties. Flashes of earlier events and homilies continued to cause undue excitement. Notwithstanding efforts to the contrary, the eyes were open.

In the midst of such restlessness, Areem amusingly recalled what Gul Meher alluded in stirring him to take additional helping of kalkool-e-fuqara. While observing that Areem was about to quit savoring of pudding, Gul Meher said, "This fuqara has been prepared with a lot of love of Mother and by astute attention of the cook. Moreover, taking fuqara, as our seniors believe, stimulates sleep at night. An additional helping will not do any harm." With that premise, both Shahram and Areem acted promptly, having a spoonful of fuqara to the delight of all.

This contemplation and reminiscing of that proved to be very mollifying for Areem. In the process, he fell asleep.

Areem was busy with office work on the following Tuesday, but his mind was preoccupied about the TV interview whose time, place, and subject matters were not a public knowledge. Areem was eager to know some of it in preparation for his much-levered audience with the Leader.

Then the bombshell befell. Its initial dubiety and subsequent intensity and impact shattered and shocked the world in varied proportions depending on animosity or sympathy for the character involved. It took the world with initial doubt and Afghani people with disbelief. International media and TV outlets continued reporting the assassination of Ahmad Shah Massoud beginning September 10, about a day after its occurrence. The United Front, the Northern Alliance's political face led by Massoud, initially denied the news. Notwithstanding the confusion, sadness overwhelmed the people at large. Panjshir was momentarily stunned. Bazarak Township came to a transitory halt while the skeleton post office was almost frozen. Most business activities were immediately suspended.

The initial denial of the assassination by the Northern Alliance created confusion and uncertainties. International media and TV outlets continued reporting the assassination notwithstanding. That coverage and indigenous local news started trickling down with identifiable sources and details. With extensive coverage based on updated information, the looming doubt was erased. Shops and restaurants remained closed. Roads continued to be deserted. Neither transports nor pedestrians were noticeable. People usually take time in absorbing and accepting unexpected realities. This case was no exception.

In that melee, the lone person approaching the post office that morning was Shahram. The assassination news of Ahmad Shah Massoud was a crushing blow for him to accept and digest.

Shahram slowly stepped in, exchanged salaam without eye contact, and took his seat. As a marked deviation, he sat on the only other chair across the table facing Areem's. Areem diligently noted that Shahram's conceit was in sharp contrast with his typical physical stoutness and past norms. It was, however, obvious to Areem that something very intense was burning within Shahram as was being manifested in subdued tremor, distress, and feeling of defeat. Areem could read his mind and, notwithstanding his own anguish, moved promptly to make his usual chai.

Contrary to others, Shahram was certain from the beginning that it happened exactly the way it was being reported. That was his pain. That was his obvious frustration. His unusual calmness, avoidance of eye contact, closing of eyes frequently, and rolling down of tears through his cheeks, and some onto his blanket, were signs of that.

Both Areem and Shahram were sitting face-to-face, motionless and speechless, while the chai, prepared by the former with care and deference, was getting cold.

Areem, dazed and baffled, was inexact as how to initiate a discussion concerning the mammoth tragedy. Devastated, Shahram was remorseful for lack of effort on his part to dissuade the Leader from having the scheduled interview and was suffering from the self-inflicted blame.

Looking at Areem, Shahram mellifluously observed, saying, "I am sorry for you. The cherished longing of yours to meet him, to learn from him, and to have guidance from him in charting your own life has tragically been snapped suddenly. The more I think about it, the more I blame myself."

Areem was staggered by the stipulated mind-set of Shahram concerning the Leader's assassination and his abortive desire. Mildly objecting, he said, "You should not blame yourself. My desire was an innocuous one irrespective of hardships I suffered and possibly will be suffering in future. The Leader's assassination ought to be part of a master plan. It happened as it was to happen. So please do not blame yourself."

Shahram looked at Areem amorously and continued, saying, "Beta, you would recall my recent unspecified absence from Bazarak. I went to Kulob to meet the Leader, and that ought not to be an ordinary consultation. Our field-level intelligence staff, trained during war with Soviets, monitored the words, movements, and locations of TV team in tandem with broad focus on al-Qaeda and Taliban. Based on information assimilated, the intelligence staff were of firm inference that the crew and journalist, having North African roots, are pretending to be Belgians and appear to be pseudo TV journalists.

"It is most likely that they have ominous intention not known to anyone. That alludes to a potent security risk. The staff were of the firm view that the interview should ideally be canceled or, at the least, be postponed for another time in the future.

"During my long meeting, I explicated the pertinent details to the Leader with submission for revocation or deferral, as he thought appropriate.

"The Leader was very serene. He listened vigilantly—cogitated the relevance of facts, including security aspects, assembled by local intelligence team—and thanked me for bringing those to his attention. Up to that point of discourse, I was very happy thinking of a positive outcome. But that was not to be.

"During that tensed discourse, the Leader kept quiet for some time and decided to perform *asr* before continuing the discussion. In that mini *jamaat*, we were only two, with the Leader performing the role of imam. After finishing the prayer, the Leader exchanged looks with me and, to utter surprise, submitted himself forthwith to a voluntary *sajdah* (prostrating to Allah in the direction of Kaaba at Mecca, a submission done numerous times during daily prayers). He was in that position for a long time.

"Freeing himself from the ritual of *sajdah*, the Leader stood up, moved to the only wooden almirah in the room, and opened it to take out his favorite SMG and *pakol* cap.

"In resuming discussions, the Leader said, 'I trusted you during Soviet invasion with my crusade and life. I always respected your prudence and valued your assessments in spite of your recent retraction from active resistance in our confrontation with al-Qaeda and Taliban. What they are propagating in the name of Islam is contrary to edicts, teachings, and practices of Islam. Al-Qaeda's Islam has created confusion and chaos among the *momins* (believers) with the future evidently bleak and uncertain. This is a situation of a pall and a pox so far as Islam and its coexistence with the rest of the world are concerned. With all previous futile efforts to moderate their extreme interpretation of Islam, we do not have options but to fight them out upfront and intrepidly. It is more relevant in case of Afghanistan as al-Qaeda has its deep roots here, and their leader bin Laden has also chosen our country for his living.'

"The Leader took a break, fondly caressed his SMG, and then said, 'I went to *sajdah* seeking divine guidance pertaining to your proposition for canceling the interview against the backdrop of intelligence outfit's conclusion relating to my security.

"'On the first point, we need to recognize that wars are no more being fought with bullets and barrels only. Media has occupied a vital role in international warfare. Presence in the media is critical to mobilize international public opinion, influence the position, and ensure the support of various governments. We definitely lack on this score.

"'I was thinking about this for a while and waiting for good coverage by a more neutral outlet. The Belgian TV, being an European media orifice, has relatively better international acceptability. So I am keen to avail this opportunity. It will be a mistake for us to miss this opening, more so by rescinding the interview with such a short notice. It can do us more harm internationally while bolstering the image of al-Qaeda, irrespective of its wrongdoing. So I am sorry that I am going to have the interview.'

"The Leader pondered before detailing his position on security concerns. Articulating his related position, the Leader said, 'You would recall our previous analysis and counting of assassination attempts by my adversaries, beginning when I was twenty-two. The first one was made by comrade Hekmatyar along with the ISI of Pakista . Now I am forty-nine. Al-Qaeda, the Taliban, ISI, Soviet KGB, and Afghan communist KHAD made numerous attempts. But I am still alive. I do not fear death. The day I have committed myself to the cause of Allahpak and the faith of Islam, I have written myself off.'

"He continued, saying, 'In our struggle against antagonists, both internal and external, we have reached a phase of confrontation where we consciously need to be little less cautious and less fearful. This ought to be a strategic decision. Apart from that, so long these SMG and *pakol* are with me, no harm will befall on me. The rest is in the hands of Allah.'"

The follow-on focus and expressions of Shahram quickly underwent a weighty transformation with rage and frustration overtaking his usual self. He kept on hoeing like a dog on a bone. Finally, in unleashing himself, Shahram said, "My extant remorse is that while I placed all facts before the Leader, I flopped in insisting on our conclusions. This inner feeling is bothering me as if I failed to act meticulously. But whatever it takes, and even if singlehandedly, I will not rest until I take proportionate revenge. And that will start with on the ground confrontation here in Bazarak with al-Qaeda."

Saying those librettos, he made a startling request, the gravity of which Areem failed to absorb at that moment. Shahram stood to leave, turned back, and said, "Not as a repayment for my love but more as a compassionate gesture, please take care of my family so long as you are here as the postmaster." He left snappily without giving any chance to Areem for comment or concurrence.

Areem had no inkling of the extent and enormity of that irritation until news started to trickle down the following noontime about sporadic wacky actions of Shahram. Areem visited Shahram's house to check on rumored news. Gul Meher, positioning herself on the inner side of mundane mud wall for the sake of modesty in the absence of her father, said, "Father was both agitated and angry . He took out his weapons from the almirah, got his set of tasbih, wrapped them in a chador, and went out just saying that he requested you to take care of us in his absence."

While returning, Areem felt a sense of disarray; his steps became lopsided and sluggish, and his mind was continuously being irritated in gauging what Shahram meant by 'taking care of them.' He sat for a while on a roadside boulder, shrugged off all peeving thoughts, and conditioned himself to act at the right time thoughtfully, always keeping his request in view.

Areem's immediate thought on retiring to bed at night was what motivated Shahram to leave with arms, and where could he go! But the pressing thought centered around the desolate voice and exasperated expressions of Gul Meher notwithstanding efforts to shroud that within the premise of traditional respect. Though restless and uncertain about the future, compounded by the thought of Gul Meher, Areem fell asleep slickly. Perhaps that was due to internal exhaustion caused by distress he was undergoing.

Soon after the post office was opened the following morning, a number of local people swarmed Areem with multiple queries, believing he was aware based on his regular interactions with Shahram. Each one had a different angle of query centering on the common issue of the murder of Bazarak's al-Qaeda chief the night before. To all and every query, Areem had a standard response of being unaware of Shahram's latest whereabouts and activities.

Areem, in his inner self, was just praying and hoping that Shahram was not involved in the murder of last night. He was scared of thinking about the family's future if Shahram was involved or alleged to be involved in this murder. Al-Qaeda, notwithstanding its lack of popular support in Panjshir, was a force to be reckoned with. Areem was scared of thinking about the enormity of al-Qaeda's possible response. He went to bed without having food.

On his travel to workplace the next morning, Areem had a strange feeling about the surroundings. The road was relatively empty. Even pedestrian traffic was less. As he was crossing the boundary of Changaram Hospital, he noticed a small group of people discussing something intensely pressing. He moved closer to the group, and the only audible word he heard was Shahram. That made Areem more nervous.

One of the part-time deputed staff, Moqbul Khan, showed up relatively early that day, markedly bearing interspersed thoughts. He was blunt and told Areem all that he knew. He was authoritative and assertive in saying, "Shahram outmaneuvered local al-Qaeda establishment last night. The mini shura of local al-Qaeda was in cloistered deliberations as a consequence of the assassination of its local amir [man of position] the previous night.

"Shahram, consistent with legendary fame he earned for carrying out effective operations with minuscular support while fighting the Russians, repeated it last night. He had only one aide with him who was used to divert the attention of two al-Qaeda security personnel guarding the shura members. By creatively taking advantage of that diversion, Shahram showed up to the shura place and opened fire. As time was of essence for his operation, Shahram withdrew quickly. While two of the shura members succumbed, one who could recognize Shahram survived. It was his and those of security personnel's narratives that are in the mouth of people traveling fast."

Depressed and baffled, Areem could not think of appropriate actions at his end and at that moment. But Shahram's departing entreat, being heavy on the mind, continued prostrating his concentration. He kept on waiting, hoping for a clue or some news about Shahram.

Areem was constantly debating whether to visit Shahram's house to console the family and to help in any respect based on need. But his vigilant reflex was against that for two reasons. First, it was too early to conclude on Shahram; and second, as he did not interact with anyone from al-Qaeda's side personally in the past, he had no reliable contact point in that camp locally. He argued with himself that his al-Qaeda credential was not enough at the moment because of the unfolding situations. Al-Qaeda followers, being enraged, might look at such visit inimically. The day for Areem passed with mixed feelings of anxiety and nerviness.

Areem fleetingly looked at his single-page calendar provided by the postal department, which he meticulously pasted on the more prominent section of the mud wall of his temporary abode. He marked September 9 with his red ball pen while fondly remembering his deceased mental idol, Ahmad Shah Massoud. Coincidentally, and after about two days, he cursorily looked at his newly acquired mundane wristwatch, and the time was 8:00 p.m. of September 11.

He started feeling hungry mostly due to inadequate ingestion of food in the recent few days because of the unexpected tragic developments all around. Areem moved in a laid-back fashion, lit his gas stove to warm the food he got from the restaurant earlier, and started eating. While the hunger was apparent, he had no yearning or palate to swallow the food. He took longer than usual time to finish eating, more due to frequent diversions in thinking about Gul Meher, her emotional state, and how she was doing.

Precipitous public jubilation outside, more in the periphery of market, unnerved Areem. He hurriedly left for the marketplace. People on the road were congratulating one another with no one having a clear clue of what actually happened. Intermittent loud and orchestrated utterance *Allahu Akbar* (Allah is the greatest) from distance filled the sky in competition with the sound of jubilant blank fires and smell of gunpowder.

Areem continued to be nervous, still unclear of what happened. He concluded this much that it was not something local and had greater implications. So he took an unanticipated turn toward the entrance of Changaram Hospital with conviction to have authentic details as to what happened. He also felt comfortable, as he knew many of hospital staff because of their frequent visits to the post office.

To his utter surprise, a small rudimentary black-and-white television was relaying PTV (Pakistan Television) telecast about multipronged aerial suicidal attacks at the heart of the USA by a group of al-Qaeda mujahids. There were numerous enthusiasts around the TV. People who knew him created space for Areem to have a better view. Areem, with concerns and anxieties bemusing him, observed with intense attention the various aerial attacks on US soils and what CNN, as being relayed by PTV, was reporting. With each of the attacks being shown as part of continuous telecast, the assembled cohorts shouted with full devotion and all intensity, "Allahu Akbar!"

A brilliant inkling suddenly hit Areem's reflex. He swiftly concluded that this euphoria was the most opportune setting to visit Gul Meher and her mother even though the time was not right. He contended with himself. "It is not an ordinary night. Populaces, irrespective of Tajik and al-Qaeda affiliations, are overwhelmed. People, both lettered and unlettered by local standard, have common conclusion about the final success of Islam, as propagated by al-Qaeda. Most people rapidly concluded that Islam has finally won the century-old struggle. The USA has been humbled and is soon to be obliterated by the force of Islam, and time has come for Islam to rule the world according to Sharia."

With that sort of assessment, Areem soon withdrew from the TV audience group, wrapped himself well by his chador to conceal his identity as feasible, and started walking toward Gul Meher's house. During the process, he acted and behaved like an ordinary Bazarakian (resident of Bazarak), nevertheless maintaining the direction of his travel.

Reaching Gul Meher's home escaping public attention was relatively easy for Areem that night but to convey his presence was congruently arduous. Calling Gul Meher loudly would be both indecorous and against established social decorum. He then smartly thought of a communication strategy in which his presence could be conveyed in a neutral way.

Areem looked around and was assured of absence of people around. He then repeatedly called for Shahram by indicating the need of communicating a message from the post office. The tenor of the voice and reference to post office drew the alert attention of Gul Meher. She, accompanied by her mother, came next to the entrance. Before Areem could act, Gul Meher said, "Oh Allah [oh my god], why you are here?" Areem responded by saying that he wanted to be assured of their safety and to ascertain whether he could be of any help to the family.

Gul Meher said, "The imam of the local mosque is a trusted friend of Father. In the past, and in many discomforting situations, he silently looked after us. The community knows about it. So do not worry. If need arises otherwise, I will send imam uncle to you. Now please go. People around are hyper at this moment. Be careful on your return journey." The discussion was snapped off without further exchange.

On his return journey, Areem was overtly happy and outshined locals in expressing happiness while dancing, shouting, hugging, and kissing unknown folks. In his bed, he was relaxed, reminiscing the sweet but concerned voice of Gul Meher. He was happy that even though partially, he could act as per the desire of Shahram.

Areem observed notable changes in approach and attitude among many people known to him. The success of major incursions at the heart of US soil elated al-Qaeda supporters beyond limits and caused conspicuous elements of arrogance among many of them. Contrary to reality of nights before, most other locals, forgetting the divide between Tajiks and Pashtuns, aligned with that enthusiasm and apparently projected each as al-Qaeda supporters.

The local shura of al-Qaeda in Bazarak held an unarranged session, ensuring full compliance with the protocol of secrecy. Two important conclusions of that deliberations were endorsement of report concerning Shahram's singular involvement in recent murders of al-Qaeda seniors and the decision to send a message to Shahram and other Tajik followers of Ahmad Shah Massoud so that such incidents would not be repeated. The objective was to stoke fear among the supporters of Massoud without risking possible erosion of recent unprecedented public support by foolish acts. It was also considered that the present exultation had the right setting for a local response without an antagonistic reaction. Consensus was also reached in that deliberation to send the messages to the community prudently avoiding possible backlash.

A follow-on surgical operation was undertaken on the residential property of Shahram in late hours of the night following the unarranged meeting of the shura. The house was badly damaged. It was done in a way to cause maximum inconvenience to the family. The two female residents were not hurt by design.

The community members as well as imam of the mosque showed up once the operation was over. There were many expressing initial empathy and concern, but no one was forthcoming to extend immediate needed material help, including that of shelter for the two ladies. It was obvious that community members were in a state of mental oscillation. The imam volunteered to take them to his home temporarily and requested the presence of community elders at a consultative discussion in the mosque after *zuhr.*

By and large, people present were loyal and sympathetic to Shahram but uncertain about the position of Tajik leadership. The immediate feeling was a sense of despair and uncertainty about how any compassionate support would be viewed by the emboldened al-Qaeda. This was aggravated by trickle-down news of movement of reinforcements, both men and weapons, from Kabul aiming at Bazarak in response to the assassination of its local leaders. Possible decisions were weighed with caution and concern.

So were the deliberations of the meeting after *zuhr.* All present were expressly caring but detached in offering needed help. Finally, and in consultation with the ladies of the house, decision was taken to relocate them in Gul Bahar's parental home. The upscale nature of that habitation, the affluence and influence enjoyed by the family in the past, the reputation and connection of the present owner though living in Karachi presently for business purpose, and consequential safety element were all pertinent factors in taking that decision. Everybody agreed with that.

The taking of the aforesaid decision was easier for the community because of the brother's known and open embrace of his sister, who was initially exorcised from the family for marrying Shahram.

Imam Shaheeb took an additional step to give cogency to that decision. He sent a messenger to bring Kazi Shaheeb of the neighboring settlement. The uniqueness of Kazi Shaheeb's social stature and the base of close relationship with Shahram and family were not clear to many. But he always exercised considerable influence on Shahram's family and always obliquely looked after the family whenever Shahram went periodically missing. The community was aware of this, and hence Kazi Shaheeb's endorsement mattered.

While the designated elders and community members accompanied the ladies to Gul Bahar's parental home with basics of life and living, Imam Shaheeb proceeded toward the post office.

Sitting on his chair in the post office loaded with fickle information about what happened last night, Areem was biting his nails, monitoring his time to close and visit Gul Meher and her mother to assess what he could do or how he could help.

Right at that moment, Imam Shaheeb entered, introduced himself briefly, and informed Areem about the community's decision to house Gul Bahar and daughter in the former's parental home until Shahram returned.

He also made one point clear: the community had sent a special messenger to Karachi to apprise Gul Bahar's brother of the local situation and about the community's decision to relocate Shahram's family in his ancestral home. As a reticent person, Imam Shaheeb immediately withdrew, keeping Areem undetermined about his roles and responsibilities.

That unfettered contemplation did not overshadow Areem's other reflections. He was engrossed in thoughts concerning how and in what manner destiny was playing with him! His yearning to talk to Gul Meher and see her had precipitously transformed into a reality now that they would be sharing the same compound. He had an implicit obligation to take care of her, including her mother. Notwithstanding his ardent contract a few nights before with himself that he would to take command of his life's journey, Areem reconciled with reality in which both luck and command play equal role in shaping a life. Reflecting on the mercy of Allahpak, Areem decided to act based on present requisites and leave the consequences to destiny.

Stepping out of the post office, one thought prevailed pronouncedly in Areem's mind. That pertained to initial hassle Gul Meher would be facing in the new setting with respect to cooking. He went to his usual *chaikhana* and ordered more-than-normal intake of food, both in terms of quantity and variety. The shopkeeper had an inquiring look. Areem smiled and said, "I am expecting some guests suddenly."

Bond

On reaching his place, Areem straightway went to the main house and knocked at the door using the chain hoist. Gul Meher was busy activating a makeshift brick-based cooking facility and was oblivious of Areem's effort to draw their attention. After a while, he banged on the door.

Gul Meher was stunned at hearing the sound of banging on the door and rapidly approached the entry point while simultaneously wiping her face to neutralize the effect of smoke. Opening the door, she was taken aback at seeing Areem standing with packets of food. She exclaimed, saying, "Oh Allah, it is you!"

"Are you expecting someone else?" quipped Areem. Such a jibe could not unnerve the bright and poised Gul Meher, who behaved and reacted all throughout naturally, notwithstanding the proximity of her sudden present relocation. The skin tone of her face, however, had undergone an involuntary shade change; and that received the full attention of Areem.

In handing over the packets containing food, Areem said, "This unexpected change is traumatic for you both, but the emotional stress is more on you. You lived most of your life in a refugee camp. And now you have been thrown out of your own home. We could not do anything. This is a small gesture in sharing your agony. You take this food, have a nice rest and sleep, and tomorrow morning, with a new dawn, you can plan your way, including having a nice clay cooking facility."

Gul Meher, without any wavering, accepted the packets, exchanged an amorous look, covered a part of her face with the dupatta as a symbolic manifestation of shyness, and said *shukria* while closing the door.

Areem had initial appalling reflex on hearing about the demolition of Shahram's residence. The inability to protest, or at the least, the absence of space to vent agonizing emotions swarmed within his inner self acutely. The possibility of relocation of Gul Meher and the mother within the same compound was beyond his wildest imagination. The news of their relocation, as told by Imam Shaheeb, did not only provide relief but equally had an intensely compelling sense of respite within his cognizance. It was not only that. This community decision was possibly the best one based on the social standing of Shahram and family. It also enabled the family to keep their head high in an adverse situation as the need for dependence on others was neutralized.

With that mooring in related comfort level, Areem enthusiastically sat on his charpoy to have dinner. The divine orientation that caused Gul Meher's relocation to her maternal uncle's location adjacent to Areem's own rented place, the upbeat facial skin tone variation during first face-to-face encounter in the new locale, the most precious one-to-one discourse while handing over food, and the countenance of bashfulness by Gul Meher while withdrawing with dinner items were too many positive upshots in too little time. The recurrent thoughts surrounding those overawed him. He lost appetite for food. Areem continued to nibble with food on the table by the side of charpoy and quit eating while half finished. He retired to bed early, being engrossed with thoughts of what all those meant in relation to him and his life. Pleasantly, though, his rapid pulsation of chest was reflective of both anxiety premised on Shahram's request of taking care of the family and challenges pertaining to traditions, more being a nonlocal. His happiness with having Gul Meher in the vicinity was overtaken by related anxieties generally surrounding Panjshir and particularly relating to the assassination of Commander Ahmed Shah Massoud by al-Qaeda.

In the main house across the courtyard, the young lady had a restless feeling in not being able to share her stances and expectations. Her relationship with Mother was always cordial, but discourses were mainly focused on traditional aphorisms and household chores. Even then, she tried to get Mother engaged in discussions pertaining to Areem.

Placing herself by the side of Mother in the master bed of her uncle, Gul Meher put one of her hands on the head of Mother and started softly moving fingers through mother's bushy hair to give some relief from the mental and physical stresses she was undergoing. The follow-on physical bearing of the mother was sufficient for Gul Meher to conclude that the gesture pleased her and she was enjoying it.

To give some relief to Mother from the excruciating tribulations she suffered during about the last twenty-four hours, Gul Meher thought of introducing a new topic. Unwittingly, she denoted the subject core to her heart. She softly said, "You never mentioned your feeling about the postmaster. To my assessment, he is a nice person of good temperament and personal traits. He really cares about us. Don't you think that getting food for tonight is a testament of that?"

The mother straightened her body, looked at Gul Meher with big open eyes, and just uttered hmm before turning again. Her only uttered words were "Turn off the light and let us sleep."

Though her last statement was premised on the need to go to sleep, in reality, mother herself was far away from that. In revisiting her own life against the backdrop of evident emotional bearing of Gul Meher, Mother started talking to herself saying, "My dear daughter, this mother of yours was also young at a given time. The feeling of youth is the impulse of age. Everything looks green and upbeat. Impossibility is obliterated by force of trance. Many a time, certain risks are lightly treated as challenges only until reality hits the bottom.

"Your father's conceit and daredevil nature, among others, overwhelmed me at that young age. I sacrificed my family to tie up with him. I firmly believed that it would comparatively be easy to tame him once we had a conjugal relationship. And that was true for the first two to three years. My quick pregnancy, the Soviet occupation on the shambles of previous order based on royalty, the rise of Commander Massoud, the unbridled rise of al-Qaeda, and the long life in refugee camp of Karachi changed most of the things I was taught and practiced. My life's focus changed to both of your well-being and grooming. Your father became secondary in life.

"In the shadowy setting of refugee camp, I, even though an illiterate individual of tribal origin, always found consolation and comfort in having exchanges with one Zubaida Khanam, fondly called Zubaida Khala by all. I do not know much about her, but to me, she was repository of wisdom and love. From being an unknown individual, she soon became my most trusted person, seeking from her advice and guidance unwaveringly on personal issues and family problems. The best part of my contact and relationship with Zubaida Khala was that she never inquired about anything and never asked me for details beyond what I told her. That was my comfort zone in a totally unknown setting.

"Honestly so, it was Zubaida Khala who encouraged me to think; to question, within limits of decency, decisions or actions not apparently palatable; to be frank; to be confident in conveying my stance; and to treat husband-wife relationship from a multidimensional perspective.

"I cannot forget what she alluded to when I raised the issue of our conjugal relationship as taking a turn contrary to what we had in the initial years of married life. She looked at me penetratingly and sensitively observed, 'Among all creations, women not only have a special place but they equally are blessed by divergent attributes of unique variances. Such traits are evident and play their roles in the form of smooth changes with each distinctive phase of her growing up. As a daughter, she fashions an aura of happiness and congeniality in the realm of family. As a wife, she not only surrenders herself before the husband physically but equally gets acquainted with and holds emotions and aspirations of the husband. But her real transformation takes place when she becomes a mother, a unique stance of unparalleled insinuations. Love, care, challenges, and concern for the offspring preponderate her thinking and actions as they grow up. But none of these are exclusive. Changes find their own way without delinking the past. A sublime phase-in becomes the norm of life.' This is where my life is and what I am."

Visiting and revisiting such thoughts in the context of what Zubaida Khala said from time to time and her own predicament concerning what the daughter wants to know, hours passed while Gul Meher was deep in sleep. Gul Bahar could sense the advent of early dawn because of the melodious sound of *azaan* from a distant mosque for *fajr* prayer. Unlike her norms and practices, and quite surprisingly, Gul Bahar opted to continue to be in the bed and soon fell asleep.

In the nearby rented accommodation, Areem coincidentally had similar sleepless hours. His concerns related to how to take care of Shahram's family given the circumstances particularly because of local culture, traditions, and practices. The presence and influence of standoffish imam of the local mosque was a matter of significant concern to Areem as he had easy access to Shahram's family.

In that agonizing scenery, proximity of Gul Meher because of community decision was the best outcome from his perspective. Areem just could not hope for a better position, and thoughts about possible happy moments and engagements kept him awake too. He was also very late in falling asleep that night.

Gul Meher woke up at the usual time and was surprised to see her mother sleeping. As a response to an evident negative thought, she closed in and moved her fingers before the nose of the mother. Being assured of normal breathing, she withdrew carefully.

She quietly prepared chai in a makeshift clay oven half completed last night. With a cup in her hand, she, nearing the exit door, paused for a while and eventually decided to act according to her intent. The yearning within her was intense, and she decided to break local restrictions without even waiting the endorsement and permission of the mother.

That determination suffered the most unexpected setback as she put her feet on the steps of Areem's accommodation. Her muscular strength suddenly weakened, and the cup started shaking on the saucer even though she tried to hold it firmly.

The front door of Areem's accommodation opened startlingly, and it was Areem standing in front of Gul Meher. Areem promptly invited her inside, more to avoid other people from noticing her. Gul Meher walked in and placed the cup on the rickety table. Placing her dupatta on the face, she took some steps out and then stopped, asking, "Why were you late in getting up?"

Areem responded very candidly, saying, "I was thinking about you and your future."

With a vivacity of an impish smile, Gul Meher retorted, saying, "But I had a nice sleep."

Areem was happy to note those light exchanges and in a still lighter tone observed, "You obviously had a nice dream."

With a fickle smile, Gul Meher repositioned her dupatta on her head, covering it fully, and stepped out hurriedly.

Her mother woke up after some time without giving any reason for the delay. She was taken aback, observing an unusually jovial and expressive Gul Meher moving around, carefree. But her quandary soon came to an end when Gul Meher voluntarily said, "Like you, the postmaster also woke up late this morning. I went out and offered him a cup of tea. To be consistent with all late risers of today, I am now offering you your cup of tea. Enjoy it as I did."

Gul Bahar was astounded in knowing the morning episode from the horse's mouth and was startled in observing the confidence and exuberance in the expressions of her daughter. It was not the daughter she knew for so long. The person in front of her was one totally unknown to her. Recalling many guidelines of life and living that Zubaida Khala articulated from time to time, Gul Bahar raised the cup of tea and sipped it for the first time. She recalled that in response to complaints about Shahram, Zubaida Khala once observed, "Look, Gul Bahar, always remember that however bad one may be, husband and wife together can only take an appropriate decision in handling critical bends of children's life." She intensely started missing the absence of Shahram, a husband against whom she always had grievances.

Suddenly, Gul Bahar found herself in a quandary. She lost her only son a few months back. Her husband was a sort of fugitive in his own land. Besides the brother, who was in faraway location of Karachi, Gul Meher was her only link and solace in this world. Thus, she opted to be quiet and noninterfering in matters related to the postmaster and only prayed for care and caution on the part of both to avoid any catastrophic consequences.

With the mother being docile and noninterfering, Gul Meher readily took a prominent role in family matters, including interactions with the postmaster. She started visiting him frequently and many a time invited him to their place for dinner and tea.

By design or sheer coincidence, one practice was meticulously followed by Gul Meher. Not only had she avoided public exposure in general but she also ensured timing of those meetings, mostly coinciding with Muslim evening prayers. That was done to ensure that the imam of their local mosque, and her father's friend who developed a practice of showing up at odd times for one or the other reason, remain completely unaware of practices within the compound. Simultaneously, Areem, with friendly and frequent contacts with Gul Meher, was both vigilant and solicitous. He devoted more time in office work and continued buying his dinner from the same restaurant though sharing it at night with Gul Meher and her mother. Anything needed by Gul Meher's family was bought either in segments or from different stores. It was easy as Imam Shaheeb used to take care of bulk provisions like flour, ghee or oil, lintels, salt, etc., which were needed by the family.

The arrangement and practice evolved voluntarily within the short time made Mother assured and happy. There were no spars around. The prevalent synergy was evidently very pleasant. The overall house environment was one of rooting. Contrary to usual practice, the postmaster did not exhibit any insidious motive. Areem's malleability and grinning approach assured the mother. She silently tolerated frequent interactions between Gul Meher and Areem, sympathizing with the daughter's need for an outlet at this stage in life besides having frequent advice from her mother, and with Areem's distance from home in Bangladesh.

Another notable and impulsive change was alteration in referring to the postmaster as *beta* Areem by the Mother. Gul Meher, however, continued with the previous one.

The following few days were passed by inhabitants luxuriating in the unexpected and equally affable setting of the compound. It appeared that the lone rented accommodation of Areem and abandoned ancestral house had a new lease of life as the compound got rejuvenated with the presence of Gul Bahar and Gul Meher. That feeling was enhanced with the news of the brother's total endorsement of action taken by the community, with imminent plan to visit them.

Areem meticulously demonstrated happiness and congeniality in all his actions within the compound, ensuring due care and caution. But that was not the case when he was out and in his work. Presence of reinforcements, both men and materials, from Kabul, aiming at Bazarak in response to the assassination of its local leaders, was a thwarting one. In addition, the apparent efficacious onslaught in the heartland of USA by al-Qaeda caused an unprecedented local euphoria in proclaiming ultimate victory over infidels.

The Pashtun-based ultraconservative Taliban movement, the other side of the same al-Qaeda coin, swapped the whole of Afghanistan in the immediate past. Successive short-lived administrations after the fall of Soviet-backed government facilitated the Taliban's accession to power, controlling about 95 percent of the territory around late 1996. They renamed the country as the Islamic Emirate of Afghanistan.

The significant exception was the northern tip of the country in general and Panjshir Province in particular. The Taliban were struggling to have a firm foothold in these areas. Related developments created the opportune moment. Al-Qaeda got engaged in storming earlier determined targets with clutching weapons. Residents were generally panicked. Many shops of the main bazaar were dented, while most others had their awning drawn. People were experiencing living in a capricious battlefield life with no law and governing authority. But they were meticulous in saying salaam to all al-Qaeda activists.

And that caused frequent uneasiness in the thinking of Areem.

As he sat in the post office one day, Areem's frustration within swelled, thinking more about the future quality of life he was destined to have relative to the acknowledged potential. To him, it appeared to be a ruse in the quest of mythical ideological pursuit, which had no end.

Areem compared his present status with that of his grandfather, who opted to embrace life about thousand miles away in a totally different geographical setting and climatic condition. He concluded that both his and grandfather's life conditions were not comparable, especially in terms family background and intellectual potential. Unwittingly, the adoring face of Gul Meher surfaced in his mind. The premise of his current thought got convoluted. Areem palpably was confused.

Right at the moment, Imam Shaheeb of the mosque near the previous settlement of Gul Meher appeared and took his seat on the lone chair across the lone table, as he did in the past many times. There was no eye contact even. After a while, he got up and left as silently as he came. These visits annoyed Areem very much. He, however, had no option but to bear with that.

That was contrary to grace and practices of Kazi Shaheeb. He never bothered Areem though he continued visiting the Shahram family periodically. Quietness of his behavior was the hallmark of that relationship.

A sudden and total transformation of affiliation, as ubiquitous in the entire Panjshir surroundings, unnerved Areem. In that backdrop, Bazarak was no exception. The beliefs, ideas, and goals of its Leader and hero, Ahmad Shah Massoud, just faded. Everyone on the street, by belief or pretention, projected himself as an al-Qaeda activist. Atrocities committed to take revenge were condoned and in many cases applauded.

The eventual quagmire resulting from recent aerial attack on civil facilities in the USA had imminent bearing on perceived and established norms of international order and peace. That was aggravated by the Taliban government's persistent refusal to hand over bin Laden for war crime trial. Because of these, and as a retaliatory response, the USA launched its military operation against Afghanistan.

The disorganized Taliban government crumbled. The basic and normal public service deliveries, including postal operations, collapsed. On a broader perspective, bin Laden took refuge in the mountain regions, while the head of the government and Taliban movement escaped the capital, sitting on the back seat of a motorcycle. Al-Qaeda activists were busy in abandoning their known identities.

The immediate impact was loud and clear. Tired of being in the office without any transaction, Areem stopped going to the post office. That created much desired space to spend more time with Gul Meher and gain the confidence of her mother.

It was the morning of tailing Friday. The locale was overcast. Copious hanging clouds overshadowed the mountain peaks. The wind was blowing with notable speed. The prevalent atmosphere was insipid one. Areem returned to his accommodation after finishing his morning tea with Gul Meher, promising an early return.

While he was performing some casual errands, the diary of the grandma fell on the floor. He fervidly picked it up and noticed that his finger was on the page where she narrated their emotions pertaining to mutual love.

Areem forgot other compulsions and commitments and started reading that section repeatedly to find a link between his present status with Gul Meher and possible progression in life.

Being herself tired of gloomy morning, Gul Meher decided to prepare desserts to surprise Areem, providing a possible prelude to brighten up their discourse once he returns.

She decided to make *halwa e sojee*. (*Halwa* means "sweet" and is generally made with butter, flour, and sugar). She made it quickly. When her mother was told about sojee preparation, she opined that in this dreary weather, one should have *sheer birinj* (creamy cardamom pudding) dessert. Gul Meher immediately prepared that too and kept on waiting for Areem with both dessert items.

Time passed by. Gul Meher continued to monitor the exit door of Areem's accommodation. There was no indication as to his movement within or out. The weather was worsening with marked acceleration of wind, rain, sleet, snow, and slush. She was both distraught and irritated.

Gul Meher became angry with herself for making desserts for an undeserving person. She was blighting herself for undertaking unnecessary troubles notwithstanding the ostensible bottlenecks. As an appropriate response to his utter insensitivity, Gul Meher, out of sheer frustration, resolutely resolved to go, even braving the worst weather, to Areem's place, and leave the desserts on his lone chest of cedar wood with a quick walk back devoid of any exchanges.

Gul Meher was prompt in acting on her thoughts. She placed adequate proportion of both desserts on one aluminum quarter plate and one similar bowl and put them on the rickety copper tray. She placed an aluminum plate on the top of desserts and additionally covered them with multifolded white dupatta as a protection against heavy rain. Gul Meher then wrapped herself from head downward in a heavy shawl and stepped out hurriedly with the tray carrying desserts.

Trying to keep her arrival a quiet one and outwardly mastering her anger and frustration, Gul Meher quietly opened the door and was astounded to see Areem deeply engaged in reading. Seeing her entering his space, Areem stood up, looked at his watch, and said, "I am sorry. I just located my grandma's diary and got engaged in reading. Time just passed."

Gul Meher was standing still inside the entry door while Areem was explaining the reasons of delay. She closed the entry door with one hand as a measure of protection against splashing rainwater, avoided eye contact, walked past Areem, put the desserts on the table, and started walking back with the tray. That silence and that indifference were too much for Areem.

As Gul Meher was walking back between the cedar chest and Areem, the latter impulsively got hold of her dangling left hand, resulting in sudden loosened grip of the right hand. That caused the tray to fall on the floor. Gul Meher made an immediate effort to retrieve the tray, and she precipitously lost balance.

He reacted in seconds. Areem's unprompted response was to extend his two hands to hold and save Gul Meher.

The immediate realization about the state of physical contact was both surprising and disconcerting for Areem. To his utter embarrassment, he found his two hands wrapping the body of Gul Meher with his two palms shielding her bulging breasts.

What bemused him was the surprising absence of any quick reaction on the part of Gul Meher conveying embarrassment, shyness, gawkiness, or unexpectedness. The marked absence of immediate effort to disengage was another factor of germaneness.

Dumbfounded, Areem sustained that physical connection for additional seconds and ventured to straighten the physique of Gul Meher in a slow motion. In the process, he was certain that Gul Meher was not embarrassed at all; rather, it so appeared that she was enjoying the physical closeness and contact.

In eventual straighten posture, both of them were cramped as one with Gul Meher's hand scratching the back of Areem's physique, while the fingers of the latter were unsnarling the lustrous straight hairs of the former. They were lost in infinite feelings, oblivious of ground realities.

Areem slowly untangled his fingers, held the face of Gul Meher with intense feeling, lifted it up, and showered her the kiss of love, a first for both.

As the nature outside was raging in speed, volume, and velocity, so were the actions and engagements within. Slowly and steadily, both moved toward the charpoy. Follow-on physical engagements were open, expressive in oral responses, and in maneuvering and variety even though it was first experience for both.

During dressing up at the culmination of maiden sexual engagement, Areem continued to be shy and nervous. He was feeling guilty for having sex prior to marriage, something he was taught from early youth as socially unethical and religiously immoral. His agony was more severe as it is tantamount to taking advantage of the unhinged family setting of Gul Meher, betraying the trust reposed in him by her parents.

That, however, was not the case with Gul Meher. Unhesitatingly, her first time to bare exposure before Areem was without expressed inhibition. She dressed up slowly. The only diversion was her occasional monitoring of weather conditions along with likely movements outside the exit door.

It was a relief for Areem to see that Gul Meher finally completed her dressing up. It was he who was more concerned about outside movement, which in that weather could only be the mother.

That relief was a transient one. What came out of the mouth of relaxed Gul Meher and the straightforwardness of that deliberation were beyond comprehension of Areem and any dictum of normalcy. Areem could never anticipate that the simple young lady of Bazarak could be that open and blunt.

Looking straight at Areem while jesting with the tray, Gul Meher, with ease and frankness, started saying, "The happiest and most contended moment of intercourse is when a man's ejaculation and a woman's orgasm coincide. That happened in our case even though it was our first engagement. But I could not enjoy that as at that precise moment, I took you as my husband with the unending rain, snow, and sleet as witnesses. So I am relaxed even though rituals were not carried out and complied with. From now on and until I breathe my last, you are my husband. I would honor and defend that at any cost and in all circumstances. I do not know about your feeling. On my side, I am very clear."

That inexorable confession had protruding impact on Areem, and most of the stinkers caused by her earlier open statement were eliminated. But Areem still agonized with the thought as to how and from whom she knew about the intricate elements of sexual pleasure. He nevertheless kept quiet, thinking intensely more about the future consequences of today's impromptu adventure.

The bashing of rain and wind continued unabated. Moving in the space available, she commented, "This is something very helpful for us. My prolonged stay in your place can easily be justified as taking excuse of adverse weather." Areem nodded even though his physical self was visibly a constrained one.

That did not avoid the attention of the ever-vigilant Gul Meher. She pointedly asked, "What is bothering you: our sexual engagement or my subsequent candid statement?"

Ameer briefly responded, saying, "Both, but without any repercussions."

With an impish smile gracing her lips, Gul Meher countered, saying, "Both of us were equal participants in the foregoing sexual engagement. That could be a reason for anxiety, but it should not lead to anguish as you are suffering. My assessment, therefore, is that the second articulation of mine is the cause of your current agitation considering my root in Bazarak."

She paused for a while and continued saying, "People have diverse views about life and living in a refugee camp and its setting. But to me, and notwithstanding specific limitations, our living and my growing up in Karachi refugee camp had significant positive impact. It enabled us to acknowledge that the world is much larger than Panjshir. Mother's contact and association with Zubaida Khala, an elderly refugee from Ghazni, was a life-changing one for an illiterate lady from Bazarak. Zubaida Khala's unprecedented aptitude to understand others, her progressive knowledge and wisdom, and her unique knack to bond with unknowns in a communication style adored by most made her soon the icon of our refugee block. My mother idolized her, but more significantly, she cared for Mother as a daughter. Both Mother and I learned a lot from Zubaida Khala.

"But I had more regular association and involvement with an illegal Bangladeshi family living on a subcontract basis in the same block of our camp. I used to address her as Rizia Khala. She was from a place known as Saidpur in Bangladesh. This is a place having dominant presence of Urdu-speaking people. Thus, most residents had largely equal proficiency in

Urdu and Bangla. Her premarital educational attainment of intermediate level made her understand functional English easily.

"She was to me what Zubaida Khala was to Mother: a friend, a philosopher, and a guide. But she was equally good to others, facilitated by her Urdu-speaking ability and functional understanding of English. Many female residents of the camp visited her to get clarifications.

"One day I was in Rizia Khala's place helping her in concocting vegetable for Bangladeshi-style cooking. That always allured me, especially the mix and match of different spices, making the curry and gravy more interesting and tastier.

"A neighborhood lady of casual acquaintance showed up with a printed paper written in Urdu with some English terms and idioms in brackets. She took her seat by the side of Rizia Khala and, oblivious of my presence, briefly referred to her conjugal problems and irritations. She said, 'I discussed this privately with the health visitor earlier, and she gave me, during follow-on visit, this paper with a few English words. She was constrained in discussing my problem in detail because of presence of other ladies. So I have come to you for help. You are my sister. Please do not share this with anyone. My husband would lose face. The family would be embarrassed.'

"Rizia Khala reacted positively, read the paper in a minute, and thinking perhaps that I was too young to understand the implications, started saying, 'You have not said much about your agony. But a plain reading indicates that your problem pertains to basic sex life of a married couple. I understand Urdu functionally, but English words like *ejaculation* and *orgasm* facilitated my clear understanding of your problem. The paper states that this is a common conjugal problem. Its first intervention is for the couple to talk to each other frankly and then try to build up confidence by acknowledging performance. If the problem persists, then see a physician.'

"Rizia Khala, in her deliberations, mentioned a number of times *ejaculation* and *orgasm*, explaining in detail in Urdu." Mentioning those, Gul Meher said, "Those two English words and their repeated mention in explaining the problem caught my imagination at that preteen age. A common mistake of elders is that they either ignore or discount children's memory and ability to understand. In most deliberations, seniors ignore the children's presence. When these children grow up, many incidents or statements recur in their thoughts and actions. Consistent with such social behavior, both the lady and Rizia Khala discussed connubial matters freely and frankly in my presence. They also casually left the printed paper, more as garbage.

"My inquisitiveness was passionate because of the sassy discussion between the lady and Rizia Khala pertaining to sex. I got hold of the paper and read it many a time later, trying to absorb the content in the context of Rizia Khala's elucidation. Initially, it did not have any impact besides imagination. But with my attaining puberty, I realized what exactly it meant and what it implied. On a deep thinking, I concluded that this is a natural thing related to sex life. So I did not hesitate to mention that in your presence as we are husband and wife. Maybe I am not as educated as you, but I distaste bigoted opinion shutting the mouth of women."

With the unleashing of those heavy words and specific opinion, Gul Meher, ignoring the adverse weather outside, hurriedly stepped out, wrapping herself with the same shawl she had when she came. Additionally, she used the tray as partial shield to protect her head. Areem was bemused.

The strong muscle tone of her legs and her confident initial steps suffered a bulging feeling while approaching their entry door and effectively were thwarted as she stepped in. Her mother had a brief cold look and refrained from asking anything. That anguished and frustrated Gul Meher. In cleaning up the kitchen area, she voluntarily said, "The postmaster was startled in seeing me entering but was exultant to have the local desserts. He was equally happy to note my make-believe statement that because of depressing weather, you prepared those for him. He expressed his thanks many a time. As the weather worsened, he asked me to stay back for a while. He was feeling very lonely and disjointed. In broken Urdu with a mix of a few Dari words, he tried to narrate his life in Bangladesh."

Mother neither responded nor reacted. Her arcane silence was unnerving for Gul Meher. That denoted apparent fundamental gap between mother and daughter. Gul Meher, though young and smart and nurtured in Karachi atmosphere, could never match the inherent instinct of a mother. Her mother had her angsts but opted to keep quiet until Gul Meher put forward plausible evidence in support of what she stated or opens up, *Allah na kare* (God forbid), with the truth.

In that psychologically traumatic moment, and within her own surroundings, the talkative and outgoing Gul Meher shrank into a reserved and lifeless individual within a short while.

Areem did not show up for lunch. Contrary to previous practice, Gul Meher refrained from taking food for him. The Mother did not make any query. Unconventional silence was intense for both but from unalike perspectives.

At the other end of the compound, Areem was engrossed in thoughts ranging from moral values to ethical parameters. His thought was burdened because of the spontaneous spark of moment's indulgence. Areem was deep in thoughts: why it ought to happen; how self-motivated participation overruled his much-cherished values; and probable options in charting a pragmatic way out.

His singular thought in isolation was depressing, confusing, and demoralizing, changing the goalpost with every new direction of reasoning.

Areem was equally worried in thinking about how Gul Meher was handling the situation of facing the piercing eyes of a mother. Looking outside, he was pleased to note a significant abating of the earlier storm.

With hesitation prevalent, resolve unceasing, and risk inherent, Areem stepped out and knocked at the entry door though it was apparently not fastened. No one showed up. Waiting a little, Areem stepped in slowly only to be greeted by the mother. Gul Meher's pensive pretention with her kitchen chores was ostensibly a pretext for avoiding interactions with Areem in the presence of her mother. That mode was at significant variance with the way Areem was greeted in the past, expressly by Gul Meher. It did not escape the attention of Gul Bahar. Ensuring cordiality, even though suspicion was dangling around her thoughts, Gul Bahar hesitantly kept quiet.

Areem stepped forward and took his usual seat. The prevailing setting was jammed by Gul Meher's total silence, Areem's nervousness, and Gul Bahar's predicament. Somehow, a very neutral query by Gul Bahar eased the situation. She innocently inquired about his not showing up for lunch.

That gave Areem a much preferred opening for a casual discourse. Areem responded, saying, "You have sent so much desserts, and I lost appetite after having those. Those were so tasty that I could not resist eating them. So I told Gul Meher about that and entreated her consideration of not taking trouble of bringing food for me either. I was equally concerned that like the late-morning experience, she might get stranded in my place again with burdening worry for you."

Hearing the related words, Gul Meher instinctively turned her face toward Areem with specific facial mien disowning those make-believe expressions. Turning her head back and in soliloquy panache, she murmured with the words, "Oh boy, what an incredible line of thought you have articulated craftily." Eventually, she was both satiated and pleased, as his expressions were conducive to ease the situation for the time being.

Things were not as smooth as both Gul Meher and Areem expected them to be. Her mother's innocuous reactions had the elements of dander and evidences of love, depending on circumstances. In practice, most of the time, they resorted to swapping bashful signals to the discomfort of neither.

Devoid of specific strategy, both Areem and Gul Meher slowly attuned to a style of dealings, which had features of restraint in front of her mother and profusion of hilarity when in Areem's place. The former entailed subservience, care, and restraint. The latter, among others, involved incessant laughter, frequent holding of hands, regular hugging, frequent kissing, and occasional sex.

The duality in living practices of these two youngsters had unique similarity with the overall national setting. USA's preoccupation with targeted air bombing of al-Qaeda strongholds, assemblies, structures, and leaderships caused disarray at the ground level. Al-Qaeda and Taliban activists were in a state of bewilderment, being unclear about their course of action. On the surface, and to avoid lethal retort of the advancing US forces, they continued behaving differently during day and night.

That was not the case with Panjshir. Followers of Ahmed Shah Massoud not only resurfaced but also played a prominent role in the interim government. During the intervening period of exercising power, a number of deaths in the community occurred. Some were innocent people like Kazi Shaheeb. Gul Bahar started witnessing disarray in regular acts and was succumbing to feeling of dismay. Having no word about Shahram and the sudden demise of brother-like Kazi Shaheeb compounded that.

In view of the breakdowns of government-administered public services, Gul Bahar's brother sent a messenger carrying his letter. The short letter mentioned briefly, and in simple term, that all formalities concerning the family's immigration to the USA had been completed. The advice from the interim embassy was for immediate travel. The letter advised Gul Bahar to complete local preparations and that he would be coming within the next month for a two days' stay and escort Gul Meher.

That message caused mixed reactions among the three inhabitants: Gul Bahar suddenly had the immense burden of shouldering the responsibility alone to let the daughter go even though Shahram had proposed this when her brother was discussing immigration options with him; Gul Meher was happy, notwithstanding the current spell of separation evident, as immigration would pave the way for permanent bonding with Areem beyond local restrictions and tribal impositions; on his part, Areem was disjointed and distressed as the future remained uncertain and convoluted. That was not a variation for him but definitely induced more uncertainty in his life, already an uncharted one.

With those variations having respective implications, all three sat together to work out preparations at the local end. Areem took the lead and opined, "In view of the prevailing impasse in national and regional life, there would be no gainsaying to retract from the agreed position. Also, there is not much to do locally except mental preparations to sustain the pain of separation."

Hesitating for a while, but without any premonition, Areem impulsively made a profound avowal that not only stunned the other two but also equally baffled himself subsequently. He said, "I came to know about your family through Janab Shahram during my occasional discourses with him in the post office. Your subsequent location to this compound drew me close to both of you in an arduous and ambiguous situation. Back in Bangladesh, I did not have anyone who loved and cared about me as both of you have done so far. I developed a close, genuine, and honest feeling and love for Gul Meher. In my thoughts and resolve, and seeking the blessings of Allah the Magnificent, I took her as my wife with surrounding nature, my grandma's diary, and her wedding sari as witnesses. I promise to you, in the name Allahpak, that I will not fail in discharging my responsibilities and obligations as husband in all situations and circumstances. And I affirm to you that Gul Meher is not only my wife for today. She would be so in my entire life even under all unlikely galling settings."

Saying those words, Areem promptly left the assembly and retreated to his space. He was both relieved and nervous. Relieved at being able to say what he wanted to say. Nervous at being unsure about Gul Bahar's reaction as she was an illiterate tribal lady. Had it been the case of a Bangladeshi mother, he would have been hopeful of having a better understanding notwithstanding the implied inferences. Bangladeshi social structure is predominantly premised on emotions in all spheres of life ranging from social interactions to political decisions, music, literature, entertainment, and so on. That definitely is in significant contrast to rigid tribal heritage and affiliations.

After a while, Gul Meher nonchalantly walked in with a tray full of food, a service palpably quite liberal compared to the past. She sat by his side and said, "This is the moment to celebrate. At least to Mother, the most important person in my life, the reality pertaining to our feelings and relationship is now clear. From her body language and few words she uttered subsequently, I believe without dithering that she is pacified by the frankness on your part and many a time reassured due to your pledges.

"After you left, she closed her eyes for a significant while and then told me to bring food for you. So I decided that we should have food together as a solemn testimony of what we are."

All they discussed during partaking of food was about Areem's forthrightness and honesty. In response, Areem stated, "I really do not know how I could be so frank before Mother. But I am happy that I could do that."

Gul Meher was not hesitant to remind Areem that some elements of his statement had close link with what she said after their first sex. Areem pleasantly agreed with that and then went on explaining the emotional bias inherent in Bangladesh culture. That was why he mentioned his grandma's diary and her wedding sari as witnesses too, as those were emotionally very relevant in his life.

As they finished eating, Gul Meher started narrating her impression of her mother's reaction, saying, "Mother imaginably noted the reality consistent with the milieu of her earlier apprehension. Her closing of eyes for a long time perhaps was apposite to her earlier discourses with Zubaida Khala, her mentor in the refugee camp. She definitely opted not to contest, and probably wished a successful culmination. Your words, expressions, and undertakings were of great solace to her. Her calm and definite direction to bring food for you is a testament to my above assessment."

They enjoyed the rest of the time of the day and following sundry days without any inhibition. In between, both of them prepared for eventual separation, sharing contact details both in Bazarak and Bangladesh with the solemn promise to be united. On his part, Areem took an extraordinary decision to present the wedding sari of his grandma to Gul Meher, fulfilling the wish of the former as written in her diary.

Both spent a lot of time thinking and discussing options of telling her uncle about taking each other as spouses without religious rituals, and their resolve to wait for a length of time as needed for Gul Meher to sponsor Areem for US immigration. Eventually, it was agreed that the best option would be to channel it though her mother.

Gul Meher slowly and cautiously permeated the idea to her mother. The focus was to raise the subject at the time of her brother's ensuing visit, highlighting, among others, the care and love demonstrated by Areem during the exasperating period, the vulnerability of both the mother and daughter in the absence of Shahram, the age of Gul Meher, and the lack of a suitable match. The highlight would be to get the brother's help in getting a document affirming their marriage.

Having reached the needed conclusion and being assured of her mother's alignment, both Gul Meher and Areem were enthused with ecstasy and exhilaration. To them, everything looked beautiful and gratifying. The sleekness of mountain peaks negated all the perils inherent on the way to its peak. On the ground, the fight between advancing US forces and retreating al-Qaeda resistance militia were discounted as peripheral. Happiness overwhelmed both within four walls of Areem's space. Outside that setting, both meticulously remained unflappable.

SLAM

The tranquility and happiness were suddenly wrecked by a bombshell, which was a matter of trepidation to them and shudder to Mother. As they celebrated the new relationship and expressed that in emotional and physical doings, the relevant sequels were not only ignored but also not even considered. Now they were face-to-face with that. The slam happened with its ugly face in the context of tribal values and Sharia legal stipulations.

After missing two consecutive monthly periods, Gul Meher became concerned and nervous. Being unclear of the implications, Areem continued to console her.

But that was not of any relevance to Gul Meher. Her own physical responses were unambiguously different. She had no option but to open up before the mother. On hearing what Gul Meher had to say, the mother's reflexes just gave in; and she spontaneously sat down on the floor, howling, "What you have done?"

Her mother's immediate reaction after wailing was an unexpectedly composed one. She remained preoccupied, pondering about the implications. Mother had two concerns agitating her mind: first, the very clear signal from the youngest son of Kazi Bhai about his passionate liking and strong yearning to have Gul Meher as wife in due course even though the latter expressed her open disapproval to such proposition and, second, the reality of sexual contact or relationship prior to marriage, which was more serious and could be devastating. The second one was treated as the grimmest offense, and the local traditions, based on Sunnah, meant stoning to death. Gul Bahar started shivering instantaneously. While moaning, her mother mentioned both of these as if she was talking to herself.

Gul Meher, the most interfering individual of the compound, was speechless. She continued looking at her mother relentlessly. Her mother's tears agitated Gul Meher immensely. She stood up immediately, went out swiftly, and returned with Areem on her side.

Taking a place near Gul Bahar, Areem started, saying, "There is nothing fundamentally wrong if she has conceived. Gul Meher is my wife. I am not shying away from that or seeking a different route. The issue we face is evidence of our marriage. For that, and to save our two lives, as well the life in the womb, we will have to find a way out. And that includes some lying, as warranted.

"Sitting alone in my space and when you were howling, I was engrossed in thought as to how to find a way out. At that time, something dawned on me. People around are familiar with your family's close association with Kazi Shaheeb. He was not only a family friend but a well wisher too. If so faced, then you should say that the Kazi Shaheeb performed the rituals in a private wedding to avoid likely social stigma for living with unknown in the same compound. At his behest, public announcements and rituals were kept pending for Shahram's presence. Since Kazi Shaheeb is dead, nobody can question this premise.

"But we need to exercise caution. Your brother should not be told about the pregnancy at this time. Let him know about this more as an eventuality, taking the plea that lack of knowledge and inexperience of Gul Meher hindered earlier conclusion.

"On the issue of eagerness of the son of Kazi Bhai for a formal relationship with Gul Meher, I do not consider that to be an issue to cause anxiety. Gul Meher and I would be able to handle that once the first issue is handled properly. He can't do any damage to us."

Areem lingered his further comments to give space to assess the reaction to what he had already articulated. He also was unsure as how to resume his deliberations until he had affirmation regarding amiability.

His attempt to assess Gul Bahar's reaction was futile as she was focusing on the floor.

He then looked at Gul Meher and was relieved in observing a sense of affability. Being comforted, Areem started saying, "My hunch insinuates that it would be better for me not to be present when discussions are held among three of you. You can always say that in view of Gul Meher's imminent departure, I was sent to trace Shahram and bring him back. This is consistent and plausible but, of course, involves another lie."

Having said so, Areem floated a fundamental proposition, saying, "For the sake of our future life and its geniality, you should get a promise from your brother that Gul Meher would be allowed to live life as per her will and decision, and no imposition would be made at any time or any circumstance. She should always be treated as an *amanat* [safekeeping in holy trust]."

Saying those words, Areem stood up to leave the meeting. The most unexpected ricochet occurred. The mother raised her face for the first time and said, "I have something to say to both of you. I have listened to what you said before, and I promise to follow those in having discussion with Brother. However, I have a point, and there would be no negotiation pertaining to that. You are to give Gul Meher your Bangladesh address and contact points first. Then, by next Friday, you are to leave us for Bangladesh incognito. You are not to look back. If both of your love is genuine, you will get reunited. But this is the best for both of you and the child in the womb of my daughter. When Imam Bhai came a day before yesterday, Gul Meher wavered in taking delivery of provisions. He winked at me with suspicion evident. I said to him that she was having loose motions for the whole night and, hence, was weak. I do not think that he was convinced and most likely would follow that up. My doubt was reinforced as Kazi Bhai's nephew came yesterday to inquire about the well-being of Gul Meher when both of you were having food. I told him that she was fast asleep and that he could come later on to meet her. That proves that Imam Bhai has already made that a talking point in the community. When moral issues are involved, religious injunctions are predominant, and no relationship or feeling matters. Religious elders will not buy the idea of private marriage. Their sticking gun would be sex prior to marriage. The consequences are known to you both. We do not have time to waste, and you must leave by the time indicated. Your absence from the scene may have needed assuaging impact."

The outspoken stance of Mother stunned and baffled both. It was beyond the thinking and assumed capability of an illiterate Bazarak lady, more known for being contained and discreet even when facing a provoking situation. In their follow-on joyous space, both of them continued to talk about the unique performance of Mother.

What Gul Meher observed in the process sounded incredulous to Areem. She said, "I am not certain as to what holds for me in the future, but Mother's performance today convinced me that there are many avenues of learning, and there is no limit of absorbing knowledge. Mother's only exposure was interactions with Zubaida Khala in the refugee camp. With Father most of the time away, Mother had plenty of time to spend with Zubaida Khala. Occasionally, I, too, used to accompany Mother. They never discussed matters related to others. Zubaida Khala had a philosophical ambiance in her deliberations. She mostly talked about life's varied problems, associated challenges, tests and tribulations of relationships, metamorphosis between expectations and realities, and so on. I did not understand most. And I always thought that my mother was on the same boat. But her performance today convinced me that her isolated self intensely absorbed most of what Zubaida Khala said. Externally, she remained a docile wife of our father, and internally, she was transformed into a discerning and impassioned lady. If I have a chance in life, I will try my best to reverse my life focusing on learning and espousing."

Areem was very happy for the resolve shown by Gul Meher. He also thanked internally Gul Bahar for bringing out the best in her, giving confidence and determination to her daughter.

The intervening period passed within a twinkle with mix of sadness, rolling tears, and occasional laughter. The time closed in. Areem, emotionally distraught, was at the point of breaking down. Learning from Mother, Gul Meher remained sturdy outside though emotionally crushed inside.

She walked in and brought out the backpack with his grandma's diary; academic certificates; residue money (Afghani currency, leftover Bangladeshi taka, Pakistani rupees, and US dollars); and his favorite *pakol* inside. Additionally, she also brought the much-needed thick shawl and the cane that Shahram used to carry always in his hand. She even did not forget to bring the *taweez* that Mr. Jatoi of Hyderabad gave him, which he promised could help him when under adverse situations.

Even if Gul Meher did not utter any word, those were sufficient indications to Areem about the need and time to leave. Handing over those to emotionally soaked Areem, Gul Meher assured him by reiterating her pledge, saying, "As I said earlier, I am married, and that is once in life for me. Wherever I may be and whatever the challenges and constraints are, I will remain your wife. I also reiterate that I will not die before handing over your child to you. Also, have my promise that I will make all efforts to make your child, whether boy or girl, a doctor, fulfilling your own desire to become one. Rest assured about that. And under all circumstances, take care of yourself in all respects, be safe and secure, and have faith in Allahpak and confidence in yourself."

After saying those words coupled with incredible emotional pressure and physical strains, she took the lead toward their home with Areem following aversely. Once he faced Gul Bahar, his hesitancy, recalling all she said earlier, gave way to unbridled resolve. He bent slowly; touched her feet, performing rituals of salaam; and left the compound, seeking her *doa* (blessings).

No words were exchanged between Gul Meher and Areem. Bending on the frame of their exit door, Gul Meher, following the vanishing physique of Areem, involuntarily relented to crying with uncontrolled tears rolling down her cheeks. The outward countenance of that feeling was murmuring verses of the Holy Quran seeking his safety and good health.

As Areem stepped out of the compound, his overbearing emotions were astonishingly turned into a resolve to live and to succeed for the love of Gul Meher and his responsibility for the child to be born. He resolved firmly to succeed and sought the *doa* of his grandparents and *raham* (benedictions) of Allahpak.

Once out of the compound, Areem wrapped himself with the heavy shawl as per Panjsharian style, realigned the *pakol*, reassured himself about the *taweez* of Mr. Jatoi hanging from his neck, and started his open-ended and unmapped journey. Quite pleasantly, he encountered a local van going to south and decided to board it to ensure his safe escape. He recalled that night before last a few youngsters from local madrassa came to the compound, inquiring his availability for a serious discussion. As it was perhaps ordained, he was taking a nap at that time, though it was past *maghrib*. His place had neither any movement nor any light. Eventually, Gul Bahar showed up following the prescribed modesty practices and, spontaneously addressing them as *beta*, said, "The postmaster was directed by Kabul to be there for discussions about resumption of the postal delivery system. He has gone there for discussion, and neither he nor we are certain when he would be back." When they turned back, Gul Bahar startlingly decided to deflect their focus and said, "Please inform your elders that we have news about Janab Shahram's current stay at Tulub and that he is returning soon." After saying those words, she slowly closed the door.

He was told about that subsequently. That concern lingered within and haunted him very much. That prompted him to decide quickly to board the van. Once in the van, Areem was relieved to note that most of the muddled passengers were nonlocals, and many of them were going to the mausoleum of leader Ahmad Shah Massoud. It so appeared that the Leader's stature and influence reemerged once the Taliban government collapsed. Areem also decided to be in the mausoleum, meeting the Leader in death even though it could not be in life.

Climbing the plateau on a semimountaintop at the edge of Bazarak, Areem followed others on foot to go inside the mausoleum, having plenty of open space. The tomb itself, made of stone (black marble), was shielded by glass panels and was placed inside the arches of a domed tower. The simplicity impressed Areem very much. He also pleasantly noted the inscription of Quranic passages on the tomb. Deep-red Persian carpets covered the area adjacent to the tomb.

Areem's original plan was to visit the tomb and then continue his journey to escape the familiar location of Bazarak. As he entered the mausoleum and reached the site of the tomb, Areem closed his eyes and involuntarily became motionless. He stood for a very long time, talking to deceased Leader Ahmed Shah Massoud. In the intervening period, scores of visitors and admirers came and left.

That experience had a unique impact on his subsequent thoughts and actions. He stayed back for another two days, mostly engaging himself, reciting quietly oratorios in the tomb. His immediate notable outdoor passion was conjuring the site of damaged and abandoned Soviet-era arms, vehicles, and tanks positioned at the bottom plains of the mountains, parallel to the access road by the side of sleek Panjshir River. His other occasional passions were: looking at the crystal-clear turquoise waters of the river surging down from glacier heights; shimmering heights and pinnacles having vegetation and greeneries with rhyme and rhythm both being fused and flawless; the cluster of majestic mountaintops mostly shrouded by mist; and the pleasant breeze touching one with unique sensation.

From a semi-mountaintop position, Areem, for the first time, realized the spectacular beauty that is naturally caused by ruggedness of the topography, which contributed manifold to the thrilling splendor of the valley located in the lap of Hindu Kush Mountains parting South Asia from its central landscape. Both rolling and receding, depending on the direction of travel, mountains at the edge of seasonal multicolored valleys; the snow on the top and sands at the bottom; the green vegetation side by side the barren grey cum black hills and mountains; cluster of mud-houses within battlements and on the laps of mountains; occasional fruit and vegetable outlets and *chaikhanas*; the flow of palate blues of the Panjshir River had all the natural elements that were both mesmerizing and mysterious. The vistas of hills and mountains from the valleys were astonishingly enchanting. Perhaps the aforesaid topographical features and settings kept the people away from orthodoxies of the north (past Soviet immensity) and faith-related firmness of the south (al-Qaeda divinations).

As Areem stayed back, he was riveted by a unique sensitivity and realization. He started harboring an unambiguous urge to live longer and to love Gul Meher fervidly, ensuring a more responsive future for the offspring.

Areem developed a unique feeling of love, which, to be real, essentially is a one-way traffic. In that iridescent surroundings, Areem argued with himself about love and its implications, recalling mostly what his grandma stipulated in her diary.

Areem related that feeling to love of his grandfather who parted with everything of his roots and its links to be with his grandma unconditionally. Based on such a realization, Areem shook off all inhibitions and mental oscillations, renewing his commitment of love for Gul Meher for all time to come.

His other insight was more heartening and stimulating. For the first time, he came to the realization that his trip to Panjshir was not in vain. In staying at the mausoleum and because of the settings all around that focused on Ahmad Shah Massoud, he was always under the thought and influence of the former. Areem could not get from Ahmad Shah Massoud what he wanted while the latter was still alive, but he got more from him than expected while he was dead. Areem consoled himself with the thought of his desire to get guidance from Ahmad Shah Massoud did materialize but more meaningfully about his own life and living. Areem expressed his gratefulness.

That rewarding feeling was momentarily tarnished by the society's overall response to a man who gave everything of his life to protect their roots, culture, and values. In a self-talking mode, Areem debated the insincere exposition of values of so-called social order. It is taken that shock and sadness, like joy and happiness, have an inbuilt element of time factor. However desolate an incident may be, over time society moves on, shadowing the inherent feeling. Not that neither the event nor the experience is forgotten but that the social system learns to live with that, attending to society's nascent commitments, desires, and responsibilities.

But the society just can't take an about turn from its destined course, and that too so soon. That precisely happened in the case of Ahmad Shah Massoud during the Taliban's presence in Panjshir and after the successful air strikes by mujahideen at the heart of the USA. That pained Areem acutely when he was having his last gaze at damaged military assets of USSR.

It precisely happened with the death of Ahmad Shah Massoud. His burial to the hilltop of his choice literally drew the line of unbearable juddering. He continued to be a part of sociopolitical discussions but did not matter to decisions taken. Life for Panjshiris goes on.

The behavior of some Panjshiris, after the reinforcement of Taliban army showed up, was an obnoxious one. Ahmad Shah Massoud, even in death, did not escape that. Partisan grandstanding, nauseating comments, and mischaracterizations hurled at him, while hardly a surprise, were nevertheless dismaying. Areem left Bazarak with the burden of that feeling, but his stay in the mausoleum and observations of devotions of followers and admirers relieved that partially.

People involved in maintaining the mausoleum were very vigilant, being conscious of the fact that the Taliban could do harm at any moment.

Cognizant of the fact that he had overstayed and normally visitors did not wander around the premise of the mausoleum without causing suspicion, Areem decided to resume his journey soon.

His aforesaid conclusion was evidently a variegated one in response to local situations and Areem's objectives in life. It nevertheless had bearings on intrinsic insight pertaining to life as experienced and obvious human behavior pattern.

JOURNEY

It was the morning of the third day. Areem walked out of the mausoleum premises with his attires and belongings. He had rejuvenated vigor, leaving behind fear and apprehension. He had no premonition. He fortified himself with a risk-facing mode irrespective of the rarefied nature of probable future encounters. Some of the phenomena he noted in his journey on foot were gradual absence of mud-brick battlements around houses, decline in small quaint villages and settlements, and frequent encounters with unexploded ordnance on the roadside.

In his walk toward south, Areem had no restraint. While walking beyond Bazarak, he maintained his own speed, stopped as he had chosen, and took rest as he liked. But one thing struck him the most. The journeys from the setting of hills and mountains to the plains, sort of valley bottom, were not as captivating as the reverse process was. Areem recalled his previous journey sitting in the Taliban truck convoy from Kandahar to Bazarak. The Yemeni driver, Jabel Hamed, a jolly and exuberant person, would draw Areem's attention to every change in scenery.

The upcoming journey towards the south had two notable features. First was the advent of dry and barren plains. And, the second was persistent casual queries from sundries about who he was, where he was going, and so on. That sounded to be standard practice of engaging with unknown in places where the population was thinning out. However, the notable specific addition was a question pertaining to any Taliban link, an identity much dreaded because of the US presence and sustained bombing.

Areem's journey back had a mix of courses and incidents never thought by him when he commenced the same. While going to Bazarak, he was not concerned about those. Neither was he familiar with the culture of

252

inhabitants, who were seminomads with penchant for talking to unknowns in determining proper identity. The speed of the truck, the driver's unceasing chatting, and the thrill of the unknown kept Areem preoccupied in his journey to Bazarak. But the return journey was not the same.

Boarding a van unto Ahmad Shah Massoud's mausoleum was the first act in his return journey and, by connotation, was an uneventful one. The remaining travel involved a long walk, occasional ride in civilian trucks, increased physical pressure caused by flow of blood because of continuous walking that rapidly impacted palms and foot, and augmented need for breaks to take rests under shades of mosques, *chaikhanas*, wayside savannas with dust-battered isolated plants, and the like. The prime focus was to find water sources as a determining factor where to rest and sleep at night.

His enthusiasm for both steady and speedy progress was thwarted once in the midst of the plains. Scorching sands and hot air of the day coupled with cool breeze and cold nights slowed down progression. Absence of regular habitation and sparseness of people compounded his agony, with sleeping becoming a major problem. Then the most inescapable scenery emerged. Nature appeared at its best.

Intermittent green fields of wheat and sporadic existence of orchards, signifying the presence of water and habitation, graced portions of the dry landscape. Rolling groves of varied fruits, shimmerig wheat fields, and patches of greens with scattered semibuilt shrubberies serving the purpose of pasture land added mind-boggling luster. Areem got invigorated.

That rejuvenation did not last long. Areem soon observed the presence and influence of both powerful and chaotic assortment of retreating Taliban clutching weapons but looking panicked. Their emotive exposition was exercising governing power without authority in the midst of cluster bombs, IEDs, and bullet casings. Beheading still continued to be their epitome of justice administration. He became a flummoxed individual in that isolated situation and was at a loss as to future course.

As providence would have it, Areem noted roaming nomadic herdsmen with their sheep moving from Hindu-Kush mountain base toward south. They stopped near the resting place of Areem. The proximity to water source was, of course, the dominant reason. After they exchanged pleasantries, the chief herdsman took interest in Areem, noting him to be isolated and different from all others. The chief also took pity, noting Areem's inability to speak reasonable Dari.

Because of abundance of water, the chief decided to camp for the night among their sheep in that place and invited Areem to join them. That association continued for three following nights as the herd's movement was slowed to ensure adequate intake of both water and grass. When they reached the vicinity of Bagram Township, Areem got separated. He reminisced that Bagram was close to Kabul. Areem's discussion with the chief herdsman convinced him about his ability to negotiate the distance easily. That appeared all the more feasible as a good number of civilian trucks also frequented these two important cities.

Areem struggled a lot in approaching Bagram, to him a vibrant township as the principal air base of the Soviets during earlier days. Of late, it also served as an establishment office of the Taliban. The US Army currently made it as their principal air operational base to root out the Taliban.

From a distance, Areem could notice the reflections of sunrays from numerous steel-framed edifices. Those shuddering reflections were in sharp contrast to reality on the ground as Areem noticed when in a nearby airbase periphery. Roads and alleys were by and large empty, and most iron shutters on storefronts were drawn. There was a sharp contrast between the hectic activities inside the barbed-wire fencing and the capricious fraught conditions outside.

Fatigued and thirsty, Areem took position in the shaded corner spot of a closed shop, dazed for a while, and fell asleep while holding a little dry fruit in his hand.

From an upraised security outpost at the edge of air base fencing, a guard, through his monitoring binocular, noted Areem in a motionless position for a long time and rapidly concluded him as being one belonging to Taliban engaged in monitoring activities around and within the base. The deduction was rapidly transmitted, and a jeepload of armed personnel showed up, promptly following prescribed military preparedness against possible upshots.

Areem was not only panicked at such turn of events but also, as immediate impulse, baffled. Without fully understanding questions with Texan intonations, he hurriedly wanted to hand over all that he had in his backpack; and in the process, some of his belongings fell on the ground. That was taken by the army to be a tricky move to deflect focus. Areem was immediately lugged to the vehicle and was handed over to an adjacent detainee center that also functioned as a torture cell for suspects.

Walking past, Areem was appalled while observing some detainees going through the torture process. He was wondering as to what was ordained for him but drew comfort in thinking that he did not do any harm to anyone or undertake any roguish act. He completely surrendered to the will of Allahpak and blessings of his grandfather.

The following day, Areem was presented before the chief interrogator of the torture cell. He was tall but unusually bulky for an army personnel. Areem yelped within himself. That alone was not the cause of Areem's fright. Apart from being a rusty army personnel with a clean-shaven face and a clean-shaven head, the chief interrogator's personality wore an unambiguously rogue manifestation with very heavy and thick mustache. His expressions and communication style heavily tuned to army lingua. His accent was very dissimilar than the one familiar to Areem. That made it difficult for Areem to understand the chief interrogator. Areem was responding to questions, as he understood them, in Bangladeshi style of speaking English that made it equally difficult for the chief interrogator to comprehend. Dari and Pashtu interpreters were of no use as Areem's proficiency in both was negligible. That evolved situation frightened Areem more and confused the interrogator greatly.

In usual army style of solving an impasse, the chief interrogator dispatched Areem to intermediate torture process to find out who he was and what made him sit outside the air base periphery for so long. A corporal of the army working in the torture interrogation center was assigned to monitor him and document words and facts that would come out from the torture.

The US invasion of Afghanistan had ended, and US presence commenced with the retreating armed Taliban continuing to survive capriciously in rural and mountain regions of Afghanistan, and hideouts in Pakistan. For the new administration, things were in their infancy. Administration structures within the command and those of civilian setup were being placed gradually.

That was the reason for the interim location of torture cell, officially named interrogation center, adjacent to Bagram air base.

The day-to-day interrogation operation was being run under the stewardship of a junior noncommissioned officer (JNCO) who happened to be the chief interrogator too; however, policies, activities, and supervision of the torture cell were under the authority of a command sergeant major of an armor brigade combat unit located in Kabul for planning sustainment of war-fighting functions. The responsibility assigned to the sergeant major was a temporary arrangement, like many other ad hoc arrangements, at the initial stage of US presence.

The assigned temporary commander in charge of the interrogation center was Sergeant Major Robert Bakely. He was on his first tour of duty in Afghanistan but earned his name and fame within a short while.

The central leaderships of the Taliban were on their heels chaotically to avoid fire and fury of US onslaught. Though the central Taliban leadership succumbed to US pressure, it was too early to have major impact locally. The foot followers, though in shock and disarray, retreated cautiously under the guidance and direction of local al-Qaeda organizational structures and claimed to have capability to confront US war machines. From a propaganda perspective, that assertion was reflective of the strength and extent of organizational structure of al-Qaeda, the backbone of its offshoot being the Taliban movement in Afghanistan.

That was evident when a camouflaged striking unit of the Taliban suddenly outmaneuvered a convoy of trucks carrying petroleum and related inflammable materials to Kabul from Kandahar. The convoy was cruising the main highway between Ghazni and Kabul while having required security details.

The unplanned focus of the Taliban attack was to neutralize the security umbrella first and then set fire on the trucks, making that a media -driven, and equally hifgh profile, show of strength.

Command Sergeant Major Beckley—who was driving his own jeep with two GIs sitting at the back, followed by additional support GIs in a follow-on armored vehicle—was returning to Kabul from a tour of Kandahar. They were following the convoy after Ghazni, looking for space to overtake. Right at the moment, the Taliban forces undertook the strike.

Without hesitating and thinking for a moment, Command Sergeant Major Beckley ordered his accompanying GIs to engage the attackers and maneuvered his vehicle to confront the enemy. The unexpected appearance of support US forces unsettled the Taliban forces even though they were successful in initially nullifying the accompanying security protection.

Command Sergeant Major Beckley and his support troops unleashed volley of firepower instantly from their automatic weapons. The Taliban insurgents did not have time to ignite fire in any of the trucks, creating the anticipated massive blaze both for making their propaganda and for sending signals to the United States and outside world. Their overenthusiastic action to open fire, aiming at the security network when they were relatively far away from the convoy, provided time for the command sergeant major to act on time.

A large number of Taliban forces were killed; and others, riding their horses, quickly withdrew into the desert plains in a spread-out manner. For Major Beckley, it was the first, even though accidental, face-to-face encounter with the Taliban. He took an intense glance at some of the dead ones to internalize their varied attributes: the way they dressed, the pattern of headgear, the way they kept their beard, and related physical features.

That quick decision and action by Command Sergeant Major Beckley minimized the damage considerably and saved a good amount of defense assets and lives. After that, Command Sergeant Major Backley was fondly addressed by all and sundry as SMB.

From his base in Kabul, SMB came to Bagram for a scheduled inspection of the interrogation center. As he was passing by the torture cell, he stopped hearing the screaming of one who was stripped of clothes except undergarment and hanged from a horizontal pole with hands tied, and cold water being poured on him to get the truth. He was shivering and crying with repeated tenuous assertions, saying, "I am not a Taliban. I do not believe in al-Qaeda mantra. I am a Bangladeshi on my way back home."

SMB continued in his earlier standstill position, observing the alleged Taliban and the ferocity of the process. He had no remorse for the process but was inquisitive about its appropriateness in the instant case. He peeped at the alleged fellow and did not find any similarity in physical posture with the dead Taliban he witnessed a few days back. He didn't have long hair, flowing beard, engaging mustache, and penetrating eyes. The latter was evident in some cases of the dead of that encounter, possibly because of the length of time involved.

He walked past without any comment and went to the corporal's office and got preliminary information about the Taliban he had observed. His face and physique flashed a number of times when SMB was having pertinent discussions with the staff. Something was bothering SMB, a childless North American of fifty years of age. He had a loving wife for the last thirty years. He had remorse for not having a child, but the love of his life and passion of army assignments kept him going and happy.

This noontime, however, was different. In between conversation with the staff, he was preoccupied with the thought of trying an alternative approach in this case: approach to and conduct of inquisition through love instead of torture.

To the utter surprise of all present, SMB floated the idea to take the detainee along with him for a few days and try to have needed opening through love and compassion with a mix of understanding. He undertook all responsibility and assured full security.

Areem, on his part, was baffled as he observed an incoming GI wearing a smiling face. All through the morning and noontime, the GI was rough, tough, and abusive fellow, shouting louder and enhancing duress every time there was a fault in complying with the command. By nature, those additional ones were gruesome, faults were plenty, and the shouting was piercing. As he went through the process, it was clear to Areem that it had a singular objective: an admission of guilt, which was predicated to link or assumed association with Taliban or al-Qaeda irrespective of truth.

The GI untied Areem with a lot of love and care, gave him fresh towel to dry up, asked him to dress up, provided his listed belongings, and civilly asked him to follow.

Areem was escorted to a waiting military jeep and was asked to wait. Soon thereafter, a military personnel, followed by two GIs, came out of an apparent office room. The GI accompanying him was speechless for so long, but on seeing the incoming higher-up, he whispered, "He is our commander named Robert Bakely."

SMB boarded the jeep, sat comfortably in the driving seat, and directed his fellow two GIs to get Areem seated in between them at the back seat. Areem voluntarily squeezed his frail body in between the two sturdy GIs. SMB noted that and was happy about the future prospect.

On reaching the assigned official accommodation in Kabul, SMB got down promptly. Without proceeding to the house, he stood there, extending his hand to ensure safe alighting of Areem.

That gesture was more than hundreds of soothing words to Areem. He was beholden to the officer assisting him and was thinking of choices to convey the same. He was also uncertain of the reasons why he was taken out of the interrogation center, what he had to do, and what his future was. As always, he reverted to the mercy of Allahpak and blessings of his grandpa.

Observing fragile and malnourished physical states of Areem, SMB deliberatively took slow steps in approaching his accommodation. In between, he said, "Oh, I forgot to introduce myself. I am Robert Bakely.

My friends and well-wishers address me as Bob. I am command sergeant major and posted in what is called Armor Brigade Command Team to help and support other fighting units in sustaining warfighting functions. That team is yet to be set up and organized. In the meantime, I have other assignments, and supervising the functioning of Interrogation Center of Bagram is one of them. By the by, you can call me by either of my names, and the choice is yours."

Showing his room, SMB said, "You take your time to freshen up. My batman, an orderly in uniform assigned to a commissioned officer, will call you at 8:00 p.m. for dinner."

Saying those words, SMB retired to his room and sat on the easy chair while his batman served him steamed hand towel, cold beers, and peeled off saltless pistachios in a service bowl.

While having his booze, SMB intensely deliberated upon strategies and options concerning the handling Areem in future to get the truth and nothing but the whole truth. Two conclusions preponderated his thought. They were trust and patience. With respect to the first one, SMB decided to give time to Areem to gain his confidence. With respect to the second one, the strategy was not to resort to unusual hurry to get to the bottom. In this respect, SMB decided to bite the bullet if so needed.

Being flabbergasted in the lonely setting of his small room for the night, having an iron–framed bed, a small table, a chair, a table lamp, and a hanging picture of a cowboy with Wild, Wild West backdrop as well an attached bathroom, Areem was wondering about what he had in his destiny. His discomfort magnified many times when he related the last few nights of sleeping under the open sky and among the sheep in made-up straw beds.

Tired and troubled, Areem sat on the chair, impulsively being engrossed in varying thoughts, and succumbed to an unintended shuteye. At the appointed time, there was knock on the door. The batman slowly opened the door and requested Areem's presence at the dining table as the sergeant major was already there.

Waking up with embarrassment, Areem hurriedly went to the washroom; splashed water on his face, neck, and hands; and set his hair, applying fingers in the absence of a comb. He then proceeded to the dining table for joining the sergeant major. The latter greeted him with a mild smile. Embarrassed for being late, Areem avoided eye contact and looked edgy.

Halfway through the dinner, SMB maneuvered to break the silence and make Areem more at ease with the new surroundings. He initiated interactions, inquiring about the food. Areem responded positively, nodding. SMB then said, "I notice that you are not only hungry but equally exhausted, needing food and rest. So eat to your heart's content and sleep as long as you want. I will instruct the batman not to disturb you. When you wake up, please look for him. His name is Nabi Baksh."

Those words did not only uplift Areem but also had an immediate notable positive impact on his physical expressions. Areem stepped away from the embarrassed feeling of immediate past and started looking at SMB, always thinking, *Who is he, and What does he have up his sleeves?* He never faced such a situation of having a present mix of comfort and care with evident unspecified turns in future that could easily be fearful and frightening.

That mind-set was both indubitably jerked and uplifted by what SMB had to say subsequently. Looking straight at Areem, he said, "I do not know you at all except a briefing about you before I saw you in a distressed situation in the torture cell. I had been known and recognized as a daredevil military guy. Softness of heart was never an attribute of mine. I do not know what happened within me in the spark of the moment when I saw you. I acted contrary to rules of engagement with terrorists and security-related practices. By taking you out of the interrogation center, I have taken a risk myself. I hope you understand it.

"I would not like to discuss anything more to night. You have a nice sleep and take rest the whole of the next day. When I return from my work, we will have free and frank discussions. Rest assured that if you live up to my expectation, I would definitely try to help you. But please bear one point in mind: you can move around within the premises of this accommodation but can't step out. That will invite perils of maximum enormity. Security personnel have been so instructed. So abide by the rules."

Having said those words, SMB winked at the batman, conveying silently for a drink to be served in his bedroom, and walked away. Areem retired to his room.

From the quiet setting of his room, sipping wine, which he did not take while having dinner to earn the trust of Muslim Areem, SMB called his wife in Minnesota and narrated in a nutshell the episode of the day. While he was talking to his wife, the emotion of the childless husband had all the spontaneity of expressions and impulsive expectations.

Responding to SMB's passionate call, the ever-loving wife, Mary Melanie, just commented, saying, "I do understand your sudden emotional upsurge at seeing the young man. I also agree with your avowal that possibly our son would have been like him had he been alive. But I request you not to draw any line purely based on feeling. Please have discussions with him tomorrow as planned and then tell me about your conclusions. I assure you that I will be with you in the future too as I was for the last thirty years."

After finishing the telephone call, Melanie went back to their married life and recalled Bob's earnest yearning to have children soon, he being one from a single-child family. He always missed interacting with siblings as his other friends used to do. So he wanted a full family where there would be more children than one. But that longing remained unfulfilled for initial many years of conjugal life. Consultations of all types and medical interventions of all forms failed to yield any result. Giving up that aspiration, they decided to enjoy life as it was, reconciling that not having children could possibly be genetic as Bob's family traditionally, so far as he could relate, had very few children.

Then something happened; and Melanie, being apprehensive of upshot, took time to share with Bob. It was the night of their wedding anniversary. Having passed a wonderful time, both of them retired to bed. Bob started to play with the shoulder lace of her long see-through nightie. Intense hugging and kissing by both followed that. However, Bob noted that Melanie was lacking her usual spontaneity and aggressiveness in such sensual interplay, particularly that night.

At the end of the foreplay, both were preparing to fall asleep. Melanie, contrary to earlier practices, was in a hurry to retire to sleep as if she were unwittingly seeking an escape. That did not distract Bob.

Sipping little water from the glass placed on the bedside table, Bob turned toward Melanie and started caressing her gleaming hair. He moved closer. Placing his lips on the ear of Melanie, he softly inquired, saying, "Are you okay?"

That was perhaps too much of love and sympathy for Melanie to endure. Without responding, she slowly raised the upper body, bent legs, put face between her two knees, and suddenly started sobbing. That took Bob not only by surprise but also with intense angst. It seldom happened in their married life. Baffled and indeterminate, he started caressing her back and said, "Please share with me your cause of anguish. Do you remember that in our wedding vow, I said, 'I promise to love you, to be your best friend, to respect and support you, to be patient with you, to work together with you to achieve our goals'? Every day of our married life, I uttered those words to register them in my ears. I will never shy away from that vow come what may. So tell me, what is bothering you?"

With feelings content in all its manifestation, Melanie just said, avoiding direct eye contact, "I missed two successive periods. I am unsure about myself. I went to consult a gynecologist the day before yesterday who said that she wouldn't rule out pregnancy in the situation. She also said that in my case, and if so, it would not be an instance of late pregnancy but it would be rated as a delayed one. She also prescribed related investigations. I delayed that for discussions with you, and hence, I always had anxiety and nervousness."

Bob drew her close as an indication of reassurance. She surrendered like a small child being relieved of penetrating anxieties. Relieving himself with a big sigh, Bob said, "We should be neither optimistic nor pessimistic. Let us have a middle course, which is often expressed as 'so far so good.' If the outcome is positive, we would welcome it. If it is negative, it does not affect us adversely as we have already conditioned ourselves to live with that. You should go for suggested investigations soon."

Those investigation results eventually confirmed pregnancy to the delight of the couple, more particularly of Bob. That multiplied many a time when prenatal ultrasound confirmed that the baby was a boy. Bob started dreaming and talking about his ardent ambition of seeing the son as a commissioned officer in the military.

Since the end of World War II, there was extensive presence of US support and protection bases in Germany. These were a combination of air force and army force units. Rhein-Main Air Base, located near the city of Frankfurt, was a prominent one and famous for playing a critical role during Berlin Airlift operation of 1948.

It was mid- nineties. A rumor was going on about the possible handover of the base to German command. And at that moment, a one-year assignment was offered to Bob in Rhein-Main Air Base. He grabbed it, further reasoning his son Jeffrey's ardent love for and competence in soccer. He told Melanie that one year's acclimatization in Germany, the citadel of world's soccer, might augment his soccer competence, a definite plus point for possible induction in the commissioned rank.

Life for Bob's family proceeded as planned. They moved to Frankfurt and settled down easily in an all-catered military accommodation within the base. Jeffrey got enrolled in school and got engaged in practicing soccer with friends, both in rain and sun, whenever time permitted.

That was a drizzling day. Jeffrey and friends were engaged in soccer practice. In that quest, enthusiasm took over competence. Jeffrey, being challenged about his ability to perform the most notable trick occasionally resorted to by Franz Beckenbauer, nicknamed Der Kaiser at being the legendary soccer player of the time, jumped up to maneuver the ball below to perform the trick. Something happened in the bat of an eye. Jeffrey not only lost balance but also fell awkwardly with his head down and without support. That was the end of Bob's dream. Being a senior noncommissioned officer himself, he was aware of the inevitability of death and absorbed the unexpected with all pain. His focus was on taking care of and extending support to Melanie.

The couple returned to the USA. Time passed. Life moved on. Bob was planning to retire after losing his dearest son and bought a small house by the side of a lake in Minnesota. More specifically, the place of their new location was known as the Lake of the Isles. It connected with the biggest inland lake of Calhoun Isles and had a circumference of about seven miles. This and the capital city, Saint Paul, are popularly known as the Twin City. The state had a nickname called Land of 10,000 Lakes because of its topography.

Preponderance of lakes, lushness of all around greens notwithstanding extreme climatic features of both cold and hot, presence of huge leafy trees, varied type of flora and fauna, spacious roads with sidewalks and bikeways looked magnificent with presence of traditional big houses and mansions. That setting would be a place of spontaneous choice for any to make life a pleasant one.

Observing downtown Minneapolis skyline and its buildings reflected in the lake awed the couple. The enormous beauty of that; the associated tranquility; the inherent peacefulness; the sublime intellectual aroma propagated by the presence of professionals of varied disciplines, traits, and demographics; and the presence of recognized educational institutions made the place a logical choice for the couple as the setting for their postretirement life.

Right at that moment, the call came for a tour of duty to Afghanistan. He was hesitant, but Melanie prevailed upon him. He was reminded of his oath to defend the sovereignty of the country and ensure its territorial integrity. The nation was under shock because of 9/11, and an affirmative decision was not difficult.

Bob moved Melanie to their new abode and settled her fully before leaving for Afghanistan. The plan was that he would retire from services soon after his return, and both would have mutually supportive life in the wonderful setting by the side of lake.

Reminiscing that phase of life in a fast-forward mode, Melanie stepped out of her home with eyes soaked. She walked slowly and sat by the side of the water of the lake, earnestly praying for peace and happiness in their days ahead. But back in Kabul, the feeling was different.

Being perched within the house was initially all right for Areem. But as hours passed by, he started feeling bored with the batman showing a reserved bearing. He noticed some books on the shelf. One, a biography of Field Marshal Montgomery, drew his attention and interest. He picked up the book and started reading it captivatingly.

Being blessed with high intellectual attribute and having a reading opportunity after a gap of months, Areem concentrated in reading that masterpiece as fast as he could while lying down on the floor. Because of strenuous effort and concentration, he fell asleep around late afternoon when the book was halfway through.

The batman showed up, addressed Areem as *sir*, and said, "Sergeant Major has come back. I will soon serve tea. Please get ready."

Embarrassed, Areem got up promptly and wondered about the impetuous twist and turn of his life. The address of 'sir' bemused him. He, however, did not have time to ponder about it. Having freshened up, he soon joined SMB for tea, initiating a discourse premised on apology. Areem apologized for picking up the book without permission and for yielding to unintended sleep on the floor.

SMB's response took Areem by surprise. He said, "It was my mistake. I should have told you about the few books I have on the shelf. I am happy that you picked up the most important among them. Now let me know whether you learned anything from the partial reading of the book."

Areem replied without taking time but with caveat centered on part reading. He said, "It is worth recognizing that Field Marshal, even though a subject of the empire where the sun never sets, had to endure posting, during his early career, in the most inhabitable place of prepartition India:

Balochistan. That taught me that hardships are part of the process to success and glory."

That reply not only made SMB exultant but also convinced him about the intellectual aptitude of the young man. He was happy to note that his first impression on seeing him was not wrong. But his yearning to know the background of the young man was pressing his immediate thought.

Being a seasoned military personnel, SMB mastered the art of managing emotions. Instead of asking the blunt question as to who he was and why he was there, SMB opted to follow a different route. He opened up briefly about himself—his married life; the accidental death of his only loving son, Jeffrey; his current status; and his future plan.

That stimulated frank and open narration by Areem as to his childhood, unpleasant growing-up life experience in Bangladesh, recognition received for academic excellence, and his sudden decision to join al-Qaeda more to know firsthand about their intent and objective. But that itself became an exasperating experience since participating in the killing operation of fellow pious people in Multan. He decided to remain with al-Qaeda for the aborted attempt to meet Commander Ahmad Shah Massoud of Panjshir, a legendary leader who had an opposite philosophy and interpretation of what Islam is all about.

Areem clarified that his participation in al-Qaeda essentially was an escape from the unfriendly reality around and influence of a close friend. Areem emphasized that notwithstanding that decision, all his ultimate intention was going back to academic life to become a physician. That specific objective was based on the fact that his mother died for lack of immediate medical attention.

To convey seriousness about pursuing studies, Areem mentioned about his stay during vacation, preparing for TOEFL as part of the process he had under consideration to study medicine in the USA.

During the ongoing chronicle, SMB remained watchful, occasionally commented, and shared briefly events of his own life to avoid any impression of investigatory focus and monologue. To be certain, SMB mentioned, "In dealing with you so far, and my related statements and comments, I have remained honest to the core so that you know fully who I am. Likewise, I expect you to be truthful and tell me the whole truth. I will never use your words against you. Rather, that will perhaps enable me to help you in life."

In follow-on oration, Areem mentioned about his grandparents and his relationship with Gul Meher of Bazarak, emphasizing that she was his wife for life even though rituals were not performed. She was presently in the early stages of pregnancy. He also touched base on the reasons for leaving her at this stage as both the society and religion do not permit premarital sex, which is known as *zina* under Sharia law. The punishment is death of both by stoning.

Areem also clarified, "Saving my life became paramount in that situation as Gul Meher is soon to leave Bazarak for the USA as an eligible dependent of her maternal uncle, a submission that has been approved. It will now be for me to join her today or tomorrow but definitely any time before death. In that quest, I am now on the run. I have not done anything wrong except succumbing to emotion pertaining to my relationship with Gul Meher. I have not committed any crime but still a hostage under your care. I am thus equally unclear about my future."

It was getting late for dinner. SMB proposed a break of thirty minutes before reassembling. That was acted upon.

Consistent with the discipline and practice of the army, SMB was in the dining table sharp past thirty minutes. Like most other civilians, Ameer showed up a few minutes late with no guilt, but he had his backpack in hand. He put it up by his side but refrained from talking about it. SMB also willfully kept quiet.

He deliberatively introduced a new topic. Drawing attention of Areem, SMB said, "I am an American, and I am a Christian too. Drinking alcohol is sanctioned by our permeating social injunctions. So I am used to having beer before dinner and wine during dinnertime. If you do not mind, I will very much like to continue that practice."

Areem could not help but burst into laughter. Embarrassed subsequently, he said, "Sir, it is your place, and you have graciously allowed me to stay. After many days, and after wandering between hills and plains and living in the midst of sheep, I had a bed and pillow last night. That is disbelieving for me. What more can I hope for? Do whatever you normally do. Do not be constrained by my presence or by my faith. My father would be of your age, or close to. So behave like a father. Command me with your wish. I will obey that without hesitation. This is a promise."

SMB was dumbfounded by such a quick turn of events. It was difficult for him to digest that an unfamiliar young man had given him the rare honor by equating him with his father. Areem, on the other hand, had a motley feeling for saying "Behave like a father." He took the initiative to explain that to his host.

After the dinner was over, both continued their discussion over respective wine and cup of tea. Areem made a dent in that by inquiring straight whether SMB felt uncomfortable for his saying "Behave like a father." Explaining the backdrop, Areem said, "As a group of people, we, Bangladeshis, are very emotional. That is embedded in our faith-related acumen, belief context, way of life, social interactions, political discourse, mode of thinking, and modality of expressions in art, literature, music, and so on.

"I was mostly on the brink of addressing you as a father for all the compassion you have shown and everything you have done during the last many hours to elevate me from the darkest moment of my life and gave me unparalleled quality of flashes of living. But I contained myself, recognizing that you are from different roots, faith, and culture. I also refrained from thinking along a similar line as that could be viewed unwelcome intrusion in the space Jeffrey, even in death, has in your mind and thought. Had you been a Bangladeshi, I would have definitely addressed you as such."

Areem was relieved at having the opportunity to unload freely and frankly his life and its events to a receptive individual of rare acumen. He was happy at being able to clarify emotional facet of growing up in a green deltaic region crisscrossed by water bodies of varied sizes and types. This influences not only seasons but also the way of thinking and articulation of people by and large.

But SMB's departing act and words took Areem by total surprise. While shaking hands as a gesture of good night, he pulled Areem toward him for a warm hug, saying, "Children are always a blessing from the Creator. However, one's own involvement in the process is equally a humble immersion in sustaining the creativity. I wish for your ultimate reunion with your wife and offspring. I am going to call Melanie, my wife, now and will tell her about you, Gul Meher, and your child in the womb." Saying those words, SMB departed.

Standing still in the same spot, Areem was beguiled, concluding that all human beings are a product of emotions. The only difference is that different segments have mottled ways and mode of expressing that.

As planned, SMB made the call to Melanie and finished his long telephone call. The positivity of that discourse quickly focused on issues pertaining to future actions. Melanie, recalling the US command's willingness to support an adoption after the sad demise of Jeffrey to relieve shattered SMB from the agony, suggested an early action on that line, iterating candidly, "Based on what you have said, I have no hesitation to embrace Areem as a son. Please convey to him that. He will be an important and meaningful addition to our retired family life."

Retiring in his bed, Areem started focusing on issues related to Gul Meher: how she was, how the baby was, whether her uncle showed up, and whether Gul Meher left with him for eventual migration to the USA. He also thought about Gul Bahar and what happened to her.

PASSAGE

While Areem was lounging in the most unexpected comfort setting of US Army facilities under the care and love of Sergeant Major Blakely, Gul Meher was in her uncle's home as part of the family experiencing challenges but equally hoping the best outcome for the family as well as self.

The uncle showed up in Bazarak with two of his associates close to the time indicated earlier. In the merry setting of reunion of siblings, he listened to what Gul Bahar had to say and decided not to contest anything as perhaps this could be their last meeting. He focused on reassuring Gul Bahar about the well-being of Gul Meher, treating her as his daughter and never imposing anything against her will. After that, he called the two accompanying fellows from their resting place and introduced them as Safiullah Saleh, one having salt-pepper flowing beard, and the other as Zabiullah Abbasi, having a clean-shaven face. He said Safiullah had a long association with him, and Zabiullah, though relatively new, had proven to be trustworthy. Instead of selling the Karachi business, he entered into a partnership with them for running the business on profit-sharing basis. He went on, stating, "Either one would visit you after every two months with 2,000 Afghani and would report back to me about your well-being."

Gul Bahar was speechless and bent down to touch the feet of her brother, showing respect and acknowledging his love. She then informed the brother about the private wedding of Gul Meher with local postmaster at the behest of the late Kazi brother.

Continuing her part of unfolding, Gul Bahar said, "The postmaster, Areem, based on a tip, has gone to Tulub in search of Gul Meher's father. The wedding was not made public due to absence of the father and

269

keeping the advice of the Kazi brother in view. We do not have any official document. I do not know what to do, a matter aggravated by sudden demise of the Kazi brother."

The brother had an operative discussion with his two associates, got the name and address of Areem from the piece of paper left behind by him for Gul Meher, handed over some money, and asked the associates to get a certificate on the government stationery with the official seal. The money handed over was to serve as grease money to facilitate the processing work on an urgent basis. He did not forget to emphasize privacy in handling the task.

Necessary headways were accomplished on time. That included having the much-needed pseudo marriage certificate and a meeting with community elites informing them about the brother's temporary absence along with Gul Meher and arrangements made to look after his only sister. He stipulated their return to Bazarak once the US citizenship issue was settled.

The community elders agreed with his arrangements but pointed out one missing link with respect to the arrangement. That related to needed day-to-day backup support for Gul Bahar's stress-free living.

Brother Fazal Abbas noted the same with thanks and evaluated possibilities. Imam Shaheeb volunteered, saying, "I would look after her periodical needs of consumable rations, as is being done presently, until Shahram returns. But she needs someone from the community, at least twice in a week, for routine tasks such as receiving and posting mails and communications and other unforeseen life and health-related challenges."

Brother Abbas expressed his unbounded gratitude to Imam Shaheeb and sought the guidance of the community on the remaining issue. The community elders, recalling the family's association with the late Kazi Shaheeb, decided that Muqquabir, the son of late Kazi Bhai, should be given the responsibility and requested his consent. That was acceded to, and everyone was happy.

The brother, Gul Meher, and the accompanying two staffs left for Karachi via Kabul. Within limited choice for reacting, Gul Bahar revisited the backdrop and the reality of her life involving, among others, the killing of her dearest son, the apparent desertion by her loving husband, and forceful marching order to her son-in-law. But the present one, Gul Meher's leaving her, based on assumed reunion with Areem in the USA, was too much for the mother to bear, though it had her consent. The stone-faced Gul Bahar, recounting some of the sayings of Zubaida Khala, held back tears in the presence of Gul Meher. She, however, succumbed to emotional pressure once Gul Meher was out of her sight. She stopped sobbing, realizing that there was no immediate one to console her anymore at the moment of her grief. She started the habit of self-talking, laughing or soothing herself as the situation warranted. But she found it extremely difficult to overcome the easygoing but veiled comment of Muqquabir, saying, "*Chachi* [Aunt], you played a game with me. I will see who finally wins and how this game ends!" That statement had all portentous insinuations.

While negotiating crossroads and in every turn, making progression of journey, Gul Meher was scanning for Areem as if he could show up any moment.

Back in Karachi, Gul Meher was initially frustrated as it was not the same familiar setting of the refugee camp. But the care of her uncle and aunt, as well as the love of her three cousins, made her acclimatization process both easy and endurable. Her early living experience in the refugee camp helped a lot in the process. Besides, the family's noninterfering attitude made the process easier and comforting. No one asked her about her marriage and her husband, least about the pregnancy that the aunt was prompt to notice.

Like other members of the family, Gul Meher got enmeshed with the preparations to leave for the USA soon. Being a product of the refugee camp, Gul Meher had no particular attachment either for Karachi or for Bazarak. So there was no emotional backlash in that preparation. Her growing up with scores of children having no roots was another factor. Gul Meher's vision of the USA, however, was much broader because of the physical presence and publicity associated with USA's invasion. Even then, her apparition was limited to Karachi but as being a place of larger scale.

Her stay in Karachi had the persistent strains of thoughts of Areem and her mother, whom she left behind alone. That continued during her settlement process as part of the uncle's family. But she had little choice. Her singular mission at that point was reconnecting with Areem in a supportive environment and rearing the baby. She recalled Areem's expressed longing to become a doctor and promised to herself to do everything to fulfill that dream through the progeny.

Gul Meher, while going to sleep every night, earnestly prayed for Areem's appearance in her dream, a wish mostly remained unfulfilled except once. Without being upset, she continued praying for his well-being and safety and made it a routine before sleep to lovingly move her palm on the belly, intuiting the sensual touch of Areem.

On his part, Areem was slowly striving to gain the confidence of SMB in his quest for a solution to his life's present conundrum, multiplied many a time for having the guilt feeling of leaving Gul Meher behind in the early phase of pregnancy.

As life-related interactions, both past and the prospect in future, between the two were being carried out as a daily feature, SMB had full understanding of rarefied nature of Areem's risk-faced problems. The former craftily conducted the said conversation to avoid causing any gratuitous expectations in the mind and thoughts of Areem. While his discussions with Areem slowly tilted from passion to pressed need and requirements for higher studies in the USA, SMB, without specific opinionated observations concerning preparations, got hold of random books and publications in matters like TOEFL (test of English as a foreign language); SAT (measurement of critical reading, writing, and mathematical abilities); and ACT (a curriculum-based multiple-choice assessment testing reading, English, mathematics, and science), being unsure of what he would need and what would be appropriate.

SMB's trajectory of exchanges with Melanie was on a different footing. Of late, he spent more time with her talking about Areem, his past, and intellectual virtuosity that, if properly nourished, despite the recent derailment, could help responding to some needs of a larger social setting. His continuous mention of how equably he bonded with and could relay to Areem started to beguile Melanie. She knew well and certain what he wanted to say but was unable to say so. She also thought that perhaps his previous vocal resistance to precipitous proposition of the command of Rhein-Main Air Base to help him adopt one on compassionate ground was the inhibiting factor in the present situation.

To spare him from any linked embarrassment, Melanie piloted that proposition with a twist as if it was her thinking. After patiently hearing the latest eulogy, she said, "I am conscious of your earlier position on adoption. But that understanding underwent a reversal at my end when I talked to Areem a few days back. I always had the feeling that I have had been interacting with someone of my own. I therefore concluded within myself without hesitation that we should take and treat him as our own and help him in pursuing his life's ambition. It also made me relaxed to find in

Areem's guise one close to your penchant. And that definitely makes you happy and me both happy and comfortable.

"So I suggest that you take action to get him a residency permission to the USA. If that entails his being sponsored by us, I will be more than happy to endorse that. If that is not possible, let us try to get for him an entry permission for higher studies, and we will give all required undertakings from financial and security perspectives. We should have the position that all our lives, we worked to keep the USA safe, and one more addition of a Bangladeshi Muslim, under our constant watch, would not make the country's security vulnerable."

Deliberately avoiding prolongation of that suggestion so that the focus was not diluted, Melanie ended the discussion promptly. She concluded it for certain that a thank-you from Bob was not that relevant. What was needed was deep deliberation and prompt action.

SMB's implicit happiness was outshined by the infinite elation of having the germane proposition from his wife about the line of action that he was harboring within himself for the last many days. That was not all. He continued to send periodic reports on Areem based on his interrogative discussions and feedback from batman and security guards. Whenever he had something interesting, he submitted a report to the Bagram Interrogation Center for onward action. That practice had twin objectives: building a case favoring political options, in addition to military intervention, to neutralize al-Qaeda influence and protecting himself from likelihood of any contentious views in the process.

In his first report, he touched base on who Areem was, his family background and growing-up experiences, his eagerness to know more about al-Qaeda and subsequent frustration, his awareness about Ahmad Shah Massoud in the process, and his sustained ambition to become a doctor, backed by his locally recognized intellectual fineness.

In the second report, he made efforts to distinguish Areem from other al-Qaeda cohorts based on intensive follow-on exchanges. Rational and evidence-based statements were recorded, establishing reasons for Areem being near Bagram Air Base on his journey back to Bangladesh with the ultimate objective to be in the USA for his cherished medicine study.

The third report moved from person to perception. It documented Areem's assessment of Afghan dilemma and its possible mitigation in the future. Many of the directional angles were not necessarily unique but certainly spoke volumes about the intellectual excellence for one of Areem's age and background, distinguishing him from other al-Qaeda followers.

SMB recorded his wonderment when Areem in a postdinner conversation observed, "I do not understand why Allied powers are still bogged down by looking at and tackling Afghanistan's current status with focus on a sort of an imposed solution. They should better be looking for options to find a sustainable way forward.

"In that pursuit, there needs to be a recognition of fact-based realities and faith-related cum culture-related practices. Among others, there are two fact-based actualities. First, the country has never been subjugated, and so it has no colonizer-ruled heritage. Second, it is a fundamental mistake to treat individuals with long loose shirts and baggy pajamas, open-breasted waist coat, turbans, tire-based footwear, and long-flowing beard as ignorant, dumb, and foolish.

"It is the same piece of geographical area where human habitations date back to thousands of years, which was a strategic link for Silk Route connecting with rich cultures either way enriching itself in the process, where the religion Zoroastrianism originated thousands of years back, and where paganism in the south and the east, Buddhism in the southeast, and Hinduism in and around Kabul were nourished before advent of Islam beginning the seventh century. This is the place that not only witnessed major military campaigns of ancient and modern Asia but also became the home of numerous dynasties establishing major empires all around.

"There is no doubt that the present scenery within Afghanistan is both disheartening and ubiquitously frightening. Prolonged history of divergent races, ethnicities, and faiths is both a pride and a problem for present Afghanistan, which was originally known as Aryana, subsequently as Khorasan, prior to its present identity.

"Focused tribal root continues to be the identity, and diversity in languages is propelling and sustaining that. People continue to be identified, both in war and peace, based on tribal roots and the languages they speak. In a chronicle of long history, these two elements could not be subjugated by higher objectives of forging national unity and the need for developing a uniform national language.

"This is the root of the current problem. Their immediate solution is a far cry. However, mitigation of those is possibly worth the try by resorting to Afghans' thousands-of-years-old genomic talents. So 'education,' forget about male and female education, should be the planning priority. Undue talk and publicity about progression in female education would certainly create misplaced apprehension in the mind of the public as it is perceptibly against the norm of prevalent social values and misplaced but pronounced religious injunctions. It needs to be recognized that once education makes general progression in the country, female education will make desired advancement without resistance.

"Second, nonlethal approach would be to explore and accentuate inherent talents and capacities of different tribes, making them block-building assets rather than arms of obliteration. That, in essence, signifies power sharing based on expertise. Generally speaking, Pashtuns, inhabitants of relative plains of southern Afghanistan and the gateway for invaders to conquer resource-rich and equally fertile India, were exposed to frequent invasions by divergent powers. That contact made them astute negotiators, which eventually made them good in national politics. Likewise, Tajiks—with proximity and close link to Russia, sharing some of the heritage—are relatively better educated and have talents and capacity for employment in administrative positions. Hazaras, the descendants of Mongol invasions, and Uzbeks, the assimilated offspring of Turko-Iranian ancestors, are possibly a natural fit to man the armed forces. Their historical link and ability may be exploited in the current setting to make them feel engaged in nation-building tasks. In that process, they will have their identities restored with emotional balance. Similar approach would possibly be helpful in the case of the remaining minor tribes."

In succeeding para of his third report, SMB mentioned, "On my query about the source of his such thoughts, he referred to a book on Afghanistan that I have in my shelf but seldom had time to read. What surprised me was that not only did he read the book but he also tried to assimilate facts and views to articulate some of his own. He was conscious of that and apologized in conclusion for talking in absolute terms. Areem concluded his oration by showing full respect to policymakers but did not hesitate to share what he had in mind."

Subsequent reports on file were mostly in support of his positive assessment about Areem and his intellectual ability, emphasizing choices between condemning him as an al-Qaeda activist or giving him a chance to excel in learning from where the society at large could benefit in the future. SMB maintained that giving Areem a chance to reshape his life might send a positive signal to many like him.

SMB had all the materials to act on Melanie's suggested line of action. He prepared a detailed and convincing submission backed by periodic reports on Areem, equally highlighting his own service to the nation and commitment to security of the country. In this regard, he also emphasized immediate response to the call of duty in Afghanistan soon after the accidental death of his only son in Germany. SMB took the opportunity to underline his denial to go for immediate adoption proposal of the army forces unit of Rhein-Main Air Base, exceptionally premised on Melanie's emotional health.

SMB further stressed in his submission by underscoring, "It is a different case and a different scenario to mention that both Melanie and Areem bonded very well during intermittent telephone discourses of recent past. The main contributing factor was the demise of Areem's mother at infancy and Melanie's losing a budding son accidentally."

This submission—augmented by justifications and supporting evidence, in addition to those mentioned earlier—was submitted to the authority concerned through designated army hierarchy and was sent to Minnesota senators and relevant congressmen as well as Rhein-Main Air Base of Frankfurt and his local command.

RESOLVE

Preoccupations entailing preparation and presentation of the case of Areem caused a vacuity in daily discourses between the two. Areem was not told anything about the current thinking of the family and actions being taken. That was to avoid unwarranted exuberance resulting in catastrophic dismay if the final decision would be a negative one. As a diversion, SMB kept on pressuring Areem for better preparation with respect to qualifying tests.

That obviously could not be a twenty-four-hour task. Even though he got involved in limited physical activities within the compound with the help of the batman and under the watchful eyes of security personnel, Areem had plenty of time to think and ponder about Gul Meher and her possible journey to the USA along with the family of her uncle whom she fondly and respectfully addressed as *mamu-jan* (dearest maternal uncle).

Mamu-jan, recognized in the community by his formal name of Fazal Abbas, was popular and respected for his occupational acumen, specifically in restaurant business. He was known for his straight-thinking ability and stability of mind. But that reputation suffered a setback for the first time when the issue of settlement in the USA came up for a decision.

Fazal Abbas's world, before becoming a refugee, rotated primarily around Kabul and occasional sojourns to Kandahar for business purposes and Bazarak to visit his roots and maintain contacts. That was the pattern while running his restaurant in Karachi too. His exposure was limited to some members of the royal family, political personalities, social elites, and diplomatic personnel of embassies. His discussions were mostly confined to variety and taste of his food. In that inhibited mingling, Fazal Abbas always kept his ears alert to pick up hints about possible social and political upshots. Though not sufficiently educated, he mastered the expertise of linking isolated words and then drawing a conclusion. Most of the time, he was right.

Fazal Abbas kept his plan for migration to the USA mostly within himself and family except two US diplomats who encouraged and guided him in the process. Their main interest was to have an authentic Afghani restaurant in Washington, DC. As the time was closing in, Fazal Abbas opened up to friends and well-wishers. That caused subsequent confusion and problems.

Friends and well-wishers came forward with specific opinions and suggestions. Many of them, like him, were never in the USA but had mostly authoritative views based on feedback from their relations and friends. Fazal Abbas got confused, and the process experienced unanticipated delay.

Times passed by with confusion getting compounded. Relatively well-versed and practical-minded Fazal Abbas had unaccustomed traumatic feeling. Decision continued to be deferred.

The high point of varied opinions was about the relative suitability of places for having a restaurant specializing in Afghan cuisine. The two diplomats who played a prominent role in motivating Fazal Abbas to migrate to the USA and helped processing his application from behind were largely for Washington, DC, as it's the seat of the government and hub of diplomatic corps. The opinions of well-wishers were at total variance based on the existence of numerous eateries in WDC of divergent preferences and tastes. The competition would be tough, and obviously the prospect was bleak. They mostly opined for Houston, with Boston as a second choice.

Eventually, it dawned on the eldest son to talk to family. He said, "Father has decided to immigrate. Necessary approvals are there. We should not be bogged down by hearsay apprehensions. We should act to leave soon. Based on earlier discourses, we should explore three cities: Houston, Boston, and Washington, DC. An early decision as to our settlement would not be difficult based on tangible experiences and eventual impressions. Once that decision is taken, we will put our best effort to succeed. MashaAllah, we are solid four individuals to be supported by Mother and sister Gul Meher. We need to take a decision."

As an exceptional gesture, Gul Meher opened up saying, "I fully agree with you, brother. There is no more justification to play with time. Let us take the dive. We would either swim or sink."

Those strong affirmative assertions caused renewed confidence within Fazal Abbas. The decision was taken to move forward without further dithering.

The extended family of Fazal Abbas landed in the George Bush Intercontinental Airport, a structure having five terminals encompassing four levels. The oversized design of the airport and long circular walk caused apprehension in the minds of new immigrants traveling with many pieces of heavy checked-in and carry-on baggages. There were noticeable question marks in the eyes of his three sons while his wife, Ambia, and niece, Gull Meher, wore confused looks. Fazal Abbas remained steadfast.

Their living in a modest rented accommodation was relatively trouble free with the generous help of and compassion shown by relatives and friends of friends in Karachi. The initial unwavering stance of Fazal Abbas, however, did not last long. He was prudent enough to assess the perils in settling down in a huge sprawled city with no public transport. He observed that most houses had more than three vehicles for mobility's sake; and he—with three sons, a niece, and himself—definitely couldn't avoid the same with recurring costs multiplying. The other thing that worried him most was his assessment of a restaurant business prospect.

The city no doubt was booming, but the demographic characteristics were not congenial. The presence of Bangladeshis, Pakistanis, Indians, Iranians, and Afghans was noticeable but evidently were overshadowed by the presence of Caucasians and African-Americans (CAAs) and a huge number of Mexicans and Vietnamese, in addition to many other ethnicities of fewer proportions. The CAAs would much prefer to taste the food of Afghan origin as occasional diversion. The other two groups had their specific culinary preferences, and a food of the type of Afghan was a no-no for them. The most disturbing finding was the behavior of subcontinental client groups. They visited restaurants more as exceptions as they preferred home-cooked food. That occasional visit was based on contact and familiarity with the owners, and the tariffs per se without necessary consideration for quality and ambiance.

Fazal Abbas continued his own assessment but preferred to discuss the matter with the family during dinnertime only. That was a cautious and calculative approach since he largely took the decision to immigrate, leaving a good business back in Karachi. And also, he wanted to avoid chipping frustration that might set in among family members in view of their experience of settling down.

His dinnertime interactions were to get honest feedback from sons who developed some contact and friendship with local youths irrespective of their ethnicities and faiths. Their presence and occasional support in helping the father in running the business in Karachi exposed them to various types and groups of people. That was very helpful in developing local contacts in Houston too.

But the most surprising similarity of what sons alluded to and what he had been observing of late unnerved Fazal Abbas for the first time. That pertained to slackening of warmth of people compared to the initial days of arrival. The sons highlighted that with the passage of days, friends started to treat them as one of the many locals; and some started taunting them indirectly, observing that many came with high hopes but eventually melted down with mundane professions.

That was what Fazal Abbas had been experiencing too. Though it was a natural consequence of regular encounter, the sharp and visible decline in warmth was noticeable. That, in some sense, was ominous too. He concluded that time was of the essence, and a decision was the most imperative need. He took his own decision and planned to advise all about that.

In a succeeding post dinner conversation, Fazal Abbas opened up himself, saying, "My experience in life and living in Kabul and Karachi made me conclude that whatever is being said, the future is uncertain and challenging for us. I had good interactions with people connected to our royal family and expatriate communities in both Kabul and Karachi. Based on that exposure and because of the enthusiasm of two American diplomats to have a genuine Afghan eatery in USA, I decided to immigrate. I do not have any regret despite the frustrating experience of the past many days. But the time has come to take a final decision.

"By all considerations, Houston is not the place for us. A few days back, I had an excellent exchange with a Bangladeshi professor of Southern University. Though she was a long-term resident herself of Houston and an ardent Houstonian, she was skeptical of the success of an Afghan eatery here. Her other opinion was that Boston, for reasons discernible, would not be the place for the type of business I have in mind. The most important reasons she referred to were seasonal variance in population related to academic schedules and dependence of the larger segment of the student body on financial assistance and scholarships, constraining their liquidity."

Fazal Abbas continued saying, "The professor further opined that based on varied nature of support factors she could reflect on, 'WDC is probably the most suitable place for you. Yes, there is no doubt that competition will be very stiff there, but also remember that both competition and opportunity are twin elements of the same encounter. There is every truth in the saying that USA is a place of opportunity and that opportunity depends on one's performance. So if you are committed to provide good food coupled with good service, nothing can stop you.'

"Saying those affirmative words, she continued her statement saying, 'One last point is, do not try to differentiate your customers based on their ethnicity, color, creed, belief, and way of dressing up and communication. Your job as the restaurant owner is to serve them and make them happy. If satisfied, they are more likely to come back.'"

After a pondering gap, the youngest son, who experienced the biggest impact of acclimatization, asked Fazal Abbas as to how he could meet the lady professor. That was very embarrassing for the other two senior brothers who grew up in Afghan and Pakistani culture of unquestioned obedience.

The father took it easy and stated, "I was in the company of your uncle Habib Ameen of Pearland a few days back. We were supposed to be going to a county to have a feel of a possible site for the restaurant, especially that being an upcoming area. As we were getting ready to leave, Habib Ameen mentioned that he was in the campus of Southern University a few days back to explore the admissions prospect of his nephew from Pakistan. The admissions office was having difficulty in understanding him. They referred him to a professor who happened to be a Bangladeshi on the perceived notion that she, being from the same geographical area, would understand him better.

"At this stage, Habib Ameen said, 'That worked very well. I am positive of a fruitful outcome.' He continued, saying, 'I was very impressed by her friendly temperament and easy style of communicating. As a long-term resident in the USA and a regular talk show participant of a number of radio Bangla programs, she has broader ideas about challenges and perils of settlement in the USA.'

"Habib Ameen continued saying 'For some odd reason, I raised your issue and your current dilemma about the settlement process. Surprisingly, she was receptive, took interest, and had follow-up queries. At my request, she agreed to meet you on a no-obligation basis at a convenient time'

Fazal Abbas resumed his part of the statement, saying, "We discussed the pros and cons and decided to meet her before going to the new site. I was motivated in getting an honest opinion from someone who is not even remotely interested in what we have as priority. That was the background and answer to your inquiry."

After saying those clarificatory words in recently used to American way, Fazal Abbas assumed the style of talking ln an authoritative posture, typical of an Afghan house master. He drew renewed attention of all, saying, "Listen to me carefully. Our decision to immigrate to the USA is one-time decision in life, and there is no turning back. We have unduly been under duress for last many days. By all consideration, WDC appears to be our best destination. Instead of wasting time and money, I have decided to settle in WDC with the dream and hope of having our Afghan restaurant there. As a family, we will work hard, serve the most authentic and delicious Afghan food, ensure the highest standard of service, and always treat customers nicely. If we can adhere to these, then nothing would be on our way to success."

The family maintained silence, which, as per culture, was reflective of their agreement. Preparations were afoot for their relocation to WDC.

The restaurant was designed having exterior melting with usual facade of local construction pattern in the chosen part of WDC, and the interior represented a typical Afghan milieu. The interior wall was pasted with colorful wallpapers reflecting features of eclectic array of its identifiable region-specific fortes.

Having his eyes on different types of clients and their different preferences based on time and demand, Fazal Abbas decided to have three sections in his leased-out longish property. The first but relatively smaller one was to cater to the taste and demands of walk-in customers for a snack-type service. Billed as the Afghan Snacks, it served selected Afghan wayside foods, including the fabulous *aloo channa chaat* made with smashed fingerling potatoes and chickpeas and served with succulent yogurt. Based on demand, this also had a side dish of sweet and spicy *chatneys* (pickles)

The middle section, fairly spacious compared to the first one and named Aram (Leisure), was designed for multifunctional uses depending on time. From morning to afternoon, it was open as a café with a franchise from Steambuck Coffee. In the next two hours, it was converted into a place serving predinner canapés and social drinks. By preference, it was kept unpolished and homey, with a counter service and just a few longish tables (akin to bar tables), each with a basket of dried hibiscus.

The third section, named Mahal (Palace), was the spacious formal dining room. Magnificent pieces of Afghan carpets with dark-maroon base and intricate designs akin to Persian ones added desirability to the ambiance of Mahal. Corduroy banquet serviettes, having smooth green and light-yellow colors resembling the carpet texture of the valleys between snow-clad mountains of northern Afghanistan, made the setting more indigenous and attractive. That was made more pleasant by having lighted *agarbatti* (incense stick) near the entrance and small presence of *attar* (oil pressed from botanical sources) on the table. The tables were designed with woodcarving of Afghan origin but had a more modern touch to avoid instant contrast. So was the case with the chairs. The tables in the dining room were placed strategically, having some preference for space to ensure relaxation and privacy.

Not only was Fazal Abbas a capable manager, but he was equally efficient in spotting points of delegation and pointers to monitor the result and performance. While physical stuffs were making progress, he concentrated on food items and service matters, including the attire of the staff.

His thought about food items was basically framed by the diaspora of reputable and traditional cuisines of Afghanistan and their international popularity. That definitely inspired him but caused concerns as the choices became restricted. He decided to keep the menu desirable with emphasis on quality and taste, decor, service, and presentation. His objective was to market the type of inconspicuous food of Afghan origin and mix and match it with eating items from nearby countries.

Principal items of Afghan diet are meat and naan. Naan is a tandoor-baked flat bread with small segments having burning signs in the process of roasting in a cylindrical clay oven fired by charcoal or wood. Generally, naans are round, but the one in Afghanistan is long.

Meat is the most consumed constituent of an Afghan meal. Meats in different forms and shapes—e.g., sliced portions, cut-up pieces, and minced—are consumed. Depending on the type of preparation, meat is smoked, braised, grilled, roasted, and juiced. In rural areas, meat kebab and naans are stable food items.

The term *kebab* popularly represents various grilled meat dishes cooked on a skewer over a fire. The lamb meat is high in demand for making kebab. But other meats like beef, chicken, and goat are also preferred with the demand being area specific. Increasingly, fruit and vegetable pieces in between the meat pieces are also being preferred with fish gradually creating its own niche. In the greater periphery, such a kebab is known as shish kebab or shashlik.

Minced meat is also consumed in the form of *kofta* (minced meat balls with a mix of mild-flavor spices like cardamom, cinnamon, turmeric, coriander, cumin, etc.). The other very popular minced meat preparation is known as *chapli* kebab, meaning flat kebab. Liberally spiced with proportions of half meat and half flour and given the shape of a patty, the *chapli* is fried on a big iron pan and is a popular barbecue meal.

Fazal Abbas discussed the suggested menu with the family. That was the outcome of his own impression concerning fondness, traits, and preferences of innate Americans. He said, "I was initially very curious about many people either eating out before going home or carrying food to be shared with the family. The need of two incomes to run a family has taken away the inherent splendor of a family setting, with each one participating in different forms. There is no gain in debating on those. This opens up a very welcome business opportunity for us. I gave a lot of thought as to what would be ideal within our capacity and ability. My earlier proposed menu was the outcome of considered deductions based on such assessment.

"Consistency in quality, taste, and service should be our topmost priority. Americans, I am told, generally do not like food preparation where the flavor of spices overtakes the flavor of basic ingredients. So we would have to be chary in determining the proportion of spices such as chili, turmeric, coriander, cumin, toasted or otherwise, in preparing our restaurant food while still ensuring Afghani taste and specialty. The essence is to retain the flavor of basic ingredients notwithstanding use of spices. By a trial-and-error process, we would be able to draw the acceptable line.

"At day's end, ordinary Americans do not have the inkling to do anything hard. They want everything prepared. They very much like to eat but seldom would exert themselves in chewing bones or anything solid. They therefore like to drink, having a special feeling of joy with each sip down their throat effortlessly. Because of a combination of factors, they prefer to have ready food at their doorsteps.

"It is therefore my view that we should have a manageable menu, have some common eating items, and cook our most items using bone stew for enriching the taste. Acknowledging the current dietary preferences, we should have fish kebab too in our menu. It is also important for us to keep in view that a large number of vegetarians reside in this city and that population is growing. We need to have preparedness to respond to orders for vegetarian foods like *bindi* [okra], *rajma* [kidney beans], dal [lentils], and *sag* [spinach]."

As was apparent, the family not only noted but also definitely endorsed what Fazal Abbas had just stated. The eldest son, as an exception to customary behavior, intervened to emphasize arrangement for home delivery as the latest marketing move for food sold by restaurants of their type. All readily endorsed that.

In the midst of prodigious penchant for unity in approach and action, the naming of the restaurant unpredictably became a contentious issue. The strong preference of Fazal Abbas was to name the restaurant according to the link with his roots as well as familiarity in the outside world. So his first choice was to name it Afghan Restaurant, with alternative choices of Kandahar and Kabul, two names he used for his restaurants in Kabul and Karachi, respectively. The sons had different views.

Gul Meher, who participated more intuitively in some of the previous discussions, made a bang in this case, siding with the brothers. Showing full respect to her maternal uncle, whom she fondly always addressed as *mamu-jan*, Gul Meher diplomatically placed her views, saying, "What you have in mind is perfectly valid and rational, but what my brothers are trying to suggest has also some merit."

Alluding to the post-9/11 French fry controversy, she observed, "Our naming of the restaurant should not be vulnerable to unforeseen happenings. So I suggest that we name the restaurant as the New Kebab House with notation below of its Afghan origin and link to Kandahar and Kabul restaurants of Kabul and Karachi respectively. It also has the advantage of a friendly-sounding acronym of NKH. From television advertisements, I find that Americans are very fond of acronyms, and NKH fits in very well in that setting."

Fazal Abbas was both amazed and exultant. Perceiving her evocative participation in earlier family homilies, particularly noting the current intervention, Fazal Abbas was very elated at being instrumental in getting

Gul Meher to the USA. Her endowment and acumen would have been a waste in Bazarak.

Bemused as well as beguiled, Fazal Abbas continued staring at Gul Meher to the utter wonderment of family members. But within himself and unknowingly, he was traversing the way of his life and gene in the physical presence and emotional aptitude of Gul Meher. He was engrossed in thoughts pertaining to his sister, Gul Bahar.

Recovering himself from that sudden sensitivity, Fazal Abbas took all present by surprise when he started saying, "I do not suffer any remorse for sponsoring Gul Meher as my dependent. My burden is lessened significantly as the decision had expressed consent of her parents. Having brought her and observing her communication competence and confidence on various issues, I have the obligation to ensure that she blossoms to her fullest potential. And more importantly, I would not like that she remains permanently a dependent. After the restaurant, that is my second project."

Everyone was contented with what Fazal Abbas had in mind. Through side comments, family members assured him their commitment and support in attaining the objectives of his second project. But what Gul Meher voiced took all by surprise. Expressing her profound thanks, she said in an emotional-laden pitch, "Mamu-jan, your decision to bring me along with the family has not only given me a new lease of life but also assured life to my yet-to-be-born progeny. The other inevitable option, as Mother told me repeatedly, was to face trial under Sharia law and be condemned to death by stoning for allegedly committing *zina*. My indebtedness to you and the family is boundless. I would like to put, whatever way I can, all my effort in helping you all in successfully running the restaurant initially. In between, I will have equal focus in looking for avenues to attain excellence in applicable fields of life. What Mamu-jan said about independent living has been in my thought too. I am indebted to this family for showering unbounded love and affection during my time of distress and dismay. But I also owe to the child to be born a life and an identity where he would proudly be able to say 'my home.' I would much prefer to have a life like that while enjoying love of you all, and expectantly awaiting a reunion with my husband."

Having said those words and without giving space for further discourse, Gul Meher bent herself to salaam her *mamani* (maternal aunt), who was in tears, as well as Mamu-jan. The latter held her head by his two hands and bestowed a kiss on her forehead, symbolically conveying his happiness and blessings. The cousins hugged her, maintaining propriety per tradition.

In the midst of such a happy ending of that evening's exchanges, Gul Meher happily returned to her bed and suddenly felt a jolt in her lower belly as if someone was trying to kick her inner self. That was a strange feeling mixed with concern and excitement. The thought of Areem resurfaced, and she shed tears for missing him on this happy experience.

The present separation did not bother Gul Meher at all. She was certain of her eventual reunion with Areem. What continued to bother her was not having any response from him despite the several letters posted at his Dhaka address. Keeping that worry parked temporarily to destiny, she was thinking of her role and effort to help Mamu-jan in having a successful restaurant business operation.

The restaurant was formally opened in mid-September, coinciding with early fall. While seasonal trees were shedding leaves, NKH entered the WDC food market with a bang and attracted an increased flow of customers. Gradual progress was also being made in Afghan Snacks window and the Aram room facility as a coffee outlet. Its home delivery initiative was a thriving business in the midst of a bitter-cold weather.

Gul Meher started working as cleaning in charge of utensils and crockeries. She soon was in charge of making the dining place ready for dinner and lunch. In this work, she had to interact with hired staff and gradually picked up speaking functional English.

Time passed. Everyone was delightful. Fazal Abbas was beaming with contentment. Gul Meher, after delivering a healthy baby boy, started working as a receptionist, receiving guests, conducting them to tables of choice, and advising one of her three cousins to attend to them with the menu.

Gul Meher's transition to the American way of life and conversation was quick. She normally attired herself in jeans and top shirts. In the evening, she used to dress up in typical Afghani outfit including traditional jewelry, with beaded hair. She applied *surma* on her eyes. Every time she did put on *surma*, she recalled specifically Areem's liking for that.

Back in Kabul, Areem was getting bored with having an indefinite restricted life even though SMB was trying best to give him time, comfort, and confidence. One specific gesture of SMB that had a deep mark in his feeling was when he unexpectedly handed over to him the telephone to talk to his wife, Melanie. What surprised Areem was the ease, frankness, care, and understanding with which Melanie talked to him right from the start as if she knew him very well. In the process, she also unloaded her own grief of losing a much-adored only son in Frankfurt. Soon, it became a regular practice. That telephone call from Melanie became the most-looked-after thing for Areem in that lonely setting, and it bonded each other emotionally: a son without mother and a mother without son.

It was like any other afternoon time. The vintage clock just produced three loud sounds, indicating 3:00 p.m. The telephone started ringing. Areem was hesitant to pick it up as the only telephone he got used of late was from Melanie. But the time was an odd one for her to call. That caused the hesitancy.

As the telephone continued to ring, Areem picked it up with much hesitation but was equally stunned hearing the voice of Melanie. Being sure that it was Melanie, Areem breathlessly shot out queries, saying, "Are you okay? Any emergency at your end? What can I do for you?"

All of Areem's queries remained unanswered. Melanie was repeating her joyous statement, "I am so happy for you! I am so delighted!" Areem repeatedly asked, "What makes you so happy? Why you are so delighted?"

The answer inevitably was "I am so happy."

As local electricity was experiencing both generation and load management problems, the power went off; and consequently, the telephone got disconnected. Emergency power was switched on, but that was of no help for telephone connectivity.

Right at that moment, SMB's military jeep stopped in front of his residence. That was not the time for SMB's homecoming. Areem was surprised at seeing him hurriedly approaching the house. Nervous, Areem stood near the door in semifrozen condition.

Excited, SMB was just going to call Areem loudly, but seeing him standing near the door, he rushed toward him, hugged him warmly, and started saying, "I am so happy!" In that exuberance, SMB lifted Areem, started to rotate with Areem being afloat, and repeated the same statement in different forms.

That undeniably was beyond what Areem could sustain. He jolted himself out of the clutches of the two hands of SMB, maintained his pause, and said, "Can you please tell me what is going on? Melanie called just a while back and was repeatedly saying, 'I am so happy,' notwithstanding my repeated inquiry about the reason. Now you have come and are repeating the same thing. May I please know what actually happened? Let me be a party to your happiness."

That unusual but straight query of Areem did the trick in calming down SMB. With sudden mood change engulfing fulfillment in all its conceivable manifestation, SMB held the hand of Areem and slowly ushered him to his favorite place of enjoying evening drinks. They took seats opposite each other. SMB winked at the batman, who was about to prepare the favorite drink of his boss. Drawing attention, SMB told his batman to serve tea for both.

While Areem's puzzlement continued unabated, SMB took the time to organize his thoughts. Finally, he opened up, saying, "As you know, we had a lot of dreams, though short-lived ones, for our son, Jeffrey. We reconciled with reality but always had a sour feeling within for failure to provide our little contribution to sustainability of Mother Nature and this beautiful world. That hurt us silently, but we continued our hushed craving for the opportunity to be worth of the creation. Then, quite accidentally, I came into contact with you. Melanie was ecstatic too after having interactions with you. We bonded ourselves with you without your knowledge. At late hours of most nights, we talked about you. Then Melanie opined that perhaps it is an ordained reality for us, compensating for the son we lost.

"So at her suggestion, I submitted a comprehensive appeal to allow us to support you in achieving your dream in life. We also emphasized that your case, under conceivable military surveillance and monitoring, may be a test case to prove that all al-Qaeda followers are not necessarily jihadis. We gave copies to the Defense Department, the command of Rhein-Main Air Base in Frankfurt, my command headquarters, Minnesota's senators, and our Congress representative. After systematic persuasions at different times and levels, our submission, as a very special case and with our full commitment to take care of all your emotional and financial needs, has been approved. You can pursue higher studies in the USA under our care. I plan to take you to Minnesota early next month. Today, I applied for a month's leave to settle you there. Then, Melanie would be able to take care of you until I return at the end of my current tour of duty."

After pausing and lifting his cup of tea, SMB resumed his oration, saying, "I forgot to explain the reason for initial confusion in communicating with you. Before I came, I called Melanie to convey the good news with indication that I am going home to inform you. In between, an urgent message came, needing immediate attention. I got delayed. But Melanie was following the earlier schedule. So when Melanie called, she rightfully assumed that you already knew. On my part, being late in coming and assuming that Melanie had already conveyed the good news, I repeated the statement. That was the confusion at our end and agony at your end. We need to align with the age-old saying that all is well that ends well."

Having said those soothing words as a foreclose to his exposure to the most positive outcome of their submission, SMB looked at Areem and was taken aback by what he saw.

Areem, being both static and reflective, was in irrepressible tears, impulsively swamping his fascia below the eyes. As he had direct eye contact with Bob, an address preferred by Areem while most others addressed him as SMB, he started sobbing with hiccups taking over soon. That was reflective of the emotional trait of Bangladeshis in general. However, in the case of Areem, it was much more than an ordinary emotional backdrop. It was the combined effect of obstacles, uncertainties, frustrations, experiences, expectations, and emotions in the way of attaining his life's objectives for intellectual attainment, including thought of possible reunion with Gul Meher.

Bob did not take much time to recognize that and approached Areem to shower him with a sincere hug, wishing him well in life. But that was forestalled by the baffling gesture of Areem.

Observing Bob approaching him, Areem bowed assiduously and touched the feet of the former, conveying gratitude and seeking blessings in the traditional way the latter was used to. Bob was not to be outdone. He promptly held Areem by his two elbows, raised him up, and gave him a warm embrace. Bob was enjoying the unlikeliest turn of events in his life, making it a challenging one for himself and equally fulfilling and exulting one for Melanie.

Bob allowed Areem the flexibility in expressing his feelings against the backdrop of most inconceivable developments centering his life. Areem's hiccups stopped, but his intermittent sobbing continued while tears were unstoppable. He wanted to talk, but his emotion-laden vocal cords appeared to be soaked.

As a happy diversion, Bob drew the attention of the batman, who, being a casual observer in that setting, had no clue of what was going on. He eventually asked for his drink and a glass of cold lemon water for Areem. That made the batman active in an otherwise dithered situation.

Sipping the water, Areem took a breath and started talking gently, saying, "There is no page of my life so far that is unrevealed to you. Since birth and in my growing-up process, I experienced disdain and dismay only in tandem with impulses pertaining to changes in tracks of life. I had my father but never had the expressed love and care from him. I lost my mother at infancy. Thus, I never had the opportunity of knowing and enjoying motherly affection and tenderness.

"Then destiny placed me in a circuitous bend of life. With no knowledge and preplan, I landed in Bazarak Township of Panjshir Valley to interact on a daily basis with armed civilians and chaotic assortment of religious activists clutching weapons but mostly bearing a look of panic. Life in that condition was merely a space between whim and a trigger. The absence of an established governing authority was most depressing. My urge to know about al-Qaeda vanished permanently.

"The lack of clarity with regard to the direction of my life and destiny coupled with the totally unaccustomed social behavior and unpredictable social order based on an orthodox interpretation of the religion of Islam made me shrink within myself in the locale of Bazarak. Outwardly, I conducted myself as a trusted government official, slowly developing a small base of contacts. That is how I came to know Gul Meher's father and, subsequently, Gul Meher.

"I experienced an emotional upshot consequent to knowing about and talking to Gul Meher, a daughter of Bazarak but born and brought up in the Afghan refugee camp of Karachi. In her mannerisms, thoughts, and actions, she had the aura that is more of urban Karachi than orthodox Bazarak. I enjoyed seeing her, meeting her, and occasionally talking to her besides relishing her interjections when her parents were talking. Unsullied human goodness in those interpolations overwhelmed me, developing within me an intense penchant for Gul Meher.

"This proclivity had enormous manifestations in inward thinking and outward behavior of mine. The initial rusty feeling within myself after encountering portions of barren mountains and other negative factors of the setting disappeared unknowingly as I got inclined toward Gul Meher. I soon started ruminating majestic mountains dotted by snow-clad numerous peaks, lush green valleys and iridescent lakes, rhythmic flow of the river with faultless rhyme, rolling olive groves, and shining wheat fields, among many others. I started liking all of them and became emotionally vulnerable and physically close to Gul Meher. The rest is known to you.

"Against that despondent backdrop, your and Melanie's consideration and action to provide an opportunity to intellectually rehabilitate me along with the possibility of getting united with my ditched family is nothing short of a miracle for me. It is challenging for me to accept that reality. For me, both of you are like angels. What both of you have done, and promised to do for me, to get into the USA is nothing one can visualize. People like you make this world beautiful and worth living in. Both of you are more than parents to me. And I promise to act, do, perform, and deliver to you both and society at large the best of everything that can be expected of me. I will live by this oath until I die."

Acknowledging the very positive and measured reflex demonstrated by Areem in handling and digesting the inconceivable way forward of his life, Bob once again stood up, hugged him, and as a diversion, said, "Let us take a little rest and join for dinner at 7:00 p.m. After we are through with that, I will call Melanie, and both of us will talk to her as a family."

Entering the room, Areem just could not be on a standing posture anymore. He felt drained and lost all his stamina and willpower. The status change from a war prisoner at Bagram to a legal resident in the USA without any prior allusion was too much to be absorbed. He was shivering. He spontaneously threw his body on the bed, closed his eyes, and got engrossed in his thoughts, which despite efforts, continued to be disoriented.

In that state of physical and mental stress, Areem impulsively recalled writing in his grandma's notebook where she recorded about the practice of his grandpa performing a few *rakat* of optional namaz whenever something positive happened in his life. Imbued by that, Areem straightway went to take shower, completed *uju* (ablution), and performed a few optional namaz following his grandpa's practice. While making a closing submission to the Almighty, he, besides expressing gratitude, especially prayed for the safety and well-being of Gul Meher and for their early reunion.

That was not straightforward and peaceful one as ordinarily expected. He was anguished for not having any reply from Gul Bahar even after repeated communications. Being unsure of her current status, Areem was thwarted. That significantly impacted his happiness pertaining to the most unexpected turn of his life. With all unforeseen adversities, he still kept on hoping for the promising outcome as the destiny had so far guided him to that path.

The two occupants of the dining table in Kabul were nibbling food with leisurely indulgence: SMB having a sense of fulfillment but more enthralled about the future responsibility and Areem dazing by the unlimited potential for attainments in the future, a reality that was a far cry from his perspective even a few hours back. He was in a state of apprehension unless what he was being told turned out to be a nightmare.

Reversely, the principal of the local elementary school, a regular customer of the New Kebab House of WDC, walked in and was warmly greeted by Gul Meher's eldest cousin, Kaiser Abbas. As he was being conducted to his familiar table of liking, the principal told Kaiser that he was expecting three other colleagues and hence would like to wait before ordering. Kaiser noted the same, withdrew quickly, and reappeared soon with a glass of freshly squeezed pomegranate juice, saying, "This is on the house, and enjoy it while waiting for friends." The principal smiled and nodded.

The dining process started merrily with the arrival of other guests. They focused more on light talk and side comments to the delight of the guidance counselor who just joined the faculty. Soon the discussion went to familiar school matters. But this particular deviation was fundamentally different from mundane matters they were mostly involved with. The subject of the discussion pertained to an emerging communication problem related to newly arriving immigrant toddlers, more specifically from beyond Kabul's periphery, both in terms of background and numbers. The communication skill of these children was limited to their native language; hence, assimilation and prompt integration was becoming difficult, constraining academic progression.

In overseeing NHK and its two associate setups, Fazal Abbas always impressed upon the need to get off-the-cuff feedback. Thus, all service personnel were motivated to selectively follow the casual conversations of customers, specifically related to NKH, its food quality, and service standard.

Kaiser was very conscious of this guidance and always believed that 'retaining a regular customer is as important as getting a new one.' Enthused by such a belief, Kaiser, while serving the principal and his guests, kept his ears alert and had a good grasp of the problem they were discussing.

Kaiser, by nature a risk taker as was evident in all discussions and decisions related to immigration, decided to talk to the group. He was a firm believer of remaining ahead of the story. So while serving Afghani green tea, he drew the attention of the principal and bluntly offered the services of his sister, Gul Meher, who was very good in Dari and Farsi. She could speak Urdu well and understood functional English. He also emphasized that Gul Meher had a natural gift of language; and during last few months of working with English-speaking workers and colleagues in this facility, she attained significant competence in English communication. She had no high school diploma but qualified enough to mitigate their existing problem until the school found a more qualified one. Kaiser concluded by saying, "I hope you do not mind my offering the services of Gul Meher, but I was motivated to do so as the problem largely affects my community in this area of WDC."

That encouraged follow-up discussions within the school administration team, and a decision was taken to try her out as a volunteer. The outcome was impressive enough to motivate a decision for her appointment as an associate. As Gul Meher's assignation was incident based and problem specific, she had plenty of free time. Being in the learning environment conscious of her inner urge, Gul Meher spent most of her time reading simple books of interest. The assigned teacher in charge noted that. She encouraged her to get a high school diploma. That, however, was not confined to suggestion. She took the time out and had an all-inclusive discussion with Gul Meher about options available for someone like her who desired to obtain a diploma without the need to follow any set schedule or classes. She referred to the availability of flexible, manageable, and supported online opportunity with unlimited one-on-one needed help from expert instructors under region-based accredited high school programs.

In explaining further, the teacher in charge stated, "Such accredited program of regional high school meets the demand of employers and colleges through accreditation process of the regional association of colleges and schools and is nationally accredited by the Distance Education Accrediting Commission. Financing and customized affordable monthly payment are also available. It thus opens up opportunities for a bright future for one like your background and talent."

Gul Meher shared the contents of that discourse with the family soon after her return, and she got their full endorsement. Lying down on the bed with the baby boy by her side, Gul Meher rekindled her life in Bazarak, especially after her relocation in Mamu-jan's ancestral house. Revisiting moments of her association and intimacy with Areem, she felt relaxed for the first time. She had nurtured the belief about their reunion as things were moving positively from her perspective. Thinking about Areem and his progression, Gul Meher fell asleep rather early in the evening.

Union

As Gul Meher was thinking and ruminating her life in conjunction with her present location and future prospect of reuniting with her husband, Areem just completed the immigration papers and formalities at his first port of entry: Chicago's O'Hare International Airport, more commonly known as ORD.

During the process of complying with immigration requirements, Areem was at the forefront. Once out of that, Bob took the lead role as the legal guardian of Areem. The subsequent connecting flight was relatively short, and their flight safely landed at the destined airport. Bob proudly gave him a short introduction of the airport, saying, "It is very ideally located within ten miles of both downtown Minneapolis and Saint Paul. So it has been named as Minneapolis-Saint Paul International Airport. This is unique as it has a common facility for both civil and military purposes. That made it tidy and efficient."

As the plane taxied and engines were switched-off, Areem unfastened his seat belt, stood up and followed Bob out of the plane and onto the gateway into one of America's finest airports--Minneapolis St. Paul International Airport, or MSP as frequent fliers refer to it. The very early evening milieu enhanced the attraction. Since that was Areem's first real exposition to modern airport, he was immediately impressed by the airport's openness, its contemporary design, and perceptible cleanliness.

They proceeded downstairs to the baggage claim area. Areem's delight bourgeoned when he saw Melanie waiting at the bottom of the escalator with a bouquet of flowers holding a sign saying, "Welcome Areem to your new home."

Melanie blessed him with an extended warm embrace, and she subsequently hugged Bob with an amorous welcome kiss.

The drive to Bob and Melanie's home was as wonderful as one could think of. Areem, sitting in the comfortable back leather seats of their teal blue metallic Mercedes sedan, was initially bemused seeing Melanie driving with Bob taking the passenger seat. Areem's perceived notion so far was that driving a car is a man's prerogative. It was the first jolt, but he took it easily concluding that it may be the first of many deviations and exceptions to the culture he had experienced up to that point.

Diverting from that sort of mundane thought, Areem started pondering the direction his life had taken so far, while Melanie and Bob were preoccupied with issues and experiences of family life in the Twin Cities of Minneapolis and St. Paul.

Bob and Melanie were fortunate to have their home in one of Minneapolis' most desirable areas, known generally as the Minneapolis Chain of Lakes. Fortunately, and as an exception, they found a modest home along Lake of the Isle's Parkway, the area generally famous for grand old homes. Their modest one somehow added startling variety to series of old grand homes of the area, thus eliciting a mollifying diversity.

For Bob, it was more to catch up, and update him. As they headed north toward downtown Minneapolis, Melanie drew Areem's attention to the Minneapolis skyline anchored by the blue reflective IDS Tower; the brown, bronze and gold of the Capella Tower; and the Wells Fargo Center. As they turned west around the south end of the city, they veered back toward the Hennepin-Lake neighborhood which Twin Citians refer to as "Uptown." But they weren't heading for the lights, noise and crowds of the Uptown scene, rather they were headed for the genteel neighborhood surrounding the most desirable of the Minneapolis lakes, Lake of the Isles.

Areem was amazed that even though the Lake of Isles is so close to a major downtown, the surroundings could be so quiet, peaceful and refined. He remarked about the beauty of the tree lined streets, the sidewalk path surrounding the lake, and the shine and light reflecting in the lake. Areem commented how beautiful Bob and Melanie's neighborhood is, especially the beauty of the blue lake. Melanie responded by saying that it charmed her too the most when she first saw it. Areem's seeming pleasure with his new surroundings made Melanie very happy.

Both Bob and Areem experienced semi jet lag for undertaking non-stop travel between Dubai International Airport [closest hub for international air travel from Kabul) and Minneapolis-Saint Paul International Airport. Bob traveled commercial airlines so he could give company to Areem. Because of their jet lag, Bob and Areem retired early that evening, and logically the breakfast of the following morning was a late one too, literally conforming to a brunch.

Bob took the initiative to retreat to patio lounge for a relaxed sitting after breakfast was over. Melanie followed him in the company of Areem. As a familiarization expose, she explained that the patio is the most used area of the house, and thus decorated by Dorchester Outdoor fully skirted seating set collection of synthetic wicker comprising of sofa and two each of coordinating chairs and ottomans.

The setting was supposed to be a relaxed one; but the center table had plenty of books, publications, and printed handouts. Melanie collected all those earlier and placed them on the table early morning as part of the plan discussed with Bob night before.

All three of them were comfortably seated against the backdrop of serene, lush green setting overlooking an unmarked spacious enclosure of the property with unobstructed view of sparkling lake water. Melanie stood up to go to the kitchen area, took a few steps, and turned back to request Areem to come along. Once in the kitchen, Melanie explained the process of igniting the electric cooking range, placing and arranging utensils and crockeries, and storing dry provisions. While taking a cold beer for Bob, she told Areem to prepare green tea for him and join them for a discussion of some thoughtful matters.

Once Areem returned to the patio with his cup of tea, Bob, with a sip of his cold beer, started his much-thought-out oration, saying, "I talked with you matters of paramount relevance in Kabul. I will briefly touch base with some of them with the physical participation of Melanie so that you are clear about our commitment in fostering the new relationship. We take you as our son, and 'not like a son,' with no material expectation but cherished desire that you should singularly try to achieve your life's objectives nurtured from childhood and fulfill your recent commitment with yourself to love and live with Gul Meher.

"Our decision to have you within the fold of our family serves us in terms of mental peace and serenity as it helps you, ushering an unexpected window of opportunity. The arrangement of sustained security surveillance should not bother you. In your case, it is a written stipulation. In most cases of new immigrants, it is a standard but unwritten operating procedure since

9/11. We are there to ensure that you continue to have the opportunity to pursue your objectives and challenges in life."

Saying those words, Bob picked up his can of beer while Melanie drew the attention of Areem to books, publications, and printed handouts on the table, saying, "Based on my discussions with Bob, I visited the neighborhood educational facilities and some related state offices of Minnesota. I discussed your case with some teachers and faculty management officials and came to the conclusion that your academic progression would better be served and in a time efficient manner through local community college. That will ensure better acclimatization with your surroundings, greater assimilation prospect, focused guidance, and efficiency in terms of time.

"Your lifelong objective is to become a physician. As perhaps Bob has already indicated to you, the enhanced standard requirement for admission to American medical schools is a pressing tedious process, which is challenging but nevertheless attainable. Essential to this is a very good result on completion of twelfth grade under the American system of education. This is generally called GED [general education development] degree. That is not enough for the purpose of medical education. The follow-on steps are admission to a reputable college for four years' undergrad education with preferably biology as one of the subjects, achievement of strong grades, and very high-level outcome in Medical College Admission Test [MCAT].

"During my last visit to our local community college, I have made appointments for you with the assistant vice president for academic affairs and college transition, student affairs, and director of student recruitment and outreach. That was done by design so that you have required clarity and understanding as to from where you start, how you can make progress in a time-efficient manner, and how the community college can be of help to you as a future student. The meetings are scheduled on next Friday, and I will accompany you to guide you to the facility but would not be present in your discussion.

"As prelude to your arrival, I have collected during earlier visits some relevant publications for your advance review and understanding. Those collections are placed on the table. Please review some of them for needed initial clarity."

Once the American residency issue was settled, Areem, while in Kabul, was preoccupied with the thought of educational prospect and requirement in his case as the minimum first requirement for higher studies in the USA was completion twelfth grade per the American system of education. He was concerned about the prospect and problem associated to his goal in life if he were to go through the lengthy process of attaining a US high school diploma (HiSET). The suggestion of Melanie was thus very significant and timely.

Reviewing some publications, Areem was exultant, noting the advantage inherent in diversity and flexibility of the US education system that really made it a great nation. Unlike other educational systems, the United States one is not exclusive. It is by design inclusive, providing avenues and options for lateral integration in most pursuits.

For those who could not complete formal high school education, or who do not meet the requirements for high school diploma, or those who are homeschooled, or those who pursued high school education outside the US education arrangement, a system has been designed for them to earn their high school equivalency credentials. This is commonly called GED and is administered by the American Council on Education based in WDC. The system involves a group of four subject tests designed to measure proficiency in mathematics, science, social studies, and reading and writing. It gives high school equivalency credentials to qualified ones. GED is equivalent to the US high school diploma.

That clarity was the most sought-after silver lining in the backdrop of a dark cloud that engulfed his life for so long. Whenever he recalled the consideration, care, and love of Bob and Melanie, he was emotionally overwhelmed, which usually drenched his expressions. Considering both of them as godsent angels in his life, he was thankful to his grandparents for their blessings, ensuring a way out in all adverse situations so far.

The thought that never vanished from his mind was that of Gul Meher and the newborn child, alternatively thinking as a girl and a boy. That thought was omnipresent. That thought was overpowering. It was difficult to express and share. It was a reality that was too personal and too poignant even though Areem was preoccupied with thought and focus of his life.

In the midst of such realization, Areem was plunged in reality that brought him back to thoughts pertaining to the immediate challenge and future life even though he had presently the most comfortable care and support of Melanie and Bob.

It was post lunchtime of Areem's first day in the Lake of the Isles, and he was immersed in reviewing the materials provided earlier by Melanie. There was no time for him to look around the neighborhood. After a gap, suddenly every minute became indispensable for him. Melanie and Bob showed up to check as how Areem was doing; and after exchanging smiles, Melanie said, "We are planning to make your first evening as a member of the family a memorable one. So both of us are going out. We will be back by about five o'clock and will have dinner together. Do not be concerned. It is very safe neighborhood."

A minute past six, Areem was asked to join them for dinner—a surprise for him. He never had dinner around that time. It was one of the many cultural deviations that he encountered and absorbed while assimilating.

But then, there was a greater surprise waiting for him. In many of his earlier exchanges with Bob, Areem casually mentioned his missing Bangladeshi food, highlighting many times his favorite cuisines. Bob listened to those and, for unlikely reference needs and possible use, occasionally noted down some of them. That became very handy in planning the surprise of the evening for Areem.

The couple went to the downtown food market and bought some favorite items of Areem from an Indian restaurant. (Most of them were Bangladeshi restaurants, but for marketing purposes, they were identified as Indian ones.)

Upon joining the couple, Areem was speechless at seeing his favorite fish curry, fried vegetable, mashed potato, and lintel along with plain white rice side by side with three crystal-cut wine glasses. As Melanie was pouring wine in two glasses, Bob was filling up the third glass with water, obviously meant for Areem.

The emotion-laden Areem was busy in wiping his eyes to hide his rolling tears. Melanie requested him to be seated and said, "We just thought that your first dinner should have Bangladeshi orientation as you missed them for about a year. Subsequently, you will be eating fast food mostly. Though we have our separate food, we also brought for us fish *kofta* [a round-shaped mashed fish after taking out bones, with a mix of herbs and mild spices] to give you company and to associate ourselves with your happiness. So no more tears. Let us start. Bon appétit. Enjoy your meal."

After the dinner, all three moved to the modest family space with a television, a wood-burning fireplace, and a few reclining settees with small-framed service pews packed together in a corner. Melanie vacated the room as soon as others were comfortably seated, cleaned the dining table, disposed restaurant containers, and made hot water for tea. Seeing her doing all those, Areem soon joined to assist her. In response to Melanie's mild observation, Areem happily replied, saying, "If Mother was doing all these, I would have done exactly the same."

Melanie smiled as a touchy response. Both of them returned to the family space with Areem holding two cups of tea and Melanie having the residue wine bottle for Bob.

It so appeared that Bob was all set to resume his oratory that, at its midpoint, was taken over by Melanie. Sipping the wine, Bob said, "Our immediate past effort to help you, our pledge to do so in the future, and our commitment to be on your side are deeply related to your actions and performances. Let there be no doubt about that. Let it also be clear that whatever we have in mind and whatever our objectives are, you do not owe anything to us.

"The second point is that both of us already decided that consistent with our approach and practice, we are, and will remain so, tolerant with all faiths and beliefs. Thus, neither are we going to change because of our adopting you, a Muslim, nor would we expect you to change. We can practice different rituals while living under the same roof. Further, if you want to go to mosque for *jumu'ah* or Eid prayers, I will be happy to drive you out, wait in nearest periphery, and bring you back as needed."

There was sudden composure in that discussion. Both Melanie and Bob gave time to Areem to ponder and react and got engaged in sipping their respective drinks.

Areem, being emotionally laden, was shaken and immersed. He opened up with his inner feelings and said, "I do not know what to say. My words are inadequate to respond to whatever you both did for me and articulated about my life with you as part of the family. I never ever been bestowed with such love, care, and understanding. In essence, it is a rebirth for me, opening up windows of new approach and fresh focus pursuing my life's objectives. I am eternally indebted to you and commit myself to be with you and support you in every turn of life, whatever the cost is."

Saying those words, Areem soaked, and his only introspective response was evident in drops of tears rolling down his face.

Melanie got up instantly, brought a glass of water, and offered that to Areem. In doing so, she said, "What I will be saying now may be hard for you to absorb. However, it is my belief and position that our successful endorsement of you enabled short-circuiting your entry to the USA. Hence, you should focus on your education presently and later on look for Gul Meher and your offspring from a stable position of life. And the time involved is the time you would have needed in any case for entry to the USA, if at all that was a possibility. In any case, she is presently under the care of her uncle, a reason for some relief. In saying so, I have looked for options instead of emotions to find a practical and viable way out for a very exultant life of you in the future."

Like people in general, Areem took the time in absorbing the unacceptable reality. On deep thought, he concluded that the suggested course was a temporary aberration with long-term beneficial implications. So he unhesitatingly accepted the proposition.

In that intensely compelling backdrop, Areem kept on waiting with long bated breath. Melanie and Bob were both curious and anxious as to what was keeping Areem so calm and quiet even though all physical expressions were indicative of subdued stress. They preferred a discreet approach toward his apparent bulging feeling and gave him time and space to reveal.

Areem had a soft and sincere exchange of looks with both of them and unhesitatingly said, "I do not have any material experience of paternal love, more that of a mother. My limited knowledge is from reading and what friends shared from time to time. Both of your unconditional love, commitment, and care for me surpassed those indicators. They are exceptional, precious, and a gift from God. I strayed in life but am on track now because of your decisions. I will do everything under the shadow of your love and care to prove worthy of the trust both of you reposed in me and in my quest to reunite with Gul Meher and my progeny."

Having said that, Areem postulated something totally unknown and unfamiliar to both Melanie and Bob. The eventual upshot stunned both of them. They never expected to hear something like what Areem had to say. That took them by surprise. The inherent sincerity overwhelmed them.

Areem continued saying, "We are used to address *mother* as *ma* and *father* as *baba*. Both these are phonetically very close to Mary Melanie and Bob. I seek your permission to address you as such, at least in private setting, so that I can always identify you both as my parents. In my culture and practice, a child is expected to salaam parents by touching their feet on the eve of any special happening in life or before facing a challenge or undertaking a noble task. Salaam, apart from submission, signifies acknowledgment that even the sands of the parents' feet are valued and honorable. So in addressing you for the first time as ma and baba, I would, if you permit, like to salaam you both."

Bob was befuddled. The sunny disposition of Melanie succumbed to controlled sobbing. Recalling Jeffrey, she rewound her life and love and, after exchanging looks with Bob, consented wholeheartedly to what Areem desired. Areem got up and performed the salaam ritual, and Melanie warmly responded by hugging him and saying, "You are our son."

Areem was overwhelmed by Melanie's addressing him as son. That propelled impulsive thoughts of his Dhaka roots with no motherly love, and the care and understanding of Gul Meher's mother in Bazarak.

Mother Gul Bahar, after a long time of lonely life and being frustrated by the continued absence of husband and drought in communication from daughter, decided to leave Bazarak for a living with Zubaida Khala in Ghazni as revenge to life. That decision almost amounted to withdrawing from life she was used to.

Fazal Abbas, the dear Mamu-jan of Gul Meher, was duly informed about it but did not have much thought about the move. He was assured of her good care, knowing from Gul Meher about her sister's depth of relationship and comfort zone in the proximity of Zubaida Khala, who before leaving refugee camp had said that any time in life, and if it so considered, her door would always remain open for Gul Bahar.

For Mamu-jan and the family, life in WDC was a constant challenge with rewarding success. Each day for them was a challenge for greater success in a new environment. With sons getting settled in life and with new arrivals in the family, their focus was on the present. They had seldom discussions about the past. That, among others, was caused by the unexpected progression of Gul Meher in pursuing life and living independently with her son.

Based on the encouragement and guidance of her teacher in charge and other faculty members, Gul Meher successfully achieved a high school diploma through the region-based accredited program, meeting school demand for employment. Her appointment as associate was made permanent with structured compensation, including insurance coverage.

In this backdrop, she floated the idea of living independently. During postdinner discussion, Gul Meher recalled saying, "Mamu-jan achieved full success in his first project of restaurant business. His second project is about me, my progression, and to have a life of my own. I am confident that I am inching forward to that. The regularization of my employment with full benefits paved the way to that process. My son, Abrar, is now about five and needs to attend pre-primary school. I acknowledge profoundly

Mamu-jan's love and guidance and my brothers' help in this journey. Also, this journey would not have been possible without the care and consideration of the revered mami-jan taking full-time care of Abrar while growing up as I was preoccupied with my job and preparation for the high school diploma.

"Consistent with Mamu-jan's stipulation in Houston, while making a decision to move to WDC, I now plan to have an independent living with my son, Abrar. This is to give him his own identity with a place that he would be able to call his home.

"I am not separating from the family. Physically, we will be away, but mentally, we will be closer to you all. My proposition, subject to the approval of Mamu-jan, will be sad for all but more traumatic for Mama-ni due to her intimate bonding with Abrar since birth. Mashallah, Mamani-jan has now two more grandchildren. Her plate is full. Nevertheless, I solemnly assure all that Abrar will spend most of his leisure time with family and Mama-ni."

Laying the proposition she had in mind, Gul Meher looked at Mamu-jan for his reaction. Fazal Abbas, without hesitation, smilingly responded, saying, "Yes, I recall what I stipulated in Houston, and I would abide by that. I do not have any regret for sponsoring Gul Meher though it amounted to delinking her from the family. Her very common and ordinary assimilation in this setup would have pained me. I now take pride for doing that based on my close interactions with her in the USA setting. She is intellectually of stupendous caliber to be wasted among the hills and valleys of Bazarak. So I give my full consent with a caveat: wherever you are, you and your son will remain an inclusive part of this family. I will urge my sons to remember this always."

Having said that, Mamu-jan lost himself in a deep thought. Other family members were oblivious of that mood change. They were preoccupied in congratulating Gul Meher in her new journey, saying repeatedly *mubarak* ("congratulations") and reiterating all care and attention in the future.

Everyone was under the impression that it was the end of discussion on the subject. But Fazal Abbas had something else in his mind. Against all reasoning, he decided to break promise he had given to his sister, which was not to meddle in the personal life of Gul Meher. He opened up, saying, "The family and I never raised any issue concerning your marriage and current depth and level of communication with your husband. That was as per the promise given to your mother. But at this major turn in your life, I want to be assured of your contact with him."

Keeping her eyes focused on the floor, Gul Meher stated, "I have sent many letters to Areem's Dhaka address with no response. That not only disturbed me but also tore my love and relationship into pieces. My mentor in the school, the teacher in charge, consoled me by saying, 'Something is wrong.' As we were preparing for parent-teacher conference about two years back, she told me to have Areem's Dhaka telephone number with me on the conference day. After the conference, she called the Dhaka office of Areem's father. The person at the other end introduced himself as the manager. The manger appeared to be a very nice person with love and feelings for Areem. As she inquired about Areem, he frankly said that they did not have any information about him for many years. One particular lady from the USA used to write to him in his Dhaka office address. His younger brother tore all those letters. He even did not bother to open them. That's all I know. If you can trace him, please let us know as his father is seriously ill, experiencing a deteriorating health condition since knowing of Areem's leaving Bangladesh. My anguish subsided. I remain worried about him but have firm belief that he is alive, and we will reunite."

On being apprised, Fazal Abbas lamented, saying, "What an irony it is! I was earlier advised by my Karachi associate, Saifullah Saleh, about what is going on in Bazarak. During his latest visit to sister Gul Bahar to hand over money as stipulated, he took the opportunity to visit the post office to make arrangements for delivering the money if he was constrained to take that option. He explained that travel between Karachi and Bazarak of late has become hazardous. So he wanted to explore the option, if that becomes necessary.

"When he entered the post office, the postmaster was having exchanges with a young man. The subject was the tearing off a letter addressed to Gul Bahar without even opening the envelope. On query by the postmaster, the young man, without any mortification, loudly said, 'Do not question me. I know the contents of the letter. Moreover, I am the authorized person to handle all related mailing matters. I will keep Gul Bahar *chachi* informed, as was done in the past, about this letter too.'

"As the young man walked out with resentment, Saifullah introduced himself with my reference, explaining the purpose of visit. While taking leave, he casually asked the identity of the young man. The postmaster said that he was an upcoming local Bazarak leader known by the name

Muqquabir and more commonly known as the son of the late Kazi Shaheeb, a social luminary of his time. Gul Bahar had no knowledge about scores of letters shredded by Muqquabir. That is perhaps the reason, in despair, to take shelter to her only resort: Zubaida Khala."

Gul Meher paused for a while even though she could not hold her tears any more. She said, "I could not open up before you all. Neither could you raise the issue with me due to your promise to Mother. I suffered the trauma all by myself. I spent all these nights and days being pestered by sadness and despair. I am all finished within myself, outwardly maintaining a smiling and tranquil posture. My only worry now is about the future of Abrar if I succumb to this agony."

In a joint response, the family said, "Please do not stress yourself on this disquiet. Nothing will happen to you. You are a strong and confident person. Moreover, we all are here even if you live independently."

Gul Meher, relaxed and reassured, stood up and performed salaam as a demonstration of her gratitude.

One thing in life is beyond jurisdiction as well irreversible. That is time. Once gone, it can't be recovered. So all decided, and Gul Meher reconciled, to look forward for an eventual reunion, praying for the safety and security of Areem. Life moved on all fronts.

Earlier, Areem completed all requisites for admission to the community college, excelled in academic pursuits, and moved to the University of Minnesota after the second year. That journey of him in the quest of an earnest objective of his life was both smooth and rewarding. But the process had some interesting occurrences too. He laughed at himself while recounting them in the midst of sustained agony concerning Gul Meher and his offspring.

One of those was his initial struggle related to acclimatization while in the community college. In the earlier days in school, he was a subject of amusement for fellow students. Areem started feeling dismayed.

One of his classmates noted the same, simultaneously recognizing his intellectual proficiency from questions asked during the class deliberations. She was Porsha Richardson, a lanky yet proportionate and attractive African-American of Somalian origin. She had a gregarious and confident personality with matching cerebral capability and an open mind. It took her no time to discover Areem. She became friendly with him and during preliminary exchanges opined that Areem should focus on two things simultaneously besides academic pursuits: (1) keep ears and brain receptive to acquire local accent and (2) listen, absorb, and pick up local slangs.

Areem not only followed those but also always looked for time and opportunity to interact with her. With improved pronunciation skill and communication ability in tandem with academic results, he soon became the center of attention to many. Porsha, on her part, was receptive to Areem's emotional advances. As he was having the pressing desire to be close to Porsha, he decided to be candid to her concerning his life and involvement with Gul Meher.

In an ardently choked situation, Areem was propelled to open up one day. He told all that would be needed for someone like Porsha to comprehend his dilemma in furthering relationship with her.

Contrary to Areem's anticipation, Poshra, without any backlash of frustration, remained normal with an impish smile. Looking at Areem straightway, she said, "I am emotionally receptive to you and will remain so in the future too. This has nothing to do with romanticism. Your losing a mother at early childhood and wretched growing-up experiences have drawn me close to you besides your academic acumen. You are talking to someone who lost her father early at the onslaught of the civil war in Somalia. So I understand your torment. Your new mother's continuous efforts to malign you agitated me. That is the reason you have my support. To me, you are my friend with whom I can share my own grievances and frustrations. For your information, I have a boyfriend in this institution, and we are steady for the last three years. Senior to me, he is a current junior faculty member of our college. So I just lend my shoulder with passion. There is no other agenda. Let us remain as friends, supporting each other. We should always remember that belonging to the past is no answer for the future. Rather, a rewarding future may help to minimize a lot of past deficiencies."

That was another unique incident helping Areem's integration process. He was charmed at being able to know, accept, and appreciate that boy-girl friendship can be a normal proposition beyond gender-related attractions and vulnerability. Areem was equally impressed by the dictum drawn with respect to past and future. He was thankful to Poshra for helping him in his societal assimilation process beyond love and care of Bob and Melanie. Both remained good friends.

Meanwhile, Areem accomplished all needed requirements, processes, and procedures for admission into the University of Minnesota for completing his last two years of undergrad education. At his informal farewell party, Poshra showed up with her boyfriend; and both most warmly hugged him and wished him well in life with a promise that he would introduce Gul Meher once they were united.

Destiny more than compensated Areem in his progression to achieve his life's ultimate objective. He got accepted in most of the top medical schools as well as in the medical school of the University of Minnesota (UMN). Against all opinions and persistence of Melanie and Bob, Areem opted for UMN, considering the deteriorating health conditions of Melanie. He assured both that he would put in his best efforts to be professionally as competent as the ones from top-ranking schools. But it was his desire to be around them now, not as repaying for past debt but as an obligation to his parents.

In between studies and needed support to Bob in managing the home and related errands, Areem devoted his attention in taking care of Melanie. While helping her in changing her attire one evening and noticing her apparent mortification, Areem, looking at her eyes, softly and lovingly said, "It is reality that you are not my biological mother. I had not been in this tummy for hypothetical ten months and ten days. But the fact is that your nexus with me is much beyond and above the biological bond. I am a part of your own self. So please do not feel otherwise."

That brought tears in the eyes of Melanie, who was known for her very intense personality. She surrendered herself to the occasional nursing of Areem but did not hesitate expressing apprehension as how much of that was impacting his studies. Areem assured her to the contrary, saying, "I am conscious of my academic challenges and obligations. I am not doing anything at the cost of that." Knowing Areem during the last few years, she contentedly accepted that pledge, remembering Jeffrey too.

Predictably, Melanie succumbed to the ultimate call one fine morning when Areem was serving her mashed breakfast eatables and Bob was standing with her favorite cappuccino while simultaneously holding a straw. As the last service was done, Melanie looked at Bob and Areem with passion and pathos and bore a waning smile; and her eyelids involuntarily closed, signifying her eternal journey to the disarray of both standing by the side.

With that tragedy behind them, Bob, the daredevil stout military guy otherwise known by his acronym SMB, slowly yielded to emotional heaviness, needing help and support in day-to-day living. Areem, in the midst of academic pursuits, doubled down his efforts in taking care of Bob, to both his pleasure and anguish. In due time, Areem got into the dual-degree program, combining his medical education program with a degree in medical research, known otherwise as MD/PhD, to the glee and ecstasy of Bob.

Gul Meher made progress in her independent living with confidence, still hoping for eventual reunion with Areem. Her only visible handicap was her lack of driving skill, but she mastered the art of travel within WDC by using bus and metro train services. In very demanding situations, her cousins and their spouses always responded unhesitatingly to her call.

As Abrar was growing up, and to overcome her agonizing mind-set, Gul Meher started talking with him more about Areem: his roots, childhood experiences, personal qualities, commitment, and the most tragic journey in life with unbridled ambition to become a doctor because of losing his mother early in life. She did not hesitate in detailing her involvement in his life, explaining simultaneously the reasons that compelled them to choose different tracks in pursuing life. She, many a time, mentioned her promise not to die before reuniting Abrar with his father and ingraining an urge within Abrar's mind to become a physician himself, fulfilling the ambition of his father.

That left a deep mark in the growing-up process of Abrar. That was magnified many a time when Abrar silently observed his mother uttering in her submissions to Allahpak after every prayer (*monazat*) for safety and security of Areem, their eventual reunion, and the continued success of Abrar in life.

Abrar showed mettle of commitment and excellence from early childhood. He, like his father, demonstrated academic excellence from very early childhood and had been to accelerate courses in all his classes. Gul Meher soon became more known as the mother of Abrar. She was receiving kudos from her colleagues, friends, and the family. That made Gul Meher blissful. She invigorated her effort and commitment in grooming up Abrar but nevertheless concentrated her internal commitment and prayer for reunion with Areem early.

Of late, she became more concerned about her health due to internalizing sustained concern and frustration against the backdrop of intimidating uncertainty for possible reunion. The passage of time with hope against hope crippled her within while putting all effort to be at ease in her daily life. That was more so to keep young Abrar away from related worries.

On his part, Areem was happy at seeing Bob gradually adjusting with the absence of his love, Melanie. He started talking more about Areem's father in Dhaka and mother-in-law in Bazarak, with the focus to track Gul Meher in the USA.

On completion of his MD and pursuit of PhD, there was a break of about fifteen days. At Bob's behest and financing, Areem undertook an exploratory journey to Dhaka and Bazarak with the new name of Areem Masud Bakely.

During his US citizenship oath-taking process, Areem, as in other cases, was given the option to change name if he wanted to. Without any inkling of thought, he agreed to do so and opted for Areem Masud Bakely. Returning home, he told that to Bob, expressing sorrow for not having the opportunity to consult him and getting his consent for adopting his name. Bob was overwhelmed, stood up, and hugged him with uncontrollable sobbing, an act very rare in the persona of the tough military guy known as SMB. His only comment was "Your mother in heaven must be ecstatic." In a sense, that was indicative of his approval and happiness. Areem soon came to be known among friends and colleagues as AMB.

Landing in Dhaka, Areem took the earliest opportunity to go to their house near Banani Township. On reaching the familiar house, he was stunned to note the name change of the house. On query, the *chokidar* (akin to a security guard) said this house was on auction for default in repaying bank loans, and the present owner bought this.

He had full sense of what happened but still decided to visit the business premises of his father. Again, there was a new name in the business office. Areem stepped in and requested a meeting with the owner. His second shock was a distressing one. The person showing up was none other than the second brother of the new mother. Keeping the owner in a guessing game about his own identity, Ameer asked for his father by his formal name; and the answer was similar to what he had in mind since seeing the house name. "Oh, he died about four years back. We do not know about his eldest son. In initial years of his disappearance, a lady from the USA used to write regularly to him. The second son will throw them in the trash or burn them. He inherited the business but could not handle the same, and it went into bankruptcy. I am the present owner."

On reaching Kabul, Areem visited the US embassy and told them about his plan for a short visit to Bazarak where he lived some years back. This had been planned as a nostalgic side trip as he was in Asia. He was given some contact numbers and a mobile phone with additional built-in technical feature for tracking it. With the help of local staff of the embassy, Areem bought some local outfits and started traveling to Bazarak in a bus. The other passenger of the same two-seater appeared to be a lettered one with penchant for social interactions. Being by the side of Areem, he was jubilant for having a seat next to an educated person. He started the conversation, saying, "I am from Kabul and working presently in the Bazarak post office."

For Areem, emotionally stressed and equally apprehensive of what he was about to face, those utterances of an unknown copassenger first unnerved him and then caused an unexpected inquisitiveness in his mind. Areem slowly opened up, first smiling to create a sense of ease in the copassenger's mind and then saying, "I am from Karachi. I have a friend there who was once in charge of newly established post office of Bazarak. On hearing that I will soon be visiting Kabul for business purpose, he requested me to check on one Gul Bahar and her family in Bazarak as his many letters remained unanswered."

The copassenger looked at him and said, "I have heard about the lady, and her mail-related matters are a common story in our post office. I do not recall anything about the letters coming from Karachi. As I have heard, she used to receive plenty of letters from the USA. Her agent, one, Muqquabir, regularly received them and used to tear them publicly. As he was the son of a prominent deceased person of the community and an upcoming local leader, no one dared to contest that. His common reply was that he was aware of the contents, and there was no need to pester *chachi* with old matters. I am told that as time passed, frequency and receipt of letters decelerated and finally stopped. Gul Bahar, the lady, also left Bazarak permanently for an unknown destination. The house is still there, but encroachments of the property are visible."

There was momentary lull in their discourse as Areem was comprehending the backdrop of no communication in response to his letters. It also sort of confirmed that Gul Meher left Bazarak as planned and was most likely in the USA.

The copassenger maneuvered his hand-carry, brought out dates, and offered some to Areem as a demonstration of typical Afghani hospitality. Areem obliged him by taking two.

While masticating the dates, the passenger, having no other subject of common interest, started narrating to Areem the topographical features of Panjshir as the bus was making progression through its hills and mountains. Areem was unmindful of the chattering but maintained continued exchange of looks with him as an indication of interest and attention. In his mind, he thanked Allahpak for making his visit so easy and satisfying even before reaching Bazarak. He also thanked his grandpa for his unbounded blessings.

On reaching Bazarak township, Areem and other passengers disembarked. He took leave from his copassenger, thanking him profusely for the company and for his dates.

Areem had all his information even without any effort but felt compelled to have a look at Gul Bahar's ancestral home, which was his place of living in the warm embrace of Gul Meher. Taking slow and emotional steps, he reached the vintage property and had an intense look, reminiscing his period of stay in a photo-finish manner. In every such thought, he felt the overt presence of Gul Meher and felt her touch.

As the next bus back to Kabul was to leave about half an hour later, Areem, being hungry too, decided to visit his favorite *chaikhana* for food. As a precaution, he covered his face as much as he could and took a corner seat.

His return trip was an uneventful one, sharing a seat with a typical Afghan, who was oozing an unfavorable smell from his blanket. He consoled himself, feeling that it was much better than sleeping among hordes of sheep during his last journey years back. He smiled as a reaction to that.

On return, he briefed Bob. In expressing sympathy for the loss of his father and dismay for the vanquished business, he told Areem, "We are almost certain that Gul Meher is now in the USA. But recalling Melanie's last advice, I too would suggest that you concentrate in successfully finishing your PhD course. After that, both of us—you through your civil connections and me through my army contacts—would launch concerted efforts to locate her. Son, you are at the end of the tunnel. So please do not get distracted." Areem unhesitatingly accepted that proposition.

Areem's acumen in research and trying out a multiprotocol treatment plan not limiting to single modality as vaccine, drug, or other monotherapy, integrating treatment modules enhancing one another, had earned him a name and fame even during his PhD academic persuasion and challenges. To Areem, enhanced supplements and effective treatment procedures go a long way in combating cancer.

On attaining his PhD, he devoted his time and energy, among others, in exploring more effective methods for multidrug treatment approaches for cancer based on case-to-case situations. His prognostic acumen coupled with innate instinct earned him heightened fame soon. Areem's consultative visits to various hospitals for diagnostic opinions and for seminars took a lot of his time besides professional practice and research.

Simultaneously, Bob and Areem commenced taking actions through respective contacts and connections to locate Gul Meher.

The energetic and committed Gul Meher suddenly started feeling depressed, feeble, and pained. She lost energy and appetite. She slowed down in life to the notice of many, especially her colleagues and associates. Consultations with family physician and other referred doctors were of no remedy. She tried to be ebullient outwardly, more for the comfort of Abrar. In her limited conversations, she always reminded him to be a doctor.

Her family became worried. Mamu-jan insisted on her and Abrar"s temporary relocation to his home. Gul Meher reluctantly agreed. As her health condition continued to deteriorate, she went on medical leave from the school. She did not miss her school environment—her latest passion—much as her colleagues started visiting her by rotation and updating her about the school.

All of them were shocked at how fast her health deteriorated and, together with family, convinced her for admission to the hospital. Tests and investigations confirmed that to be a case of acute cancer affecting various sections of her body. She started to have breathing problems with poor response even to aggressive medications.

The few words she would occasionally say focused on Abrar's roots, the name of his father, and her departing promise to Areem to make his offspring a medical practitioner. Those repeated assertions, despite the pain and weakness, distressed all in the family, more due to feedback from doctors. That logically caused an emotional setting of pathos in Gul Meher's known circle and family. Abrar became aware that his mother was ailing but had no inkling to comprehend the upshot. His only visible reactions were sustained looks at his mother with his big eyes and occasional holding of her hands.

Areem was in WDC to attend a day's workshop on the emerging protocols for treatment of acute multilevel cancer cases. That seminar was being held in the hospital where Gul Meher was admitted to.

Seminar deliberations were at a closing phase. The senior oncologist of the hospital presented a case of a patient of the hospital who was not responding to medications. He further said, "It is a unique case. The patient is young, and the ailment is not more than six months old. Due to worsening breathing problems, we have put her on oxygen. Because of her fast-worsening situation, it would be imperative to put the patient on life support. Before such a decision is taken, we will appreciate if you would have a look. In anticipation of the benefit of your prognosis, we requested the family's presence for discussion about life support option."

Areem readily agreed but said that before physically seeing the patient, he would like to have her full genomic information as well as the protocols followed.

The oncologist opened his laptop, and the projector was activated to present related information. The name appeared, and that was Gul Meher Masud, along with her ward number.

To the disarray of all present, Dr. Areem sprang up and started running, asking random people about the location of the ward. Most participants followed him. It was momentary chaos and confusion.

Areem and many of his fellow seminar participants rushed into the ward to the shock and surprise of Gul Meher's family and friends present as well as other patients. Stopping momentarily halfway through, he had a full look at the patient with oxygen mask, having uncontrolled tears rolling down. He took measured steps but could not hold himself stable. Involuntarily bending by the side of the hospital bed, he picked up her right hand and in the midst of irresistible sobbing said, "Gul Meher, look at me. I have become a doctor. I renew my promise in Bazarak that I will take care of you and will look after you always. Also, you are still my only wife whom I was looking for everywhere."

Bewilderingly, and to the disbelief of the attending physician, Gul Meher opened her eyes, smiled faintly, looked at Areem, and later on looked around and signaled for the removal of oxygen mask. With the consent of the attending physician, Areem, with all love and care, passionately removed that. Gul Meher unleashed tears of happiness. She signaled to something kept under her pillow. Areem diligently took out wrapped clothing and opened that at Gul Meher's indication. Once opened, it was his grandma's saree which he had given to Gul Meher as a departing memento before leaving Bazarak. He could not stop howling. At her indication, Areem put the saree on Gul Meher's fragile upper body with a portion of the tail end partially covering her head and face. She was just looking like a new Bangladeshi bride.

It was evident to all that Gul Meher was under intense breathing pressure, and she needed immediate oxygen support.

Oblivious of that prognosis, she focused on Abrar, holding the tail end of his grandma's dupatta. By signaling, she desired him to be near the bed. Once close by, Gul Meher slightly lifted her left hand to hold the right hand of Abrar and placed that on the right hand of Areem, which was on her body.

To the astonished eyes of Abrar, who had a baffled expression, Gul Meher winked and nodded to indicate that he was his father. The baffled father and son continued to hold their respective hands as Gul Meher placed them.

Soon thereafter, she looked at Areem once again and palely smiled, and her eyes succumbed to involuntary closure with her face to the east. A slight tear dripped in. Both passion and pathos prevailed in life.

About the Author

Born and grown up in Sonapur habitation of Noakhali civil district in Bangladesh, Jahed Rahman joined government service in early youth. In his retired life in Chicago, after serving in the Asian Development Bank and the World Bank, he considers himself a misfit in professional world watching his three children frequently working from home and other informal places wearing shorts and t-shirts with lap top and I-phone being the main vehicles. So he started writing to remain engaged in life. This is his latest publication of the four so far.

Printed in the United States
By Bookmasters